The

KATHERINE MANSFIELD

And after all the weather was ideal. They could not have had a more perfect day for a garden-party if they had ordered it. Windless, warm, the sky without a cloud. Only the blue was veiled with a haze of light gold, as it is sometimes in early summer. The gardener had been up since dawn, mowing the lawns and sweeping them, until the grass and the dark flat rosettes where the daisy plants had been seemed to shine. As for the roses, you could not help feeling they understood that roses are the only flowers that impress people at garden-parties; the only flowers that everybody is certain of knowing. Hundreds, yes, literally hundreds, had come out in a single night; the green bushes bowed down as though they had been visited by archangels.

Breakfast was not yet over before the men came to put up the marquee.

"Where do you want the marquee put, mother?"

"My dear child, it's no use asking me. I'm determined to leave everything to you children this year. Forget I am your mother. Treat me as an honoured guest."

But Meg could not possibly go and supervise the men. She had washed her hair before breakfast, and she sat drinking her coffee in a green turban, with a dark wet curl stamped on each cheek. Jose, the butterfly, always came down in a silk petticoat and a kimono jacket.

"You'll have to go, Laura; you're the artistic one."

Away Laura flew, still holding her piece of bread-and-butter. It's so delicious to have an excuse for eating out of doors and, besides, she loved having to arrange things; she always felt she could do it so much better than anybody else.

Four men in their shirt-sleeves stood grouped together on the garden path. They carried staves covered with rolls of canvas and they had big tool-bags slung on their backs. They looked impressive. Laura wished now that she was not holding that piece of bread-and-butter, but there was nowhere to put it and she couldn't possibly throw it away. She blushed and tried to look severe and even a little bit short-sighted as she came up to them.

"Good morning," she said, copying her mother's voice. But that sounded so fearfully affected that she was ashamed, and stammered like a little girl, "Oh—er—have you come—is it about the marquee?"

"That's right, miss," said the tallest of the men, a lanky, freckled fellow, and he shifted his tool-bag, knocked back his straw hat and smiled down at her. "That's about it."

His smile was so easy, so friendly, that Laura recovered. What nice eyes he had, small, but such a dark blue! And now she looked at the others, they were smiling too. "Cheer up, we won't bite," their smile seemed to say. How very nice workmen were! And what a beautiful morning! She mustn't mention the morning; she must be business-like. The marquee.

"Well, what about the lily-lawn? Would that do?"

And she pointed to the lily-lawn with the hand that didn't hold the bread-and-butter. They turned, they stared in the

PARTIES AND PASSIONS

Classic Short Stories from Around the World

PARTIES AND PASSIONS

Classic Short Stories from Around the World

Selection by
ELENA RICHARDS

MACMILLAN COLLECTOR'S LIBRARY

This collection first published 2025 by Macmillan Collector's Library
an imprint of Pan Macmillan
The Smithson, 6 Briset Street, London ECIM 5NR
EU representative: Macmillan Publishers Ireland Ltd, 1st Floor,
The Liffey Trust Centre, 117–126 Sheriff Street Upper,
Dublin 1 DOI YC43
Associated companies throughout the world

ISBN 978-1-0350-5856-3

Selection copyright © Macmillan Publishers International Ltd. 2025

The permissions acknowledgements on p. 349 constitute an
extension of this copyright page.

1 3 5 7 9 8 6 4 2

A CIP catalogue record for this book is available from the British Library.

Typeset in Plantin by Six Red Marbles UK, Thetford, Norfolk
Printed and bound in the UK using 100% Renewable Electricity by CPI Group (UK) Ltd

The text of this book remains true to the original in every way and is reflective of the
language and period in which it was originally written. Readers should be aware that there
may be hurtful or indeed harmful phrases and terminology that were prevalent at the time
these stories were written and in the context of the historical setting of these stories.

Macmillan believes changing the text to reflect today's world would undermine the
authenticity of the original, so has chosen to leave the text in its entirety. This does not,
however, constitute an endorsement of the characterization, content or language used.

Visit **www.panmacmillan.com** to read more
about all our books and to buy them.

Contents

KATHERINE MANSFIELD
The Garden-Party 1

L. M. MONTGOMERY
Aunt Susanna's Thanksgiving Dinner 21

EDITH NESBIT
John Charrington's Wedding 33

GEORGE RANDOLPH CHESTER
Bargain Day at Tutt House 43

NELLA LARSEN
The Wrong Man 73

NATHANIEL HAWTHORNE
Dr. Heidegger's Experiment 81

F. SCOTT FITZGERALD
The Bridal Party 95

SAKI
Tobermory 121

EDGAR ALLAN POE
The Masque of the Red Death 131

RYUNOSUKE AKUTAGAWA
The Ball 139

EDITH WHARTON
After Holbein 149

A. A. MILNE
Birthday Party 181

ALEXANDRE DUMAS
A Bal Masqué 199

ELIZA LESLIE

The Watkinson Evening 211

KATE CHOPIN

Wiser Than a God 233

O. HENRY

Lost on Dress Parade 247

JAMES JOYCE

The Dead 255

WASHINGTON IRVING

The Spectre Bridegroom 309

LEO TOLSTOY

After the Ball 329

BROTHERS GRIMM

The Twelve Dancing Princesses 343

Permissions Acknowledgements 349

PARTIES AND PASSIONS

Classic Short Stories from Around the World

direction. A little fat chap thrust out his underlip and the tall fellow frowned.

"I don't fancy it," said he. "Not conspicuous enough. You see, with a thing like a marquee"—and he turned to Laura in his easy way—"you want to put it somewhere where it'll give you a bang slap in the eye, if you follow me."

Laura's upbringing made her wonder for a moment whether it was quite respectful of a workman to talk to her of bangs slap in the eye. But she did quite follow him.

"A corner of the tennis-court," she suggested. "But the band's going to be in one corner."

"H'm, going to have a band, are you?" said another of the workmen. He was pale. He had a haggard look as his dark eyes scanned the tennis-court. What was he thinking?

"Only a very small band," said Laura gently. Perhaps he wouldn't mind so much if the band was quite small. But the tall fellow interrupted.

"Look here, miss, that's the place. Against those trees. Over there. That'll do fine."

Against the karakas. Then the karaka trees would be hidden. And they were so lovely, with their broad, gleaming leaves, and their clusters of yellow fruit. They were like trees you imagined growing on a desert island, proud, solitary, lifting their leaves and fruits to the sun in a kind of silent splendour. Must they be hidden by a marquee?

They must. Already the men had shouldered their staves and were making for the place. Only the tall fellow was left. He bent down, pinched a sprig of lavender, put his thumb and fore-finger to his nose and snuffed up the smell. When Laura saw that gesture she forgot all about the karakas in her wonder at him caring for things like that—caring for the smell of lavender. How many men that she knew would have done such a thing. Oh, how extraordinarily nice workmen were, she thought. Why couldn't she have workmen for friends rather than the silly boys she danced with and who came to Sunday night supper? She would get on much better with men like these.

It's all the fault, she decided, as the tall fellow drew something on the back of an envelope, something that was to be looped up or left to hang, of these absurd class distinctions. Well, for her part, she didn't feel them. Not a bit, not an atom . . . And now there came the chock-chock of wooden hammers. Someone whistled, someone sang out, "Are you right there, matey?" "Matey!" The friendliness of it, the—the—Just to prove how happy she was, just to show the tall fellow how at home she felt, and how she despised stupid conventions, Laura took a big bite of her bread-and-butter as she stared at the little drawing. She felt just like a work-girl.

"Laura, Laura, where are you? Telephone, Laura!" a voice cried from the house.

"Coming!" Away she skimmed, over the lawn, up the path, up the steps, across the veranda and into the porch. In the hall her father and Laurie were brushing their hats ready to go to the office.

"I say, Laura," said Laurie very fast, "you might just give a squiz at my coat before this afternoon. See if it wants pressing."

"I will," said she. Suddenly she couldn't stop herself. She ran at Laurie and gave him a small, quick squeeze. "Oh, I do love parties, don't you?" gasped Laura.

"Ra-ther," said Laurie's warm, boyish voice, and he squeezed his sister too and gave her a gentle push. "Dash off to the telephone, old girl."

The telephone. "Yes, yes; oh yes. Kitty? Good morning, dear. Come to lunch? Do, dear. Delighted, of course. It will only be a very scratch meal—just the sandwich crusts and broken meringue-shells and what's left over. Yes, isn't it a perfect morning? Your white? Oh, I certainly should. One moment—hold the line. Mother's calling." And Laura sat back. "What, mother? Can't hear."

Mrs. Sheridan's voice floated down the stairs. "Tell her to wear that sweet hat she had on last Sunday."

"Mother says you're to wear that *sweet* hat you had on last Sunday. Good. One o'clock. Bye-bye."

Laura put back the receiver, flung her arms over her head, took a deep breath, stretched and let them fall. "Huh," she sighed, and the moment after the sigh she sat up quickly. She was still, listening. All the doors in the house seemed to be open. The house was alive with soft, quick steps and running voices. The green baize door that led to the kitchen regions swung open and shut with a muffled thud. And now there came a long, chuckling absurd sound. It was the heavy piano being moved on its stiff castors. But the air! If you stopped to notice, was the air always like this? Little faint winds were playing chase in at the tops of the windows, out at the doors. And there were two tiny spots of sun, one on the inkpot, one on a silver photograph frame, playing too. Darling little spots. Especially the one on the inkpot lid. It was quite warm. A warm little silver star. She could have kissed it.

The front door bell pealed and there sounded the rustle of Sadie's print skirt on the stairs. A man's voice murmured;

Sadie answered, careless, "I'm sure I don't know. Wait. I'll ask Mrs. Sheridan."

"What is it, Sadie?" Laura came into the hall.

"It's the florist, Miss Laura."

It was, indeed. There, just inside the door, stood a wide, shallow tray full of pots of pink lilies. No other kind. Nothing but lilies—canna lilies, big pink flowers, wide open, radiant, almost frighteningly alive on bright crimson stems.

"O-oh, Sadie!" said Laura, and the sound was like a little moan. She crouched down as if to warm herself at that blaze of lilies; she felt they were in her fingers, on her lips, growing in her breast.

"It's some mistake," she said faintly. "Nobody ever ordered so many. Sadie, go and find mother."

But at that moment Mrs. Sheridan joined them. "It's quite right," she said calmly. "Yes, I ordered them. Aren't they lovely?" She pressed Laura's arm. "I was passing the shop yesterday, and I saw them in the window. And I suddenly thought for once in my life I shall have enough canna lilies. The garden-party will be a good excuse."

"But I thought you said you didn't mean to interfere," said Laura. Sadie had gone. The florist's man was still outside at his van. She put her arm round her mother's neck and gently, very gently, she bit her mother's ear.

"My darling child, you wouldn't like a logical mother, would you? Don't do that. Here's the man."

He carried more lilies still, another whole tray.

"Bank them up, just inside the door, on both sides of the porch, please," said Mrs. Sheridan. "Don't you agree, Laura?"

"Oh, I *do*, mother."

In the drawing-room Meg, Jose and good little Hans had at last succeeded in moving the piano.

"Now, if we put this chesterfield against the wall and move everything out of the room except the chairs, don't you think?"

"Quite."

"Hans, move these tables into the smoking-room, and bring a sweeper to take these marks off the carpet and—one moment, Hans—" Jose loved giving orders to the servants and they loved obeying her. She always made them feel they were taking part in some drama. "Tell mother and Miss Laura to come here at once."

"Very good, Miss Jose."

She turned to Meg. "I want to hear what the piano sounds like, just in case I'm asked to sing this afternoon. Let's try over 'This Life is Weary.'"

Pom! Ta-ta-ta *Tee-ta!* The piano burst out so passionately that Jose's face changed. She clasped her hands. She looked mournfully and enigmatically at her mother and Laura as they came in.

> This Life is *Wee*-ary,
> A Tear—a Sigh.
> A Love that *Chan*-ges,
> This Life is *Wee*-ary,
> A Tear—a Sigh.
> A Love that *Chan*-ges,
> And then . . . Good-bye!

But at the word "Good-bye," and although the piano sounded more desperate than ever, her face broke into a brilliant, dreadfully unsympathetic smile.

"Aren't I in good voice, mummy?" she beamed.

> This Life is *Wee*-ary,
> Hope comes to Die.
> A Dream—a *Wa*-kening.

But now Sadie interrupted them. "What is it, Sadie?"

"If you please, m'm, cook says have you got the flags for the sandwiches?"

"The flags for the sandwiches, Sadie?" echoed Mrs. Sheridan dreamily. And the children knew by her face that she hadn't got them. "Let me see." And she said to Sadie firmly, "Tell cook I'll let her have them in ten minutes."

Sadie went.

"Now, Laura," said her mother quickly, "come with me into the smoking-room. I've got the names somewhere on the back of an envelope. You'll have to write them out for me. Meg, go upstairs this minute and take that wet thing off your head. Jose, run and finish dressing this instant. Do you hear me, children, or shall I have to tell your father when he comes home to-night? And—and, Jose, pacify cook if you do go into the kitchen, will you? I'm terrified of her this morning."

The envelope was found at last behind the dining-room clock, though how it had got there Mrs. Sheridan could not imagine.

"One of you children must have stolen it out of my bag, because I remember vividly—cream-cheese and lemon-curd. Have you done that?"

"Yes."

"Egg and—" Mrs. Sheridan held the envelope away from her. "It looks like mice. It can't be mice, can it?"

"Olive, pet," said Laura, looking over her shoulder.

"Yes, of course, olive. What a horrible combination it sounds. Egg and olive."

They were finished at last, and Laura took them off to the kitchen. She found Jose there pacifying the cook, who did not look at all terrifying.

"I have never seen such exquisite sandwiches," said Jose's rapturous voice. "How many kinds did you say there were, cook? Fifteen?"

"Fifteen, Miss Jose."

"Well, cook, I congratulate you."

Cook swept up crusts with the long sandwich knife, and smiled broadly.

"Godber's has come," announced Sadie, issuing out of the pantry. She had seen the man pass the window.

That meant the cream puffs had come. Godber's were famous for their cream puffs. Nobody ever thought of making them at home.

"Bring them in and put them on the table, my girl," ordered cook.

Sadie brought them in and went back to the door. Of course Laura and Jose were far too grown-up to really care about such things. All the same, they couldn't help agreeing that the puffs looked very attractive. Very. Cook began arranging them, shaking off the extra icing sugar.

"Don't they carry one back to all one's parties?" said Laura.

"I suppose they do," said practical Jose, who never liked to be carried back. "They look beautifully light and feathery, I must say."

"Have one each, my dears," said cook in her comfortable voice. "Yer ma won't know."

Oh, impossible. Fancy cream puffs so soon after breakfast. The very idea made one shudder. All the same, two minutes later Jose and Laura were licking their fingers with that absorbed inward look that only comes from whipped cream.

"Let's go into the garden, out by the back way," suggested Laura. "I want to see how the men are getting on with the marquee. They're such awfully nice men."

But the back door was blocked by cook, Sadie, Godber's man and Hans.

Something had happened.

"Tuk-tuk-tuk," clucked cook like an agitated hen. Sadie had her hand clapped to her cheek as though she had toothache. Hans's face was screwed up in the effort to understand. Only Godber's man seemed to be enjoying himself; it was his story.

"What's the matter? What's happened?"

"There's been a horrible accident," said cook. "A man killed."

"A man killed! Where? How? When?"

But Godber's man wasn't going to have his story snatched from under his very nose.

"Know those little cottages just below here, miss?" Know them? Of course she knew them. "Well, there's a young chap living there, name of Scott, a carter. His horse shied at a traction-engine, corner of Hawke Street this morning, and he was thrown out on the back of his head. Killed."

"Dead!" Laura stared at Godber's man.

"Dead when they picked him up," said Godber's man with relish. "They were taking the body home as I come up here." And he said to the cook, "He's left a wife and five little ones."

"Jose, come here." Laura caught hold of her sister's sleeve and dragged her through the kitchen to the other side of the green baize door. There she paused and leaned against it. "Jose!" she said, horrified, "however are we going to stop everything?"

"Stop everything, Laura!" cried Jose in astonishment. "What do you mean?"

"Stop the garden-party, of course." Why did Jose pretend?

But Jose was still more amazed. "Stop the garden-party? My dear Laura, don't be so absurd. Of course we can't do anything of the kind. Nobody expects us to. Don't be so extravagant."

"But we can't possibly have a garden-party with a man dead just outside the front gate."

That really was extravagant, for the little cottages were in a lane to themselves at the very bottom of a steep rise that led up to the house. A broad road ran between. True, they were far too near. They were the greatest possible eyesore and they had no right to be in that neighbourhood at all. They were little mean dwellings painted a chocolate brown. In the garden patches there was nothing but cabbage stalks, sick hens and tomato cans. The very smoke coming out of their chimneys was poverty-stricken. Little rags and shreds of smoke, so unlike the great silvery plumes that uncurled from the Sheridans' chimneys. Washerwomen lived in the lane and sweeps and a cobbler and a man whose house-front was studded all over with minute bird-cages. Children swarmed. When the Sheridans were little they were forbidden to set foot there because of the revolting language and of what they might catch. But since they were grown up Laura and Laurie on their prowls sometimes walked through. It was disgusting and sordid. They came out with a shudder. But still one must go everywhere; one must see everything. So through they went.

"And just think of what the band would sound like to that poor woman," said Laura.

"Oh, Laura!" Jose began to be seriously annoyed. "If you're going to stop a band playing every time someone has an accident, you'll lead a very strenuous life. I'm every bit as sorry about it as you. I feel just as sympathetic." Her eyes hardened. She looked at her sister just as she used to when they were little and fighting together. "You won't bring a drunken workman back to life by being sentimental," she said softly.

"Drunk! Who said he was drunk?" Laura turned furiously on Jose. She said just as they had used to say on those occasions, "I'm going straight up to tell mother."

"Do, dear," cooed Jose.

"Mother, can I come into your room?" Laura turned the big glass door-knob.

"Of course, child. Why, what's the matter? What's given you such a colour?" And Mrs. Sheridan turned round from her dressing-table. She was trying on a new hat.

"Mother, a man's been killed," began Laura. "*Not* in the garden?" interrupted her mother.

"No, no!"

"Oh, what a fright you gave me!" Mrs. Sheridan sighed with relief and took off the big hat and held it on her knees.

"But listen, mother," said Laura. Breathless, half choking, she told the dreadful story. "Of course, we can't have our party, can we?" she pleaded. "The band and everybody arriving. They'd hear us, mother; they're nearly neighbours!"

To Laura's astonishment her mother behaved just like Jose;

it was harder to bear because she seemed amused. She refused to take Laura seriously.

"But, my dear child, use your common sense. It's only by accident we've heard of it. If someone had died there normally—and I can't understand how they keep alive in those poky little holes—we should still be having our party, shouldn't we?"

Laura had to say "yes" to that, but she felt it was all wrong. She sat down on her mother's sofa and pinched the cushion frill.

"Mother, isn't it really terribly heartless of us?" she asked.

"Darling!" Mrs. Sheridan got up and came over to her, carrying the hat. Before Laura could stop her she had popped it on. "My child!" said her mother, "the hat is yours. It's made for you. It's much too young for me. I have never seen you look such a picture. Look at yourself!" And she held up her hand-mirror.

"But, mother," Laura began again. She couldn't look at herself; she turned aside.

This time Mrs. Sheridan lost patience just as Jose had done.

"You are being very absurd, Laura," she said coldly. "People like that don't expect sacrifices from us. And it's not very sympathetic to spoil everybody's enjoyment as you're doing now."

"I don't understand," said Laura, and she walked quickly out of the room into her own bedroom. There, quite by chance, the first thing she saw was this charming girl in the mirror, in her black hat trimmed with gold daisies and a long black velvet ribbon. Never had she imagined she could look like that. Is mother right? she thought. And now she hoped her mother was right. Am I being extravagant? Perhaps it was extravagant. Just for a moment she had another glimpse of that poor woman and those little children and the body being carried into the house. But it all seemed blurred, unreal, like a picture in the newspaper. I'll remember it again after the party's over, she decided. And somehow that seemed quite the best plan . . .

Lunch was over by half-past one. By half-past two they were all ready for the fray. The green-coated band had arrived and was established in a corner of the tennis-court.

"My dear!" trilled Kitty Maitland, "aren't they too like frogs for words? You ought to have arranged them round the pond with the conductor in the middle on a leaf."

Laurie arrived and hailed them on his way to dress. At the sight of him Laura remembered the accident again. She wanted to tell him. If Laurie agreed with the others, then it was bound to be all right. And she followed him into the hall.

"Laurie!"

"Hallo!" He was half-way upstairs, but when he turned round and saw Laura he suddenly puffed out his cheeks and goggled his eyes at her. "My word, Laura! You do look stunning," said Laurie. "What an absolutely topping hat!"

Laura said faintly "Is it?" and smiled up at Laurie and didn't tell him after all.

Soon after that people began coming in streams. The band struck up; the hired waiters ran from the house to the marquee. Wherever you looked there were couples strolling, bending to the flowers, greeting, moving on over the lawn. They were like bright birds that had alighted in the Sheridans' garden for this one afternoon, on their way to—where? Ah, what happiness it is to be with people who all are happy, to press hands, press cheeks, smile into eyes.

"Darling Laura, how well you look!"

"What a becoming hat, child!"

"Laura, you look quite Spanish. I've never seen you look so striking."

And Laura, glowing, answered softly, "Have you had tea? Won't you have an ice? The passion-fruit ices really are rather special." She ran to her father and begged him: "Daddy darling, can't the band have something to drink?"

And the perfect afternoon slowly ripened, slowly faded, slowly its petals closed.

"Never a more delightful garden-party . . ." "The greatest success . . ." "Quite the most . . ."

Laura helped her mother with the good-byes. They stood side by side in the porch till it was all over.

"All over, all over, thank heaven," said Mrs. Sheridan. "Round up the others, Laura. Let's go and have some fresh coffee. I'm exhausted. Yes, it's been very successful. But oh, these parties, these parties! Why will you children insist on giving parties!" And they all of them sat down in the deserted marquee.

"Have a sandwich, daddy dear. I wrote the flag."

"Thanks." Mr. Sheridan took a bite and the sandwich was gone. He took another. "I suppose you didn't hear of a beastly accident that happened to-day?" he said.

"My dear," said Mrs. Sheridan, holding up her hand, "we did. It nearly ruined the party. Laura insisted we should put it off."

"Oh, mother!" Laura didn't want to be teased about it.

"It was a horrible affair all the same," said Mr. Sheridan. "The chap was married too. Lived just below in the lane, and leaves a wife and half a dozen kiddies, so they say."

An awkward little silence fell. Mrs. Sheridan fidgeted with her cup. Really, it was very tactless of father . . .

Suddenly she looked up. There on the table were all those sandwiches, cakes, puffs, all uneaten, all going to be wasted. She had one of her brilliant ideas.

"I know," she said. "Let's make up a basket. Let's send that poor creature some of this perfectly good food. At any rate, it will be the greatest treat for the children. Don't you agree? And she's sure to have neighbours calling in and so on. What a point to have it all ready prepared. Laura!" She jumped up. "Get me the big basket out of the stairs cupboard."

"But, mother, do you really think it's a good idea?" said Laura.

Again, how curious, she seemed to be different from them all. To take scraps from their party. Would the poor woman really like that?

"Of course! What's the matter with you to-day? An hour or two ago you were insisting on us being sympathetic."

Oh well! Laura ran for the basket. It was filled, it was now heaped by her mother.

"Take it yourself, darling," said she. "Run down just as you are. No, wait, take the arum lilies too. People of that class are so impressed by arum lilies."

"The stems will ruin her lace frock," said practical Jose.

So they would. Just in time. "Only the basket, then. And, Laura!"—her mother followed her out of the marquee—"don't on any account—"

"What, mother?"

No, better not put such ideas into the child's head! "Nothing! Run along."

16

It was just growing dusky as Laura shut their garden gates. A big dog ran by like a shadow. The road gleamed white, and down below in the hollow the little cottages were in deep shade. How quiet it seemed after the after-noon. Here she was going down the hill to somewhere where a man lay dead, and she couldn't realise it. Why couldn't she? She stopped a minute. And it seemed to her that kisses, voices, tinkling spoons, laughter, the smell of crushed grass were somehow inside her. She had no room for anything else. How strange! She looked up at the pale sky, and all she thought was, "Yes, it was the most successful party."

Now the broad road was crossed. The lane began, smoky and dark. Women in shawls and men's tweed caps hurried by. Men hung over the palings; the children played in the doorways. A low hum came from the mean little cottages. In some of them there was a flicker of light, and a shadow, crab-like, moved across the window. Laura bent her head and hurried on. She wished now she had put on a coat. How her frock shone! And the big hat with the velvet streamer—if only it was another hat! Were the people looking at her? They must be. It was a mistake to have come; she knew all along it was a mistake. Should she go back even now?

No, too late. This was the house. It must be. A dark knot of people stood outside. Beside the gate an old, old woman with a crutch sat in a chair, watching. She had her feet on a newspaper. The voices stopped as Laura drew near. The group parted. It was as though she was expected, as though they had known she was coming here.

Laura was terribly nervous. Tossing the velvet ribbon over her shoulder, she said to a woman standing by, "Is this

Mrs. Scott's house?" and the woman, smiling queerly, said, "It is, my lass."

Oh, to be away from this! She actually said, "Help me, God," as she walked up the tiny path and knocked. To be away from those staring eyes, or to be covered up in anything, one of those women's shawls even. I'll just leave the basket and go, she decided. I shan't even wait for it to be emptied.

Then the door opened. A little woman in black showed in the gloom.

Laura said, "Are you Mrs. Scott?" But to her horror the woman answered, "Walk in, please, miss," and she was shut in the passage.

"No," said Laura, "I don't want to come in. I only want to leave this basket. Mother sent—"

The little woman in the gloomy passage seemed not to have heard her. "Step this way, please, miss," she said in an oily voice, and Laura followed her.

She found herself in a wretched little low kitchen, lighted by a smoky lamp. There was a woman sitting before the fire.

"Em," said the little creature who had let her in. "Em! It's a young lady." She turned to Laura. She said meaningly, "I'm 'er sister, miss. You'll excuse 'er, won't you?"

"Oh, but of course!" said Laura. "Please, please don't disturb her. I—I only want to leave—"

But at that moment the woman at the fire turned round. Her face, puffed up, red, with swollen eyes and swollen lips, looked terrible. She seemed as though she couldn't understand why Laura was there. What did it mean? Why was this stranger standing in the kitchen with a basket? What was it all about? And the poor face puckered up again.

"All right, my dear," said the other. "I'll thenk the young lady."

And again she began, "You'll excuse her, miss, I'm sure," and her face, swollen too, tried an oily smile.

Laura only wanted to get out, to get away. She was back in the passage. The door opened. She walked straight through into the bedroom, where the dead man was lying.

"You'd like a look at 'im, wouldn't you?" said Em's sister, and she brushed past Laura over to the bed. "Don't be afraid, my lass"—and now her voice sounded fond and sly, and fondly she drew down the sheet—" 'e looks a picture. There's nothing to show. Come along, my dear."

Laura came.

There lay a young man, fast asleep—sleeping so soundly, so deeply, that he was far, far away from them both. Oh, so remote, so peaceful. He was dreaming. Never wake him up again. His head was sunk in the pillow, his eyes were closed; they were blind under the closed eyelids. He was given up to his dream. What did garden-parties and baskets and lace frocks matter to him? He was far from all those things. He was wonderful, beautiful. While they were laughing and while the band was playing, this marvel had come to the lane. Happy . . . happy . . . All is well, said that sleeping face. This is just as it should be. I am content.

But all the same you had to cry, and she couldn't go out of the room without saying something to him. Laura gave a loud childish sob.

"Forgive my hat," she said.

And this time she didn't wait for Em's sister. She found her way out of the door, down the path past all those dark people. At the corner of the lane she met Laurie.

He stepped out of the shadow. "Is that you, Laura?"

"Yes."

"Mother was getting anxious. Was it all right?"

"Yes, quite. Oh, Laurie!" She took his arm, she pressed up against him.

"I say, you're not crying, are you?" asked her brother.

Laura shook her head. She was.

Laurie put his arm round her shoulder. "Don't cry," he said in his warm, loving voice. "Was it awful?"

"No," sobbed Laura. "It was simply marvellous. But, Laurie—" She stopped, she looked at her brother. "Isn't life," she stammered, "isn't life—" But what life was she couldn't explain. No matter. He quite understood.

"*Isn't* it, darling?" said Laurie.

Aunt Susanna's Thanksgiving Dinner

L. M. MONTGOMERY

"Here's Aunt Susanna, girls," said Laura who was sitting by the north window—nothing but north light does for Laura who is the artist of our talented family.

Each of us has a little pet new-fledged talent which we are faithfully cultivating in the hope that it will amount to something and soar highly some day. But it is difficult to cultivate four talents on our tiny income. If Laura wasn't such a good manager we never could do it.

Laura's words were a signal for Kate to hang up her violin and for me to push my pen and portfolio out of sight. Laura had hidden her brushes and water colors as she spoke. Only Margaret continued to bend serenely over her Latin grammar. Aunt Susanna frowns on musical and literary and artistic ambitions but she accords a faint approval to Margaret's desire for an education. A college course, with a tangible diploma at the end, and a sensible pedagogic aspiration is something Aunt Susanna can understand when she tries hard. But she cannot understand messing with paints, fiddling, or scribbling, and she has only unmeasured contempt for messers, fiddlers, and scribblers. Time was when we had paid no attention to Aunt Susanna's views on these points; but ever since she had, on one incautious day when she was in high good humor, dropped a pale, anemic little hint that she might send Margaret to college if she were a good girl we had been bending all our energies towards securing Aunt Susanna's approval. It was not enough that Aunt Susanna should approve of Margaret; she must approve of the whole four of us or she would not help Margaret. That is Aunt Susanna's way. Of late we had been growing a little discouraged. Aunt Susanna had recently read a magazine article which stated that the higher education of women was ruining our country and that a woman who was a B. A. couldn't, in the very nature of things, ever be a housewifely, cookly creature. Consequently, Margaret's chances looked a little foggy; but we hadn't quite given up hope. A very little thing might sway Aunt Susanna one way or the other, so that we walked very softly and tried to mingle serpents' wisdom and doves' harmlessness in practical proportions.

When Aunt Susanna came in Laura was crocheting, Kate was sewing, and I was poring over a recipe book. That was not deception at all, since we did all these things frequently—much more frequently, in fact, than we painted or fiddled or wrote. But Aunt Susanna would never believe it. Nor did she believe it now.

She threw back her lovely new sealskin cape, looked around the sitting-room and then smiled—a truly Aunt Susannian smile.

"What a pity you forgot to wipe that smudge of paint off your nose, Laura," she said sarcastically. "You don't seem to get on very fast with your lace. How long is it since you began it? Over three months, isn't it?"

"This is the third piece of the same pattern I've done in three months, Aunt Susanna," said Laura presently. Laura is an old duck. She never gets cross and snaps back. I do; and it's so hard not to with Aunt Susanna sometimes. But I generally manage it for I'd do anything for Margaret. Laura did not tell Aunt Susanna that she sold her lace at the Women's Exchange in town and made enough to buy her new hats. She makes enough out of her water colors to dress herself.

Aunt Susanna took a second breath and started in again.

"I notice your violin hasn't quite as much dust on it as the rest of the things in this room, Kate. It's a pity you stopped playing just because I came in. I don't enjoy fiddling much but I'd prefer it to seeing anyone using a needle who isn't accustomed to it."

Kate is really a most dainty needlewoman and does all the fine sewing in our family. She colored and said nothing—that being the highest pitch of virtue to which our Katie, like myself, can attain.

"And there's Margaret ruining her eyes over books," went on Aunt Susanna severely. "Will you kindly tell me, Margaret Thorne, what good you ever expect Latin to do you?"

"Well, you see, Aunt Susanna," said Margaret gently—Magsie and Laura are birds of a feather—"I want to be a teacher if I can manage to get through, and I shall need Latin for that."

All the girls except me had now got their accustomed rap, but I knew better than to hope I should escape.

"So you're reading a recipe book, Agnes? Well, that's better than poring over a novel. I'm afraid you haven't been at it very long though. People generally don't read recipes upside down—and besides, you didn't quite cover up your portfolio. I see a corner of it sticking out. Was genius burning before I came in? It's too hard if I quenched the flame."

"A cookery book isn't such a novelty to me as you seem to think, Aunt Susanna," I said, as meekly as it was possible for me. "Why, I'm a real good cook—'if I do say it as hadn't orter.'"

I am, too.

"Well, I'm glad to hear it," said Aunt Susanna skeptically, "because that has to do with my errand here today. I'm in a peck of troubles. Firstly, Miranda Mary's mother has had to go and get sick and Miranda Mary must go home to wait on her. Secondly, I've just had a telegram from my sister-in-law who has been ordered west for her health, and I'll have to leave on to-night's train to see her before she goes. I can't get back until the noon train Thursday, and that is Thanksgiving, and I've invited Mr. and Mrs. Gilbert to dinner that day. They'll come on the same train. I'm dreadfully worried. There doesn't seem to be anything I can do except get one of you girls to go up to the Pinery Thursday morning and cook the dinner for us. Do you think you can manage it?"

We all felt rather dismayed, and nobody volunteered with a rush. But as I had just boasted that I could cook it was plainly my duty to step into the breach, and I did it with fear and trembling.

"I'll go, Aunt Susanna," I said.

"And I'll help you," said Kate.

"Well, I suppose I'll have to try you," said Aunt Susanna with the air of a woman determined to make the best of a bad business. "Here is the key of the kitchen door. You'll find everything in the pantry, turkey and all. The mince pies are all ready made so you'll only have to warm them up. I want dinner sharp at twelve for the train is due at 11:50. Mr. and Mrs. Gilbert are very particular and I do hope you will have things right. Oh, if

I could only be home myself! Why will people get sick at such inconvenient times?"

"Don't worry, Aunt Susanna," I said comfortingly. "Kate and I will have your Thanksgiving dinner ready for you in tiptop style."

"Well I'm sure I hope so. Don't get to mooning over a story, Agnes. I'll lock the library up and fortunately there are no fiddles at the Pinery. Above all, don't let any of the McGinnises in. They'll be sure to be prowling around when I'm not home. Don't give that dog of theirs any scraps either. That is Miranda Mary's one fault. She will feed that dog in spite of all I can do and I can't walk out of my own back door without falling over him."

We promise to eschew the McGinnises and all their works, including the dog, and when Aunt Susanna had gone we looked at each other with mingled hope and fear.

"Girls, this is the chance of your lives," said Laura. If you can only please Aunt Susanna with this dinner it will convince her that you are good cooks in spite of your nefarious bent for music and literature. I consider the illness of Miranda Mary's mother a Providential interposition—that is, if she isn't too sick."

"It's all very well for you to be pleased, Lolla," I said dolefully. "But I don't feel jubilant over the prospect at all. Something will probably go wrong. And then there's our own nice little Thanksgiving celebration we've planned, and pinched and economized for weeks to provide. That is half spoiled now."

"Oh, what is that compared to Margaret's chance of going to college?" exclaimed Kate. "Cheer up, Aggie. You know we can cook. I feel that it is now or never with Aunt Susanna."

I cheered up accordingly. We are not given to pessimism which is fortunate. Ever since father died four years ago we have struggled on here, content to give up a good deal just to keep our home and be together. This little gray house—oh, how we do love it and its apple trees—is ours and we have, as aforesaid, a tiny income and our ambitions; not very big ambitions but big enough to give zest to our lives and hope to the future. We've been very happy as a rule. Aunt Susanna has a big house and lots of money but she isn't as happy as we are. She nags us a good deal—just as she used to nag father—but we don't mind it very much after all. Indeed, I sometimes suspect that we really like Aunt Susanna tremendously if she'd only leave us alone long enough to find it out.

Thursday morning was an ideal Thanksgiving morning—bright, crisp and sparkling. There had been a white frost in the night, and the orchard and the white birch wood behind it looked like fairyland. We were all up early. None of us had slept well, and both Kate and I had had the most fearful dreams of spoiling Aunt Susanna's Thanksgiving dinner.

"Never mind, dreams always go by contraries, you know," said Laura cheerfully. "You'd better go up to the Pinery early and get the fires on, for the house will be cold. Remember the McGinnises and the dog. Weigh the turkey so that you'll know exactly how long to cook it. Put the pies in the oven in time to get piping hot—lukewarm mince pies are an abomination. Be sure—"

"Laura, don't confuse us with any more cautions," I groaned, "or we shall get hopelessly fuddled. Come on, Kate, before she has time to."

It wasn't very far up to the Pinery—just ten minutes' walk,

and such a delightful walk on that delightful morning. We went through the orchard and then through the white birch wood where the loveliness of the frosted boughs awed us. Beyond that there was a lane between ranks of young, balsamy, white misted firs and then an open pasture field, sere and crispy. Just across it was the Pinery, a lovely old house with dormer windows in the roof, surrounded by pines that were dark and glorious against the silvery morning sky.

The McGinnis dog was sitting on the back-door steps when we arrived. He wagged his tail ingratiatingly, but we ruthlessly pushed him off, went in and shut the door in his face. All the little McGinnises were sitting in a row on their fence, and they whooped derisively. The McGinnis manners are not those which appertain to the caste of Vere de Vere; but we rather like the urchins—there are eight of them—and we would probably have gone over to talk to them if we had not had the fear of Aunt Susanna before our eyes.

We kindled the fires, weighed the turkey, put it in the oven and prepared the vegetables. Then we set the dining-room table and decorated it with Aunt Susanna's potted ferns and dishes of lovely red apples. Everything went so smoothly that we soon forgot to be nervous. When the turkey was done, we took it out, set it on the back of the range to keep warm and put the mince pies in. The potatoes, cabbage and turnips were bubbling away cheerfully, and everything was going as merrily as a marriage bell. Then, all at once, things happened.

In an evil hour we went to the yard window and looked out. We saw a quiet scene. The McGinnis dog was still sitting on his haunches by the steps, just as he had been sitting all the morning. Down in the McGinnis yard everything wore an unusually peaceful aspect. Only one McGinnis was in sight—Tony, aged eight, who was perched up on the edge of the well box, swinging his legs and singing at the top of his melodious Irish voice. All at once, just as we were looking at him, Tony went over backward and apparently tumbled head foremost down his father's well.

Kate and I screamed simultaneously. We tore across the kitchen, flung open the door, plunged down over Aunt Susanna's yard, scrambled over the fence and flew to the well. Just as we reached it, Tony's red head appeared as he climbed serenely out over the box. I don't know whether I felt more relieved or furious. He had merely fallen on the blank guard inside the box: and there are times when I am tempted to think he fell on purpose because he saw Kate and me looking out at the window. At least he didn't seem at all frightened, and grinned most impishly at us.

Kate and I turned on our heels and marched back in as dignified a manner as was possible under the circumstances. Half way up Aunt Susanna's yard we forgot dignity and broke into a run. We had left the door open and the McGinnis dog had disappeared.

Never shall I forget the sight we saw or the smell we smelled when we burst into that kitchen. There on the floor was the McGinnis dog and what was left of Aunt Susanna's Thanksgiving turkey. As for the smell, imagine a commingled odor of scorching turnips and burning mince pies, and you have it.

The dog fled out with a guilty yelp. I groaned and snatched the turnips off. Kate threw open the oven door and dragged out the pies. Pies and turnips were ruined as irretrievably as the turkey.

"Oh, what shall we do?" I cried miserably. I knew Margaret's chance of college was gone forever.

"Do!" Kate was superb. She didn't lose her wits for a second. "We'll go home and borrow the girls' dinner. Quick—there's just ten minutes before train time. Throw those pies and turnips into this basket—the turkey too—we'll carry them with us to hide them."

I might not be able to evolve an idea like that on the spur of the moment, but I can at least act up to it when it is presented. Without a moment's delay we shut the door and ran. As we went I saw the McGinnis dog licking his chops over in their yard. I have been ashamed ever since of my feelings toward that dog. They were murderous. Fortunately I had no time to indulge them.

It is ten minutes walk from the Pinery to our house, but you can run it in five. Kate and I burst into the kitchen just as Laura and Margaret were sitting down to dinner. We had neither time nor breath for explanations. Without a word I grasped the turkey platter and the turnip tureen. Kate caught one hot mince pie from the oven and whisked a cold one out of the pantry.

"We've—got—to have—them," was all she said.

I've always said that Laura and Magsie would rise to any occasion. They saw us carry their Thanksgiving dinner off under their very eyes and they never interfered by word or motion. They didn't even worry us with questions. They realized that something desperate had happened and that the emergency called for deed not words.

"Aggie," gasped Kate behind me as we tore through the birch wood, "the border—of these pies—is crimped—differently—from Aunt Susanna's."

"She—won't know—the difference," I panted. "Miranda—Mary—crimps them."

We got back to the Pinery just as the train whistle blew. We had ten minutes to transfer turkey and turnips to Aunt Susanna's dishes, hide our own, air the kitchen, and get back our breath. We accomplished it. When Aunt Susanna and her guests came we were prepared for them; we were calm—outwardly—and the second mince pie was getting hot in the oven. It was ready by the time it was needed. Fortunately our turkey was the same size as Aunt Susanna's, and Laura had cooked a double supply of turnips, intending to warm them up the next day. Still, all things considered, Kate and I didn't enjoy that dinner much. We kept thinking of poor Laura and Magsie at home, dining off potatoes on Thanksgiving!

But at least Aunt Susanna was satisfied. When Kate and I were washing the dishes she came out quite beamingly.

"Well, my dears, I must admit that you made a very good job of the dinner, indeed. The turkey was done to perfection. As for the mince pies—well, of course Miranda Mary made them, but she must have had extra good luck with them, for they were excellent and heated to just the right degree. You didn't give anything to the McGinnis dog, I hope?"

"No, we didn't give him anything," said Kate.

Aunt Susanna did not notice the emphasis.

When we had finished the dishes we smuggled our platter and tureen out of the house and went home. Laura and Margaret were busy painting and studying and were just as sweet-tempered as if we hadn't robbed them of their dinner. But we had to tell them the whole story before we even took off our hats.

30

"There is a special Providence for children and idiots," said Laura gently. We didn't ask her whether she meant us or Tony McGinnis or both. There are some things better left in obscurity. I'd have probably said something much sharper than that if anybody had made off with my Thanksgiving turkey so unceremoniously.

Aunt Susanna came down the next day and told Margaret that she would send her to college. Also she commissioned Laura to paint her a water color for her dining-room and said she'd pay her five dollars for it.

Kate and I were rather left out in the cold in this distribution of favors, but when you come to reflect that Laura and Magsie had really cooked that dinner, it was only just.

Anyway, Aunt Susanna has never since insinuated that we can't cook, and that is as much as we deserve.

John Charrington's Wedding

EDITH NESBIT

No one ever thought that May Forster would marry John Charrington; but he thought differently, and things which John Charrington intended had a queer way of coming to pass. He asked her to marry him before he went up to Oxford. She laughed and refused him. He asked her again next time he came home. Again she laughed, tossed her dainty blonde head, and again refused. A third time he asked her; she said it was becoming a confirmed bad habit, and laughed at him more than ever.

John was not the only man who wanted to marry her: she was the belle of our village coterie, and we were all in love with her more or less; it was a sort of fashion, like masher collars or Inverness capes. Therefore we were as much annoyed as surprised when John Charrington walked into our little local Club—we held it in a loft over the saddler's, I remember—and invited us all to his wedding.

"Your wedding?"

"You don't mean it?"

"Who's the happy pair? When's it to be?"

John Charrington filled his pipe and lighted it before he replied. Then he said—

"I'm sorry to deprive you fellows of your only joke—but Miss Forster and I are to be married in September."

"You don't mean it?"

"He's got the mitten again, and it's turned his head."

"No," I said, rising, "I see it's true. Lend me a pistol someone—or a first-class fare to the other end of Nowhere. Charrington has bewitched the only pretty girl in our twenty-mile radius. Was it mesmerism, or a love-potion, Jack?"

"Neither, sir, but a gift you'll never have—perseverance—and the best luck a man ever had in this world."

There was something in his voice that silenced me, and all chaff of the other fellows failed to draw him further.

The queer thing about it was that when we congratulated Miss Forster, she blushed and smiled, and dimpled, for all the world as though she were in love with him, and had been in love with him all the time. Upon my word, I think she had. Women are strange creatures.

We were all asked to the wedding. In Brixham every one who was anybody knew everybody else who was any one. My sisters were, I truly believe, more interested in the *trousseau* than the bride herself, and I was to be best man. The coming marriage was much canvassed at afternoon tea-tables, and at our little Club over the saddler's, and the question was always asked: "Does she care for him?"

I used to ask that question myself in the early days of their engagement, but after a certain evening in August I never asked it again. I was coming home from the Club through the church-yard. Our church is on a thyme-grown hill, and the turf about it is so thick and soft that one's footsteps are noiseless.

I made no sound as I vaulted the low lichened wall, and threaded my way between the tombstones. It was at the same instant that I heard John Charrington's voice, and saw her face.

May was sitting on a low flat gravestone with the full splendour of the western sun upon her *mignonne* face. Its expression ended, at once and for ever, any question of her love for him; it was transfigured to a beauty I should not have believed possible, even to that beautiful little face.

John lay at her feet, and it was his voice that broke the stillness of the golden August evening.

"My dear, my dear, I believe I should come back from the dead if you wanted me!"

I coughed at once to indicate my presence, and passed on into the shadow fully enlightened.

The wedding was to be early in September. Two days before I had to run up to town on business. The train was late, of course, for we are on the South-Eastern, and as I stood grumbling with my watch in my hand, whom should I see but John Charrington and May Forster. They were walking up and down the unfrequented end of the platform, arm in arm, looking into each other's eyes, careless of the sympathetic interest of the porters.

Of course I knew better than to hesitate a moment before burying myself in the booking-office, and it was not till the train drew up at the platform, that I obtrusively passed the pair with my Gladstone, and took the corner in a first-class smoking-carriage. I did this with as good an air of not seeing them as I could assume. I pride myself on my discretion, but if John were travelling alone I wanted his company. I had it.

"Hullo, old man," came his cheery voice as he swung his bag into my carriage; "here's luck; I was expecting a dull journey!"

"Where are you off to?" I asked, discretion still bidding me turn my eyes away, though I saw, without looking, that hers were red-rimmed.

"To old Branbridge's," he answered, shutting the door and leaning out for a last word with his sweetheart.

"Oh, I wish you wouldn't go, John," she was saying in a low, earnest voice. "I feel certain something will happen."

"Do you think I should let anything happen to keep me, and the day after to-morrow our wedding-day?"

"Don't go," she answered, with a pleading intensity which would have sent my Gladstone on to the platform and me after it. But she wasn't speaking to me. John Charrington was made differently; he rarely changed his opinions, never his resolutions.

He only stroked the little ungloved hands that lay on the carriage door.

"I must, May. The old boy's been awfully good to me, and now he's dying I must go and see him, but I shall come home in time for——" the rest of the parting was lost in a whisper and in the rattling lurch of the starting train.

"You're sure to come?" she spoke as the train moved.

"Nothing shall keep me," he answered; and we steamed out. After he had seen the last of the little figure on the platform he leaned back in his corner and kept silence for a minute.

When he spoke it was to explain to me that his godfather, whose heir he was, lay dying at Peasmarsh Place, some fifty miles away, and had sent for John, and John had felt bound to go.

"I shall be surely back to-morrow," he said, "or, if not, the day after, in heaps of time. Thank Heaven, one hasn't to get up in the middle of the night to get married nowadays!"

"And suppose Mr. Branbridge dies?"

"Alive or dead I mean to be married on Thursday!" John answered, lighting a cigar and unfolding the *Times*.

At Peasmarsh station we said "good-bye," and he got out, and I saw him ride off; I went on to London, where I stayed the night.

When I got home the next afternoon, a very wet one, by the way, my sister greeted me with—

"Where's Charrington?"

"Goodness knows," I answered testily. Every man, since Cain, has resented that kind of question.

I thought you might have heard from him," she went on, "as you're to give him away to-morrow."

"Isn't he back?" I asked, for I had confidently expected to find him at home.

"No, Geoffrey,"—my sister Fanny always had a way of jumping to conclusions, especially such conclusions as were least favourable to her fellow-creatures—"he has not returned, and, what is more, you may depend upon it he won't. You mark my words, there'll be no wedding to-morrow."

My sister Fanny has a power of annoying me which no other human being possesses.

"You mark my words," I retorted with asperity, "you had better give up making such a thundering idiot of yourself. There'll be more wedding to-morrow than ever you'll take the first part in." A prophecy which, by the way, came true.

But though I could snarl confidently to my sister, I did not feel so comfortable when, late that night, I, standing on the doorstep of John's house, heard that he had not returned. I went home gloomily through the rain. Next morning brought a brilliant blue sky, gold sun, and all such softness of air and beauty of cloud as go to make up a perfect day. I woke with a vague feeling of having gone to bed anxious, and of being rather averse to facing that anxiety in the light of full wakefulness.

But with my shaving-water came a note from John which relieved my mind and sent me up to the Forsters with a light heart.

May was in the garden. I saw her blue gown through the hollyhocks as the lodge gates swung to behind me. So I did not go up to the house, but turned aside down the turfed path.

"He's written to you too," she said, without preliminary greeting, when I reached her side.

"Yes, I'm to meet him at the station at three, and come straight on to the church."

Her face looked pale, but there was a brightness in her eyes, and a tender quiver about the mouth that spoke of renewed happiness.

"Mr. Branbridge begged him so to stay another night that he had not the heart to refuse," she went on. "He is so kind, but I wish he hadn't stayed."

I was at the station at half-past two. I felt rather annoyed with John. It seemed a sort of slight to the beautiful girl who loved him, that he should come as it were out of breath, and with the dust of travel upon him to take her hand, which some of us would have given the best years of our lives to take.

But when the three o'clock train glided in, and glided out again having brought no passengers to our little station, I was more than annoyed. There was no other train for thirty-five minutes; I calculated that, with much hurry, we might just get to the church in time for the ceremony; but, oh, what a fool to miss that first train! What other man could have done it?

That thirty-five minutes seemed a year, as I wandered round the station reading the advertisements and the time-tables, and the company's bye-laws, and getting more and more angry with John Charrington. This confidence in his own power of getting everything he wanted the minute he wanted it was leading him too far. I hate waiting. Everyone does, but I believe I hate it more than anyone else. The three thirty-five was late, of course.

I ground my pipe between my teeth and stamped with impatience as I watched the signals. Click. The signal went down. Five minutes later I flung myself into the carriage that I had brought for John.

"Drive to the church!" I said, as someone shut the door. "Mr. Charrington hasn't come by this train."

Anxiety now replaced anger. What had become of the man? Could he have been taken suddenly ill? I had never known him have a day's illness in his life. And even so he might have telegraphed. Some awful accident must have happened to him. The thought that he had played her false never—no, not for a moment, entered my head. Yes, something terrible had happened to him, and on me lay the task of telling his bride. I tell you, I almost wished the carriage would upset and break my head so that someone else might tell her, not I, who—but that's nothing to do with the story.

It was five minutes to four as we drew up at the churchyard gate. A double row of eager on-lookers lined the path from lych-gate to porch. I sprang from the carriage and passed up between them. Our gardener had a good front place near the door. I stopped.

"Are they waiting still, Byles?" I asked, simply to gain time, for of course I knew they were by the waiting crowd's attentive attitude.

"Waiting, sir? No no, sir, why it must be over by now."

"Over! Then Mr. Charrington's come?"

"To the minute, sir; must have missed you somehow, and, I say, sir," lowering his voice, "I never see Mr. John the least bit so afore, but my opinion is he's been drinking pretty free. His clothes was all dusty and his face like a sheet. I tell you I didn't like the looks of him at all, and the folks inside are saying all sorts of things. You'll see, something's gone very wrong with Mr. John, and he's tried liquor. He looked like a ghost, and in he went with his eyes straight before him, with never a look or a word for none of us; him that was always such a gentleman!"

I had never heard Byles make so long a speech. The crowd in the churchyard were talking in whispers and getting ready rice and slippers to throw at the bride and bridegroom. The ringers were ready with their hands on the ropes to ring out the merry peal as the bride and bridegroom should come out.

A murmur from the church announced them; out they came, Byles was right. John Charrington did not look himself. There was dust on his coat, his hair was disarranged. He seemed to have been in some row, for there was a black mark above his eye-brow. He was deathly pale. But his pallor was not greater than that of the bride, who might have been carved in ivory—dress, veil, orange blossoms and all.

As they passed out the ringers stooped—there were six of them—and then, on the ears expecting the gay wedding peal, came the slow tolling of the passing bell.

A thrill of horror at so foolish a jest from the ringers passed through us all. But the ringers themselves dropped the ropes and fled like rabbits down the belfry stairs. The bride shuddered, and grey shadows came about her mouth, but the bridegroom led her on down the path where the people stood with the handfuls of rice; but the handfuls were never thrown, and the wedding-bells never rang. In vain the ringers were urged to remedy their mistake: they protested with many whispered expletives that they would see themselves further first.

In a hush like the hush in the chamber of death the bridal pair passed into their carriage and its door slammed behind them.

Then the tongues were loosed. A babel of anger, wonder, conjecture from the guests and the spectators.

"If I'd seen his condition, sir," said old Forster to me as we drove off, "I would have stretched him on the floor of the church, sir, by Heaven I would, before I'd have let him marry my daughter!"

Then he put his head out of the window.

"Drive like fury," he cried to the coachman; "don't spare the horses."

He was obeyed. We passed the bride's carriage. I forbore to look at it, and old Forster turned his head away and swore. We reached home before it.

We stood in the hall doorway, in the blazing afternoon sun, and in about half a minute we heard wheels crunching the gravel. When the carriage stopped in front of the steps old Forster and I ran down.

"Great Heaven, the carriage is empty! And yet——"

I had the door open in a minute, and this is what I saw—

No sign of John Charrington; and of May, his wife, only a

huddled heap of white satin lying half on the floor of the carriage and half on the seat.

"I drove straight here, sir," said the coachman, as the bride's father lifted her out; "and I'll swear no one got out of the carriage."

We carried her into the house in her bridal dress and drew back her veil. I saw her face. Shall I ever forget it? White, white and drawn with agony and horror, bearing such a look of terror as I have never seen since except in dreams. And her hair, her radiant blonde hair, I tell you it was white like snow.

As we stood, her father and I, half mad with the horror and mystery of it, a boy came up the avenue—a telegraph boy. They brought the orange envelope to me. I tore it open.

"Mr. Charrington was thrown from his horse on his way to the station at half-past one. Killed on the spot!"

And he was married to May Forster in our parish church at half-past three, in presence of half the parish.

"I shall be married, dead or alive!"

What had passed in that carriage on the homeward drive? No one knows—no one will ever know. Oh, May! Oh, my dear!

Before a week was over they laid her beside her husband in our little churchyard on the thyme-covered hill—the churchyard where they had kept their love-trysts.

Thus was accomplished John Charrington's wedding.

Bargain Day at Tutt House

GEORGE RANDOLPH CHESTER

I

Just as the stage rumbled over the rickety old bridge creaking and groaning, the sun came from behind the clouds that had frowned all the way, and the passengers cheered up a bit. The two richly-dressed matrons, who had been so utterly and unnecessarily oblivious to the presence of each other, now suspended hostilities for the moment by mutual and unspoken consent, and viewed with relief the little, golden-tinted valley and the tree-clad road just beyond. The respective husbands of these two ladies exchanged a mere glance, no more, of comfort. They, too, were relieved, though more by the momentary truce than by anything else. They regretted very much to be compelled to hate each other, for each had reckoned up his *vis-à-vis* as a rather proper sort of fellow, probably a man of some achievement, used to good living and good company.

Extreme iciness was unavoidable between them, however. When one stranger has a splendidly-preserved blonde wife and the other a splendidly-preserved brunette wife, both of whom have won social prominence by years of hard fighting and aloofness, there remains nothing for the two men but to follow the lead, especially when directly under the eyes of the leaders.

The son of the blonde matron smiled cheerfully as the welcome light flooded the coach.

He was a nice looking young man, of about twenty-two one might judge, and he did his smiling, though in a perfectly impersonal and correct sort of manner, at the pretty daughter of the brunette matron. The pretty daughter also smiled, but her smile was demurely directed at the trees outside, clad as they were in all the flaming glory of their autumn tints, glistening with the recent rain and dripping with gems that sparkled and flashed in the noonday sun as they fell.

It is marvelous how much one can see out of the corner of the eye, while seeming to view mere scenery.

The driver looked down, as he drove safely off the bridge, and shook his head at the swirl of water that rushed and eddied, dark and muddy, close up under the rotten planking; then he cracked his whip, and the horses sturdily attacked the little hill.

Thick, overhanging trees on either side now dimmed the light again, and the two plump matrons once more glared past the opposite shoulders, profoundly unaware of each other. The husbands took on the politely surly look required of them. The blonde son's eyes still sought the brunette daughter, but it was furtively done and quite unsuccessfully, for the daughter was now doing a little glaring on her own account. The blonde matron had just swept her eyes across the daughter's skirt, estimating the fit and material of it with contempt so artistically veiled that it could almost be understood in the dark.

44

II

The big bays swung to the brow of the hill with ease, and dashed into a small circular clearing, where a quaint little two-story building, with a mossy watering-trough out in front, nestled under the shade of majestic old trees that reared their brown and scarlet crowns proudly into the sky. A long, low porch ran across the front of the structure, and a complaining sign hung out announcing, in dim, weather-flecked letters on a cracked board, that this was the "Tutt House." A gray-headed man, in brown overalls and faded blue jumper, stood on the porch and shook his fist at the stage as it whirled by.

"What a delightfully old-fashioned inn!" exclaimed the pretty daughter. "How I should like to stop there over night!"

"You would probably wish yourself away before morning, Evelyn," replied her mother indifferently. "No doubt it would be a mere siege of discomfort."

The blonde matron turned to her husband. The pretty daughter had been looking at the picturesque "inn" between the heads of this lady and her son.

"Edward, please pull down the shade behind me," she directed. "There is quite a draught from that broken window."

The pretty daughter bit her lip. The brunette matron continued to stare at the shade in the exact spot upon which her gaze had been before directed, and she never quivered an eyelash. The young man seemed very uncomfortable, and he tried to look his apologies to the pretty daughter, but she could not see him now, not even if her eyes had been all corners.

They were bowling along through another avenue of trees when the driver suddenly shouted, "Whoa there!"

The horses were brought up with a jerk that was well nigh fatal to the assortment of dignity inside the coach. A loud roaring could be heard, both ahead and in the rear, a sharp splitting like a fusillade of pistol shots, then a creaking and tearing of timbers. The driver bent suddenly forward.

"Gid ap!" he cried, and the horses sprang forward with a lurch. He swung them around a sharp bend with a skillful hand and poised his weight above the brake as they plunged at terrific speed down a steep grade. The roaring was louder than ever now, and it became deafening as they suddenly emerged from the thick under-brush at the bottom of the declivity.

"Caught, by gravy!" ejaculated the driver, and, for the second time, he brought the coach to an abrupt stop.

"Do see what is the matter, Ralph?" said the blonde matron impatiently.

Thus commanded, the young man swung out and asked the driver about it.

"Paintsville dam's busted," he was informed. "I been a lookin' fer it this many a year, an' this here freshet done it. You see the holler there? Well, they's ten foot o' water in it, an' it had ort to be stone dry. The bridge is tore out behind us, an' we're stuck here till that water runs out. We can't git away till to-morry, anyways."

He pointed out the peculiar topography of the place, and Ralph got back in the coach.

"We're practically on a flood-made island," he exclaimed, with one eye on the pretty daughter, "and we shall have to stop over night at that quaint, old-fashioned inn we passed a few moments ago."

The pretty daughter's eyes twinkled, and he thought he caught a swift, direct gleam from under the long lashes—but he was not sure.

"Dear me, how annoying," said the blonde matron, but the brunette matron still stared, without the slightest trace of interest in anything else, at the infinitesimal spot she had selected on the affronting window-shade.

The two men gave sighs of resignation, and cast carefully concealed glances at each other, speculating on the possibility of a cigar and a glass, and maybe a good story or two, or possibly even a game of poker after the evening meal. Who could tell what might or might not happen?

III

When the stage drew up in front of the little hotel, it found Uncle Billy Tutt prepared for his revenge. In former days the stage had always stopped at the Tutt House for the noonday meal. Since the new railway was built through the adjoining county, however, the stage trip became a mere twelve-mile, cross-country transfer from one railroad to another, and the stage made a later trip, allowing the passengers plenty of time for "dinner" before they started. Day after day, as the coach flashed by with its money-laden passengers, Uncle Billy had hoped that it would break down. But this was better, much better. The coach might be quickly mended, but not the flood.

"I'm agoin' t'charge 'em till they squeal," he declared to the timidly protesting Aunt Margaret, "an' then I'm goin' t'charge 'em a least mite more, drat 'em!

He retreated behind the rough wooden counter that did duty as a desk, slammed open the flimsy, paper-bound "cash book" that served as a register, and planted his elbows uncompromisingly on either side of it.

"Let 'em bring in their own traps," he commented, and Aunt Margaret fled, ashamed and conscience-smitten, to the kitchen. It seemed sinful.

The first one out of the coach was the husband of the brunette matron, and, proceeding under instructions, he waited neither for luggage nor women folk, but hurried straight into the Tutt House. The other man would have been neck and neck with him in the race, if it had not been that he paused to seize two suit cases and had the misfortune to drop one which burst open and scattered a choice assortment of lingerie from one end of the dingy coach to the other.

In the confusion of rescuing the fluffery, the owner of the suit case had to sacrifice her hauteur and help her husband and son block up the aisle, while the other matron had the ineffable satisfaction of being *kept waiting*, at last being enabled to say, sweetly and with the most polite consideration:

"Will you kindly allow me to pass?"

The blonde matron raised up and swept her skirts back perfectly flat. She was pale but collected. Her husband was pink but collected. Her son was crimson and uncollected. The brunette daughter could not have found an eye anywhere in his countenance as she rustled out after her mother.

"I do hope that Belmont has been able to secure choice quarters," the triumphing matron remarked as her daughter joined her on the ground. "This place looks so very small that there can scarcely be more than one comfortable suite in it."

It was a vital thrust. Only a splendidly cultivated self-control prevented the blonde matron from retaliating upon the unfortunate who had muddled things. Even so, her eyes spoke whole shelves of volumes.

The man who first reached the register wrote, in a straight, black scrawl, "J. Belmont Van Kamp, wife, and daughter." There being no space left for his address, he put none down.

"I want three adjoining rooms, en suite if possible," he demanded.

"Three!" exclaimed Uncle Billy, scratching his head. "Won't two do ye? I ain't got but six bedrooms in th' house. Me an' Marge't sleeps in one, an' we're a gittin' too old fer a shake down on th' floor. I'll have t'save one room fer th' driver, an' that leaves four. You take two now—"

Mr. Van Kamp cast a hasty glance out of the window. The other man was getting out of the coach. His own wife was stepping on the porch.

"What do you ask for meals and lodging until this time tomorrow?" he interrupted.

The decisive moment had arrived. Uncle Billy drew a deep breath.

"Two dollars a head!" he defiantly announced. There! It was out! He wished Margaret had staid to hear him say it.

The guest did not seem to be seriously shocked, and Uncle Billy was beginning to be sorry he had not said three dollars, when Mr. Van Kamp stopped the landlord's own breath.

"I'll give you fifteen dollars for the three best rooms in the house," he calmly said, and landlord Tutt gasped as the money fluttered down under his nose.

"Jis' take yore folks right on up, Mr. Kamp," said Uncle Billy, pouncing on the money. "Th' rooms is th' three right along th' hull front o' th' house. I'll be up and make on a fire in a minute. Jis' take th' *Jonesville Banner* an' th' *Uticky Clarion* along with ye."

As the swish of skirts marked the passage of the Van Kamps up the wide hall stairway, the other party swept into the room.

The man wrote, in a round flourish, "Edward Eastman Ellsworth, wife, and son."

"I'd like three choice rooms, en suite," he said.

"Gosh!" said Uncle Billy, regretfully. "That's what Mr. Kamp wanted, fust off, an' he got it. They hain't but th' little room over th' kitchen left. I'll have to put you an' your wife in that, an' let your boy sleep with th' driver."

The consternation in the Ellsworth party was past calculating by any known standards of measurement. The thing was an outrage! It was not to be borne! They would not submit to it!

Uncle Billy, however, secure in his mastery of the situation, calmly quartered them as he had said: "An' let 'em splutter all they want to," he commented comfortably to himself.

IV

The Ellsworths were holding a family indignation meeting on the broad porch when the Van Kamps came contentedly down for a walk, and brushed by them with unseeing eyes.

"It makes a perfectly fascinating suite," observed Mrs. Van

Kamp, in a pleasantly conversational tone that could be easily overhead by anyone impolite enough to listen. "That delightful old-fashioned fireplace in the middle apartment makes it an ideal sitting-room, and the beds are so roomy and comfortable."

"I just knew it would be like this!" chirruped Miss Evelyn. "I remarked as we passed the place, if you will remember, how charming it would be to stop in this dear, quaint old inn over night. All my wishes seem to come true this year."

These simple and, of course, entirely unpremeditated remarks were as vinegar and wormwood to Mrs. Ellsworth, and she gazed after the retreating Van Kamps with a glint in her eye that would make one understand Lucretia Borgia at last.

Her son also gazed after the retreating Van Kamp. She had an exquisite figure, and she carried herself with a most delectable grace. As the party drew away from the inn she dropped behind the elders and wandered off into a side path to gather autumn leaves.

Ralph, too, started off for a walk, but naturally not in the same direction.

"Edward!" suddenly said Mrs. Ellsworth. "I want you to turn those people out of that suite before night!"

"Very well," he replied with a sigh, and got up to do it. He had wrecked a railroad and made one, and had operated successful corners in nutmegs and chicory. No task seemed impossible. He walked in to see the landlord.

"What are the Van Kamps paying you for those three rooms?" he asked.

"Fifteen dollars," Uncle Billy informed him, smoking one of Mr. Van Kamp's good cigars, and twiddling his thumbs in huge content.

"I'll give you thirty for them. Just set their baggage outside and tell them the rooms are occupied."

"No sir-ree!" rejoined Uncle Billy. "A bargain's a bargain, an' I allus stick to one I make."

Mr. Ellsworth withdrew, but not defeated. He had never supposed that such an absurd proposition would be accepted. It was only a feeler, and he had noticed a wince of regret in his landlord. He sat down on the porch and lit a strong cigar. His wife did not bother him. She gazed complacently at the flaming foliage opposite, and allowed him to think. Getting impossible things was his business in life, and she had confidence in him.

"I want to rent your entire house for a week," he announced to Uncle Billy a few minutes later. It had occurred to him that the flood might last longer than they anticipated.

Uncle Billy's eyes twinkled.

"I reckon it kin be did," he allowed. "I reckon a *bo*-tel man's got a right to rent his hull house ary minute."

"Of course he has. How much do you want?"

Uncle Billy had made one mistake in not asking this sort of folks enough, and he reflected in perplexity.

"Make me a offer," he proposed. "Ef it hain't enough I'll tell ye. You want to rent th' hull place, back lot an' all?"

"No, just the mere house. That will be enough," answered the other with a smile. He was on the point of offering a hundred dollars, when he saw the little wrinkles about Mr. Tutt's eyes, and he said seventy-five.

"Sho, ye're jokin'!" retorted Uncle Billy. He had been considered a fine horse-trader in that part of the country. "Make it a hundred and twenty-five, an' I'll go ye."

Mr. Ellsworth counted out some bills.

"Here's a hundred," he said. "That ought to be about right."

"Fifteen more," insisted Uncle Billy.

With a little frown of impatience the other counted off the extra money and handed it over. Uncle Billy gravely handed it back.

"Them's the fifteen dollars Mr. Kamp give me," he explained. "You've got the hull house fer a week, an' o' course, all th' money that's token in is your'n. You kin do as ye please about rentin' out rooms to other folks, I reckon. A bargain's a bargain, an' I allus stick to one I make."

V

Ralph Ellsworth stalked among the trees, feverishly searching for squirrels, scarlet leaves, and the glint of a brown walking-dress, this last not being so easy to locate in sunlit autumn woods. Time after time he quickened his pace, only to find that he had been fooled by a patch of dogwood, a clump of haw bushes or even a leaf-strewn knoll, but at last he unmistakably saw the dress, and then he slowed down to a careless saunter.

She was reaching up for some brilliantly-colored maple leaves, and was entirely unconscious of his presence, especially after she had seen him. Her pose showed her pretty figure to advantage, but, of course, she did not know that. How should she?

Ralph admired the picture very much. The hat, the hair, the gown, the dainty shoes, even the narrow strip of silken hose that was revealed as she stood a tip toe, were all of a deep, rich brown that proved an exquisite foil for the pink and cream of her cheeks. He remembered that her eyes were almost the same shade, and wondered how it was that women-folk happened on combinations in dress that so well set off their natural charms. The fool!

He was about three trees away, now, and a panic akin to that which hunters describe as "buck ague" seized him. He decided that he really had no excuse for coming any nearer. It would not do, either, to be seen staring at her if she should happen to turn her head, so he veered off, intending to regain the road. It would be impossible to do this without passing directly in her range of vision, and he did not intend to try to avoid it. He had a fine, manly figure of his own.

He had just passed the nearest radius to her circle and was proceeding along the tangent that he had laid out for himself, when the unwitting maid looked carefully down and saw a tangle of roots at her very feet. She was so unfortunate, a second later, as to slip her foot in this very tangle and give her ankle ever so slight a twist.

"Oh!" cried Miss Van Kamp, and Ralph Ellsworth flew to the rescue. He had not been noticing her at all, and yet he had started to her side before she had even cried out, which was strange. She had a very attractive voice.

"May I be of assistance?" he anxiously inquired.

"I think not, thank you," she replied, compressing her lips to keep back the intolerable pain, and half-closing her eyes to show the fine lashes. Declining the proffered help, she extricated her foot, picked up her autumn branches, and turned away. She was intensely averse to anything that could be construed as a flirtation, even of the mildest, he could certainly see that. She took a step, swayed slightly, dropped the leaves, and clutched out her hand to him.

"It is nothing," she assured him in a moment, withdrawing the hand after he had held it quite long enough. "Nothing whatever. I gave my foot a slight wrench, and turned the least bit faint for a moment."

"You must permit me to walk back, at least to the road, with you," he insisted, gathering up her arm-load of branches. "I couldn't think of leaving you here alone."

As he stooped to raise the gay woodland treasures he smiled to himself, ever so slightly. This was not *his* first season out, either.

"Delightful spot, isn't it?" he observed as they regained the road and sauntered in the direction of the Tutt House.

"Quite so," she reservedly answered. She had noticed that smile as he stooped. He must be snubbed a little. It would be so good for him.

"You don't happen to know Billy Evans, of Boston, do you?" he asked.

"I think not. I am but very little acquainted in Boston."

"Too bad," he went on. "I was rather in hopes you knew Billy. All sorts of a splendid fellow, and knows everybody."

"Not quite, it seems," she reminded him, and he winced at the error. In spite of the sly smile that he had permitted to himself, he was unusually interested.

He tried the weather, the flood, the accident, golf, books and three good, substantial, warranted jokes, but the conversation lagged in spite of him. Miss Van Kamp would not for the world have it understood that this unconventional meeting, made allowable by her wrenched ankle, could possibly fulfill the functions of a formal introduction.

"What a ripping, queer old building that is!" he exclaimed, making one more brave effort as they came in sight of the hotel.

"It is, rather," she assented. "The rooms in it are as quaint and delightful as the exterior, too."

She looked as harmless and innocent as a basket of peaches as she said it, and never the suspicion of a smile deepened the dimple in the cheek toward him. The smile was glowing cheerfully away inside, though. He could feel it, if he could not see it, and he laughed aloud.

"Your crowd rather got the better of us there," he admitted with the keen appreciation of one still quite close to college days.

"Of course, the mater is furious, but I rather look on it as a lark."

She thawed like an April icicle.

"It's perfectly jolly," she laughed with him. "Awfully selfish of us, too, I know, but such loads of fun."

They were close to the Tutt House now, and her limp, that had entirely disappeared as they emerged from the woods, now became quite perceptible. There might be people looking out of the windows, though it is hard to see why that should affect a limp.

Ralph was delighted to find that a thaw had set in, and he made one more attempt to establish at least a proxy acquaintance.

"You don't happen to know Peyson Kingsley, of Philadelphia, do you?"

"I'm afraid I don't," she replied. "I know so few Philadelphia people, you see." She was rather regretful about it this time. He really was a clever sort of a fellow, in spite of that smile.

The center window in the second floor of the Tutt House swung open, its little squares of glass flashing jubilantly in the sunlight. Mrs. Ellsworth leaned out over the sill, from the quaint old sitting-room of the *Van Kamp apartments!*

"Oh, Ralph!" she called in her most dulcet tones. "Kindly excuse yourself and come right on up to our suite for a few moments!"

VI

It is not nearly so easy to take a practical joke as to perpetrate one. Evelyn was sitting thoughtfully on the porch when her father and mother returned. Mrs. Ellsworth was sitting at the center window above, placidly looking out. Her eyes swept carelessly over the Van Kamps, and unconcernedly passed on to the rest of the landscape.

Mrs. Van Kamp gasped and clutched the arm of her husband. There was no need. He, too, had seen the apparition. Evelyn now, for the first time, saw the real humor of the situation. She smiled as she thought of Ralph. She owed him one, but she never worried about her debts. She always managed to get them paid, principal and interest.

Mr. Van Kamp suddenly glowered and strode into the Tutt House. Uncle Billy met him at the door, reflectively chewing a straw, and handed him an envelope. Mr. Van Kamp tore it open and drew out a note. Three five-dollar bills came out with it and fluttered to the porch floor. This missive confronted him:

Mr. J. Belmont Van Kamp.

Dear Sir:—This is to notify you that I have rented the entire Tutt House, for the ensuing week, and am compelled to assume possession of the three second-floor front rooms. Herewith I am enclosing the fifteen dollars you paid to secure the suite. You are quite welcome to make use, as my guest, of the small room over the kitchen. You will find your luggage in that room. Regretting any inconvenience that this transaction may cause you, I am

YOURS RESPECTFULLY,

EDWARD EASTMAN ELLSWORTH.

Mr. Van Kamp passed the note to his wife and sat down on a large chair. He was glad that the chair was comfortable and roomy. Evelyn picked up the bills and tucked them into her waist. She never overlooked any of her perquisites. Mrs. Van Kamp read the note, and the tip of her nose became white. She also sat down, but she was the first to find her voice.

"Atrocious!" she exclaimed. "Atrocious! Simply atrocious, Belmont. This is a house of public entertainment. They *can't* turn us out in this high-minded manner! Isn't there a law or something to that effect?"

"It wouldn't matter if there was," he thoughtfully replied. "This fellow Ellsworth would be too clever to be caught by it. He would say that the house was not a hotel but a private residence during the period for which he has rented it."

Personally, he rather admired Ellsworth. Seemed to be a resourceful sort of chap who knew how to make money behave itself, and do its little tricks without balking in the harness.

"Then you can make him take down the sign!" his wife declared.

He shook his head decidedly.

"It wouldn't do, Belle," he replied. "It would be spite, not retaliation, and not at all sportsmanlike. The course you suggest would belittle us more than it would annoy them. There must be some other way."

He went in to talk with Uncle Billy.

"I want to buy this place," he stated. "Is it for sale?"

"It sartin is!" replied Uncle Billy. He did not merely twinkle this time. He grinned.

"How much?"

"Three thousand dollars." Mr. Tutt was used to charging by this time, and he betrayed no hesitation.

"I'll write you out a check at once," and Mr. Van Kamp reached in his pocket with the reflection that the spot, after all, was an ideal one for a quiet summer retreat.

"Air you a goin' t' scribble that there three thousan' on a piece o' paper?" inquired Uncle Billy, sitting bolt upright. "Ef you air a figgerin' on that, Mr. Kamp, jis' you save yore time. I give a man four dollars fer one o' them check things oncet, an' I owe myself them four dollars yit."

Mr. Van Kamp retired in disorder, but the thought of his wife and daughter waiting confidently on the porch stopped him. Moreover, the thing had resolved itself rather into a contest between Ellsworth and himself, and he had done a little making and breaking of men and things in his own time. He did some Gatling-gun thinking out by the newel-post, and presently rejoined Uncle Billy.

"Mr. Tutt, tell me just exactly what Mr. Ellsworth rented, please," he requested.

"Th' hull house," replied Billy, and then he somewhat sternly added: "Paid me spot cash fer it, too."

Mr. Van Kamp took a wad of loose bills from his trousers pocket, straightened them out leisurely, and placed them in his bill book, along with some smooth yellowbacks of eye-bulging denominations. Uncle Billy sat up and stopped twiddling his thumbs.

"Nothing was said about the furniture, was there?" suavely inquired Van Kamp.

Uncle Billy leaned blankly back in his chair. Little by little the light dawned on the ex-horse-trader. The crow's feet reappeared about his eyes, his mouth twitched, he smiled, he grinned, then he slapped his thigh and haw-hawed.

"No!" roared Uncle Billy. "No, there wasn't, by gum!"

"Nothing but the house?"

"His very own words!" chuckled Uncle Billy. "'Jis' th' mere house,' says he, an' he gits it. A bargain's a bargain, an' I allus stick to one I make."

"How much for the furniture for the week?"

"Fifty dollars!" Mr. Tutt knew how to do business with this kind of people now, you bet.

Mr. Van Kamp promptly counted out the money.

"Drat it!" commented Uncle Billy to himself. "I could a got more!"

"Now, where can we make ourselves comfortable with this furniture?"

Uncle Billy chirked up. All was not yet lost.

"Wall," he reflectively drawled, "there's th' new barn. It

hain't been used for nothin' yit, senct I built it two years ago. I jis' hadn't th' heart t' put th' critters in it as long as th' ole one stood up."

The other smiled at this flash-light on Uncle Billy's character, and they went out to look at the barn.

VII

Uncle Billy came back from the "Tutt House Annex," as Mr. Van Kamp dubbed the barn, with enough more money to make him love all the world until he got used to having it. Uncle Billy belongs to a large family.

Mr. Van Kamp joined the women on the porch, and explained the attractively novel situation to them. They were chatting gaily when the Ellsworths came down the stairs. Mr. Ellsworth paused for a moment to exchange a word with Uncle Billy.

"Mr. Tutt," said he laughing, "if we go for a bit of exercise will you guarantee us the possession of our rooms when we come back?"

"Yes-sir-ree!" Uncle Billy assured him. "They shan't nobody take them rooms away from you fer money, marbles, ner chalk. A bargain's a bargain, an' I allus stick to one I make," and he virtuously took a chew of tobacco while he inspected the afternoon sky with a clear conscience.

"I want to get some of those splendid autumn leaves to decorate our cozy apartments," Mrs. Ellsworth told her husband as they passed in hearing of the Van Kamps. "Do you know those old-time rag-rugs are the most oddly decorative effects that

I have ever seen. They are so rich in color and so exquisitely blended."

There were reasons why this poisoned arrow failed to rankle, but the Van Kamps did not trouble to explain. They were waiting for Ralph to come out and join his parents. Ralph, it seemed however, had decided not to take a walk. He had already fatigued himself, he had explained, and his mother had favored him with a significant look. She could readily believe him, she had assured him, and had then left him in scorn.

The Van Kamps went out to consider the arrangement of the barn. Evelyn returned first and came out on the porch to find a handkerchief. It was not there, but Ralph was. She was very much surprised to see him, and she intimated as much.

"It's dreadfully damp in the woods," he explained. "By the way, you don't happen to know the Whitleys, of Washington, do you? Most excellent people."

"I'm quite sorry that I do not," she replied. "But you will have to excuse me. We shall be kept very busy with arranging our apartments."

Ralph sprang to his feet with a ludicrous expression.

"Not the second floor front suite!" he exclaimed.

"Oh, no! Not at all," she reassured him. He laughed lightly.

"Honors are about even in that game," he said.

"Evelyn," called her mother from the hall. "Please come and take those front suite curtains down to the barn."

"Pardon me while we take the next trick," remarked Evelyn with a laugh quite as light and gleeful as his own, and disappeared into the hall.

He followed her slowly, and was met at the door by her father.

"You are the younger Mr. Ellsworth, I believe," politely said Mr. Van Kamp.

"Ralph Ellsworth. Yes, sir."

"Here is a note for your father. It is unsealed. You are quite at liberty to read it."

Mr. Van Kamp bowed himself away, and Ralph opened the note, which read:

Edward Eastman Ellsworth, Esq.

Dear Sir:—This is to notify you that I have rented the entire furniture of the Tutt House for the ensuing week, and am compelled to assume possession of that in the three second floor front rooms, as well as all the balance not in actual use by Mr. and Mrs. Tutt and the driver of the stage. You are quite welcome, however, to make use of the furnishings in the small room over the kitchen. Your luggage you will find undisturbed. Regretting any inconvenience that this transaction may cause you. I remain

> Yours Respectfully,
> J. Belmont Van Kamp.

Ralph scratched his head in amused perplexity. It devolved upon him to even up the affair a little before his mother came back. He must support the family reputation for resourcefulness, but it took quite a bit of scalp irritation before he aggravated the right idea into being. As soon as the idea came, he went in and made a hide-bound bargain with Uncle Billy, then he went out into the hall and waited until Evelyn came down with a huge arm-load of window curtains.

"Honors are still even," he remarked. "I have just bought all the edibles about the place, whether in the cellar, the house or any of the surrounding structures, in the ground, above the ground, dead or alive, and a bargain's a bargain as between man and man."

"Clever of you, I'm sure," commented Miss Van Kamp, reflectively. Suddenly her lips parted with a smile that revealed a double row of most beautiful teeth. He meditatively watched the curve of her lips.

"Isn't that rather a heavy load?" he suggested. "I'd be delighted to help you move the things, don't you know."

"It is quite kind of you, and what the men would call 'game,' I believe, under the circumstances," she answered, "but really it will not be necessary. We have hired Mr. Tutt and the driver to do the heavier part of the work, and the rest of it will be really a pleasant diversion."

"No doubt," agreed Ralph, with an appreciative grin. "By the way, you don't happen to know Maud and Dorothy Partridge, of Baltimore, do you? Stunning pretty girls, both of them, and no end of swells."

"I know so very few people in Baltimore," she murmured, and tripped on down to the barn.

Ralph went out on the porch and smoked. There was nothing else that he could do.

VIII

It was growing dusk when the elder Ellsworth returned, almost hidden by great masses of autumn boughs.

"You should have been with us, Ralph," enthusiastically said his mother. "I never saw such gorgeous tints in all my life. We have brought nearly the entire woods with us."

"It was a good idea," said Ralph. "A stunning good idea. They may come in handy to sleep on."

Mrs. Ellsworth turned cold.

"What do you mean?" she gasped.

"Ralph," sternly demanded his father, "you don't mean to tell us that you let the Van Kamps jockey us out of those rooms after all?"

"Indeed no," he airily responded. "Just come right on up and see."

He led the way into the suite and struck a match. One solitary candle had been left upon the mantel shelf. Ralph thought that this had been overlooked, but his mother afterwards set him right about that. Mrs. Van Kamp had cleverly left it so that the Ellsworths could see how dreadfully bare the place was. One candle in three rooms is drearier than darkness anyhow.

Mrs. Ellsworth took in all the desolation, the dismal expanse of the now enormous apartments, the shabby walls, the hideous bright spots where pictures had hung, the splintered flooring, the great, gaunt windows—and she gave in. She had met with snub after snub, and cut after cut, in her social climb, she had had the cook quit in the middle of an important dinner, she had had every disconcerting thing possible happen to her, but this—this was the last *bale* of straw. She sat down on a suit case, in the middle of the biggest room, and cried!

Ralph, having waited for this, now told about the food transaction, and she hastily pushed the last-coming tear back into her eye.

"Good!" she cried. "They will be up here soon. They will

be compelled to compromise, and they must not find me with red eyes."

She cast a hasty glance around the room, then, in a sudden panic seized the candle and explored the other two. She went wildly out into the hall, back into the little room over the kitchen, down-stairs, everywhere, and returned in consternation.

"There's not a single mirror left in the house!" she moaned.

Ralph heartlessly grinned. He could appreciate that this was a characteristic woman trick, and wondered admiringly whether Evelyn or her mother had thought of it. However, this was a time for action.

"I'll get you some water to bathe your eyes," he offered, and ran into the little room over the kitchen to get a pitcher. A cracked shaving-mug was the only vessel that had been left, but he hurried down into the yard with it. This was no time for fastidiousness.

He had barely creaked the pump handle when Mr. Van Kamp hurried up from the barn.

"I beg your pardon, sir," said Mr. Van Kamp, "but this water belongs to us. My daughter bought it, all that is in the ground, above the ground, or that may fall from the sky upon these premises."

IX

The mutual siege lasted until after seven o'clock, but it was rather one-sided. The Van Kamps could drink all the water they liked, it made them no hungrier. If the Ellsworths ate anything, however, they grew thirstier, and, moreover, water was necessary if anything worth while was to be cooked. They knew all this, and resisted until Mrs. Ellsworth was tempted and fell. She ate a sandwich and choked. It was heartbreaking, but Ralph had to be sent down with a plate of sandwiches and an offer to trade them for water.

Half way between the pump and the house he met Evelyn coming with a small pail of the precious fluid. They both stopped stock still; then, seeing that it was too late to retreat, both laughed and advanced.

"Who wins now?" bantered Ralph as they made the exchange.

"It looks to me like a misdeal," she gaily replied, and was moving away when he called her back.

"You don't happen to know the Gatelys, of New York, do you?" he was quite anxious to know.

"I am truly sorry, but I am acquainted with so few people in New York. We are from Chicago, you know."

"Oh," said he blankly, and took the water up to the Ellsworth suite.

Mrs. Ellsworth cheered up considerably when she heard that Ralph had been met half way, but her eyes snapped when he confessed that it was Miss Van Kamp who had met him.

"I hope you are not going to carry on a flirtation with that over-dressed creature," she blazed.

"Why mother," exclaimed Ralph, shocked beyond measure. "What right have you to accuse either this young lady or myself of flirting? Flirting!"

Mrs. Ellsworth suddenly attacked the fire with quite unnecessary energy.

X

Down at the barn, the wide threshing floor had been covered with gay rag-rugs, and strewn with tables, couches, and chairs in picturesque profusion. Roomy box-stalls had been carpeted deep with clean straw, curtained off with gaudy bed-quilts, and converted into cozy sleeping apartments. The mow and the stalls had been screened off with lace curtains and blazing counterpanes, and the whole effect was one of Oriental luxury and splendor. Alas, it was only an "effect!" The red-hot parlor stove smoked abominably, and the pipe carried other smoke out through the hay-mow window, only to let it blow back again. Chill cross-draughts whistled in from cracks too numerous to be stopped up, and the miserable Van Kamps could only cough and shiver, and envy the Tutts and the driver, non-combatants who had been fed two hours before.

Up in the second floor suite there was a roaring fire in the big fireplace, but there was a chill in the room that no mere fire could drive away—the chill of absolute emptiness.

A man can outlive hardships that would kill a woman, but a woman can endure discomforts that would drive a man crazy.

Mr. Ellsworth went out to hunt up Uncle Billy, with an especial solace in mind. The landlord was not in the house, but the yellow gleam of a lantern revealed his presence in the woodshed, and Mr. Ellsworth stepped in upon him just as he was pouring something yellow and clear into a tumbler from a big jug that he had just taken from under the flooring.

"How much do you want for that jug and its contents?"

he asked, with a sigh of gratitude that this supply had been overlooked.

Before Mr. Tutt could answer, Mr. Van Kamp hurried in at the door.

"Wait a moment!" he cried. "I want to bid on that!"

"This here jug hain't fer sale at no price," Uncle Billy emphatically announced, nipping all negotiations right in the bud. "It's too pesky hard to sneak this here licker in past Marge't, but I reckon it's my treat, gents. Ye kin have all ye want."

One minute later Mr. Van Kamp and Mr. Ellsworth were seated, one on a saw-buck and the other on a nail-keg, comfortably eyeing each other across the work bench, and each was holding up a tumbler one-third filled with the golden yellow liquid.

"Your health, sir," courteously proposed Mr. Ellsworth.

"And to you, sir," gravely replied Mr. Van Kamp.

XI

Ralph and Evelyn happened to meet at the pump, quite accidentally, after the former had made half a dozen five-minute-apart trips for a drink. It was Miss Van Kamp, this time, who had been studying on the mutual acquaintance problem.

"You don't happen to know the Tylers, of Parkersburg, do you?" she asked.

"The Tylers! I should say I do!" was the unexpected and enthusiastic reply. "Why, we are on our way now to Miss Georgiana Tyler's wedding to my friend Jimmy Carston. I'm to be best man."

"How delightful!" she exclaimed. "We are on the way there, too. Georgiana was my dearest chum at school, and I am to be her 'best girl.'"

"Let's go around on the porch and sit down," said Ralph.

XII

Mr. Van Kamp, back in the woodshed, looked about him with an eye of content.

"Rather cozy for a woodshed," he observed. "I wonder if we couldn't scare up a little session of dollar limit?"

Both Uncle Billy and Mr. Ellsworth were willing. Death and poker level all Americans. A fourth hand was needed, however. The stage driver was in bed and asleep, and Mr. Ellsworth volunteered to find the extra player.

"I'll get Ralph," he said. "He plays a fairly stiff game."

He finally found his son on the porch, apparently alone, and stated his errand.

"Thank you, but I don't believe I care to play this evening," was the astounding reply, and Mr. Ellsworth looked closer. He made out, then, a dim figure on the other side of Ralph.

"Oh! Of course not!" he blundered, and went back to the woodshed.

Three-handed poker is a miserable game, and it seldom lasts long. It did not in this case. After Uncle Billy had won the only jack-pot deserving of the name, he was allowed to go blissfully to sleep with his hand on the handle of the big jug.

After poker there is only one other always available amusement for men, and that is business. The two travelers were quite well acquainted when Ralph put his head in at the door.

"Thought I'd find you here," he explained. "It just occurred to me to wonder whether you gentlemen had discovered, as yet, that we are all to be house guests at the Carston-Tyler wedding."

"Why, no!" exclaimed his father in pleased surprise. "It is a most agreeable coincidence. Mr. Van Kamp, allow me to introduce my son, Ralph. Mr. Van Kamp and myself, Ralph, have found out that we shall be considerably thrown together in a business way from now on. He has just purchased control of the Metropolitan and Western string of Interurbans."

"Delighted, I'm sure," murmured Ralph, shaking hands, and then he slipped out as quickly as possible. Some one seemed to be waiting for him.

Perhaps another twenty minutes had passed, when one of the men had an illuminating idea that resulted, later on, in pleasant relations for all of them. It was about time, for Mrs. Ellsworth, up in the bare suite, and Mrs. Van Kamp, down in the draughty barn, both wrapped up to the chin and both still chilly, had about reached the limit of patience and endurance.

"Why can't we make things a little more comfortable for all concerned?" suggested Mr. Van Kamp. "Suppose, as a starter, that we have Mrs. Van Kamp give a shiver party down in the barn?"

"Good idea," agreed Mr. Ellsworth. "A little diplomacy will do it. Each one of us will have to tell his wife that the other fellow made the first abject overtures."

Mr. Van Kamp grinned understandingly, and agreed to the infamous ruse.

"By the way," continued Mr. Ellsworth, with a still happier thought, "you must allow Mrs. Ellsworth to furnish the dinner for Mrs. Van Kamp's shiver party."

"Dinner!" gasped Mr. Van Kamp. "By all means!"

Both men felt an anxious yawning in the region of the appetite, and a yearning moisture wetted their tongues. They looked at the slumbering Uncle Billy and decided to see Mrs. Tutt themselves about a good, hot dinner for six.

"Law me!" exclaimed Aunt Margaret when they appeared at the kitchen door. "I swan I thought you folks 'ud never come to yore senses. Here I've had a big pot o' stewed chicken ready on the stove fer two mortal hours. I kin give ye that, an' smashed taters an' chicken gravy, an' dried corn, an' hot corn-pone, an' currant jell, an' strawberry preserves, an' my own cannin' o' peaches, an' pumpkin-pie an' coffee. Will that do ye?" Would it *do! Would* it do!!

As Aunt Margaret talked, the kitchen door swung wide, and the two men were stricken speechless with astonishment. There, across from each other at the kitchen table, sat the utterly selfish and traitorous younger members of the rival houses of Ellsworth and Van Kamp, deep in the joys of chicken, and mashed potatoes, and gravy, and hot corn-pone, and all the other "fixings," laughing and chatting gaily like chums of years' standing. They had seemingly just come to an agreement about something or other, for Evelyn, waving the shorter end of a broken wish-bone, was vivaciously saying to Ralph:

"A bargain's a bargain, and I always stick to one I make."

The Wrong Man

NELLA LARSEN

The room blazed with color. It seemed that the gorgeous things which the women were wearing had for this once managed to subdue the strident tones of the inevitable black and white of the men's costumes. Tonight they lent just enough of preciseness to add interest to the riotously hued scene. The place was crowded but cool, for a gentle breeze blew from the Sound through the large open windows and doors, now and then stirring some group of flowers.

Julia Romley, in spite of the smoke-colored chiffon gown (ordered specially for the occasion) which she was wearing, seemed even more flamingly clad than the rest. The pale indefinite gray but increased the flaring mop of her hair; scarlet, a poet had called it. The satiny texture of her skin seemed also to reflect in her cheeks a cozy tinge of that red mass.

Julia, however, was not happy tonight. A close observer would have said that she was actively disturbed. Faint abstraction, trite remarks nervously offered, and uncontrolled restlessness marred her customary perfect composure. Her dreamy gray eyes stole frequently in the direction of Myra Redmon's party. Myra always had a lion in tow, but why that particular man? She shook a little as she wondered.

Suddenly, the orchestra blared into something wild and impressionistic, with a primitive staccato understrain of jazz.

The buzz of conversation died, strangled by the savage strains of the music. The crowd stirred, broke, coalesced into twos, and became a whirling mass. A partner claimed Julia and they became part of the swaying mob.

"Some show, what?" George Hill's drawling voice was saying, while he secretly wondered what had got into Julia; she was so quiet, not like herself at all.

Julia let her eyes wander over the moving crowd. Young men, old men, young women, older women, slim girls, fat women, thin men, stout men, glided by. The old nursery rhyme came into her mind. She repeated it to George in a singsong tone:

> "Rich man, poor man,
> Beggar man, thief,
> Doctor, lawyer,
> Indian chief."

George nodded. "Yes, that's it. Everybody's here and a few more. And look, look! There's the 'Indian chief.' Wonder who he is? He certainly looks the part."

Julia didn't look; she knew what she would see. A tall, thin man, his lean face yellowed and hardened as if by years in the tropics; a man, perhaps, a bit unused to scenes of this kind, purposely a little aloof and, one suspected, more than a little contemptuous.

She felt a flash of resentful anger against Myra. Why was she always carting about impossible people? It was disgusting. It was worse—it was dangerous. Certainly it was about to become dangerous to her, Julia Romley, erstwhile . . . She let the thought die unfinished, it was too unpleasant.

She had been so happy, so secure, and now this: Ralph Tyler, risen from the past to shatter the happiness which she had grasped for herself. Must she begin all over again? She made a hasty review of her life since San Francisco days: Chicago and the art school where she had studied interior decorating with the money that Ralph Tyler had given her; New York, her studio and success; Boston, and marriage to Jim Romley. And now this envied gay life in one of Long Island's most exclusive sets. Yes, life had been good to her at last, better than she had ever dreamed. Was she about to lose everything—love, wealth, and position? She shivered.

"Cold?" Again George's drawling voice dragging her back to the uncertain present.

"No, not cold. Just someone walking over my grave," she answered laughingly. "I'm rotten company tonight, George. I'm sorry; I'll do better. It's the crowd, I guess."

Her husband claimed her for the next dance. A happy married pair, their obvious joy in each other after five wedded years was the subject of amused comment and mild jokes among their friends. "The everlasting lovers," they were dubbed, and the name suited them as perfectly as they suited each other.

"What's wrong, Julie, old girl?" asked Jim after a few minutes' baffled scrutiny. "Tired?"

"Nothing, nothing. I just feel small, so futile in this crush; sort of trapped, you know. Why *do* the Arnolds have so many people to their things?" Quickly regretting her display of irritation, she added: "It's wonderful, though—the people, the music, the color, and these lovely rooms, like a princess's ball in a fairy tale."

"Yes, great," he agreed. "Lots of strangers here, too; most of them distinguished people from town."

"Who's the tall browned man with Myra, who looks like—well, like an Indian chief?" She laughed a little at her own pleasantry, just to show Jim that there was nothing troubling her.

"Doesn't he, though? Sort of self-sufficient and superior and a bit indifferent, as if he owned us all and despised the whole tribe of us. I guess you can't blame him much. He probably thinks we're a soft, lazy, self-pampering lot. He's Ralph Tyler, an explorer, just back from some godforsaken place on the edge of nowhere. Been head of some expedition lost somewhere in Asia for years, given up for dead. Discovered a buried city or something; great contribution to civilization and all that, you know. They say he brought back some emeralds worth a king's ransom."

"Do you know him, Jim?"

"Yes; knew him years ago in college. Didn't think he'd remember me after such a long time and all those thrilling adventures, but he did. Honestly, you could have knocked me over with a feather when he came over to me and put out his hand and said, 'Hello there, Jim Romley.' Nice, wasn't it?" Jim's handsome face glowed. He was undoubtedly flattered by the great man's remembrance. He went on enthusiastically: "I'm going to have him out to the house, Julie; that is, if I can get him. Small, handpicked dinner party. What say?"

She shivered again.

"Cold?"

"No, not cold. Just someone walking over my grave." She

laughed, amused at the double duty of the superstition in one evening, and glad too that Jim had not noticed that his question had passed unanswered.

Dance followed dance. She wasn't being a success tonight. She knew it, but somehow she couldn't make small talk. Her thoughts kept wandering to that tall browned man who had just come back from the world's end. One or two of her partners, after trying in vain to draw her out, looked at her quizzically, wondering if the impossible had happened. Had Julia and old Jim quarreled?

At last she escaped to a small deserted room on an upper floor, where she could be alone to think. She groped about in her mind for some way to avoid that dinner party. It spelled disaster. She must find some way to keep Ralph Tyler from finding out that she was the wife of his old schoolmate. But if he were going to be here for any length of time, and Jim seemed to think that he would, she would have to meet him. Perhaps she could go away? . . . No, she dared not; anything might happen. Better to be on hand to ward off the blow when it fell. She sighed, suddenly weary and beaten. It was hopeless. And she had been so happy! Just a faint shadow of uneasiness, at first, which had gradually faded as the years slipped away.

She sat for a long time in deep thought. Her face settled into determined lines; she made up her mind. She would ask, plead if necessary, for his silence. It was the only way. It would be hard, humiliating even, but it must be done if she were to continue to be happy in Jim's love. She couldn't bear to look ahead to years without him.

She crossed the room and wrote a note to Ralph Tyler,

asking him to meet her in the summerhouse in one of the gardens. She hesitated a moment over the signature, finally writing *Julia Hammond*, in order to prepare him a little for the meeting.

After she had given the note into the hand of a servant for delivery "to Mr. Tyler, the man with Mrs. Redmon," she experienced a slight feeling of relief. "At least I can try," she thought as she made her way to the summerhouse to wait. "Surely, if I tell him about myself and Jim, he'll be merciful."

The man looked curiously at the woman sitting so motionless in the summerhouse in the rock garden. Even in the darkness she felt his gaze upon her, though she lacked the courage to raise her eyes to look at him. She waited expectantly for him to speak.

After what seemed hours but was, she knew, only seconds, she understood that he was waiting for her to break the silence. So she began to speak in a low hesitating voice.

"I suppose you think it strange, this request of mine to meet me here alone; but I had to see you, to talk to you. I wanted to tell you about my marriage to Jim Romley. You know him?"

"Yes, I know him."

"Well," she went on, eagerly now, "you see, we're so happy! Jim's so splendid, and I've tried to be such a good wife. And I thought—I thought—you see, I thought—" The eager voice trailed off on a note of entreaty.

"Yes, you thought?" prompted the man in a noncommittal tone.

"Well, you see, I thought that if you knew how happy we were, and how much I love him, and that since you know Jim, that you—you—"

She stopped. She couldn't go on, she simply couldn't. But she must. There he stood like a long, menacing shadow between her and the future. She began again, this time with insinuating flattery:

"You have so much yourself now—honor, fame, and money—and you've done such splendid things! You've suffered too. How you must have suffered! Oh, I'm glad of your success; you deserve it. You're a hero, a great man. A little thing like that can't matter to you now and it means everything to me, everything. Please spare me my little happiness. Please be kind!"

"But I don't understand." The man's voice was puzzled. "How 'kind'? What is it you're asking?"

Reading masked denial in the question, Julia began to sob softly.

"Don't tell Jim! Please, don't tell Jim! I'll do anything to keep him from knowing, anything."

"But aren't you making a mistake? I—"

"Mistake?" She laughed bitterly. "I see; you think I should have told him. You think that even now I should tell him that I was your mistress once. You don't know Jim. He'd never forgive that. He wouldn't understand that, when a girl has been sick and starving on the streets, anything can happen to her; that she's grateful for food and shelter at any price. You won't tell him, will you?"

"But I'm sure," stammered the tall figure, fumbling for cigarettes, "I'm sure you've made a mistake. I'm sorry. I've been trying to—"

Julia cut him off. She couldn't bear to hear him speak the refusing words, his voice seemed so grimly final. She knew it was useless, but she made a last desperate effort:

"I was so young, so foolish, and so hungry; but Jim wouldn't understand." She choked over the last words.

He shook his head—impatiently, it seemed to the agonized woman.

"Mrs. Romley, I've been trying to tell you that you've made a mistake. I'm sorry. However, I can assure you that your secret is safe with me. It will never be from my lips that Jim Romley hears you have been—er—what you say you have been."

Only the woman's sharply drawn quivering breath indicated that she had heard. A match blazed for a moment as he lighted his cigarette with shaking hands. Julia's frightened eyes picked out his face in the flickering light. She uttered a faint dismayed cry.

She had told the wrong man.

Dr. Heidegger's Experiment

NATHANIEL HAWTHORNE

That very singular man, old Dr. Heidegger, once invited four venerable friends to meet him in his study. There were three white-bearded gentlemen, Mr. Medbourne, Colonel Killigrew, and Mr. Gascoigne, and a withered gentlewoman, whose name was the Widow Wycherly. They were all melancholy old creatures, who had been unfortunate in life, and whose greatest misfortune it was, that they were not long ago in their graves. Mr. Medbourne, in the vigor of his age, had been a prosperous merchant, but had lost his all by a frantic speculation, and was now little better than a mendicant. Colonel Killigrew had wasted his best years, and his health and substance, in the pursuit of sinful pleasures, which had given birth to a brood of pains, such as the gout, and divers other torments of soul and body. Mr. Gascoigne was a ruined politician, a man of evil fame, or at least had been so, till time had buried him from the knowledge of the present generation, and made him obscure instead of infamous. As for the Widow Wycherly, tradition tells us that she was a great beauty in her day; but, for a long while past, she had lived in deep seclusion, on account of certain scandalous stories, which had prejudiced the gentry of the town against her. It is a circumstance worth mentioning, that each of these three old gentlemen, Mr. Medbourne, Colonel Killigrew, and Mr. Gascoigne, were early lovers of the Widow

Wycherly, and had once been on the point of cutting each other's throats for her sake. And, before proceeding farther, I will merely hint, that Dr. Heidegger and all his four guests were sometimes thought to be a little beside themselves; as is not unfrequently the case with old people, when worried either by present troubles or woeful recollections.

'My dear old friends,' said Dr. Heidegger, motioning them to be seated, 'I am desirous of your assistance in one of those little experiments with which I amuse myself here in my study.'

If all stories were true, Dr. Heidegger's study must have been a very curious place. It was a dim, old-fashioned chamber, festooned with cobwebs, and besprinkled with antique dust. Around the walls stood several oaken bookcases, the lower shelves of which were filled with rows of gigantic folios, and blackletter quartos, and the upper with little parchment covered duodecimos. Over the central bookcase was a bronze bust of Hippocrates, with which, according to some authorities, Dr. Heidegger was accustomed to hold consultations, in all difficult cases of his practice. In the obscurest corner of the room stood a tall and narrow oaken closet, with its door ajar, within which doubtfully appeared a skeleton. Between two of the bookcases hung a looking-glass, presenting its high and dusty plate within a tarnished gilt frame. Among many wonderful stories related of this mirror, it was fabled that the spirits of all the doctor's deceased patients dwelt within its verge, and would stare him in the face whenever he looked thitherward. The opposite side of the chamber was ornamented with the full-length portrait of a young lady, arrayed in the faded magnificence of silk, satin, and brocade, and with a visage as faded as her dress. Above half a century ago, Dr. Heidegger had been on the point of marriage with this young lady; but, being affected with some slight disorder, she had swallowed one of her lover's prescriptions, and died on the bridal evening. The greatest curiosity of the study remains to be mentioned; it was a ponderous folio volume, bound in black leather, with massive silver clasps. There were no letters on the back, and nobody could tell the title of the book. But it was well known to be a book of magic; and once, when a chambermaid had lifted it, merely to brush away the dust, the skeleton had rattled in its closet, the picture of the young lady had stepped one foot upon the floor, and several ghastly faces had peeped forth from the mirror; while the brazen head of Hippocrates frowned, and said—'Forbear!'

Such was Dr. Heidegger's study. On the summer afternoon of our tale, a small round table, as black as ebony, stood in the centre of the room, sustaining a cut-glass vase, of beautiful form and elaborate workmanship. The sunshine came through the window, between the heavy festoons of two faded damask curtains, and fell directly across this vase; so that a mild splendor was reflected from it on the ashen visages of the five old people who sat around. Four champagne glasses were also on the table.

'My dear old friends,' repeated Dr. Heidegger, 'may I reckon on your aid in performing an exceedingly curious experiment?'

Now Dr. Heidegger was a very strange old gentleman, whose eccentricity had become the nucleus for a thousand fantastic stories. Some of these fables, to my shame be it spoken, might possibly be traced back to mine own veracious self; and if any passages of the present tale should startle the reader's faith, I must be content to bear the stigma of a fiction-monger.

When the doctor's four guests heard him talk of his proposed experiment, they anticipated nothing more wonderful than the murder of a mouse in an air-pump, or the examination of a cobweb by the microscope, or some similar nonsense, with which he was constantly in the habit of pestering his intimates. But without waiting for a reply, Dr. Heidegger hobbled across the chamber, and returned with the same ponderous folio, bound in black leather, which common report affirmed to be a book of magic. Undoing the silver clasps, he opened the volume, and took from among its blackletter pages a rose, or what was once a rose, though now the green leaves and crimson petals had assumed one brownish hue, and the ancient flower seemed ready to crumble to dust in the doctor's hands.

'This rose,' said Dr. Heidegger, with a sigh, 'this same withered and crumbling flower, blossomed five-and-fifty years ago. It was given me by Sylvia Ward, whose portrait hangs yonder; and I meant to wear it in my bosom at our wedding. Five-and-fifty years it has been treasured between the leaves of this old volume. Now, would you deem it possible that this rose of half a century could ever bloom again?'

'Nonsense!' said the Widow Wycherly, with a peevish toss of her head. 'You might as well ask whether an old woman's wrinkled face could ever bloom again.'

'See!' answered Dr. Heidegger.

He uncovered the vase, and threw the faded rose into the water which it contained. At first, it lay lightly on the surface of the fluid, appearing to imbibe none of its moisture. Soon, however, a singular change began to be visible. The crushed and dried petals stirred, and assumed a deepening tinge of crimson, as if the flower were reviving from a death-like slumber; the slender stalk and twigs of foliage became green; and there was the rose of half a century, looking as fresh as when Sylvia Ward had first given it to her lover. It was scarcely full-blown; for some of its delicate red leaves curled modestly around its moist bosom, within which two or three dew-drops were sparkling.

'That is certainly a very pretty deception,' said the doctor's friends; carelessly, however, for they had witnessed greater miracles at a conjurer's show: 'pray how was it effected?'

'Did you never hear of the "Fountain of Youth?"' asked Dr. Heidegger, 'which Ponce De Leon, the Spanish adventurer, went in search of, two or three centuries ago?'

'But did Ponce De Leon ever find it?' said the Widow Wycherly.

'No,' answered Dr. Heidegger, 'for he never sought it in the right place. The famous Fountain of Youth, if I am rightly informed, is situated in the southern part of the Floridian peninsula, not far from Lake Macaco. Its source is overshadowed by several gigantic magnolias, which, though numberless centuries old, have been kept as fresh as violets, by the virtues of this wonderful water. An acquaintance of mine, knowing my curiosity in such matters, has sent me what you see in the vase.'

'Ahem!' said Colonel Killigrew, who believed not a word of the doctor's story: 'and what may be the effect of this fluid on the human frame?'

'You shall judge for yourself, my dear colonel,' replied Dr. Heidegger; 'and all of you, my respected friends, are welcome to so much of this admirable fluid, as may restore to you the bloom of youth. For my own part, having had much trouble in growing old, I am in no hurry to grow young again. With your permission, therefore, I will merely watch the progress of the experiment.'

While he spoke, Dr. Heidegger had been filling the four champagne glasses with the water of the Fountain of Youth. It was apparently impregnated with an effervescent gas, for little bubbles were continually ascending from the depths of the glasses, and bursting in silvery spray at the surface. As the liquor diffused a pleasant perfume, the old people doubted not that it possessed cordial and comfortable properties; and, though utter skeptics as to its rejuvenescent power, they were inclined to swallow it at once. But Dr. Heidegger besought them to stay a moment.

'Before you drink, my respectable old friends,' said he, 'it would be well that, with the experience of a life-time to direct you, you should draw up a few general rules for your guidance, in passing a second time through the perils of youth. Think what a sin and shame it would be, if, with your peculiar advantages, you should not become patterns of virtue and wisdom to all the young people of the age!'

The doctor's four venerable friends made him no answer, except by a feeble and tremulous laugh; so very ridiculous was the idea, that, knowing how closely repentance treads behind the steps of error, they should ever go astray again.

'Drink, then,' said the doctor, bowing: 'I rejoice that I have so well selected the subjects of my experiment.'

With palsied hands, they raised the glasses to their lips. The liquor, if it really possessed such virtues as Dr. Heidegger imputed to it, could not have been bestowed on four human beings who needed it more woefully. They looked as if they had never known what youth or pleasure was, but had been the offspring of Nature's dotage, and always the gray, decrepit, sapless, miserable creatures, who now sat stooping round the doctor's table, without life enough in their souls or bodies to be animated even by the prospect of growing young again. They drank off the water, and replaced their glasses on the table.

Assuredly there was an almost immediate improvement in the aspect of the party, not unlike what might have been produced by a glass of generous wine, together with a sudden glow of cheerful sunshine, brightening over all their visages at once. There was a healthful suffusion on their cheeks, instead of the ashen hue that had made them look so corpse-like. They gazed at one another, and fancied that some magic power had really begun to smooth away the deep and sad inscriptions which Father Time had been so long engraving on their brows. The Widow Wycherly adjusted her cap, for she felt almost like a woman again.

'Give us more of this wondrous water!' cried they, eagerly. 'We are younger—but we are still too old! Quick!—give us more!'

'Patience, patience!' quoth Dr. Heidegger, who sat watching the experiment, with philosophic coolness. 'You have been a long time growing old. Surely, you might be content to grow young in half an hour! But the water is at your service.'

Again he filled their glasses with the liquor of youth, enough of which still remained in the vase to turn half the old people in the city to the age of their own grandchildren. While the bubbles were yet sparkling on the brim, the doctor's four guests snatched their glasses from the table, and swallowed the contents at a single gulp. Was it delusion! Even while the draught was passing down their throats, it seemed to have wrought a change on their whole systems. Their eyes grew clear and bright; a dark shade deepened among their silvery locks; they sat around the table, three gentlemen, of middle age, and a woman, hardly beyond her buxom prime.

'My dear widow, you are charming!' cried Colonel Killigrew, whose eyes had been fixed upon her face, while the shadows of age were flitting from it like darkness from the crimson daybreak.

The fair widow knew, of old, that Colonel Killigrew's compliments were not always measured by sober truth; so she started up and ran to the mirror, still dreading that the ugly visage of an old woman would meet her gaze. Meanwhile, the three gentlemen behaved in such a manner, as proved that the water of the Fountain of Youth possessed some intoxicating qualities; unless, indeed, their exhilaration of spirits were merely a lightsome dizziness, caused by the sudden removal of the weight of years. Mr. Gascoigne's mind seemed to run on political topics, but whether relating to the past, present, or future, could not easily be determined, since the same ideas and phrases have been in vogue these fifty years. Now he rattled forth full-throated sentences about patriotism, national glory, and the people's right; now he muttered some perilous stuff or other, in a sly and doubtful whisper, so cautiously that even his own conscience could scarcely catch the secret; and now, again, he spoke in measured accents, and a deeply deferential tone, as if a royal ear were listening to his well-turned periods. Colonel Killigrew all this time had been trolling forth a jolly bottle-song, and ringing his glass in symphony with the chorus, while his eyes wandered toward the buxom figure of the Widow Wycherly. On the other side of the table, Mr. Medbourne was involved in a calculation of dollars and cents, with which was strangely intermingled a project for supplying the East Indies with ice, by harnessing a team of whales to the polar icebergs.

As for the Widow Wycherly, she stood before the mirror, curtseying and simpering to her own image, and greeting it as the friend whom she loved better than all the world beside. She thrust her face close to the glass, to see whether some long-remembered wrinkle or crows-foot had indeed vanished. She examined whether the snow had so entirely melted from her hair, that the venerable cap could be safely thrown aside. At last, turning briskly away, she came with a sort of dancing step to the table.

'My dear old doctor,' cried she, 'pray favor me with another glass!'

'Certainly, my dear madam, certainly!' replied the complaisant doctor; 'see! I have already filled the glasses.'

There, in fact, stood the four glasses, brim-full of this wonderful water, the delicate spray of which, as it effervesced from the surface, resembled the tremulous glitter of diamonds. It was now so nearly sunset, that the chamber had grown duskier than ever; but a mild and moon-like splendor gleamed from within the vase, and rested alike on the four guests, and on the doctor's venerable figure. He sat in a high-backed, elaborately-carved, oaken arm-chair, with a gray dignity of aspect that might have well befitted that very Father Time, whose power had never been disputed, save by this fortunate company. Even while quaffing the third draught of the Fountain of Youth, they were almost awed by the expression of his mysterious visage.

But, the next moment, the exhilarating gush of young life shot through their veins. They were now in the happy prime of youth. Age, with its miserable train of cares, and sorrows, and diseases, was remembered only as the trouble of a dream, from which they had joyously awoke. The fresh gloss of the soul, so early lost, and without which the world's successive scenes had been but a gallery of faded pictures, again threw its enchantment over all their prospects. They felt like new-created beings, in a new-created universe.

'We are young! We are young!' they cried, exultingly.

Youth, like the extremity of age, had effaced the strongly marked characteristics of middle life, and mutually assimilated them all. They were a group of merry youngsters, almost maddened with the exuberant frolicksomeness of their years. The most singular effect of their gaiety was an impulse to mock the infirmity and decrepitude of which they had so lately been the victims. They laughed loudly at their old-fashioned attire, the wide-skirted coats and flapped waistcoats of the young men, and the ancient cap and gown of the blooming girl. One limped across the floor, like a gouty grandfather; one set a pair of spectacles astride of his nose, and pretended to pore over the blackletter pages of the book of magic; a third seated himself in an arm-chair, and strove to imitate the venerable dignity of Dr. Heidegger. Then all shouted mirthfully, and leaped about the room. The Widow Wycherly—if so fresh a damsel could be called a widow—tripped up to the doctor's chair, with a mischievous merriment in her rosy face.

'Doctor, you dear old soul,' cried she, 'get up and dance with me!' And then the four young people laughed louder than ever, to think what a queer figure the poor old doctor would cut.

'Pray excuse me,' answered the doctor, quietly. 'I am old

and rheumatic, and my dancing days were over long ago. But either of these gay young gentlemen will be glad of so pretty a partner.'

'Dance with me, Clara!' cried Colonel Killigrew.

'No, no, I will be her partner!' shouted Mr. Gascoigne.

She promised me her hand, fifty years ago!' exclaimed Mr. Medbourne.

They all gathered round her. One caught both her hands in his passionate grasp—another threw his arm about her waist—the third buried his hand among the glossy curls that clustered beneath the widow's cap. Blushing, panting, struggling, chiding, laughing, her warm breath fanning each of their faces by turns, she strove to disengage herself, yet still remained in their triple embrace. Never was there a livelier picture of youthful rivalship, with bewitching beauty for the prize. Yet, by a strange deception, owing to the duskiness of the chamber, and the antique dresses which they still wore, the tall mirror is said to have reflected the figures of the three old, gray, withered grandsires, ridiculously contending for the skinny ugliness of a shriveled granddam.

But they were young: their burning passions proved them so. Inflamed to madness by the coquetry of the girl-widow, who neither granted nor quite withheld her favors, the three rivals began to interchange threatening glances. Still keeping hold of the fair prize, they grappled fiercely at one another's throats. As they struggled to and fro, the table was overturned, and the vase dashed into a thousand fragments. The precious Water of Youth flowed in a bright stream across the floor, moistening the wings of a butterfly, which, grown old in the decline of summer, had alighted there to die. The insect fluttered lightly through the chamber, and settled on the snowy head of Dr. Heidegger.

'Come, come, gentlemen!—come, Madam Wycherly,' exclaimed the doctor, 'I really must protest against this riot.'

They stood still, and shivered; for it seemed as if gray Time were calling them back from their sunny youth, far down into the chill and darksome vale of years. They looked at old Dr. Heidegger, who sat in his carved arm-chair, holding the rose of half a century, which he had rescued from among the fragments of the shattered vase. At the motion of his hand, the four rioters resumed their seats; the more readily, because their violent exertions had wearied them, youthful though they were.

'My poor Sylvia's rose!' ejaculated Dr. Heidegger, holding it in the light of the sunset clouds: 'it appears to be fading again.'

And so it was. Even while the party were looking at it, the flower continued to shrivel up, till it became as dry and fragile as when the doctor had first thrown it into the vase. He shook off the few drops of moisture which clung to its petals.

'I love it as well thus, as in its dewy freshness,' observed he, pressing the withered rose to his withered lips. While he spoke, the butterfly fluttered down from the doctor's snowy head, and fell upon the floor.

His guests shivered again. A strange chillness, whether of the body or spirit they could not tell, was creeping gradually over them all. They gazed at one another, and fancied that each fleeting moment snatched away a charm, and left a deepening furrow where none had been before. Was it an illusion? Had the changes of a life-time been crowded into so brief a space, and were they now four aged people, sitting with their old friend, Dr. Heidegger?

'Are we grown old again, so soon!' cried they, dolefully.

In truth, they had. The Water of Youth possessed merely a virtue more transient than that of wine. The delirium which it created had effervesced away. Yes! They were old again. With a shuddering impulse, that showed her a woman still, the widow clasped her skinny hands before her face, and wished that the coffin-lid were over it, since it could be no longer beautiful.

'Yes, friends, ye are old again,' said Dr. Heidegger; 'and lo! The Water of Youth is all lavished on the ground. Well—I bemoan it not; for if the fountain gushed at my very door-step, I would not stoop to bathe my lips in it—no, though its delirium were for years instead of moments. Such is the lesson ye have taught me!'

But the doctor's four friends had taught no such lesson to themselves. They resolved forthwith to make a pilgrimage to Florida, and quaff at morning, noon, and night, from the Fountain of Youth.

The Bridal Party

F. SCOTT FITZGERALD

There was the usual insincere little note saying: "I wanted you to be the first to know." It was a double shock to Michael, announcing, as it did, both the engagement and the imminent marriage; which, moreover, was to be held, not in New York, decently and far away, but here in Paris under his very nose, if that could be said to extend over the Protestant Episcopal Church of the Holy Trinity, Avenue George Cinq. The date was two weeks off, early in June.

At first Michael was afraid and his stomach felt hollow. When he left the hotel that morning, the *femme de chambre*, who was in love with his fine, sharp profile and his pleasant buoyancy, scented the hard abstraction that had settled over him. He walked in a daze to his bank, he bought a detective story at Smith's on the Rue de Rivoli, he sympathetically stared for a while at a faded panorama of the battlefields in a tourist-office window and cursed a Greek tout who followed him with a half-displayed packet of innocuous post cards warranted to be very dirty indeed.

But the fear stayed with him, and after a while he recognized it as the fear that now he would never be happy. He had met Caroline Dandy when she was seventeen, possessed her young heart all through her first season in New York, and then lost her, slowly, tragically, uselessly, because he had no money and

95

could make no money; because, with all the energy and good will in the world, he could not find himself; because, loving him still, Caroline had lost faith and begun to see him as something pathetic, futile and shabby, outside the great, shining stream of life toward which she was inevitably drawn.

Since his only support was that she loved him, he leaned weakly on that; the support broke, but still he held on to it and was carried out to sea and washed up on the French coast with its broken pieces still in his hands. He carried them around with him in the form of photographs and packets of correspondence and a liking for a maudlin popular song called 'Among My Souvenirs'. He kept clear of other girls, as if Caroline would somehow know it and reciprocate with a faithful heart. Her note informed him that he had lost her forever.

It was a fine morning. In front of the shops in the Rue de Castiglione, proprietors and patrons were on the sidewalk gazing upward, for the Graf Zeppelin, shining and glorious, symbol of escape and destruction—of escape, if necessary, through destruction—glided in the Paris sky. He heard a woman say in French that it would not her astonish if that commenced to let fall the bombs. Then he heard another voice, full of husky laughter, and the void in his stomach froze. Jerking about, he was face to face with Caroline Dandy and her fiancé.

"Why, Michael! Why, we were wondering where you were. I asked at the Guaranty Trust, and Morgan and Company, and finally sent a note to the National City—"

Why didn't they back away? Why didn't they back right up, walking backward down the Rue de Castiglione, across the Rue de Rivoli, through the Tuileries Gardens, still walking backward as fast as they could till they grew vague and faded out across the river?

"This is Hamilton Rutherford, my fiancé."

"We've met before."

"At Pat's, wasn't it?"

"And last spring in the Ritz Bar."

"Michael, where have you been keeping yourself?"

"Around here." This agony. Previews of Hamilton Rutherford flashed before his eyes—a quick series of pictures, sentences. He remembered hearing that he had bought a seat in 1920 for a hundred and twenty-five thousand of borrowed money, and just before the break sold it for more than half a million. Not handsome like Michael, but vitally attractive, confident, authoritative, just the right height over Caroline there—Michael had always been too short for Caroline when they danced.

Rutherford was saying: "No, I'd like it very much if you'd come to the bachelor dinner. I'm taking the Ritz Bar from nine o'clock on. Then right after the wedding there'll be a reception and breakfast at the Hotel George Cinq."

"And, Michael, George Packman is giving a party day after tomorrow at Chez Victor, and I want you to be sure and come. And also to tea Friday at Jebby West's; she'd want to have you if she knew where you were. What's your hotel, so we can send you an invitation? You see, the reason we decided to have it over here is because mother has been sick in a nursing home here and the whole clan is in Paris. Then Hamilton's mother's being here too——"

The entire clan; they had always hated him, except her mother; always discouraged his courtship. What a little counter he was in this game of families and money! Under his hat his brow sweated with the humiliation of the fact that for all his misery he was worth just exactly so many invitations. Frantically he began to mumble something about going away.

Then it happened—Caroline saw deep into him, and Michael knew that she saw. She saw through to his profound woundedness, and something quivered inside her, died out along the curve of her mouth and in her eyes. He had moved her. All the unforgettable impulses of first love had surged up once more; their hearts had in some way touched across two feet of Paris sunlight. She took her fiancé's arm suddenly, as if to steady herself with the feel of it.

They parted. Michael walked quickly for a minute; then he stopped, pretending to look in a window, and saw them farther up the street, walking fast into the Place Vendôme, people with much to do.

He had things to do also—he had to get his laundry.

"Nothing will ever be the same again," he said to himself. "She will never be happy in her marriage and I will never be happy at all any more."

The two vivid years of his love for Caroline moved back around him like years in Einstein's physics. Intolerable memories arose—of rides in the Long Island moonlight; of a happy time at Lake Placid with her cheeks so cold there, but warm just underneath the surface; of a despairing afternoon in a little café on Forty-eighth Street in the last sad months when their marriage had come to seem impossible.

"Come in," he said aloud.

The concierge with a telegram; brusque because Mr. Curly's clothes were a little shabby. Mr. Curly gave few tips; Mr. Curly was obviously a *petit client*.

Michael read the telegram.

"An answer?" the concierge asked.

"No," said Michael, and then, on an impulse: "Look."

"Too bad—too bad," said the concierge. "Your grandfather is dead."

"Not too bad," said Michael. "It means that I come into a quarter of a million dollars."

Too late by a single month; after the first flush of the news his misery was deeper than ever. Lying awake in bed that night, he listened endlessly to the long caravan of a circus moving through the street from one Paris fair to another.

When the last van had rumbled out of hearing and the corners of the furniture were pastel blue with the dawn, he was still thinking of the look in Caroline's eyes that morning—the look that seemed to say: "Oh, why couldn't you have done something about it? Why couldn't you have been stronger, made me marry you? Don't you see how sad I am?"

Michael's fists clenched.

"Well, I won't give up till the last moment," he whispered. "I've had all the bad luck so far, and maybe it's turned at last. One takes what one can get, up to the limit of one's strength, and if I can't have her, at least she'll go into this marriage with some of me in her heart."

II

Accordingly he went to the party at Chez Victor two days later, upstairs and into the little salon off the bar where the party was to assemble for cocktails. He was early; the only other occupant was a tall lean man of fifty. They spoke.

"You waiting for George Packman's party?"

"Yes. My name's Michael Curly."

"My name's——"

Michael failed to catch the name. They ordered a drink, and Michael supposed that the bride and groom were having a gay time.

"Too much so," the other agreed, frowning. "I don't see how they stand it. We all crossed on the boat together; five days of that crazy life and then two weeks of Paris. You"—he hesitated, smiling faintly—"you'll excuse me for saying that your generation drinks too much."

"Not Caroline."

"No, not Caroline. She seems to take only a cocktail and a glass of champagne, and then she's had enough, thank God. But Hamilton drinks too much and all this crowd of young people drink too much. Do you live in Paris?"

"For the moment," said Michael.

"I don't like Paris. My wife—that is to say, my ex-wife, Hamilton's mother—lives in Paris."

"You're Hamilton Rutherford's father?"

"I have that honor. And I'm not denying that I'm proud of what he's done; it was just a general comment."

"Of course."

Michael glanced up nervously as four people came in. He felt suddenly that his dinner coat was old and shiny; he had ordered a new one that morning. The people who had come in were rich and at home in their richness with one another—a dark, lovely girl with a hysterical little laugh whom he had met before; two confident men whose jokes referred invariably to last night's scandal and tonight's potentialities, as if they had important rôles in a play that extended indefinitely into the past and the future. When Caroline arrived, Michael had scarcely a moment of her, but it was enough to note that, like all the others, she was strained and tired. She was pale beneath her rouge; there were shadows under her eyes. With a mixture of relief and wounded vanity, he found himself placed far from her and at another table; he needed a moment to adjust himself to his surroundings. This was not like the immature set in which he and Caroline had moved; the men were more than thirty and had an air of sharing the best of this world's goods. Next to him was Jebby West, whom he knew; and, on the other side, a jovial man who immediately began to talk to Michael about a stunt for the bachelor dinner: They were going to hire a French girl to appear with an actual baby in her arms, crying: "Hamilton, you can't desert me now!" The idea seemed stale and unamusing to Michael, but its originator shook with anticipatory laughter.

Farther up the table there was talk of the market—another drop today, the most appreciable since the crash; people were kidding Rutherford about it: "Too bad, old man. You better not get married, after all."

Michael asked the man on his left, "Has he lost a lot?"

"Nobody knows. He's heavily involved, but he's one of the smartest young men in Wall Street. Anyhow, nobody ever tells you the truth."

It was a champagne dinner from the start, and toward the end it reached a pleasant level of conviviality, but Michael saw that all these people were too weary to be exhilarated by any ordinary stimulant; for weeks they had drunk cocktails before meals like Americans, wines and brandies like Frenchmen, beer like Germans, whisky-and-soda like the English, and as they were no longer in the twenties, this preposterous *mélange*, that was like some gigantic cocktail in a nightmare, served only to make them temporarily less conscious of the mistakes of the night before. Which is to say that it was not really a gay party; what gayety existed was displayed in the few who drank nothing at all.

But Michael was not tired, and the champagne stimulated him and made his misery less acute. He had been away from New York for more than eight months and most of the dance music was unfamiliar to him, but at the first bars of the Painted Doll, to which he and Caroline had moved through so much happiness and despair the previous summer, he crossed to Caroline's table and asked her to dance.

She was lovely in a dress of thin ethereal blue, and the proximity of her crackly yellow hair, of her cool and tender gray eyes, turned his body clumsy and rigid; he stumbled with their first step on the floor. For a moment it seemed that there was nothing to say; he wanted to tell her about his inheritance, but the idea seemed abrupt, unprepared for.

"Michael, it's so nice to be dancing with you again."

He smiled grimly.

"I'm so happy you came," she continued. "I was afraid maybe you'd be silly and stay away. Now we can be just good friends and natural together. Michael, I want you and Hamilton to like each other."

The engagement was making her stupid; he had never heard her make such a series of obvious remarks before.

"I could kill him without a qualm," he said pleasantly," but he looks like a good man. He's fine. What I want to know is, what happens to people like me who aren't able to forget?"

As he said this he could not prevent his mouth from drooping suddenly, and glancing up, Caroline saw, and her heart quivered violently, as it had the other morning.

"Do you mind so much, Michael?"

"Yes."

For a second as he said this, in a voice that seemed to have come up from his shoes, they were not dancing; they were simply clinging together. Then she leaned away from him and twisted her mouth into a lovely smile.

"I didn't know what to do at first, Michael. I told Hamilton about you—that I'd cared for you an awful lot—but it didn't worry him, and he was right. Because I'm over you now—yes, I am. And you'll wake up some sunny morning and be over me just like that."

He shook his head stubbornly.

"Oh, yes. We weren't for each other. I'm pretty flighty, and I need somebody like Hamilton to decide things. It was that more than the question of—of——"

"Of money." Again he was on the point of telling her what had happened, but again something told him it was not the time.

"Then how do you account for what happened when we met the other day," he demanded helplessly—"what happened just now? When we just pour toward each other like we used to—as if we were one person, as if the same blood was flowing through both of us?"

"Oh, don't," she begged him. "You mustn't talk like that; everything's decided now. I love Hamilton with all my heart. It's just that I remember certain things in the past and I feel sorry for you—for us—for the way we were."

Over her shoulder, Michael saw a man come toward them to cut in. In a panic he danced her away, but inevitably the man came on.

"I've got to see you alone, if only for a minute," Michael said quickly. "When can I?"

"I'll be at Jebby West's ten tomorrow," she whispered as a hand fell politely upon Michael's shoulder.

But he did not talk to her at Jebby West's tea. Rutherford stood next to her, and each brought the other into all conversations. They left early. The next morning the wedding cards arrived in the first mail.

Then Michael, grown desperate with pacing up and down his room, determined on a bold stroke; he wrote to Hamilton Rutherford, asking him for a rendezvous the following afternoon. In a short telephone communication Rutherford agreed, but for a day later than Michael had asked. And the wedding was only six days away.

They were to meet in the bar of the Hotel Jena. Michael knew what he would say: "See here, Rutherford, do you realize the responsibility you're taking in going through with this marriage? Do you realize the harvest of trouble and regret you're sowing in persuading a girl into something contrary to the instincts of her heart?" He would explain that the barrier between Caroline and himself had been an artificial one and was now removed, and demand that the matter be put up to Caroline frankly before it was too late.

Rutherford would be angry, conceivably there would be a scene, but Michael felt that he was fighting for his life now.

He found Rutherford in conversation with an older man, whom Michael had met at several of the wedding parties.

"I saw what happened to most of my friends," Rutherford was saying, "and I decided it wasn't going to happen to me. It isn't so difficult; if you take a girl with common sense, and tell her what's what, and do your stuff damn well, and play decently square with her, it's a marriage. If you stand for any nonsense at the beginning, it's one of these arrangements—within five years the man gets out, or else the girl gobbles him up and you have the usual mess."

"Right!" agreed his companion enthusiastically. "Hamilton, boy, you're right."

Michael's blood boiled slowly.

"Doesn't it strike you," he inquired coldly, "that your attitude went out of fashion about a hundred years ago?"

"No, it didn't," said Rutherford pleasantly, but impatiently. "I'm as modern as anybody. I'd get married in an aeroplane next Saturday if it'd please my girl."

"I don't mean that way of being modern. You can't take a sensitive woman——"

"Sensitive? Women aren't so darn sensitive. It's fellows like you who are sensitive; it's fellows like you they exploit—all your devotion and kindness and all that. They read a couple of books and see a few pictures because they haven't got anything else to do, and then they say they're finer in grain than you are, and to prove it they take the bit in their teeth and tear off for a fare-you-well—just about as sensitive as a fire horse."

"Caroline happens to be sensitive," said Michael in a clipped voice.

At this point the other man got up to go; when the dispute

about the check had been settled and they were alone, Rutherford leaned back to Michael as if a question had been asked him.

"Caroline's more than sensitive," he said. "She's got sense."

His combative eyes, meeting Michael's, flickered with a gray
light. "This all sounds pretty crude to you, Mr. Curly, but it
seems to me that the average man nowadays just asks to be made
a monkey of by some woman who doesn't even get any fun out
of reducing him to that level. There are darn few men who pos-
sess their wives any more, but I am going to be one of them."

To Michael it seemed time to bring the talk back to the actual
situation: "Do you realize the responsibility you're taking?"

"I certainly do," interrupted Rutherford. "I'm not afraid
of responsibility. I'll make the decisions—fairly, I hope, but
anyhow they'll be final."

"What if you didn't start right?" said Michael impetuously.
"What if your marriage isn't founded on mutual love?"

"I think I see what you mean," Rutherford said, still pleasant. "And since you've brought it up, let me say that if you and
Caroline had married, it wouldn't have lasted three years. Do
you know what your affair was founded on? On sorrow. You got
sorry for each other. Sorrow's a lot of fun for most women and
for some men, but it seems to me that a marriage ought to be
based on hope." He looked at his watch and stood up.

"I've got to meet Caroline. Remember, you're coming to the
bachelor dinner day after tomorrow."

Michael felt the moment slipping away. "Then Caroline's
personal feelings don't count with you?" he demanded fiercely.

"Caroline's tired and upset. But she has what she wants, and
that's the main thing."

"Are you referring to yourself?" demanded Michael incredulously.

"Yes."

"May I ask how long she's wanted you?"

"About two years." Before Michael could answer, he was gone.

During the next two days Michael floated in an abyss of helplessness. The idea haunted him that he had left something undone that would sever this knot drawn tighter under his eyes. He phoned Caroline, but she insisted that it was physically impossible for her to see him until the day before the wedding, for which day she granted him a tentative rendezvous. Then he went to the bachelor dinner, partly in fear of an evening alone at his hotel, partly from a feeling that by his presence at that function he was somehow nearer to Caroline, keeping her in sight.

The Ritz Bar had been prepared for the occasion by French and American banners and by a great canvas covering one wall, against which the guests were invited to concentrate their proclivities in breaking glasses.

At the first cocktail, taken at the bar, there were many slight spillings from many trembling hands, but later, with the champagne, there was a rising tide of laughter and occasional bursts of song.

Michael was surprised to find what a difference his new dinner coat, his new silk hat, his new, proud linen made in his estimate of himself; he felt less resentment toward all these people for being so rich and assured. For the first time since he had left college he felt rich and assured himself; he felt that he was part of all this, and even entered into the scheme of

Johnson, the practical joker, for the appearance of the woman betrayed, now waiting tranquilly in the room across the hall.

"We don't want to go too heavy," Johnson said, "because I imagine Ham's had a pretty anxious day already. Did you see Fullman Oil's sixteen points off this morning?"

"Will that matter to him?" Michael asked, trying to keep the interest out of his voice.

"Naturally. He's in heavily; he's always in everything heavily. So far he's had luck; anyhow, up to a month ago."

The glasses were filled and emptied faster now, and men were shouting at one another across the narrow table. Against the bar a group of ushers was being photographed, and the flash light surged through the room in a stifling cloud.

"Now's the time," Johnson said. "You're to stand by the door, remember, and we're both to try and keep her from coming in—just till we get everybody's attention."

He went on out into the corridor, and Michael waited obediently by the door. Several minutes passed. Then Johnson reappeared with a curious expression on his face.

"There's something funny about this."

"Isn't the girl there?"

"She's there all right, but there's another woman there, too; and it's nobody we engaged either. She wants to see Hamilton Rutherford, and she looks as if she had something on her mind."

They went out into the hall. Planted firmly in a chair near the door sat an American girl a little the worse for liquor, but with a determined expression on her face. She looked up at them with a jerk of her head.

"Well, j'tell him?" she demanded. "The name is Marjorie

Collins, and he'll know it. I've come a long way, and I want to see him now and quick, or there's going to be more trouble than you ever saw." She rose unsteadily to her feet.

"You go in and tell Ham," whispered Johnson to Michael. "Maybe he'd better get out. I'll keep her here."

Back at the table, Michael leaned close to Rutherford's ear and, with a certain grimness, whispered:

"A girl outside named Marjorie Collins says she wants to see you. She looks as if she wanted to make trouble."

Hamilton Rutherford blinked and his mouth fell ajar; then slowly the lips came together in a straight line and he said in a crisp voice:

"Please keep her there. And send the head barman to me right away."

Michael spoke to the barman, and then, without returning to the table, asked quietly for his coat and hat. Out in the hall again, he passed Johnson and the girl without speaking and went out into the Rue Cambon. Calling a cab, he gave the address of Caroline's hotel.

His place was beside her now. Not to bring bad news, but simply to be with her when her house of cards came falling around her head.

Rutherford had implied that he was soft—well, he was hard enough not to give up the girl he loved without taking advantage of every chance within the pale of honor. Should she turn away from Rutherford, she would find him there.

She was in; she was surprised when he called, but she was still dressed and would be down immediately. Presently she appeared in a dinner gown, holding two blue telegrams in her hand. They sat down in armchairs in the deserted lobby.

"But, Michael, is the dinner over?"

"I wanted to see you, so I came away."

"I'm glad." Her voice was friendly, but matter-of-fact. "Because I'd just phoned your hotel that I had fittings and rehearsals all day tomorrow. Now we can have our talk after all."

"You're tired," he guessed. "Perhaps I shouldn't have come."

"No. I was waiting up for Hamilton. Telegrams that may be important. He said he might go on somewhere, and that may mean any hour, so I'm glad I have someone to talk to."

Michael winced at the impersonality in the last phrase.

"Don't you care when he gets home?"

"Naturally," she said, laughing, "but I haven't got much say about it, have I?"

"Why not?"

"I couldn't start by telling him what he could and couldn't do."

"Why not?"

"He wouldn't stand for it."

"He seems to want merely a housekeeper," said Michael ironically.

"Tell me about your plans, Michael," she asked quickly.

"My plans? I can't see any future after the day after tomorrow. The only real plan I ever had was to love you."

Their eyes brushed past each other's, and the look he knew so well was staring out at him from hers. Words flowed quickly from his heart:

"Let me tell you just once more how well I've loved you, never wavering for a moment, never thinking of another girl. And now when I think of all the years ahead without you, without any hope, I don't want to live, Caroline darling. I used to dream about our home, our children, about holding you in my arms and touching your face and hands and hair that used to belong to me, and now I just can't wake up."

Caroline was crying softly. "Poor Michael—poor Michael." Her hand reached out and her fingers brushed the lapel of his dinner coat. "I was so sorry for you the other night. You looked so thin, and as if you needed a new suit and somebody to take care of you." She sniffled and looked more closely at his coat. "Why, you've got a new suit! And a new silk hat! Why, Michael, how swell!" She laughed, suddenly cheerful through her tears. "You must have come into money, Michael; I never saw you so well turned out."

For a moment, at her reaction, he hated his new clothes.

"I have come into money," he said. "My grandfather left me about a quarter of a million dollars."

"Why, Michael," she cried, "how perfectly swell! I can't tell you how glad I am. I've always thought you were the sort of person who ought to have money."

"Yes, just too late to make a difference."

The revolving door from the street groaned around and Hamilton Rutherford came into the lobby. His face was flushed, his eyes were restless and impatient.

"Hello, darling; hello, Mr. Curly." He bent and kissed Caroline. "I broke away for a minute to find out if I had any telegrams. I see you've got them there." Taking them from her, he remarked to Curly, "That was an odd business there in the bar, wasn't it? Especially as I understand some of you had a joke fixed up in the same line." He opened one of the telegrams, closed it and turned to Caroline with the divided expression of a man carrying two things in his head at once.

"A girl I haven't seen for two years turned up," he said. "It seemed to be some clumsy form of blackmail, for I haven't and never have had any sort of obligation toward her whatever."

"What happened?"

"The head barman had a Sûreté Générale man there in ten minutes and it was settled in the hall. The French blackmail laws make ours look like a sweet wish, and I gather they threw a scare into her that she'll remember. But it seems wiser to tell you."

"Are you implying that I mentioned the matter?" said Michael stiffly.

"No," Rutherford said slowly. "No, you were just going to be on hand. And since you're here, I'll tell you some news that will interest you even more."

He handed Michael one telegram and opened the other.

"This is in code," Michael said.

"So is this. But I've got to know all the words pretty well this last week. The two of them together mean that I'm due to start life all over."

Michael saw Caroline's face grow a shade paler, but she sat quiet as a mouse.

"It was a mistake and I stuck to it too long," continued Rutherford. "So you see I don't have all the luck, Mr. Curly. By the way, they tell me you've come into money."

"Yes," said Michael.

"There we are, then." Rutherford turned to Caroline. "You understand, darling, that I'm not joking or exaggerating. I've lost almost every cent I had and I'm starting life over."

Two pairs of eyes were regarding her—Rutherford's non-committal and unrequiring, Michael's hungry, tragic, pleading. In a minute she had raised herself from the chair and with a little cry thrown herself into Hamilton Rutherford's arms.

"Oh, darling," she cried, "what does it matter! It's better; I like it better, honestly I do! I want to start that way; I want to! Oh, please don't worry or be sad even for a minute!"

"All right, baby," said Rutherford. His hand stroked her hair gently for a moment; then he took his arm from around her.

"I promised to join the party for an hour," he said. "So I'll say good night, and I want you to go to bed soon and get a good sleep. Good night, Mr. Curly. I'm sorry to have let you in for all these financial matters."

But Michael had already picked up his hat and cane. "I'll go along with you," he said.

III

It was such a fine morning. Michael's cutaway hadn't been delivered, so he felt rather uncomfortable passing before the cameras and moving-picture machines in front of the little church on the Avenue George Cinq.

It was such a clean, new church that it seemed unforgivable not to be dressed properly, and Michael, white and shaky after a sleepless night, decided to stand in the rear. From there he looked at the back of Hamilton Rutherford, and the lacy, filmy back of Caroline, and the fat back of George Packman, which looked unsteady, as if it wanted to lean against the bride and groom.

The ceremony went on for a long time under the gay flags

and pennons overhead, under the thick beams of June sunlight slanting down through the tall windows upon the well-dressed people.

As the procession, headed by the bride and groom, started down the aisle, Michael realized with alarm he was just where everyone would dispense with their parade stiffness, become informal and speak to him.

So it turned out. Rutherford and Caroline spoke first to him; Rutherford grim with the strain of being married, and Caroline lovelier than he had ever seen her, floating all softly down through the friends and relatives of her youth, down through the past and forward to the future by the sunlit door.

Michael managed to murmur, "Beautiful, simply beautiful," and then other people passed and spoke to him—old Mrs. Dandy, straight from her sickbed and looking remarkably well, or carrying it off like the very fine old lady she was; and Rutherford's father and mother, ten years divorced, but walking side by side and looking made for each other and proud. Then all Caroline's sisters and their husbands and her little nephews in Eton suits, and then a long parade, all speaking to Michael because he was still standing paralyzed just at that point where the procession broke.

He wondered what would happen now. Cards had been issued for a reception at the George Cinq; an expensive enough place, heaven knew. Would Rutherford try to go through with that on top of those disastrous telegrams? Evidently, for the procession outside was streaming up there through the June morning, three by three and four by four. On the corner the long dresses of girls, five abreast, fluttered many-colored in the wind. Girls had become gossamer again, perambulatory flora; such lovely fluttering dresses in the bright noon wind.

Michael needed a drink; he couldn't face that reception line without a drink. Diving into a side doorway of the hotel, he asked for the bar, whither a *chasseur* led him through half a kilometer of new American-looking passages.

But—how did it happen?—the bar was full. There were ten—fifteen men and two—four girls, all from the wedding, all needing a drink. There were cocktails and champagne in the bar; Rutherford's cocktails and champagne, as it turned out, for he had engaged the whole bar and the ballroom and the two great reception rooms and all the stairways leading up and down, and windows looking out over the whole square block of Paris. By and by Michael went in and joined the long, slow drift of the receiving line. Through a flowery mist of "Such a lovely wedding," "My dear, you were simply lovely," "You're a lucky man, Rutherford" he passed down the line. When Michael came to Caroline, she took a single step forward and kissed him on the lips, but he felt no contact in the kiss; it was unreal and he floated on away from it. Old Mrs. Dandy, who had always liked him, held his hand for a minute and thanked him for the flowers he had sent when he heard she was ill.

"I'm so sorry not to have written; you know, we old ladies are grateful for——" The flowers, the fact that she had not written, the wedding—Michael saw that they all had the same relative importance to her now; she had married off five other children and seen two of the marriages go to pieces, and this scene, so poignant, so confusing to Michael, appeared to her simply a familiar charade in which she had played her part before.

A buffet luncheon with champagne was already being served at small tables and there was an orchestra playing in the empty ballroom. Michael sat down with Jebby West; he was still a little embarrassed at not wearing a morning coat, but he perceived now that he was not alone in the omission and felt better. "Wasn't Caroline divine?" Jebby West said. "So entirely self-possessed. I asked her this morning if she wasn't a little nervous at stepping off like this. And she said, 'Why should I be? I've been after him for two years, and now I'm just happy, that's all.'"

"It must be true," said Michael gloomily.

"What?"

"What you just said."

He had been stabbed, but, rather to his distress, he did not feel the wound.

He asked Jebby to dance. Out on the floor, Rutherford's father and mother were dancing together.

"It makes me a little sad, that," she said. "Those two hadn't met for years; both of them were married again and she divorced again. She went to the station to meet him when he came over for Caroline's wedding, and invited him to stay at her house in the Avenue du Bois with a whole lot of other people, perfectly proper, but he was afraid his wife would hear about it and not like it, so he went to a hotel. Don't you think that's sort of sad?"

An hour or so later Michael realized suddenly that it was afternoon. In one corner of the ballroom an arrangement of screens like a moving-picture stage had been set up and photographers were taking official pictures of the bridal party. The bridal party, still as death and pale as wax under the bright lights, appeared, to the dancers circling the modulated semi-darkness of the ballroom, like those jovial or sinister groups that one comes upon in The Old Mill at an amusement park.

After the bridal party had been photographed, there was a group of the ushers; then the bridesmaids, the families, the children. Later, Caroline, active and excited, having long since abandoned the repose implicit in her flowing dress and great bouquet, came and plucked Michael off the floor.

"Now we'll have them take one of just old friends." Her voice implied that this was best, most intimate of all. "Come here, Jebby, George—not you, Hamilton; this is just my friends—Sally——"

A little after that, what remained of formality disappeared and the hours flowed easily down the profuse stream of champagne. In the modern fashion, Hamilton Rutherford sat at the table with his arm about an old girl of his and assured his guests, which included not a few bewildered but enthusiastic Europeans, that the party was not nearly at an end; it was to reassemble at Zelli's after midnight. Michael saw Mrs. Dandy, not quite over her illness, rise to go and become caught in polite group after group, and he spoke of it to one of her daughters, who thereupon forcibly abducted her mother and called her car. Michael felt very considerate and proud of himself after having done this, and drank much more champagne.

"It's amazing," George Packman was telling him enthusiastically. "This show will cost Ham about five thousand dollars, and I understand they'll be just about his last. But did he countermand a bottle of champagne or a flower? Not he! He happens to have it—that young man. Do you know that T. G. Vance offered him a salary of fifty thousand dollars a year ten minutes before the wedding this morning? In another year he'll be back with the millionaires."

The conversation was interrupted by a plan to carry Rutherford out on communal shoulders—a plan which six of them put into effect, and then stood in the four-o'clock sunshine waving good-by to the bride and groom. But there must have been a mistake somewhere, for five minutes later Michael saw both bride and groom descending the stairway to the reception, each with a glass of champagne held defiantly on high.

"This is our way of doing things," he thought. "Generous and fresh and free; a sort of Virginia-plantation hospitality, but at a different pace now, nervous as a ticker tape."

Standing unself-consciously in the middle of the room to see which was the American ambassador, he realized with a start that he hadn't really thought of Caroline for hours. He looked about him with a sort of alarm, and then he saw her across the room, very bright and young, and radiantly happy. He saw Rutherford near her, looking at her as if he could never look long enough, and as Michael watched them they seemed to recede as he had wished them to do that day in the Rue de Castiglione—recede and fade off into joys and griefs of their own, into the years that would take the toll of Rutherford's fine pride and Caroline's young, moving beauty; fade far away, so that now he could scarcely see them, as if they were shrouded in something as misty as her white, billowing dress.

Michael was cured. The ceremonial function, with its pomp and its revelry, had stood for a sort of initiation into a life where even his regret could not follow them. All the bitterness melted out of him suddenly and the world reconstituted itself out of the youth and happiness that was all around him, profligate as the spring sunshine. He was trying to remember which one of the bridesmaids he had made a date to dine with tonight as he walked forward to bid Hamilton and Caroline Rutherford good-by.

Tobermory

SAKI

It was a chill, rain-washed afternoon of a late August day, that indefinite season when partridges are still in security or cold storage, and there is nothing to hunt – unless one is bounded on the north by the Bristol Channel, in which case one may lawfully gallop after fat red stags. Lady Blemley's house-party was not bounded on the north by the Bristol Channel, hence there was a full gathering of her guests round the tea-table on this particular afternoon. And, in spite of the blankness of the season and the triteness of the occasion, there was no trace in the company of that fatigued restlessness which means a dread of the pianola and a subdued hankering for auction bridge. The undisguised open-mouthed attention of the entire party was fixed on the homely negative personality of Mr Cornelius Appin. Of all her guests, he was the one who had come to Lady Blemley with the vaguest reputation. Someone had said he was 'clever,' and he had got his invitation in the moderate expectation, on the part of his hostess, that some portion at least of his cleverness would be contributed to the general entertainment. Until tea-time that day she had been unable to discover in what direction, if any, his cleverness lay. He was neither a wit nor a croquet champion, a hypnotic force nor a begetter of amateur theatricals. Neither did his exterior suggest the sort of man in whom women are willing to pardon a generous measure of mental deficiency. He had subsided into mere Mr Appin, and the Cornelius seemed a piece of transparent baptismal bluff. And now he was claiming to have launched on the world a discovery beside which the invention of gunpowder, of the printing press, and of steam locomotion were inconsiderable trifles. Science had made bewildering strides in many directions during recent decades, but this thing seemed to belong to the domain of miracle rather than to scientific achievement.

'And do you really ask us to believe,' Sir Wilfrid was saying, 'that you have discovered a means for instructing animals in the art of human speech, and that dear old Tobermory has proved your first successful pupil?'

'It is a problem at which I have worked for the last seventeen years,' said Mr Appin, 'but only during the last eight or nine months have I been rewarded with glimmerings of success. Of course I have experimented with thousands of animals, but latterly only with cats, those wonderful creatures which have assimilated themselves so marvellously with our civilisation while retaining all their highly developed feral instincts. Here and there among cats one comes across an outstanding superior intellect, just as one does among the ruck of human beings, and when I made the acquaintance of Tobermory a week ago I saw at once that I was in contact with a "Beyond-cat" of extraordinary intelligence. I had gone far along the road to success in recent experiments; with Tobermory, as you call him, I have reached the goal.'

Mr Appin concluded his remarkable statement in a voice which he strove to divest of a triumphant inflection. No one said 'Rats,' though Clovis's lips moved in a monosyllabic contortion which probably invoked those rodents of disbelief.

'And do you mean to say,' asked Miss Resker, after a slight pause, 'that you have taught Tobermory to say and understand easy sentences of one syllable?'

'My dear Miss Resker,' said the wonder-worker patiently, 'one teaches little children and savages and backward adults in that piecemeal fashion; when one has once solved the problem of making a beginning with an animal of highly developed intelligence one has no need for those halting methods. Tobermory can speak our language with perfect correctness.'

This time Clovis very distinctly said, 'Beyond-rats!' Sir Wilfrid was more polite, but equally sceptical.

'Hadn't we better have the cat in and judge for ourselves?' suggested Lady Blemley.

Sir Wilfrid went in search of the animal, and the company settled themselves down to the languid expectation of witnessing some more or less adroit drawing-room ventriloquism.

In a minute Sir Wilfrid was back in the room, his face white beneath its tan and his eyes dilated with excitement.

'By Gad, it's true!'

His agitation was unmistakably genuine, and his hearers started forward in a thrill of awakened interest. Collapsing into an armchair he continued breathlessly: 'I found him dozing in the smoking-room and called out to him to come for his tea. He blinked at me in his usual way, and I said, "Come on, Toby; don't keep us waiting"; and, by Gad! he drawled out in a most horribly natural voice that he'd come when he dashed well pleased! I nearly jumped out of my skin!' Appin had preached to absolutely incredulous hearers; Sir Wilfrid's statement carried instant conviction. A Babel-like chorus of startled exclamation arose, amid which the scientist sat mutely enjoying the first fruit of his stupendous discovery.

In the midst of the clamour Tobermory entered the room and made his way with velvet tread and studied unconcern across to the group seated round the tea-table.

A sudden hush of awkwardness and constraint fell on the company. Somehow there seemed an element of embarrassment in addressing on equal terms a domestic cat of acknowledged dental ability.

'Will you have some milk, Tobermory?' asked Lady Blemley in a rather strained voice.

'I don't mind if I do,' was the response, couched in a tone of even indifference. A shiver of suppressed excitement went through the listeners, and Lady Blemley might be excused for pouring out the saucerful of milk rather unsteadily.

'I'm afraid I've spilt a good deal of it,' she said apologetically.

'After all, it's not my Axminster,' was Tobermory's rejoinder.

Another silence fell on the group, and then Miss Resker, in her best district-visitor manner, asked if the human language had been difficult to learn. Tobermory looked squarely at her for a moment and then fixed his gaze serenely on the middle distance. It was obvious that boring questions lay outside his scheme of life.

'What do you think of human intelligence?' asked Mavis Pellington lamely.

'Of whose intelligence in particular?' asked Tobermory coldly.

'Oh, well, mine for instance,' said Mavis, with a feeble laugh.

'You put me in an embarrassing position,' said Tobermory, whose tone and attitude certainly did not suggest a shred of embarrassment. 'When your inclusion in this house-party was suggested Sir Wilfrid protested that you were the most brainless woman of his acquaintance, and that there was a wide distinction between hospitality and the care of the feeble-minded. Lady Blemley replied that your lack of brain-power was the precise quality which had earned you your invitation, as you were the only person she could think of who might be idiotic enough to buy their old car. You know, the one they call "The Envy of Sisyphus", because it goes quite nicely uphill if you push it.'

Lady Blemley's protestations would have had greater effect if she had not casually suggested to Mavis only that morning that the car in question would be just the thing for her down at her Devonshire home.

Major Barfield plunged in heavily to effect a diversion.

'How about your carryings-on with the tortoiseshell puss up at the stables, eh?'

The moment he had said it everyone realised the blunder.

'One does not usually discuss these matters in public,' said Tobermory frigidly. 'From a slight observation of your ways since you've been in this house I should imagine you'd find it inconvenient if I were to shift the conversation on to your own little affairs.'

The panic which ensued was not confined to the Major.

'Would you like to go and see if cook has got your dinner ready?' suggested Lady Blemley hurriedly, affecting to ignore the fact that it wanted at least two hours to Tobermory's dinner-time.

'Thanks,' said Tobermory, 'not quite so soon after my tea. I don't want to die of indigestion.'

'Cats have nine lives, you know,' said Sir Wilfrid heartily.

'Possibly,' answered Tobermory; 'but only one liver.'

'Adelaide!' said Mrs Cornett, 'do you mean to encourage that cat to go out and gossip about us in the servants' hall?'

The panic had indeed become general. A narrow ornamental balustrade ran in front of most of the bedroom windows at the Towers, and it was recalled with dismay that this had formed a favourite promenade for Tobermory at all hours, whence he could watch the pigeons – and heaven knew what else besides. If he intended to become reminiscent in his present outspoken strain the effect would be something more than disconcerting. Mrs Cornett, who spent much time at her toilet table, and whose complexion was reputed to be of a nomadic though punctual disposition, looked as ill at ease as the Major. Miss Scrawen, who wrote fiercely sensuous poetry and led a blameless life, merely displayed irritation; if you are methodical and virtuous in private you don't necessarily want everyone to know it. Bertie van Than, who was so depraved at seventeen that he had long ago given up trying to be any worse, turned a dull shade of gardenia white, but he did not commit the error of dashing out of the room like Odo Finsberry, a young gentleman who was understood to be reading for the Church and who was possibly disturbed at the thought of scandals he might hear concerning other people. Clovis had the presence of mind to maintain a composed exterior; privately he was calculating how long it would take to procure a box of fancy mice through the agency of the *Exchange and Mart* as a species of hush-money. Even in a delicate situation like the present, Agnes Resker could not endure to remain too long in the background.

'Why did I ever come down here?' she asked dramatically.

Tobermory immediately accepted the opening. 'Judging by

what you said to Mrs Cornett on the croquet-lawn yesterday, you were out for food. You described the Blemleys as the dullest people to stay with that you knew, but said they were clever enough to employ a first-rate cook; otherwise they'd find it difficult to get anyone to come down a second time.'

'There's not a word of truth in it! I appeal to Mrs Cornett –' exclaimed the discomfited Agnes.

'Mrs Cornett repeated your remark afterwards to Bertie van Than,' continued Tobermory, 'and said, "That woman is a regular Hunger Marcher; she'd go anywhere for four square meals a day," and Bertie van Tahn said –'

At this point the chronicle mercifully ceased. Tobermory had caught a glimpse of the big yellow Tom from the Rectory working his way through the shrubbery towards the stable wing. In a flash he had vanished through the open French window.

With the disappearance of his too brilliant pupil Cornelius Appin found himself beset by a hurricane of bitter upbraiding, anxious enquiry, and frightened entreaty. The responsibility for the situation lay with him, and he must prevent matters from becoming worse. Could Tobermory impart his dangerous gift to other cats? was the first question he had to answer. It was possible, he replied, that he might have initiated his intimate friend the stable puss into his new accomplishment, but it was unlikely that his teaching could have taken a wider range as yet.

'Then,' said Mrs Cornett, 'Tobermory may be a valuable cat and a great pet; but I'm sure you'll agree, Adelaide, that both he and the stable cat must be done away with without delay.'

'You don't suppose I've enjoyed the last quarter of an hour, do you?' said Lady Blemley bitterly. 'My husband and I are very fond of Tobermory – at least, we were before this horrible accomplishment was infused into him; but now, of course, the only thing is to have him destroyed as soon as possible.'

'We can put some strychnine in the scraps he always gets at dinner-time,' said Sir Wilfrid, 'and I will go and drown the stable cat myself. The coachman will be very sore at losing his pet, but I'll say a very catching form of mange has broken out in both cats and we're afraid of its spreading to the kennels.'

'But my great discovery!' expostulated Mr Appin; 'after all my years of research and experiment –'

'You can go and experiment on the short-horns at the farm, who are under proper control,' said Mrs Cornett, 'or the elephants at the Zoological Gardens. They're said to be highly intelligent, and they have this recommendation, that they don't come creeping about our bedrooms and under chairs, and so forth.'

An archangel ecstatically proclaiming the Millennium, and then finding that it clashed unpardonably with Henley and would have to be indefinitely postponed, could hardly have felt more crestfallen than Cornelius Appin at the reception of his wonderful achievement. Public opinion, however, was against him – in fact, had the general voice been consulted on the subject it is probable that a strong minority vote would have been in favour of including him in the strychnine diet.

Defective train arrangements and a nervous desire to see matters brought to a finish prevented an immediate dispersal of the party, but dinner that evening was not a social success. Sir Wilfrid had had rather a trying time with the stable cat and subsequently with the coachman. Agnes Resker ostentatiously limited her repast to a morsel of dry toast, which she bit as though it were a personal enemy; while Mavis Pellington maintained a vindictive silence throughout the meal. Lady Blemley kept up a flow of what she hoped was conversation, but her attention was fixed on the doorway. A plateful of carefully dosed fish scraps was in readiness on the sideboard, but sweets and savoury and dessert went their way, and no Tobermory appeared either in the dining-room or kitchen.

The sepulchral dinner was cheerful compared with the subsequent vigil in the smoking-room. Eating and drinking had at least supplied a distraction and cloak to the prevailing embarrassment. Bridge was out of the question in the general tension of nerves and tempers, and after Odo Finsberry had given a lugubrious rendering of 'Melisande in the Wood' to a frigid audience, music was tacitly avoided. At eleven the servants went to bed, announcing that the small window in the pantry had been left open as usual for Tobermory's private use. The guests read steadily through the current batch of magazines, and fell back gradually on the *Badminton Library* and bound volumes of *Punch*. Lady Blemley made periodic visits to the pantry, returning each time with an expression of listless depression which forestalled questioning.

At two o'clock Clovis broke the dominating silence.

'He won't turn up tonight. He's probably in the local newspaper office at the present moment, dictating the first instalment of his reminiscences. Lady What's-her-name's book won't be in it. It will be the event of the day.'

Having made this contribution to the general cheerfulness, Clovis went to bed. At long intervals the various members of the house-party followed his example.

The servants taking round the early tea made a uniform

announcement in reply to a uniform question. Tobermory had not returned.

Breakfast was, if anything, a more unpleasant function than dinner had been, but before its conclusion the situation was relieved. Tobermory's corpse was brought in from the shrubbery, where a gardener had just discovered it. From the bites on his throat and the yellow fur which coated his claws it was evident that he had fallen in unequal combat with the big Tom from the Rectory.

By midday most of the guests had quitted the Towers, and after lunch Lady Blemley had sufficiently recovered her spirits to write an extremely nasty letter to the Rectory about the loss of her valuable pet.

Tobermory had been Appin's one successful pupil, and he was destined to have no successor. A few weeks later an elephant in the Dresden Zoological Garden, which had shown no previous signs of irritability, broke loose and killed an Englishman who had apparently been teasing it. The victim's name was variously reported in the papers as Appin and Eppelin, but his front name was faithfully rendered Cornelius.

'If he was trying German irregular verbs on the poor beast,' said Clovis, 'he deserved all he got.'

The Masque of the Red Death

EDGAR ALLAN POE

The 'Red Death' had long devastated the country. No pestilence had ever been so fatal, or so hideous. Blood was its Avatar and its seal – the redness and the horror of blood. There were sharp pains, and sudden dizziness, and then profuse bleeding at the pores, with dissolution. The scarlet stains upon the body and especially upon the face of the victim, were the pest ban which shut him out from the aid and from the sympathy of his fellow-men. And the whole seizure, progress, and termination of the disease, were the incidents of half an hour.

But the Prince Prospero was happy and dauntless and sagacious. When his dominions were half depopulated, he summoned to his presence a thousand hale and light-hearted friends from among the knights and dames of his court, and with these retired to the deep seclusion of one of his castellated abbeys. This was an extensive and magnificent structure, the creation of the prince's own eccentric yet august taste. A strong and lofty wall girdled it in. This wall had gates of iron. The courtiers, having entered, brought furnaces and massy hammers and welded the bolts. They resolved to leave means neither of ingress or egress to the sudden impulses of despair or of frenzy from within. The abbey was amply provisioned. With such precautions the courtiers might bid defiance to contagion. The external world could take care of itself. In the meantime it was folly to grieve, or to think. The prince had provided all the appliances of pleasure. There were buffoons, there were improvisatori, there were ballet-dancers, there were musicians, there was beauty, there was wine. All these and security were within. Without was the 'Red Death'.

It was toward the close of the fifth or sixth month of his seclusion, and while the pestilence raged most furiously abroad, that the Prince Prospero entertained his thousand friends at a masked ball of the most unusual magnificence.

It was a voluptuous scene, that masquerade. But first let me tell of the rooms in which it was held. There were seven – an imperial suite. In many palaces, however, such suites form a long and straight vista, while the folding doors slide back nearly to the walls on either hand, so that the view of the whole extent is scarcely impeded. Here the case was very different, as might have been expected from the duke's love of the bizarre. The apartments were so irregularly disposed that the vision embraced but little more than one at a time. There was a sharp turn at every twenty or thirty yards, and at each turn a novel effect. To the right and left, in the middle of each wall, a tall and narrow Gothic window looked out upon a closed corridor which pursued the windings of the suite. These windows were of stained glass, whose colour varied in accordance with the prevailing hue of the decorations of the chamber into which it opened. That at the eastern extremity was hung, for example, in blue – and vividly blue were its windows. The second chamber was purple in its ornaments and tapestries, and here the panes were purple. The third was green throughout, and so were the casements. The fourth was furnished and lighted with orange – the fifth with white – the sixth with violet. The seventh apartment was closely shrouded in black velvet tapestries that hung all over the ceiling and down the walls, falling in heavy folds upon a carpet of the same material and hue. But in this chamber only the colour of the windows failed to correspond with the decorations. The panes here were scarlet – a deep blood colour. Now in no of the seven apartments was there any lamp or candelabrum, amid the profusion of golden ornaments that lay scattered to and fro, or depended from the roof. There was no light of any kind emanating from lamp or candle within the suite of chambers. But in the corridors that followed the suite, there stood, opposite to each window, a heavy tripod, bearing a brazier of fire, that projected its rays through the tinted glass, and so glaringly illumined the room. And thus were produced a multitude of gaudy and fantastic appearances. But in the western or black chamber the effect of the firelight that streamed upon the dark hangings through the blood-tinted panes, was ghastly in the extreme, and produced so wild a look upon the countenances of those who entered, that there were few of the company bold enough to set foot within its precincts at all.

It was in this apartment, also, that there stood against the western wall a gigantic clock of ebony. Its pendulum swung to and fro with a dull, heavy, monotonous clang; and when the minute-hand made the circuit of the face, and the hour was to be stricken, there came from the brazen lungs of the clock a sound which was clear and loud and deep and exceedingly musical; but of so peculiar a note and emphasis that, at each lapse of an hour, the musicians of the orchestra were constrained to pause, momentarily, in their performance, to hearken to the sound; and thus the waltzers perforce ceased their evolutions; and there was a brief disconcert of the whole gay company; and, while the chimes of the clock yet rang, it was observed that the giddiest grew pale, and the more aged and sedate passed their hands over their brows as if in confused reverie or meditation. But when the echoes had fully ceased, a light laughter at once pervaded the assembly; the musicians looked at each other and smiled as if at their own nervousness and folly, and made whispering vows, each to the other, that the next chiming of the clock should produce in them no similar emption; and then, after the lapse of sixty minutes (which embrace three thousand and six hundred seconds of the Time that flies), there came yet another chiming of the clock, and then were the same disconcert and tremulousness and meditation as before.

But, in spite of these things, it was a gay and magnificent revel. The tastes of the duke were peculiar. He had a fine eye for colours and effects. He disregarded the *decora* of mere fashion. His plans were bold and fiery, and his conceptions glowed with barbaric lustre. There are some who would have thought him mad. His followers felt that he was not. It was necessary to hear and see and touch him to be *sure* that he was not.

He had directed, in great part, the movable embellishments of the seven chambers, upon occasion of this great fête; and it was his own guiding taste which had given character to the masqueraders. Be sure they were grotesque. There were much glare and glitter and piquancy and phantasm – much of what has been since seen in *Hernani*. There were arabesque figures with unsuited limbs and appointments. There were delirious fancies as the madman fashions. There were much of the beautiful, much of the wanton, much of the bizarre, something of the terrible, and not a little of that which might have excited disgust. To and fro in the seven chambers there stalked, in fact, a multitude of dreams. And these – the dreams – writhed in and about, taking hue from the rooms, and causing the wild music of the orchestra to seem as the echo of their steps. And, anon, there strikes the ebony clock which stands in the hall of the velvet. And then, for a moment, all is still, and all is silent save the voice of the clock. The dreams are stiff-frozen as they stand. But the echoes of the chime die away – they have endured but an instant – and a light, half-subdued laughter floats after them as they depart. And now again the music swells, and the dreams live, and writhe to and fro more merrily than ever, taking hue from the many tinted windows through which stream the rays from the tripods. But to the chamber which lies most west-wardly of the seven, there are now none of the maskers who venture; for the night is waning away; and there flows a rud-dier light through the blood-coloured panes; and the blackness of the sable drapery appals; and to him whose foot falls upon the sable carpet, there comes from the near clock of ebony a muffled peal more solemnly emphatic than any which reaches *their* ears who indulge in the more remote gaieties of the other apartments.

But these other apartments were densely crowded, and in them beat feverishly the heart of life. And the revel went whirlingly on, until at length there commenced the sounding of midnight upon the clock. And then the music ceased, as I have told; and the evolutions of the waltzers were quieted; and there was an uneasy cessation of all things as before. But now there were twelve strokes to be sounded by the bell of the clock; and thus it happened, perhaps, that more of thought crept, with more of time, into the meditations of the thoughtful among those who revelled. And thus, too, it happened, perhaps, that before the last echoes of the last chime had utterly sunk into silence, there were many individuals in the crowd who had found leisure to become aware of the presence of a masked figure which had arrested the attention of no single individual before. And the rumour of this new presence having spread itself whisperingly around, there arose at length from the whole company a buzz, or murmur, expressive of disapprobation and surprise – then, finally, of terror, of horror, and of disgust.

In an assembly of phantasms, such as I have painted, it may well be supposed that no ordinary appearance could have excited such sensation. In truth the masquerade license of the night was nearly unlimited; but the figure in question had out-Heroded Herod, and gone beyond the bounds of even the prince's indefinite decorum. There are chords in the hearts of the most reckless which cannot be touched without emotion. Even with the utterly lost, to whom life and death are equally jests, there are matters of which no jests can be made. The whole company, indeed, seemed now deeply to feel that in the costume and bearing of the stranger neither wit nor propriety existed. The figure was tall and gaunt, and shrouded from head to foot in the habiliments of the grave. The mask which concealed the visage was made so nearly to resemble the countenance of a stiffened corpse that the closest scrutiny must have had difficulty in detecting the cheat. And yet all this might have been endured, if not approved, by the mad revellers around. But the mummer had gone so far as to assume the type of the Red Death. His vesture was dabbled in *blood* – and his broad brow, with all the features of the face, was besprinkled with the scarlet horror.

When the eyes of Prince Prospero fell upon this spectral image (which with a slow and solemn movement, as if more fully to sustain its *rôle*, stalked to and fro among the waltzers), he was seen to be convulsed, in the first moment, with a strong shudder either of terror or distaste; but, in the next, his brow reddened with rage.

'Who dares?' he demanded hoarsely of the courtiers who stood near him – 'who dares insult us with this blasphemous mockery? Seize him and unmask him – that we may know whom we have to hang at sunrise from the battlements!'

It was in the eastern or blue chamber in which stood the Prince Prospero as he uttered these words. They rang throughout the seven rooms loudly and clearly – for the prince was a bold and robust man, and the music had become hushed at the waving of his hand.

It was in the blue room where stood the prince with a group of pale courtiers by his side. At first, as he spoke, there was a slight rushing movement of this group in the direction of the intruder, who, at the moment, was also near at hand, and now, with deliberate and stately step, made closer approach to the speaker. But from a certain nameless awe with which the mad assumptions of the mummer had inspired the whole party, there were found none who put forth hand to seize him; so that, unimpeded, he passed within a yard of the price's person; and, while the vast assembly, as if with one impulse, shrank from the centres of the rooms to the walls, he made his way uninterruptedly, but with the same solemn and measured step which had distinguished him from the first, through the blue chamber to the purple – through the purple to the green – through the green to the orange – through this again to the white – and even thence to the violet, ere a decided movement had been made to arrest him. It was then, however, that the Prince Prospero, maddened with rage and the shame of his own momentary cowardice, rushed hurriedly through the six chambers, while none followed him on account of a deadly terror that had seized upon all. He bore aloft a drawn dagger, and had approached, in rapid impetuosity, to within three or four feet of the retreating figure, when the latter, having attained the extremity of the velvet apartment, turned suddenly and confronted his pursuer. There was a sharp cry – and the dagger dropped gleaming upon the sable carpet, upon which, instantly afterwards, fell prostrate in death the Prince Prospero. Then, summoning the wild courage of despair, a throng of the revellers at once threw themselves into the black apartment, and, seizing the mummer, whose tall figure stood erect and motionless within the shadow of the ebony clock, gasped in unutterable horror at finding the grave cerements and corpse-like mask which they handled with so violent a rudeness, untenanted by any tangible form.

And now was acknowledged the presence of the Red Death. He had come like a thief in the night. And one by one dropped the revellers in the blood-bedewed halls of their revel, and died each in the despairing posture of his fall. And the life of the ebony clock went out with that of the last of the gay. And the flames of the tripods expired. And Darkness and Decay and the Red Death held illimitable dominion over all.

The Ball

RYUNOSUKE AKUTAGAWA

I

It was the night of the third day of the eleventh month of the nineteenth year of Meiji (1886). Akiko, the seventeen-year-old daughter of the distinguished family of ——, accompanied by her bald-headed father, climbed the stairs of the Rokumeikan, where the ball that night was to be held. Great chrysanthemum blossoms, which seemed almost to be artificial, formed three-fold hedges up the sides of the broad, brightly gas-lighted stairs. The petals of the chrysanthemums, those at the back pink, those in the middle deep yellow, and those in front pure white, were all tousled like flag tassels. And near where the banks of chrysanthemums came to an end, already floated out incessantly from the ball-room at the top of the stairs lively orchestra music like an irrepressible sigh of happiness.

Akiko had early been taught to speak French and dance. But to-night she was going to attend a formal ball for the first time in her life. Wherefore in the carriage, when her father spoke to her from time to time, she returned only absent-minded answers. Thus deeply had an unsettled feeling that may well be defined as a glad uneasiness taken root in her breast. Till the carriage finally came to a stop in front of the Rokumeikan, time and again she lifted impatient eyes and gazed out of the window at the scanty lights of the Tōkyō streets drifting by outside.

But immediately she entered the Rokumeikan, she experienced that which made her forget her uneasiness. When half way up the stairs, she and her father overtook some Chinese officials ascending just ahead of them. And as the officials separated in their fatness to let them go ahead, they cast surprised glances at Akiko. In good truth, with her simple rose-colored ball gown, a light blue ribbon around her well-formed neck and a single rose exhaling perfume from her dark hair, Akiko that night was fully possessed of the beauty of the girls of enlightened Japan, a beauty that might well startle the eyes of these Chinese officials with their long pigtails hanging down their backs. And just as she noticed this, a young Japanese in swallow-tails came hurrying down the steps and, as he passed them, turned his head in a slight reflex action and likewise gave a glace of surprise after Akiko as she went on. Then for some reason, as if suddenly having an idea, he put his hand up to his white necktie and went on hurriedly down through the chrysanthemums toward the entrance.

When they got to the top of the stairs, at the door of the ball-room on the second floor they found a count with gray whiskers, who was the host of the evening, with his chest covered with decorations, and the countess, older than himself, dressed to the last degree of perfection in a Louis XV gown, extending a dignified welcome to the guests of the evening. Akiko did not fail to see the momentary look of naïve admiration that appeared and faded away somewhere in the crafty old face even of this count when he saw her. Her good-natured father, with a happy smile, introduced her briefly to the count and countess. She experienced a succession of the feelings of shame and pride. But meanwhile she had just time to notice that there was a touch of vulgarity in the haughty features of the countess.

In the ball-room, too, chrysanthemums blossomed in beautiful profusion everywhere. And everywhere the lace and flowers and ivory fans of the ladies waiting for their partners moved like soundless waves in the refreshing sweetness of perfume. Akiko soon separated from her father and joined one of the groups of gorgeous women. They were all girls of about the same age dressed in similar light blue and rose-colored ball gowns. When they turned to welcome her, they chirped softly like birds and spoke with admiration of her beauty that night.

But no sooner had she joined the group than a French naval officer she had never seen before walked quietly up to her. And with his two arms hanging down to his knees, he politely made her a Japanese bow. Akiko was faintly conscious of the blood mounting to her cheeks. But the meaning of that bow was clear without any asking. So she looked round at the girl standing beside her in a light blue gown to get her to hold her fan. As she turned, to her surprise, the French naval officer, with a smile flitting across his cheek, said distinctly to her in Japanese with a strange accent,

"Won't you dance with me?"

In a moment Akiko was dancing the Blue Danube Waltz with the French naval officer. He had tanned cheeks, clear-cut features and a heavy mustache. She was too short to reach up and put her long-gloved hand on the left shoulder of his uniform. But the experienced officer handled her deftly and danced her lightly through the crowd. And at times he even whispered amiable flatteries into her ear in French.

Repaying his gentle words with a bashful smile, she looked from time to time about the ball-room in which they danced. She could see between the sea of people flashes of curtains of purple silk crape with the Imperial crest dyed into them, and the gay silver or sober gold of the chrysanthemums in the vases under Chinese flags on which blue claw-spread dragons writhed. And the sea of people, stirred up by the wind of gay melody from the German orchestra that came bubbling over it like champagne, never stopped for a moment its dizzy commotion. When she and one of her friends, also dancing, saw each other, they nodded happily as they went busily by. But at that moment, another dancer, whirling like a big moth, appeared between them from nowhere in particular.

But meanwhile, she realized that the naval officer was watching her every movement. This simply showed how much interest this foreigner, unaccustomed to Japan, took in her vivacious dancing. Did this beautiful young lady, too, live like a doll in a house of paper and bamboo? And with slender metal chopsticks did she pick up grains of rice out of a teacup as big as the palm of your hand with a blue flower painted on it and eat them? Such doubts, together with an affectionate smile, seemed ever and anon to come and go in his eyes. If this was amusing to Akiko, it was at the same time gratifying. So every time his surprised gaze fell to her feet, her slender little rose-colored dancing pumps went sliding the more lightly over the slippery floor.

But finally the officer seemed to notice that this kitten-like

young lady showed signs of fatigue, and peering into her face
with kindly eyes, he asked,

"Shall we go on dancing?"

"*Non, merci,*" said Akiko in excitement, this time clearly.

Then the French naval officer, continuing the steps of the
waltz, wove his way through the waves of lace and flowers
moving back and forth and right and left, and guided her leisurely up to the chrysanthemums in vases by the wall. And after
the last revolution, he seated her neatly in a chair there and,
having once thrown out his chest in his military uniform, again
respectfully made her a deep Japanese bow.

Then after dancing a polka and a mazurka, Akiko took
the arm of this French naval officer and went down the stairs
between the walls of white and yellow and pink chrysanthemums to a large hall.

Here in the midst of swallow-tails and white shoulders
moving to and fro unceasingly, many tables loaded with silver
and glass utensils were piled high with meat and truffles, or
pinnacled with towers of sandwiches and ice-cream, or built
up into pyramids of pomegranates and figs. Especially beautiful
was a gilt lattice with skilfully made artifical grape vines twining
their green leaves through it on the wall at one side of the room
above the piled-up chrysanthemums. And among the leaves,
bunches of grapes like wasps' nests hung in purple abundance.
In front of this gilt lattice, Akiko found her bald-headed father,
with another gentleman of the same age, smoking a cigar. When
he saw her, he nodded slightly with evident satisfaction, aud
without taking further notice of her, turned to his companion
and went on smoking.

The French naval officer went to one of the tables with

Akiko, and they began to eat ice-cream. As they ate, she noticed that ever and anon his eyes were drawn to her hands or her hair or her neck with the light blue ribbon round it. This did not, of course, make her unhappy. But at one moment a womanly doubt could not but flash forth in her. Then, as two young women who looked like Germans went by with red camellias on their black velvet breasts, in order to hint at this doubt, she exclaimed,

"Really how beautiful western women are!"

When the naval officer heard this, contrary to her expectation, he shook his head seriously.

"Japanese women are beautiful, too. Especially you—"

"I'm no such thing."

"No, I'm not flattering. You could appear at a Parisian ball just as you are. If you did, everybody would be surprised. For you're like the princess in Watteau's picture."

Akiko did not know who Watteau was. So the beautiful vision of the past called up for the naval officer by his words—the vision of a fountain in a dusky grove and a fading rose—could only disappear without a trace and be lost. But this girl of unusual sensibility, as she plied her ice-cream spoon, did not forget to stick to just one more thing she wanted to speak of.

"I should like to go to a Parisian ball and see what they're like."

"No, a Parisian ball is exactly the same as this."

As he said this, the naval officer looked round at the sea of people and the chrysanthemums surrounding the table where they stood; then suddenly, as a cynical smile seemed to move like a little wave in the depths of his eyes, he put down his ice-cream spoon and added as if half to himself,

"Not only Paris. Balls are just the same everywhere."

An hour later, Akiko and the French naval officer stood arm in arm on a balcony off the ball-room under the starlight with many other Japanese and foreigners.

Out beyond the balcony railing the pines that covered the extensive garden stood hushed with their branches interwoven, and here and there among their twigs shone the lights of little red paper lanterns.

In the bottom of the chilly air the fragrance of the moss and fallen leaves rising from the garden below seemed to set adrift faintly the breath of lonely autumn. And in the ball-room behind them, that same sea of lace and flowers went on ceaselessly moving under the curtains of purple silk crape with the sixteen petaled chrysanthemums dyed into them. And still up over the sea of people, the whirlwind of high-pitched orchestra music mercilessly goaded them on.

Of course from the balcony, too, lively talk and laughter stirred the night air ceaselessly. More, when beautiful fireworks shot up into the sky over the pines, a sound almost like a shout came from the throats of the people on the balcony. Standing in their midst, Akiko had been exchanging light chit-chat with some young lady friends of hers near them. But she finally bethought herself, and turning to the French naval officer, found him with his arm still supporting hers, gazing silently into the starry sky up over the garden. It seemed to her somehow that he was experiencing a touch of homesickness. So looking furtively up into his face, she said half teasingly,

"You're thinking of your own country, aren't you?"

Then the naval officer, with a smile in his eyes as always,

looked round at her quietly. And instead of saying *"Non,"* he shook his head like a child.

"But you seem to be musing on something."

"Guess what."

Just then among the people on the veranda arose again for a time a noise like a wind. As if by agreement, Akiko and the naval officer stopped talking and looked up into the night sky that pressed down heavily on the pines of the garden. There a red and blue firework, throwing its spider legs out against the darkness, was just on the verge of dying away. To Akiko, for some reason or other, that firework was so beautiful that it almost made her sad.

"I was thinking of the fireworks. The fireworks, like our lives," said the French naval officer, looking gently down into Akiko's face and speaking as if teaching her.

II

It was autumn in the seventh year of Taisho (1918). The Akiko of that time, on her way back to her villa at Kamakura, met by chance on the train a young novelist with whom she was slightly acquainted. The young man put a bunch of chrysanthemums which he was taking to a friend in Kamakura up into the rack. Then Akiko, who was now the elderly Madame H——, told him that there was a story of which she was always reminded whenever she saw chrysanthemums and recounted to him in detail her reminiscences of the ball at the Rokumeikan. He could not but feel a deep interest when he heard such reminiscences from the mouth of the woman herself.

When the story was over, he casually asked,

146

"Madame, do you not know the name of that French naval officer?"

Then old Madame H—— gave him an unexpected answer.

"Of course I do. His name was Julien Viaud."

"Then it was Loti, wasn't it? It was Pierre Loti, who wrote 'Madame Chrysantheme', wasn't it?"

The young man felt an agreeable excitement. But old Madame H—— simply looked into his face wonderingly and murmured over and over,

"No, his name wasn't Loti. It was Julien Viaud."

After Holbein

EDITH WHARTON

Anson Warley had had his moments of being a rather remarkable man, but they were only intermittent; they recurred at ever-lengthening intervals, and between times he was a small poor creature, chattering with cold inside, in spite of his agreeable and even distinguished exterior.

He had always been perfectly aware of these two sides of himself—which, even in the privacy of his own mind, he contemptuously refused to dub a dual personality—and as the rather remarkable man could take fairly good care of himself, most of Warley's attention was devoted to ministering to the poor wretch who took longer and longer turns at bearing his name and was more and more insistent on accepting the invitations which New York, for more than thirty years, had tirelessly poured out on him.

It was in the interest of this lonely, fidgety unemployed self that Warley, in his younger days, had frequented the gaudiest restaurants and the most glittering Palace Hotels of two hemispheres, subscribed to the most advanced literary and artistic reviews, bought the pictures of the young painters who were being the most vehemently discussed, missed few of the showiest first nights in New York, London or Paris, sought the company of the men and women—especially the women—most conspicuous in fashion, scandal, or any other form of social notoriety, and thus tried to warm the shivering soul within him at all the passing bonfires of success.

The original Anson Warley had begun by staying at home in his little flat, with his books and his thoughts, when the other poor creature went forth, but gradually—he hardly knew when or how—he had slipped into the way of going, too, till finally he made the bitter discovery that he and the creature had become one, except on the increasingly rare occasions when, detaching himself from all casual contingencies, he mounted to the lofty watershed which fed the sources of his scorn. The view from there was vast and glorious; the air was icy, but exhilarating; but soon he began to find the place too lonely and too difficult to get to, especially as the lesser Anson not only refused to go up with him but began to sneer, at first ever so faintly, then with increasing insolence, at this affectation of a taste for the heights.

"What's the use of scrambling up there anyhow? I could understand it if you brought down anything worth while—a poem or a picture of your own. But just climbing and staring, what does it lead to? Fellows with the creative gift have got to have their occasional Sinais; I can see that. But for a mere looker-on like you, isn't that sort of thing rather a pose? You talk awfully well, brilliantly, even—oh, my dear fellow, no false modesty between you and me, please!—but who the devil is there to listen to you, up there among the glaciers? And some-times, when you come down, I notice that you're rather—well, heavy and tongue-tied. Look out, or they'll stop asking us to dine! And sitting at home every evening—b-r-r! Look here, by the way; if you've got nothing better for tonight, come along with me to Chrissy Torrance's, or the Bob Briggses', or Prin-cess Kate's—anywhere where there's lots of racket and sparkle;

places that people go to in limousines and that are smart and hot and overcrowded and you have to pay a lot, in one way or another, to get in."

Once and again, it is true, he still dodged his double and slipped off on a tour to remote uncomfortable places where there were churches or pictures to be seen, or shut himself up at home for a good bout of reading, or, in sheer disgust at his companion's platitudes, spent an evening with people who were doing or thinking real things. This happened seldomer than of old, however, and more clandestinely; so that at last he used to sneak away to spend two or three days with an archæologically minded friend or an evening with a quiet scholar, as furtively as if he were stealing to a lovers' tryst; which, as lovers' trysts were now always kept in the limelight, was, after all, a fair exchange. But he always felt rather apologetic to the other Warley about these escapades and, if the truth were known, rather bored and restless before they were over. And in the back of his mind there lurked an increasing dread of missing something hot and noisy and overcrowded, when he went off to one of his mountain tops.

"After all, that highbrow business has been awfully overdone, now, hasn't it?" the little Warley would insinuate, rummaging for his pearl studs and consulting his flat evening watch as nervously as if it were a railway time-table, "If only we haven't missed something really jolly by all this backing and filling."

"Oh, you poor creature, you! Always afraid of being left out, aren't you? Well, just for once, to humor you, and because I happen to be feeling rather stale myself. But only to think of a sane man's wanting to go to places just because they're hot and smart and overcrowded!" And off they would dash together.

II

All that was long ago. It was years now since there had been two distinct Anson Warleys. The lesser one had made away with the other, done him softly to death without shedding of blood; and only a few people suspected—and they no longer cared—that the pale white-haired man, with the small slim figure, the ironic smile and the perfect evening clothes, whom New York still indefatigably invited, was nothing less than a murderer.

Anson Warley—Anson Warley! No party was complete without Anson Warley. He no longer went abroad now—too stiff in the joints and there had been two or three slight attacks of dizziness. Nothing to speak of, nothing to think of, even, but somehow one dug oneself into one's comfortable quarters and felt less and less like moving out of them, except to motor down to Long Island for week-ends, or to Newport for a few visits in summer. A trip to the Hot Springs, to get rid of the stiffness, had not helped much, and the aging Anson Warley—who really, otherwise, felt as young as ever—had developed a growing dislike for the promiscuities of hotel life and the monotony of hotel food.

Yes, he was growing more fastidious as he grew older. A good sign, he thought. Fastidious not only about food and comfort but about people also. It was still a privilege, a distinction, to have him to dine. His old friends were faithful, and the new people fought for him and often failed to get him; to do so, they had to offer very special inducements in the way of cuisine, conversation or beauty. Young beauty—yes, that would do it. He did like to sit and watch a lovely face and call laughter into lovely eyes. But no dull dinners for him, even if they fed you off gold. As to that, he was as firm as the other Warley, the distant aloof one with whom he had—er—well, parted company—oh, quite amicably—a good many years ago.

On the whole, since that parting, life had been much easier and pleasanter, and by the time he was sixty-three, he found himself looking forward with equanimity to an eternity of New York dinners.

Oh, but only at the right houses—always at the right houses; that was understood! The right people, the right setting, the right wines. He smiled a little over his perennial enjoyment of them; said "Nonsense, Filmore," to his devoted, tiresome man-servant, who was beginning to hint that, really, every night, sir, and sometimes a dance afterward, was too much, especially when you kept at it for months on end, and Doctor——

"Oh, damn your doctors!" Warley snapped. He was seldom ill-tempered; he knew it was foolish and upsetting to lose one's self-control. But the man began to be a nuisance, nagging him, preaching at him—as if he himself wasn't the best judge.

Besides, he chose his company. He'd stay at home any time rather than risk a boring evening. Rot—what Filmore said about his going out every night. Not like poor old Mrs. Jaspar, for instance. He smiled self-approvingly as he evoked her tottering image.

"That's the kind of fool Filmore takes me for," he chuckled, his good humor restored by an analogy that was so much to his advantage.

Poor old Evelina Jaspar! In his youth, and even in his

prime, she had been New York's chief entertainer—"leading hostess," the newspapers called her. Her big house on Fifth Avenue had been an entertaining machine. She had lived, breathed, invested and reinvested her millions to no other end. At first her pretext had been that she had to marry her daughters and amuse her sons, but when sons and daughters had married and left her she had seemed hardly aware of it; she had just gone on entertaining. Hundreds—no, thousands of dinners—on gold plate, of course, and with orchids and all the delicacies that were out of season—had been served in that vast pompous dining room which one had only to close one's eyes to transform into a railway buffet for millionaires, at a big junction, before the invention of restaurant trains.

Warley closed his eyes and did so picture it. He lost himself in amused computation of the annual number of guests, of saddles of mutton, of legs of lamb, of terrapin, canvasbacks, magnums of champagne, and pyramids of hothouse fruit that must have passed through that room in the last forty years.

And even now, he thought, hadn't one of old Evelina's nieces told him the other day, half bantering, half shivering at the avowal, that the poor old lady, who was gently dying of softening of the brain, still imagined herself to be New York's leading hostess, still sent out invitations—which, of course, were never delivered—still ordered terrapin, champagne and orchids, and still came down every evening to her great shrouded drawing-rooms, with her tiara askew on her purple wig, to receive a stream of imaginary guests?

Rubbish, of course—a macabre pleasantry of the extravagant

Nelly Pierce, who had always had her joke at Aunt Evelina's expense—but Warley could not help smiling at the thought that those dull monotonous dinners were still going on in their hostess' clouded imagination. "Poor old Evelina," he thought. In a way she was right. There was really no reason why that kind of standardized entertaining should ever cease; a performance so undiscriminating, so undifferentiated that one could almost imagine, in the hostess' tired brain, all the dinners she had ever given merging into one Gargantuan pyramid of food and drink, with the same faces—perpetually the same faces—gathered stolidly about the same gold plate.

Thank heaven, Anson Warley had never conceived of social values in terms of mass and volume. It was years since he had accepted an invitation to old Mrs. Jaspar's. He even felt that he was not above reproach in that respect. Two or three times in the past he had accepted her invitations, always sent out weeks ahead, and then chucked her at the eleventh hour for something more amusing. Finally, to avoid such risks, he had made it a rule always to refuse her dinners. He had even, he remembered, been rather funny about it once, when someone had told him that Mrs. Jaspar couldn't understand; was a little hurt; said it couldn't be true that he always had another engagement the nights she asked him.

"True? Is the truth what she wants? All right! Then the next time I get a 'Mrs. Jaspar requests the pleasure,' I'll answer it with a 'Mr. Warley declines the boredom.' Think she'll understand that, eh?"

And the phrase became a catchword in his little set that winter. "'Mr. Warley declines the boredom'—good, good, good!" "Dear Anson, I do hope you won't decline the

EDITH WHARTON

boredom of coming to lunch next Sunday to meet the new Hindu yogi"—or the new saxophone soloist, or that genius of a mulatto boy who plays negro spirituals on a toothbrush, and so on, and so on. He only hoped poor old Evelina never heard of it.

"Certainly I shan't stay at home tonight. Why, what's wrong with me?" he snapped, swinging round on Filmore.

The valet's long face, about as expressive as the sole of a snowshoe, grew longer. His way of answering such questions was always to pull out his face; it was his only means of putting any expression into it. He turned away into the bedroom and Warley sat alone by his library fire. Now what did the man see that was wrong with him, he wondered. He had felt a little confusion that morning when he was doing his daily sprint around the park—his exercise was reduced to that—but it had been only a passing flurry, of which Filmore could of course know nothing. And as soon as it was over, his mind had seemed more lucid, his eye keener than ever, as sometimes, he reflected, the electric light in his library lamps would blaze up too brightly after a break in the current and he would say to himself, wincing a little in the sudden glare on the page he was reading: "That means that it'll go out again in a minute."

Yes, his mind, at that moment, had been quite piercingly clear and perceptive; his eye had passed with a renovating glitter over every detail of the daily scene. He stood still for a minute under the leafless trees of the Mall and, looking about him with the sudden insight of age, understood that he had reached the time of life when Alps and cathedrals became as transient as flowers.

Everything was fleeting, fleeting. Yes, that was what had

given him the vertigo. The doctors, poor fools, called it the stomach or high blood pressure, but it was only the dizzy plunge of the sands in the hourglass, the everlasting plunge that emptied one of heart and bowels, like the drop of an elevator from the top floor of a skyscraper.

Certainly, after that moment of revelation, he had felt a little more tired than usual for the rest of the day; the light had flagged in his mind as it sometimes did in his lamps. At Chrissy Torrance's, where he had lunched, they had accused him of being silent; his hostess had said he looked pale; but he had retorted with a joke and thrown himself into the talk with a feverish loquacity. It was the only thing to do, for he could not tell all these people at the luncheon table that that very morning he had arrived at the turn in the path from which mountains look as transient as flowers, and that one after another they would all arrive there too.

He leaned his head back and closed his eyes, but not in sleep. He did not feel sleepy, but keyed up and alert. In the next room he heard Filmore reluctantly, protestingly, laying out his evening clothes. He had no fear about the dinner tonight—a quiet, intimate little affair at an old friend's house. Just two or three congenial men and Elfmann, the pianist, who would probably play, and that lovely Ethelred Flight. The fact that people asked him to dine, to meet Ethelred Flight seemed to prove pretty conclusively that he was still in the running. He chuckled softly at Filmore's pessimism. "Well, after all, I suppose no man seems young to his valet. . . . Time to dress very soon," he thought, and luxuriously postponed getting up out of his chair.

III

"She's worse than usual tonight," said the day nurse, laying down the evening paper as her colleague joined her. "Absolutely determined to have her jewels out."

The night nurse, fresh from a long sleep and an afternoon at the movies with a gentleman friend, threw down her fancy bag, tossed off her hat and rumpled up her hair before old Mrs. Jaspar's tall toilet mirror.

"Oh, I'll settle that; don't you worry," she said brightly.

"Don't you fret her, though, Miss Cress," said the other, getting wearily out of her chair. "We're very well off here, take it as a whole, and I don't want her pressure rushed up for nothing."

Miss Cress, still looking at herself in the glass, smiled reassuringly at Miss Dunn's pale reflection behind her. She and Miss Dunn got on very well together and knew on which side their bread was buttered. But at the end of the day Miss Dunn was always fagged out and fearing the worst. The patient wasn't so hard to handle as all that. Just let her ring for her old maid, old Lavinia, and say: "My sapphire velvet tonight, with the diamond stars," and Lavinia would know exactly how to manage her.

Miss Dunn had put on her hat and coat, crammed her knitting and the newspaper into her bag, which, unlike Miss Cress', was capacious and shabby, but she still loitered, undecided, on the threshold.

"I could stay with you till ten as easy as not."

She looked almost reluctantly about the big high-studded

dressing room—everything in the house was high studded—
with its rich dusky carpet and curtains, and its monumental
dressing table draped with lace and laden with gold-backed
brushes and combs, gold-stoppered toilet bottles and all the
charming paraphernalia of beauty at her glass. Old Lavinia even
renewed, every morning, the roses and carnations in the slim
crystal vases between the powder boxes and the nail polishers.
Since the family had shut down the hothouses at the uninhab-
ited country place on the Hudson, Miss Cress suspected that
old Lavinia bought these flowers out of her own pocket.

"Cold out tonight?" queried Miss Dunn from the door.

"Fierce. Reg'lar blizzard at the corners. Say, shall I lend you
my fur scarf?"

Miss Cress, pleased with the memory of her afternoon—
they'd be engaged soon, she thought—and with the drowsy
prospect of an evening in a deep armchair near the warm
gleam of the dressing-room fire, was disposed to kindliness
toward that poor thin Dunn girl, who supported her mother
and her brother's idiot twins. And she wanted Miss Dunn to
notice her new fur.

"My, isn't it lovely? No, not for worlds, thank you." Her
hand on the door knob, Miss Dunn repeated: "Don't you cross
her now"—and was gone.

Lavinia's bell rang furiously twice; then the door between
the dressing room and Mrs. Jaspar's bedroom opened, and
Mrs. Jaspar herself emerged.

"Lavinia!" she called in a high irritated voice; then, seeing
the nurse, who had slipped into her print dress and starched
cap, she added in a lower tone: "Oh, Miss Lemoine, good
evening." Her first nurse, it appeared, had been called Miss

Lemoine, and she gave the same name to all the others, quite
unaware that there had been any changes in the staff.

"I heard talking and carriages driving up. Have people
begun to arrive?" she asked nervously. "Where is Lavinia? I still
have my jewels to put on."

She stood before the nurse, the same petrifying apparition which always, at this hour, struck Miss Cress to silence.
Mrs. Jaspar was tall; she had been broad; and her bones
remained impressive, though the flesh had withered on them.
Lavinia had incased her, as usual, in her low-necked purple
velvet dress, nipped in at the waist in the old-fashioned way,
expanding in voluminous folds about the hips and flowing in a
long train over the darker velvet of the carpet.

Mrs. Jaspar's swollen feet could no longer be pushed into the
high-heeled satin slippers which went with the dress, but her
skirts were so long and spreading that, by taking short steps,
she managed—so Lavinia daily assured her—entirely to conceal
the broad round tips of her black orthopedic shoes.

"Your jewels, Mrs. Jaspar? Why, you've got them on," said
Miss Cress brightly.

Mrs. Jaspar turned her dark porphyry-tinted face to Miss
Cress and looked at her with a glassy, incredulous gaze. Her
eyes, Miss Cress thought, were the worst. She lifted one
stony old hand, veined and knobbed as a raised map, to her
elaborate purple-black wig, groped among the puffs and curls
and undulations—queer, Miss Cress thought, that it never
occurred to her to look into the glass—and, after an interval,
affirmed:

"You must be mistaken, my dear. Don't you think you ought
to have your eyes examined?"

The door opened again, and a very old woman—so old as to make Mrs. Jaspar appear almost young—hobbled in with fluttering sidelong steps.

"Excuse me, madam. I was downstairs when the bell rang."

Lavinia had probably always been small and slight; now, beside her towering mistress, she looked a mere feather—a straw. Everything about her had dried, contracted, been volatilized into nothingness, except her watchful gray eyes, in which intelligence and comprehension burned like two fixed stars.

"Do excuse me, madam," she repeated.

Mrs. Jaspar looked at her despairingly. "I hear carriages driving up. And Miss Lemoine says I have my jewels on, and I know I haven't."

"With that lovely necklace!" Miss Cress ejaculated.

Mrs. Jaspar's twisted hand rose again, this time to her denuded shoulders, which were as stark and barren as the rock from which the hand might have been broken. She felt and felt, and tears rose in her lashless eyes.

"Why do you lie to me?" she burst out passionately.

Lavinia softly intervened. "Miss Lemoine meant how lovely you'll be when you get the necklace on, madam."

"Diamonds—diamonds," said Mrs. Jaspar, with an awful smile.

"Of course, madam."

Mrs. Jaspar sat down at the dressing table, and Lavinia, with eager random hands, began to adjust the *point de Venise* about her mistress' shoulders and to repair the havoc wrought in the purple-black wig by its wearer's gropings for her tiara.

"Now you do look lovely, madam," she sighed with conviction.

Mrs. Jaspar was on her feet again, stiff but incredibly active—"Like a cat, she is," Miss Cress used to relate. "I do hear carriages—or is it a motor? The Magraws, I know, have one of those newfangled motors. And now I hear the front door opening. Quick, Lavinia! My fan, my gloves, my handkerchief! How often have I got to tell you? I used to have a perfect maid——"

Lavinia's eyes brimmed. "That was me, madam," she said, bending her tremulous knees to straighten out the folds of the long purple velvet train.

"To watch the two of 'em," Miss Cress used to tell a circle of appreciative friends, "is a lot better than any circus."

Mrs. Jaspar paid no attention. She twitched the train out of Lavinia's vacillating hold, swept to the door, and then paused there as if stopped by a jerk of her constricted muscles.

"Oh, but my diamonds! You cruel woman, you! You're letting me go down without my diamonds!" Her ruined face puckered up in a grimace like a newborn baby's, and she began to sob despairingly: "Everybody—everybody's against me." She wept in her powerless misery.

Lavinia helped herself to her feet and tottered across the floor. It was almost more than she could bear—to see her mistress in distress.

"Madam—madam, if you'll just wait till they're got out of the safe," she entreated.

The woman she saw before her, the woman she was entreating and consoling, was not the old petrified Mrs. Jaspar, with porphyry face and wig awry, whom Miss Cress stood watching with a smile, but a young, proud creature, commanding and splendid in her Paris gown of amber moire, who, years ago, had burst into just such furious sobs because, as she was sweeping down to receive her guests, the doctor had told her that little Grace, with whom she had been playing all the afternoon, had a diphtheritic throat and no one must be allowed to enter. "Everybody's against me—everybody," she had sobbed in her fury; and the young Lavinia, stricken by such Olympian anger, had stood speechless, longing to comfort her and secretly indignant with little Grace and the doctor.

"If you'll just wait, madam, while I go down and ask Munson to open the safe. There's no one come yet, I do assure you."

Munson was the old butler, the only person who knew the combination of the safe in Mrs. Jaspar's bedroom. Lavinia had once known it, too, but now she was no longer able to remember it. The worst of it was that she feared lest Munson, who had been spending the day with his family in the Bronx, might not have returned. Munson was growing old, too, and he did sometimes forget about these dinner parties of Mrs. Jaspar's, and then the stupid footman, George, had to announce the names; and you couldn't be sure that Mrs. Jaspar wouldn't notice Munson's absence and be excited and angry. These dinner-party nights were killing old Lavinia, and she did so want to keep alive; she wanted to live long enough to wait on Mrs. Jaspar to the last.

She disappeared, and Miss Cress poked up the fire and persuaded Mrs. Jaspar to sit down in an armchair and tell her who was coming. It always amused Mrs. Jaspar to say over the long list of her guests' names, and generally she remembered them fairly well, for they were always the same—the last people, Lavinia and Munson said, who dined at the house the very night before her stroke. With recovered complacency, she began, counting over one after another on her ring-laden fingers:

"The Italian Ambassador, the bishop, Mr. and Mrs. Torrington Bligh, Mr. and Mrs. Fred Amesworth, Mr. and Mrs. Mitchell Magraw, Mr. and Mrs. Torrington Bligh——"

"You've said them before," Miss Cress interpolated, getting out her fancy knitting—a necktie for her friend—and beginning to count the stitches.

And Mrs. Jaspar, distressed and bewildered by the interruption, had to repeat over and over: "Torrington Bligh—Torrington Bligh," till the connection was re-established and she went on again swimmingly with: "Mr. and Mrs. Fred Amesworth, Mr. and Mrs. Mitchell Magraw, Miss Laura Ladew, Mr. Harold Ladew, Mr. and Mrs. Benjamin Bronx, Mr. and Mrs. Torrington Bl——No, I mean, Mr. Anson Warley. Yes, Mr. Anson Warley; that's it," she ended complacently.

Miss Cress smiled and interrupted her counting. "No, that's not it."

"What do you mean, my dear—not it?"

"Mr. Anson Warley. He's not coming."

Mrs. Jaspar's jaw fell and she stared at the nurse's coldly smiling face. "Not coming?"

"No. He's not coming. He's not on the list." That old list! As if Miss Cress didn't know it by heart! Everybody in the house did, except the booby, George, who heard it reeled off every other night by Munson and who was always stumbling over the names and having to refer to the written paper.

"Not on the list?" Mrs. Jaspar gasped.

Miss Cress shook her pretty head.

Signs of uneasiness gathered on Mrs. Jaspar's face, and her

lip began to tremble. It always amused Miss Cress to give her these little jolts, though she knew Miss Dunn and the doctors didn't approve of her doing so. She knew, also, that it was against her own interests, and she did try to bear in mind Miss Dunn's oft-repeated admonition about not sending up the patient's blood pressure, but when she was in high spirits, as she was tonight—they would certainly be engaged—it was irresistible to get a rise out of the old lady. And she thought it funny—this new figure unexpectedly appearing among those timeworn guests.

"I wonder what the rest of 'em 'll say to him," she giggled inwardly.

"No, he's not on the list." Mrs. Jaspar, after pondering deeply, announced the fact with an air of recovered composure.

"That's what I told you," snapped Miss Cress.

"He's not on the list, but he promised me to come. I saw him yesterday," continued Mrs. Jaspar mysteriously.

"You saw him—where?"

She considered. "Last night, at the Fred Amesworths' dance."

"Ah," said Miss Cress with a little shiver, for she knew that Mrs. Amesworth was dead, and she was the intimate friend of the trained nurse who was keeping alive, by dint of *piqûres* and high frequency, the inarticulate and inanimate Mr. Amesworth. "It's funny," she remarked to Mrs. Jaspar, "that you'd never invited Mr. Warley before."

"No, I hadn't; not for a long time. I believe he felt I'd neglected him, for he came up to me last night and said he was so sorry he hadn't been able to call. It seems he's been ill, poor fellow. Not so young as he was! So, of course, I invited him. He was very much gratified."

Mrs. Jaspar smiled at the remembrance of her little triumph, but Miss Cress' attention had wandered, as it always did when the patient became docile and reasonable. She thought: "Where's old Lavinia? I bet she can't find Munson." And she got up and crossed the floor to look into Mrs. Jaspar's bedroom, where the safe was.

There an astonishing sight met her. Munson, as she had expected, was nowhere visible, but Lavinia, on her knees before the safe, was in the act of opening it herself, her twitching hand slowly moving about the mysterious dial.

"Why, I thought you'd forgotten the combination!" Miss Cress exclaimed.

Lavinia turned a startled face over her shoulder. "So I had, miss. But I've managed to remember it, thank God. I had to, you see, because Munson's forgot to come home."

"Oh," said the nurse incredulously. "Old fox," she thought. "I wonder why she's always pretended she'd forgotten it." For Miss Cress did not know that the age of miracles is not yet past.

Joyous, trembling, her cheeks wet with grateful tears, the little old woman was on her feet again, clutching to her breast the diamond stars, the necklace of solitaires, the tiara, the earrings. One by one she spread them out on the velvet-lined tray in which they always used to be carried from the safe to the dressing room; then, with her flighty rambling fingers, she managed to lock the safe again and put the keys in the drawer where they belonged, while Miss Cress continued to stare at her in amazement.

"I don't believe the old witch is as shaky as she makes out,"

AFTER HOLBEIN

was her reflection as Lavinia passed her, bearing the jewels
to the dressing room, where Mrs. Jaspar, lost in pleasant
memories, was still computing: "The Italian Ambassador, the
bishop, the Torrington Blighs, the Mitchell Magraws, the Fred
Amesworths——"

Mrs. Jaspar was allowed to go down to the drawing-room
alone on dinner-party evenings, because it would have mortified her too much to receive her guests with a maid or a nurse
at her elbow, but Miss Cress and Lavinia always leaned over
the stair rail to watch her descent and make sure it was accomplished in safety.

"She do look lovely yet when all her diamonds is on,"
Lavinia sighed, her purblind eyes bedewed with memories as
the bedizened wig and purple velvet disappeared at the last
bend of the stairs. Miss Cress, with a shrug, turned back to
the fire and picked up her knitting, while Lavinia set about the
slow ritual of tidying up her mistress' room. From below they
heard the sound of George's stentorian monologue: "Mr. and
Mrs. Torrington Bligh, Mr. and Mrs. Mitchell Magraw,
Mr. Ladew, Miss Laura Ladew——"

IV

Anson Warley, who had always prided himself on his equable
temper, was conscious of being on edge that evening. But it was
an irritability which did not frighten him—in spite of what the
doctors always said about the importance of keeping calm—
because he knew it was due merely to the unusual lucidity of
his mind. He was, in fact, feeling uncommonly well, his brain
clear and all his perceptions so alert that he could positively

hear the thoughts passing through his manservant's mind on the other side of the door as Filmore grudgingly laid out the evening clothes.

Smiling at the man's obstinacy, he thought: "I shall have to tell them tonight that Filmore thinks I'm no longer fit to go into society." It was always pleasant to hear the incredulous laugh with which his younger friends received any allusion to his supposed senility. "What—you? Well, that's a good one!" And he thought it was, himself.

And then, the moment he was in his bedroom, dressing, the sight of Filmore made him lose his temper again. "No, not those studs, confound it! The black onyx ones; haven't I told you a hundred times? Lost them, I suppose? Sent them to the wash again in a soiled shirt, that it?" He laughed nervously and, sitting down before his dressing table, began to brush back his hair with short, angry strokes.

"Above all," he shouted out suddenly, "don't stand there staring at me as if you were watching to see exactly at what minute to telephone for the undertaker!"

"The under——Oh, sir!" gasped Filmore.

"The—the——Damn it, are you deaf too? Who said 'undertaker'? I said 'taxi'; can't you hear what I say?"

"You want me to call a taxi, sir?"

"No, I don't. I've already told you so. I'm going to walk." Warley straightened his tie, rose and held out his arms toward his dinner jacket.

"It's bitter cold, sir. Better let me call a taxi, all the same."

Warley gave a short laugh. "Out with it now! What you'd really like to suggest is that I should telephone to say I can't dine out. You'd scramble me some eggs instead, eh?"

"I wish you would stay in, sir. There's eggs in the house."

"My overcoat!" snapped Warley.

"Or else let me call a taxi; now do, sir."

Warley slipped his arms into his overcoat, tapped his chest to see if his watch—the thin evening watch—and his note case were in their proper pockets, turned back to put a dash of cologne on his handkerchief, and walked with stiff, quick steps toward the front door of his flat.

Filmore, abashed, preceded him to ring for the lift; and then, as it quivered upward through the long shaft, said again: "It's a bitter cold night, sir, and you've had a good deal of exercise today."

Warley leveled a contemptuous glance at him.

"Dare say that's why I'm feeling so fit," he retorted as he entered the lift.

It was bitter cold; the icy air hit him in the chest when he stepped out of the overheated building, and he halted on the doorstep and took a long breath. "Filmore's missed his vocation; ought to be nurse to a paralytic," he thought. "He'd love to have to wheel me about in a chair."

After the first shock of the biting air he began to find it exhilarating, and walked along at a good pace, dragging one leg ever so little after the other. The masseur had promised him that he'd soon be rid of that stiffness. Yes, decidedly a fellow like himself ought to have a young valet—a more cheerful one, anyhow. He felt like a young 'un himself this evening. As he turned into Fifth Avenue he rather wished he could meet someone he knew, some man who'd say afterward at his club: "Warley? Why, I saw him sprinting up Fifth Avenue the other night like a two-year-old—that night it was four or five below." He needed a good counter-irritant for Filmore's gloom. "Always have young people about you," he thought as he walked along, and at the words his mind turned to Ethelred Flight, next to whom he would soon be sitting in a warm, pleasantly lit dining room—where?

It came as abruptly as that—the gap in his memory. He pulled up at it as if his advance had been checked by a chasm in the pavement at his feet. Where the dickens was he going to dine? And with whom was he going to dine? God! But things didn't happen in that way—a sound, strong man didn't suddenly have to stop in the middle of the street and ask himself where he was going to dine.

"Perfect in mind, body and understanding"—the old legal phrase bobbed up inconsequently into his thoughts. Less than two minutes ago he had answered in every particular to that description; what was he now? He put his hand to his forehead, which was bursting; then he lifted his hat and let the cold air blow for a while on his overheated temples. It was queer, how hot he'd got, walking. Fact was, he'd been sprinting along at a damned good pace. In future he must try to remember not to hurry. Hang it, one more thing to remember! Well, but what was all the fuss about? Of course, as people got older, their memories were subject to these momentary lapses; he'd noticed it often enough among his contemporaries. And, brisk and alert though he still was, it wouldn't do to imagine himself totally exempt from human ills.

Where was it he was dining? Why, somewhere farther up Fifth Avenue; he was perfectly sure of that. With that lovely—that lovely——No, better not make any further effort for the moment. Just keep calm and stroll slowly along in the right direction. When he came to the street corner, of course he'd spot it, and then everything would be perfectly clear again. He walked on more deliberately, trying to empty his mind of all thoughts.

"Above all," he said to himself, "don't worry."

He tried to think of amusing things. "Decline the boredom——" He thought he might get off that joke tonight. "Mrs. Jaspar requests the pleasure—Mr. Warley declines the boredom." Not so bad, really; and he had an idea he'd never told it to the people—what in hell was their name?—the people he was on his way to dine with. "Mrs. Jaspar requests the pleasure." Poor old Mrs. Jaspar! Again it occurred to him that he hadn't always been very civil to her in old times. When everybody's running after a fellow it's pardonable now and then to chuck a boring dinner at the last minute; but, all the same, as one grew older, one understood better how an unintentional slight of that sort might cause offense, cause even pain. And he hated to cause people pain. He thought perhaps he'd better call on Mrs. Jaspar some afternoon. She'd be surprised! Or ring her up, poor old girl, and propose himself, just informally, for dinner. One dull evening wouldn't kill him, and how pleased she'd be! "Yes," he thought, "decidedly." When he got to be her age he could imagine how much he'd like it if somebody still in the running should ring him up unexpectedly and say——

He stopped and looked up slowly, wonderingly, at the wide illuminated façade of the house he was approaching. Queer coincidence—it was the Jaspar house. And all lit up—for a dinner evidently. And that was queerer yet, almost uncanny; for here he was, in front of the door, as the clock struck a quarter past eight, and of course—he remembered it quite clearly now—it was just here, it was with Mrs. Jaspar that he was dining. Those little lapses of memory never lasted more than a second or two. How right he'd been not to let himself worry! He pressed his hand on the doorbell.

"It's good to get in out of the cold," he thought, as the double doors swung open at his ring.

V

In that hushed, sonorous house the sound of the doorbell was as loud to the two women upstairs as if it had rung in the next room.

Miss Cress raised her head in surprise, and Lavinia dropped Mrs. Jaspar's other false set—the more comfortable one—with a clatter, on the marble washstand. She stumbled across the dressing room and hastened out to the landing. With Munson absent, there was no knowing how George might muddle things.

Miss Cress joined her. "Who is it?" she whispered excitedly. Below, they heard the sound of a hat and a walking stick being laid down on the big marble-topped table in the hall and then George's stentorian drone: "Mr. Anson Warley."

"It is—it is! I can see him," Miss Cress whispered, hanging over the stair rail.

"Good gracious—mercy me! And Munson not here! Oh, whatever—whatever shall we do?" Lavinia was trembling so violently that she had to clutch the stair rail to prevent herself from falling. Miss Cress thought, with her cold lucidity: "She's a good deal sicker than the old woman."

"What shall we do, Miss Cress? That fool of a George—he's showing him in! Who could have thought it?" Miss Cress knew the images that were whirling through Lavinia's brain—the vision of Mrs. Jaspar's having another stroke at the sight of this mysterious intruder; of Mr. Anson Warley's seeing her there, in her impotence and her abasement; of the family's being summoned and rushing in to exclaim, to question, to be horrified and furious—and all because poor old Munson's memory was going, like his mistress', like Lavinia's, and because he had forgotten that it was one of the dinner nights. Oh, misery! The tears were running down Lavinia's cheeks, and Miss Cress knew she was thinking: "If the daughters sack him—and they will—where's he going to, old and deaf as he is? Oh, if only he can hold till she dies, and get his pension."

Lavinia recovered herself, with one of her supreme efforts.

"Miss Cress, we must go down at once—at once! Something dreadful's going to happen." She began to totter toward the little velvet-lined lift in the corner of the landing.

Miss Cress took pity on her. "Come along," she said, sustaining her. "But nothing dreadful's going to happen. You'll see."

"Oh, thank you, Miss Cress. But the shock—the awful shock to her—of seeing that strange gentleman walk in."

"Not a bit of it." Miss Cress laughed as she stepped into the lift. "He's not a stranger. She's expecting him."

"Expecting him? Expecting Mr. Warley?"

"Sure she is. She told me so just now. She says she invited him yesterday."

"But, Miss Cress, what are you thinking of? Invite him—how? When you know she can't write nor telephone?"

"Well, she says she saw him; she saw him last night at a dance."

173

"Oh, God," murmured Lavinia, covering her eyes with her hands.

"At a dance at the Fred Amesworths'—that's what she said," Miss Cress pursued, feeling the same little shiver run down her back as when Mrs. Jaspar had made the statement to her.

"The Amesworths—not the Amesworths—not the Amesworths?" Lavinia echoed, shivering too. She dropped her hands from her stricken face and followed Miss Cress out of the lift. Her expression had become less anguished, and the nurse wondered why. In reality, she was thinking, in a sort of dreary beatitude: "But if she's suddenly got as much worse as this, she'll go before me, after all, my poor lady, and I'll see to it she's properly laid out and dressed, and nobody but Lavinia's hands 'll touch her."

"You'll see—if she was expecting him, as she says, it won't give her a shock, anyhow, Only, how did he know?" Miss Cress whispered, with an acuter renewal of her shiver.

She followed Lavinia, with muffled steps, down the passage to the pantry, and from there the two women stole into the dining room and placed themselves noiselessly behind the tall Coromandel screen, through the cracks of which they could peep into the empty room.

The long table was set, as Mrs. Jaspar always insisted that it should be on these occasions, but, old Munson not having returned, the gold plate, which his mistress also insisted on, had not been got out, and all down the table, as Lavinia saw with horror, George had laid the coarse blue-and-white plates from the servants' hall. The electric wall lights were on and the candles lit in the branching Sèvres candelabra—so much at least had been done. But the flowers in the great central dish of rose Du Barry porcelain and in the smaller dishes which accompanied it—the flowers—oh, shame—had been forgotten! They were no longer real flowers; the family had long since suppressed that expense—and no wonder, for Mrs. Jaspar always insisted on orchids. But Grace, the youngest daughter, who was the kindest, had hit on the clever device of arranging three beautiful clusters of artificial orchids and maidenhair, which had only to be lifted from their shelf in the pantry and set in the dishes—only, of course, that imbecile footman had forgotten or had not known where to find them. And—oh, horror—realizing his oversight too late, no doubt, to appeal to Lavinia, he had taken some old newspapers and bunched them up into something that he probably thought resembled a bouquet, and crammed one into each of the priceless rose Du Barry dishes!

Lavinia clutched at Miss Cress' arm. "Oh, look—look what he's done. I shall die of the shame of it. Oh, miss, hadn't we better slip round to the drawing-room and try to coax my poor lady upstairs again, afore ever she notices?"

Miss Cress, peering through the crack of the screen, could hardly suppress a giggle; for at that moment the double doors of the dining room were thrown open and George, shuffling about in a baggy livery inherited from a long-departed predecessor, of more commanding build, bawled out in his loud singsong:

"Dinner is served, madam."

"Oh, it's too late," moaned Lavinia. Miss Cress signed to her to keep silent, and the two watchers glued their eyes to their respective cracks of the screen.

What they saw, far off down the vista of empty drawing-rooms, and after an interval during which, as Lavinia knew, the imaginary guests were supposed to file in and take their seats, was the entrance, at the end of the ghostly cortège, of a very old woman, still tall and towering, on the arm of a man somewhat smaller than herself, with a fixed smile on a darkly pink face and a slim, erect figure clad in perfect evening clothes, who advanced with short measured steps, profiting, Miss Cress noticed, by the support of the arm he was supposed to sustain.

"Well, I never!" was the nurse's inward comment.

The couple continued to advance, with rigid smiles and eyes starting ahead. Neither turned to the other, neither spoke. All their attention was concentrated on the immense, the almost unachievable effort of reaching that point, halfway down the long dinner table, opposite the big Du Barry dish, where George was drawing back an armchair for Mrs. Jaspar. At last they reached it, and Mrs. Jaspar seated herself and waved a stony hand to Mr. Warley.

"On my right."

He gave a little bow, like the bend of a jointed doll, and, with infinite precaution, let himself down into his chair. Beads of perspiration were standing on his forehead, and Miss Cress saw him draw out his cambric handkerchief and wipe them stealthily away. He then turned his head somewhat stiffly toward his hostess.

"What beautiful flowers!" he said, with great precision and perfect gravity, waving his hand toward the bunched-up newspaper in the bowl of Sèvres.

Mrs. Jaspar received the tribute with complacency. "So glad. From High Lawn every morning," she simpered.

"Mar-vellows," Mr. Warley completed.

"I always say to the bishop——" Mrs. Jaspar continued.

"Ha, of course!" Mr. Warley warmly assented.

"Not that I don't think——"

"Ha, rather!"

George had reappeared from the pantry, with a blue crockery dish of mashed potatoes. This he handed in turn to one after another of the imaginary guests and finally presented to Mrs. Jaspar and her right-hand neighbor.

They both helped themselves cautiously, and Mrs. Jaspar addressed an arch smile to Mr. Warley. " 'Nother month, no more oysters."

"Ha, no more!"

George, with a bottle of Apollinaris wrapped in a napkin, was saying to each guest in turn: "Perrier-Jouet, 'ninety-five." He had picked that up, thought Miss Cress, from hearing old Munson repeat it so often.

"Hang it—well, then, just a sip," murmured Mr. Warley.

"Old times," bantered Mrs. Jaspar; and the two turned to each other and bowed their heads and touched glasses.

"I often tell Mrs. Amesworth——" Mrs. Jaspar continued, bending to an imaginary presence across the table.

"Ha, ha!" Mr. Warley approved.

George reappeared and slowly encircled the table, with a dish of spinach. After the spinach the Apollinaris also went the rounds again, announced successively as "Château Lafite, 'seventy-four," and "the old Newbold Madeira." Each time that George approached his glass, Mr. Warley made the feint of lifting a defensive hand, and then smiled and yielded. "Might as well—hanged for a sheep," he remarked gayly; and Mrs. Jaspar giggled.

Finally a dish of Malaga grapes and apples was handed. Mrs. Jaspar, now growing perceptibly languid and nodding with more and more effort at Mr. Warley's pleasantries, transferred a bunch of grapes to her plate, but nibbled only two or three.

"Tired," she said suddenly, in a whimper like a child's; and she rose, lifting herself up by the arms of her chair and leaning over to catch the eye of an invisible lady, presumably Mrs. Amesworth, seated opposite to her.

Mr. Warley was on his feet, too, supporting himself by resting one hand on the table in a jaunty attitude. Mrs. Jaspar waved to him to be reseated.

"Join us, after cigars," she smilingly ordained; and with a great and concentrated effort, he bowed to her as she passed toward the double doors which George was throwing open.

Slowly, majestically, the purple velvet train disappeared down the long enfilade of illuminated rooms, and the last door closed behind her.

"Well, I do believe she's enjoyed it!" chuckled Miss Cress, taking Lavinia by the arm to help her back to the hall. Lavinia, for weeping, could not answer.

VI

Anson Warley found himself in the hall again, getting into his fur-lined overcoat. He remembered suddenly thinking that the rooms had been intensely overheated and that all the other guests had talked very loud and laughed inordinately.

"Very good talk, though, I must say," he had to acknowledge.

In the hall, as he got his arms into his coat—rather a job, too, after that Perrier-Jouet—he remembered saying to somebody—perhaps it was the old butler—"Slipping off early. Going on; 'nother engagement," and thinking to himself the while that when he got out into the fresh air again he would certainly remember where the other engagement was. He smiled a little, while the servant, who seemed a clumsy fellow, fumbled with the fastening of the door. "And Filmore, who thought I wasn't even well enough to dine out—ass!—what would he say if he knew I was going on?"

The door opened, and with an immense sense of exhilaration Mr. Warley issued forth from the house and drew in a first deep breath of night air. He heard the door closed and bolted behind him, and continued to stand motionless on the step, expanding his chest and drinking in the icy draught.

"Spose it's about the last house where they give you 'ninety-five Perrier-Jouet," he thought; and then: "Never heard better talk either."

He smiled again, with satisfaction, at the memory of the wine and the wit. Then he took a step forward, to where a moment before the pavement had been—and where now there was nothing.

Birthday Party

A. A. MILNE

1

David Alistair Shawn Baker came into the world at half-past three on an April morning; and at four o'clock William Henry Baker was kneeling at his wife's bed, her hand, wet with his tears, held against his cheek.

'Oh, Will,' she sighed.

'Oh, Maggie!' he sobbed, and felt for his handkerchief with his left hand.

'Have you seen him?' she asked faintly.

'Yes, no, it's only you, Maggie, that's all that matters.'

'Well, that's a nice thing to say of your son and heir,' put in Mrs Shawn from the basket wherein David Alistair Shawn lay. Maggie, she considered, had had a very easy time, much easier than her own had been when Maggie was born. All her emotion was for her first grandchild.

'You must see him, darling.'

He kissed her hand; he wanted to go on kissing it for ever, but knew that he couldn't. He got up clumsily, and went over to the basket, wiping his eyes. He looked at his son, and felt, as other husbands have felt looking at their firstborn, 'All that for this; so small, so ugly; and yet what a burden to have borne.'

'Hallo!' he said, and had an absurd impulse to chuck it

under the chin, but restrained himself, no obvious chin being there. He looked from his son to his wife, wondering at the miracle of their union.

'Now you must be off,' said Mrs Shawn. 'Try to get some sleep, and you may come and say good-bye just before you catch your train.'

He bent down and kissed his wife's forehead, whispering, 'Thank you, Maggie dear.' She gave him a loving smile, so tired, so remote, that the tears came back into his eyes, and he felt again for his handkerchief. He went back to the campbed in what was going to be the nursery. 'Bars on the windows,' he said to himself. 'I mustn't forget that. Oh well, there's no hurry.'

He had a few minutes with her alone before he caught his train. She had come back into the world, she was herself again; proud and happy.

'You promise to have a really good dinner, darling? I don't mean a midday dinner. Proper dinner, and drink David's health.'

He had had it made clear to him by Mrs Shawn that there was enough to do in the house without looking after a grown-up man who could look after himself. He was to have his meal in town, and come back by a late train. Orders.

'I will, Maggie. I shall be thinking of you both all day.'

'You'll tell them at the office? They knew he was coming, didn't they?'

He said 'Yes' to both questions, and asked again, 'You did want a boy, didn't you, dear?' as if he would have changed it even now if it had not been satisfactory.

'Of course! Didn't you?'

He nodded proudly.

William Henry Baker was nearly forty when David was born, and he had been married for ten years. Because his son had been so long in coming, he had been more than usually frightened. He would have been frightened in any case, for he was a timid little man, and his love for Maggie was almost the whole of his life. He had longed for a son: a son, a Shawn Baker, who would not be timid, would not be ineffectual, as he knew himself to be; would not be a clerk in an office who was treated with a tolerant, only just not contemptuous, familiarity by his fellow-clerks. Shawn Baker would be one of those big, strong, masterful men: an explorer, perhaps: a statesman, a great general. That was why Mr Baker had insisted—well, not insisted, he could never do that—had wanted the Shawn in his boy's name. There must be a hundred David Bakers about, but Shawn Baker was unique. He sounded like somebody. Perhaps, when he became Lord Mayor of London, David would hyphen the name: Sir David Shawn-Baker.

Yes, he had told his fellow-clerks that the baby was coming; far too often, most of them would have said. Never had a baby been so generously shared. The brighter spirits had suggested a sweepstake on the day and hour of its arrival; anything to make a commonplace event more interesting. There had been opportunities for humour which the humorous had not missed. At times Mr Baker wished that he had been more reticent; at other times he was glad to think that Shawn Baker was being talked about already. He pictured them in after years: young Henderson, an elderly man now, managing director of the firm, perhaps, saying to an important client: 'Yes, I remember the very day he was born, his father coming into the office as pleased as Punch—oh, yes, Shawn Baker's father was with us then—just an ordinary sort of fellow, you'd never have thought he'd have had such a brilliant son.' And Miss Clissold, retired and living in the country, saying proudly to the Vicar: 'Oh, yes, I knew Sir David's dear father *very* well. Quite a little excitement, I remember, when Sir David was born. We all drank his health—oh, only in tea, of course.'

But there was another reason why he was sometimes glad and sometimes sorry that he had confided in them. The elder married men were comforting. 'Pooh, old man, it's nothing. Danger? Nonsense! In the old days, perhaps, but not to-day. Well, I suppose you and I wouldn't like it much, but I always say women don't feel pain in the way men do. Not so sensitive. Besides, they give 'em anaesthetics now. Easy. No, it's the damned expense of it that's the real trouble. You're not having anything to do with these blasted nursing-homes? Quite right. It's a racket.' But the younger ones told agonizing stories of what they had suffered (and, by inference, their wives) through the long hours of labour. They went into clinical details which both terrified and outraged him; as if, in some way, by talking of these intimate things, the speaker was admitting himself to intimacy with Maggie. Then he wished with all his heart that he had kept his secret to himself.

And the jokes. Horrible.

So now, as he hurried to the station, it came over him suddenly that he did not want to tell them, not to-day. His happiness, his pride, his relief, were too great to share with strangers who could feel none of these things. Just for to-day it would be his secret. Miss Clissold would raise enquiring eyebrows, and he would shrug his shoulders. Henderson would say: 'Well, old boy, any news of the twins?' and he wouldn't answer. He would just be smiling quietly to himself.

He smiled now as he thought of the private happiness which would be his; of the secret which he would carry with him throughout the day.

2

At 6.45 that evening Mr Baker was walking up and down outside the entrance to the Savoy Grill, looking at his watch from time to time, and giving the impression of a man of the world, a well-known clubman, who preferred to meet the Lady Patricia (late as usual) as her Rolls-Royce drew up, and personally to conduct her inside. The Lady Patricia might be a little bewildered, left to herself, having always dined at the Ritz before; might be uncertain of the way into the restaurant—as, indeed, Mr Baker was. He was also not quite sure whether evening dress was necessary. He proposed, therefore, to follow the first arrivals obviously not in evening dress through the swing door with the air of being in their party, leaving his hat and coat where they left theirs, and accompanying them into the restaurant. Up till now he had somehow failed to do this. Each time that the opportunity had come he had told himself that it was still a little before his usual hour for dinner and that there was just time for one more saunter to the Strand and back. In this way, if he were lucky, he would miss the next opportunity also.

The terrifying decision to dine at the Savoy had been taken at lunch that morning. The cup of coffee slopped into the saucer, the baked beans overrunning the side of the plate, the stained marble-topped table which had satisfied William Henry Baker for so long, suddenly disgusted the father of Shawn Baker. Not in these surroundings, not even in the homely comfort of a City chop-house, should Sir David's health be drunk. To go West into the bright world of fashion, and be one with the heroes and heroines of so many serialized meals was indeed an alarming adventure to him; but to Shawn Baker it would be routine, and the friendly 'Good evening, Sir David,' of head-waiters a familiar sound in his ears. Perhaps Mr Baker's ideas of heredity were a little muddled. Perhaps he was wrong in thinking that a sudden, uncharacteristic display of moral courage by the father can influence the character of a son already born. Perhaps he was right in thinking that a post-natal virtue, if some sign of it could be achieved, would at least be evidence of a latent virtue such as a son might have inherited and would bring to maturity. Right or wrong, fearfully he had pledged himself to dine in style that evening; right or wrong, he had told himself that on the keeping of his pledge the whole future of David Alistair Shawn Baker depended.

The Savoy was the obvious tourney-ground. It was nearest to the familiar City, which was in itself a sort of comfort; it was the most advertised in novels. Moreover, young Dugdale, son of old Dugdale and now taken into partnership, who had begun his career in the clerks' room (in order to 'start at the bottom and work my way sideways', as he put it cheerfully) had spoken so often of the girls he had taken to the Savoy that he had given it a solidity which made the adventure a little more plausible. Mr Baker was one of the firm, dining, as was the firm's custom, at the Savoy. What was there frightening in that? Nothing. He had the money in his pocket, he was ready for anything, afraid of nobody.

A taxi drew up at the door, and a man and a girl got out. With a weak feeling at the knees and a sick feeling in the stomach, Mr Baker followed them in.

3

The man was Mr Basil St John Wender, and the girl was Miss Charmian Flyte. Unlike David Alistair Shawn Baker, they had chosen (and who better?) their own names. Mr Wender was good-looking in a business-like way; a solid man of fifty with what he thought of (and hoped you would think of) as a Roman nose commanding a strongly coloured face, the red of a sanguine temperament fighting it out with the blue-black of a jaw which, for all his care, never seemed freshly shaved. To make up for this there was always an air of eau-de-Cologne about him. His hands were beautifully manicured; as indeed they should have been, seeing that Miss Charmian Flyte herself attended to them every week. She was what he would have called a pretty little thing; with more character of her own and less admiration for his than he supposed. This was the first time he had taken her out to dinner. Being a man of generous impulses where his own tastes were concerned, he had ordered champagne, and, as a result, they amused each other a good deal.

They also found easy amusement in others. In Mr William Henry Baker, for instance.

He was at a little table in the gangway, alone. With their backs to the glass screen separating them from the lounge they had him under their eyes; had so had him all through his dinner. It would not be true to say that Mr Baker was particularly conscious of them, for he felt that the eyes of all the early diners were upon him, that all the waiters were whispering about him; that, in short, what he was undergoing was not a romantic adventure, but an unpleasant ordeal. The prices of the strangely named foods were far beyond what he had expected, prices more suited to a purchase of the whole animal (whatever it was) from which the dish came. Conveying as best he could the suggestion that he was under doctor's orders, he chose the most moderately priced dish he could identify, to be followed by the most translatable sweet; and, since wine was essential for the drinking of David's health, he added a half-bottle of the cheapest Burgundy, telling himself, as he did so, that he was throwing money away, had been a fool to come, and that David's chance of inheriting anything worth while from his father was now remote. Perhaps he would be like his mother, sons often were, and Maggie was perfect. What would she say when he confessed how wickedly extravagant he had been? He would have to tell her; he had never had any secrets from Maggie.

Some, but not all, of his emotions were visible to Mr Wender and Miss Flyte. As Miss Flyte so well put it, the poor little man seemed like a fish out of water; and though neither of them had seen a fish out of water except on a fishmonger's slab, when it bore little resemblance to Mr Baker, they agreed laughingly that this was exactly what he did look like.

'Thought it was an A.B.C.,' suggested Mr Wender, 'and then found too late that it wasn't. Having a little difficulty with his French, isn't he?' This was when Mr Baker was deeply involved in the menu. 'Wonder what he'll make of the wine-list?'

'That's easy, darling. He just says "25", and there you are.'

'*I* may be, but he isn't. "25" is champagne. He won't be

having champagne,' said Mr Wender, with the simple ostenta-
tion of one who was. 'Well, girlie, enjoying yourself?'

She nodded. 'I always say there's nothing like the dear old
Savoy. It's sort of different, if you know what I mean.'

'Another glass of Pommery?'

'Just what Mother ordered,' laughed Miss Flyte, as he picked
up the bottle.

All through his dinner Mr Wender's eyes invited the attention of his neighbours. The pretty girl he was entertaining, the
lavishness of his entertainment, the forceful personality of the
entertainer, were shared with them; even the people drinking
cocktails in the lounge behind him could look enviously, admiringly, through the glass screen. Picking up the second bottle, he
flicked an eye in that direction so as to include them, said 'Good
God!' suddenly, and put the bottle down.

'What's the matter?' asked Miss Flyte.

His hand to his cheek, his head averted, he told her.

4

It might have been Sir David Shawn Baker himself who lay
back in his chair twirling his empty glass. He was at ease with
the world. He saw himself taking Maggie to the Savoy on
her next birthday. He imagined somebody asking him—not
that anybody would—what he thought of the Ritz, and heard
himself answering, 'Well, personally, I prefer the Savoy,' and
perhaps something about 'my usual table'. He wondered why
he had ever been frightened. The whole thing was so easy.
You just decided where you would dine that night, went there,
chose your dinner (and, of course, your bottle of wine) and

dined. There was one trifling impediment which escaped him for the moment. Something which, in certain circumstances, might prevent full enjoyment of the evening. No, not Maggie's absence; she and David had been with him all the time; at first encouraging him, then, as the half-bottle did its work, sharing his pride and satisfaction. But there had been a moment, a little while back, just before he had begun that second glass of Burgundy, when the roseate cloud in his mind had suddenly darkened. It couldn't have been very important, because now everything was rosy again. Still, it was silly not to remember . . .

The folded bill on his plate caught his eyes. Ah, that was it. He couldn't pay the bill. All these potatoes and things added up surprisingly, and the waiter seemed to have made a mistake about the number of the Burgundy. 'My son, Sir David, will pay it next time he comes in.' Doubtless something could be arranged. He would give his mind to it directly. Just now it was resting with its feet up in a cosy warmth of contentment.

A big important-looking man was coming to his table. Probably—what was that fellow's name in that book?—Prince Florizel of Bohemia. Mr Baker was glad to see him.

'How *are* you?' said Mr Wender genially, holding out a large white hand.

Mr Baker, shaking it, said that he was very well. Never better, in fact.

'That's good. I noticed that you were dining alone. My friend,' he indicated her over his shoulder, and added confidentially, 'one of the most famous actresses from the Comédie Française, is most anxious to meet you. I wonder if you would give us the great pleasure of finishing your meal at our table?'

Mr Baker said that in fact he had finished it, three, or possibly four, minutes ago.

'Still,' smiled Mr Wender, in the persuasive voice which had launched a thousand companies, 'you will let us give you a glass of champagne, a cigar, and a cup of coffee.' He stopped a passing waiter and said, 'Sir Joseph is dining with me. Just put that,' he indicated the bill carelessly, 'on to mine.' He bowed to Mr Baker. 'If you will give me that great pleasure?'

Mr Baker made it clear that he was glad—in a sense, relieved—to give it to him.

'And now,' said Mr Wender, helping his guest up, 'we will join Mademoiselle de—but no. For reasons which you will understand she wishes to remain incognito while in London. By the way, she talks English perfectly—unless, of course, you insist on conversing with her in own language.' He waited a moment in case Mr Baker insisted, and went on, 'Should it be necessary to refer to her by name I am permitted to call her Lady Witterman. You won't mind my introducing you as Sir Joseph?'

(Undoubtedly Prince Florizel of Bohemia.)

'Well, actually, my name is——'

Mr Wender waggled a genial hand.

'No names, no pack-drill, as we used to say in the Guards.'

(Or the Duke of Westminster?)

They came, arm-in-arm, to the table by the glass screen.

'This, darling,' said Mr Wender, 'is Sir Joseph.'

Miss Flyte nodded sulkily.

'A glass of Pommery, Sir Joseph?'

Mr Baker wondered if champagne went well with Burgundy, and didn't see why it shouldn't try.

'Your very good health. My dear, we must drink Sir Joseph's health.'

Miss Flyte, her mouth still sullen, raised her glass to Mr Baker. Then, seeing something in his insignificant face, something which she didn't see in the faces of the men who made love to her, she gave him a sudden warming smile, and said, 'All the best.'

'The same to you,' said Mr Baker, 'both of you,' he explained, remembering that the Duke was paying his bill. But, as he drank, he was drinking to Maggie and David. He was drinking their healths in champagne. Real champagne. Pommery. What an evening!

The Pommery seemed to like the Burgundy. It reminded the Burgundy of a very funny thing which their lessor knew about and nobody else did. That was what made it so funny. That was what made Mr Baker laugh so surprisingly.

'Yes?' said Mr Wender encouragingly. His eyes went round again to the doorway.

'What,' Mr Baker invited them to tell him, 'do they know of England who only England know?'

'What?' wondered Miss Flyte, assuming that it was a riddle.

'That wasn't what I said,' he explained with a happy smile. 'What I said was nobody knows what happened this morning. Now why does nobody know what happened this morning? Because it's a profound secret.'

'What did happen?' asked Miss Flyte.

'When I say nobody, I mean nobody-but-three. No,' said Mr Baker, working it out, 'four. Probably five. Or six or seven. Things get about. Have you ever,' he asked on a different note, 'come across Sir David Shawn Baker in Paris or elsewhere?'

'I seem to have heard of him,' said Miss Flyte, feeling that it was expected of her. 'I've never actually met him.'

'I have. Just for a moment.'

'What's he like?'

Mr Baker reflected for a little.

'On the short side,' he said, summing it up.

Mr Wender rose to his feet. One felt that he had been waiting for this moment. Three people in evening dress were coming in. The big woman who led the way, magnificently under-gowned and over-jewelled, glanced at Mr Wender, stood for a moment in surprise, committed Miss Flyte and Mr Baker to memory, and inclined her head to Mr Wender's bow. The party moved on. Mr Wender sat down and poured himself out the rest of the champagne. 'I think that's all right,' he murmured, gulping it down.

The waiter brought the bill. Mr Wender put a £10 note on the plate.

'Look, girlie,' he said, 'I think I'll just go and say a word to those people, while you powder your nose. I'll meet you both outside.'

They all got up. Mr Baker, surprised to find that he could walk, not only effectively but with a certain dignity, followed Miss Flyte out. She turned to him as soon as they were through the doorway.

'Hat and coat!' she snapped. 'Quick!' She indicated the cloak-room. Then, as soon as he was ready, 'Come on!'

'But what about Mr—er——'

'Come on!' She led the way. 'Ask for a taxi. Tell him Victoria.'

Completely bewildered, Mr Baker, as so often before in his

life, obeyed instructions. As he took his place in the taxi beside her he was still saying, 'What about Mr—er——'

'To hell with him!' said Miss Flyte bitterly. 'Thinking he was going to get away with *that*!'

5

The fresh air through the open window was doing Mr Baker good. He still wondered why he was there, but now he felt benevolently and intelligently interested in his position.

'Married men!' said Miss Flyte. 'They make me sick.'

Mr Baker waited for further details.

'He asks me to have dinner with him. Well, why shouldn't I have dinner with him? What else did he think he was going to get? Not bloody likely. (That's a quotation, ducky, you needn't look shocked.) And then suddenly there's his darling wife in the lounge, plastered with Koh-i-noors and looking like the Queen of Sheba's Aunt Rachel. He's told her, see, that he's dining with Sir Joseph Wotsit so's to discuss a—what's that thing men like that discuss, financiers I mean?'

'Well, they might discuss so many things. Would it be a merger?'

'Something like that. So now when she comes in and sees him—well, am I going to look like I'm discussing a merger with darling hubby? So I've got to be explained somehow, see? Well, he's a quick thinker, I will say that for him. Well, you see, we'd noticed you at your table—"I wonder who that nice-looking man is," I said, "seems sort of lonely"—I'd just passed the remark, not thinking any more of it, so now he gets his idea. Because once you're at our table, he's all right. There he is, dining with Sir Joseph, and if Sir Joseph brings his wife along, well he can't help it, can he? So he gets up and bows to her— don't suppose you noticed, you were telling me about that secret of yours—and then goes up to her table and says, all smiles and handwash, I can just hear him saying it, "Sir Joseph brought the wife along, used to be his secretary, knows all the ins and outs of the business; well, I must be getting along, got to get back to his flat, he's left some papers behind; how are you, John, how are you, Mary, nice of you to look after the wife while I'm so busy." Cah! It makes me sick. I'm as good as she is, aren't I?'

'But not as married to him as she is,' said Mr Baker mildly.

'Who said I was, and who wants to be? He asked me to come out with him, didn't he? I didn't ask *him*. What's it matter to *me* what his wife thinks? If he couldn't stand up to her, he oughtn't to of asked me. How did I know he had a wife at all? What would he of thought if I'd said, "Don't look now but there's my husband over there, you'd better pretend to be the Archbishop of Canterbury"? What sort of a way is that of having a nice little dinner together?'

Mr Baker didn't feel competent to answer any of these questions, nor did he suppose that an answer was expected. All that mattered was that he had dined at the Savoy and had drunk David's health in Burgundy and champagne. Now he was sitting in a taxi with an extremely pretty girl. All this on David's birthday. Miss Flyte seemed to remember suddenly that he was there, and that she had certain obligations towards him.

'Victoria all right for you?' she asked.

'Yes. Oh, yes.' He looked at his watch. 'Catch my train nicely.'

'I'm on the District. Ealing. D'you know that part?'

'No.'

'Retired Indians mostly. You know what I mean. Not blacks. Nice part, near the Common where we are. Married, I suppose?'

'Yes.' She knew by the way he said it that he was in love with his wife.

'What I said about married men making me sick, of course I didn't mean you.'

'I'm sure you wouldn't have said so to me, even if I had.'

'I just say anything that comes into my head when I'm angry, and if there's one thing that makes me angry, it's bad manners. What's your real name when you aren't Sir Joseph?'

He laughed and said, 'Baker.'

'Mr Baker,' she said, looking at him, pondering the name and its owner. 'Fancy! If it hadn't been for that wife of his we should never have met. Seems funny, doesn't it? What was that secret you were telling me?'

He coughed apologetically.

'I'm afraid I was a little—I must have been—it's the first time I've ever drunk champagne. And I'd already had half a bottle of Burgundy.'

'I say, you *were* going it! What will Mrs Baker say when you tell her?'

'She wanted me to have a good dinner, because, you see, she—we—we had a son early this morning.'

'First?'

'Yes.'

'Was that the secret?'

'Yes. I didn't tell them at the office, because I thought—well, it was something rather—I know this sounds silly——'

'I shan't laugh.'

'Well, sort of sacred between Maggie and me. Just for to-day. I didn't want jokes about it.'

'And now you've told *me*?'

'Yes, but that's different somehow.'

She looked at him wonderingly.

'How long have you been married?'

'Ten years.'

'What are you calling him?'

'David Alistair Shawn,' said Mr Baker shyly. 'Shawn was his mother's name.'

The taximan opened the window behind him, and said, 'Which line?'

'Main line,' said Miss Flyte, and to her companion, 'I'll pay.'

'No, no,' he protested. 'You forget, I didn't pay for my dinner.'

'D'you mean *he* paid?' Miss Flyte laughed happily. 'Well, that's a good one. That's cheered me up a lot. All the same, I'm going to pay the taxi, and you can put half a crown in David's money-box specially for me. See?'

'Oh, that *is* kind——'

She leant across to him suddenly and kissed him on the cheek.

'And that's for yourself. Because you're different from all the others. See?'

The taxi drew up at the station, and they got out.

6

Mr Baker was happy. He'd done it. He had dined where he had said he would, he had toasted David in champagne, and it hadn't cost him a penny. His son, he felt modestly, could be proud of him. The Bakers were not to be despised. When put to it, they could hold their own with the best in the land.

What a story to tell Maggie!

Except for that last moment. That, he felt instinctively, must remain untold. The fragrant memory of that touching, unexpected kiss was for himself alone. The thought of keeping anything from Maggie made him a little uneasy, but he assured himself that men and women must always have secrets from each other. When, for instance, Sir David Shawn Baker was Ambassador in Paris, there would be many matters which he would not confide to his wife.

A Bal Masqué

ALEXANDRE DUMAS

I said that I was in to no one; one of my friends forced admission.

My servant announced Mr. Anthony R——. Behind Joseph's livery I saw the corner of a black redingote; it is probable that the wearer of the redingote, from his side, saw a flap of my dressing gown; impossible to conceal myself.

"Very well! Let him enter," I said out loud. "Let him go to the Devil," I said to myself.

While working it is only the woman you love who can disturb you with impunity, for she is always at bottom interested in what you are doing.

I went up to him, therefore, with the half-bored face of an author interrupted in one of those moments of sorest self-mistrust, while I found him so pale and haggard that the first words I addressed to him were these:

"What is the matter? What has happened to you?"

"Oh! Let me take breath," said he. "I'm going to tell you all about it, besides, it's a dream perhaps, or perhaps I am mad."

He threw himself into an armchair, and let his head drop between his hands.

I looked at him in astonishment; his hair was dripping with rain; his shoes, his knees, and the bottom of his trousers were covered with mud. I went to the window; I saw at the door his servant and his cabriolet; I could make nothing out of it all.

He saw my surprise.

"I have been to the cemetery of Père-Lachaise," said he.

"At ten o'clock in the morning?"

"I was there at seven—cursed bal masqué!"

I could not imagine what a bal masqué and Père-Lachaise had to do with one another. I resigned myself, and turning my back to the mantelpiece began to roll a cigarette for him between my fingers with the phlegm and the patience of a Spaniard.

While he was coming to the point I hinted to Anthony that I, for my part, was commonly very susceptible to attentions of that kind.

He made me a sign of thanks, but pushed my hand away.

Finally I bent over to light the cigarette for myself: Anthony stopped me.

"Alexandre," he said to me, "listen, I beg of you."

"But you have been here already a quarter of an hour and have not told me anything."

"Oh! It is a most strange adventure."

I got up, placed my cigarette on the mantelpiece and crossed my arms like a man resigned; only I began to believe, as he did, that he was fast becoming mad.

"You remember the ball at the Opéra, where I met you?" he said to me after a moment's silence.

"The last one where there were at least two hundred people?"

"The very same. I left you with the intention of abandoning myself to one of those varieties of which they spoke to me as

being a curiosity even in the midst of our curious times; you
wished to dissuade me from going; a fatality drove me on. Oh!
you, why did you not see it all, you who have the knack of
observation? Why were not Hoffman or Callot there to paint
the picture as the fantastic, burlesque thing kept unrolling
itself beneath my eyes? Unsatisfied and in melancholy mood
I walked away, about to quit the Opéra; I came to a hall that
was overflowing and in high spirits: corridors, boxes, par-
terre. Everything was obstructed. I made a tour of the room;
twenty masks called me by name and told me theirs. These
were all leaders—aristocrats and merchants—in the undigni-
fied disguise of pierrots, of postilions, of merry-andrews, or of
fishwives. They were all young people of family, of culture, of
talent; and young people of family, of culture, of talent; and
there, forgetful of family, talent, breeding, they were resurrect-
ing in the midst of our sedate and serious times a soirée of
the Regency. They had told me about it, and yet I could not
have believed it!—I mounted a few steps and leaning against a
pillar, half hidden by it, I fixed my eyes on that sea of human
beings surging beneath me. Their dominoes, of all colors, their
motley costumes, their grotesque disguises formed a spectacle
resembling nothing human. The music began to play. Oh, it was
then these gargoyle creatures stirred themselves to the sound
of that orchestra whose harmony reached me only in the midst
of cries, of laughs, of hootings; they hung on to each other by
their hands, by their arms, by their necks; a long coil formed
itself, beginning with a circular motion, the dancers, men and
women, stamping with their feet, made the dust break forth
with a noise, the atoms of which were rendered visible by the
wan light of the lustres; turning at ever-increasing speed with

bizarre postures, with unseemly gestures, with cries full of abandonment; turning always faster and still faster, swaying and swinging like drunken men, yelling like lost women, with more delirium than delight, with more passion than pleasure; resembling a coil of the damned doing infernal penance under the scourge of demons! All this passed beneath my eyes, at my feet. I felt the wind of their whirling past; as they rushed by each one whom I knew flung a word at me that made me blush. All this noise, all this humming, all this confusion, all this music went on in my brain as well as in the room! I soon came to the point of no longer knowing whether that which I had before my eyes was a dream or reality; I came to the point of asking myself whether it was not I who was mad and they who were sane; I was seized with a weird temptation to throw myself into the midst of this pandemonium, like Faust through the Witches' Sabbath, and I felt that I too, would then have cries, postures, laughs like theirs. Oh! from that to madness there is but one step. I was appalled; I flung myself out of the room, followed even to the street door by shrieks that were like those cries of passion that come out of the caverns of the fallow deer.

"I stopped a moment under the portico to collect myself; I did not wish to venture into the street; with such confusion still in my soul I might not be able to find my way; I might, per- haps, be thrown under the wheels of some carriage I had not seen coming. I was as a drunken man might be who begins to recover sufficient reason in his clouded brain to recognize his condition, and who, feeling the will return but not the power, with fixed eyes and staring, leans motionless against some street post or some tree on the public promenade.

"At that moment a carriage stopped before the door, a woman alighted or rather shot herself from the doorway.

"She entered beneath the peristyle, turning her head from right to left like one who had lost her way; she was dressed in a black domino, had her face covered by a velvet mask. She presented herself at the door.

"'Your ticket,' said the door-keeper.

"'My ticket?' she replied. 'I have none.'

"'Then get one at the box-office.'

"The domino came back under the peristyle, fumbled nervously about in all her pockets.

"'No money!' she cried. 'Ah! this ring—a ticket of admission for this ring,' she said.

"'Impossible,' replied the woman who was distributing the cards; 'we do not make bargains of that kind.'

"And she pushed away the brilliant, which fell to the ground and rolled to my side.

"The domino remained still without moving, forgetting the ring, sunk in thought.

"I picked up the ring and handed it to her.

"Through her mask I saw her eyes fixed on mine.

"'You must help me to get in,' she said to me; 'You must, for pity's sake.'

"'But I am going out, madame,' I said to her.

"'Then give me six francs for this ring, and you will render me a service for which I shall bless you my life long.'

"I replaced the ring on her finger; I went to the box-office, I took two tickets. We re-entered together.

"As we arrived within the corridor I felt that she was

tottering. Then with her second hand she made a kind of ring around my arm.

"'Are you in pain?' I asked her.

"'No, no, it is nothing,' she replied, 'a dizziness, that is all—'

"She hurried me into the hall.

"We re-entered into that giddy Charenton.

"Three times we made the tour, breaking our way with great difficulty through the waves of masks that were hurling themselves one upon the other; she trembling at every unseemly word that came to her ear; I blushing to be seen giving my arm to a woman who would thus put herself in the way of such words; then we returned to the end of the hall.

"She fell upon a sofa. I remained standing in front of her, my hand leaning on the back of her seat.

"'Oh! this must seem to you very bizarre,' she said, 'but not more so than to me, I swear to you. I have not the slightest idea of all this' (she looked at the ball), 'for even in my dreams I could not imagine such things. But they wrote me, you see, that he would be here with a woman, and what sort of a woman should it be who could come to a place like this?'

"I made a gesture of surprise; she understood.

"'But *I* am here, you wish to ask, do you not? Oh! but for me that is another thing: I, I am looking for him; I, I am his wife. As for these people, it is madness and dissipation that drives them hither. But I, I, it is jealousy infernal! I have been everywhere looking for him; I have been all night in a cemetery; I have been at Grève on the day of an execution; and yet, I swear to you, as a young girl I have never once gone into the street without my mother; as a wife I have never taken one step out of doors without being followed by a lackey; and yet here I am, the same as all these women who are so familiar with the way; here I am giving my arm to a man whom I do not know, blushing under my mask at the opinion he ought to have of me! I know all this!—Have you ever been jealous, monsieur?'

"'Unhappily,' I replied to her.

"'Then you will forgive me, for you understand. You know that voice that cries out to you "Do!" as in the ear of a madman; you have felt that arm that pushes one into shame and crime, like the arm of fate. You know that at such a moment one is capable of everything, if one can only get vengeance.'

"I was about to reply; all at once she rose, her eyes fastened on two dominoes that were passing in front of us at that moment.

"'Silence!' she said.

"And she hurried me on following in their footsteps. I was thrown into the middle of an intrigue of which I understood nothing; I could feel all the threads vibrating, but could take hold of none of them by the end; but this poor wife seemed so troubled that she became interesting. I obeyed like a child, so imperious is real feeling, and we set ourselves to follow the two masks, one of which was evidently a man, the other a woman. They spoke in a low voice; the sounds reached our ears with difficulty.

"'It is he!' she murmured; 'it is his voice; yes, yes, that is his figure—'

"The latter of the two dominoes began to laugh.

"'That is his laugh,' said she; 'it is he, monsieur, it is he! The letter said true, O, mon Dieu, mon Dieu!'

"In the mean while the two masks kept on, and we followed them always. They went out of the hall, and we went out after them; they took the stairs leading to the boxes, and we ascended in their footsteps; they did not stop till they came to the boxes in the centre; we were like their two shadows. A little closed box was opened; they entered it; the door again closed upon them.

"The poor creature I was supporting on my arm frightened me by her excitement. I could not see her face, but crushed against me as she was, I could feel her heart beating, her body shivering, her limbs trembling. There was something uncanny in the way there came to me such Knowledge of unheard-of suffering, the spectacle of which I had before my very eyes, of whose victim I knew nothing, and of the cause of which I was completely ignorant. Nevertheless, for nothing in this world would I have abandoned that woman at such a moment.

"As she saw the two masks enter the box and the box close upon them, she stopped still a moment, motionless, and as if overwhelmed. Then she sprang forward to the door to listen. Placed as she was her slightest movement would betray her presence and ruin her; I dragged her back violently by the arm, I lifted the latch of the adjoining box, I drew her in after me, I lowered the grille and pulled the door to.

"'If you wish to listen,' I said to her, 'at least listen from here.'

"She fell upon one knee and flattened her ear against the partition, and I—I held myself erect on the opposite side, my arms crossed, my head bent and thoughtful.

"All that I had been able to observe of that woman seemed to me to indicate a type of beauty. The lower part of her face, which was not concealed by her mask, was youthful, velvety, and round; her lips were scarlet and delicate; her teeth, which the black velvet mask falling just above them made appear still whiter, were small, separated, and glistening; her hand was one to be modeled, her figure to be held between the fingers; her black hair, silky, escaped in profusion from beneath the hood of her domino, and the foot of a child, that played in and out under her skirt, looked as if it should have trouble in balancing her body, all lithe, all graceful, all airy as it was. Oh! what a marvelous piece of perfection must she be! Oh! he that should hold her in his arms, that should see every faculty of that spirit absorbed in loving him, that should feel the beating of her heart against his, her tremblings, her nervous palpitations, and that should be able to say: 'All of this, all of this, comes of love, of love for me, for me alone among all the millions of men, for me, angel predestined! Oh! that man!— that man!—'

"Such were my thoughts, when all at once I saw that woman rise, turn toward me, and say to me in a voice broken and fierce:

"'Monsieur, I am beautiful, I swear it; I am young, I am but nineteen. Until now I have been white as an angel of the Creation—ah, well—' she threw both arms about my neck, '—ah, well, I am yours—take me!—'

"At the same instant I felt her lips pressed close to mine, and the effect of a bite, rather than that of a kiss, ran shuddering and dismayed through my whole body; over my eyes passes a cloud of flame.

"Ten minutes later I was holding her in my arms, in a swoon, half dead and sobbing.

"Slowly she came to herself; through her mask I made out how haggard were her eyes; I saw the lower part of her pale face, I heard her teeth chatter one upon the other, as in the chill of a fever. I see it all once more.

"She remembered all that had taken place, and fell at my feet.

"'If you have any compassion,' she said to me, sobbing, 'any pity, turn away your eyes from me, never seek to know me; let me go and forget me. I will remember for two!'

"At these words she rose again; quickly, like a thought that escapes us, she darted toward the door, opened it, and coming back again, 'Do not follow me, in heaven's name, Monsieur, do not follow me!' she said.

"The door pushed violently open, closed again between her and me, stole her from my sight, like an apparition. I have never seen her more!

"I have never seen her more! And ever since, ever since the six months that have glided by, I have sought her everywhere, at balls, at spectacles, at promenades. Every time I have seen from a distance a woman with lithe figure, with a foot like a child's, with black hair, I have followed her, I have drawn near to her, I have looked into her face, hoping that her blushes would betray her. Nowhere have I found her again, in no place have I seen her again—except at night, except in my dreams! Oh! there, there she reappears; there I feel her, I feel her embraces, her biting caresses so ardent, as if she had something of the devil in her; then the mask has fallen and a face most grotesque appeared to me at times blurred as if veiled in a cloud; sometimes brilliant, as if circled by an aureole; sometimes pale, with a skull white and naked, with eyes vanished from the orbits, with teeth chattering and few. In short, ever since that night, I have ceased to live; burning with mad passion for a woman I do not know, hoping always and always disappointed at my hopes. Jealous without the right to be so, without knowing of whom to be jealous, not daring to avow such madness, and all the time pursued, preyed upon, wasted away, consumed by her."

As he finished these words he tore a letter from his breast.

"Now that I have told you everything," he said to me, "take this letter and read it."

I took the letter and read:

"Have you perhaps forgotten a poor woman who has forgotten nothing and who dies because she can not forget?

"When you receive this letter I shall be no more. Then go to the cemetery of Père-Lachaise, tell the concierge to let you see among the newest graves one that bears on its stone the simple name 'Marie,' and when you are face to face with that grave, fall on your knees and pray."

"Ah, well!" continued Anthony, "I received that letter yesterday, and I went there this morning. The concierge conducted me to the grave, and I remained two hours on my knees there, praying and weeping. Do you understand? She was there, that woman. Her flaming spirit had stolen away; the body consumed by it had bowed, even to breaking, beneath the burden of jealousy and of remorse; she was there, under my feet, and she had lived, and she had died, for me unknown; unknown!—and taking a place in my life as she had taken one in the grave; unknown!—and burying in my heart a corpse, cold and lifeless, as she had buried one in the sepulcher—Oh! Do you know anything to equal it? Do you know any event so appalling? Therefore, now, no more hope. I will see her again never. I would dig up her grave that I might recover, perhaps, some traces wherewithal to reconstruct her face; and I love her always! Do you understand, Alexandre? I love her like a madman; and I would kill myself this instant in order to rejoin her, if she were not to remain unknown to me for eternity, as she was unknown to me in this world."

With these words he snatched the letter from my hands, kissed it over and over again, and began to weep like a little child.

I took him in my arms, and not knowing what to say to him, I wept with him.

The Watkinson Evening

ELIZA LESLIE

Mrs. Morland, a polished and accomplished woman, was the widow of a distinguished senator from one of the western states, of which, also, her husband had twice filled the office of governor. Her daughter having completed her education at the best boarding-school in Philadelphia, and her son being about to graduate at Princeton, the mother had planned with her children a tour to Niagara and the lakes, returning by way of Boston. On leaving Philadelphia, Mrs. Morland and the delighted Caroline stopped at Princeton to be present at the annual commencement, and had the happiness of seeing their beloved Edward receive his diploma as bachelor of arts; after hearing him deliver, with great applause, an oration on the beauties of the American character. College youths are very prone to treat on subjects that imply great experience of the world. But Edward Morland was full of kind feeling for everything and everybody; and his views of life had hitherto been tinted with a perpetual rose-color.

Mrs. Morland, not depending altogether upon the celebrity of her late husband, and wishing that her children should see specimens of the best society in the northern cities, had left home with numerous letters of introduction. But when they arrived at New York, she found to her great regret, that having unpacked and taken out her small traveling desk, during her short stay in Philadelphia, she had strangely left it behind in the closet of her room at the hotel. In this desk were deposited all her letters, except two which had been offered to her by friends in Philadelphia. The young people, impatient to see the wonders of Niagara, had entreated her to stay but a day or two in the city of New York, and thought these two letters would be quite sufficient for the present. In the meantime she wrote back to the hotel, requesting that the missing desk should be forwarded to New York as soon as possible.

On the morning after their arrival at the great commercial metropolis of America, the Morland family took a carriage to ride round through the principal parts of the city, and to deliver their two letters at the houses to which they were addressed, and which were both situated in the region that lies between the upper part of Broadway and the North River. In one of the most fashionable streets they found the elegant mansion of Mrs. St. Leonard; but on stopping at the door, were informed that its mistress was not at home. They then left the introductory letter, (which they had prepared for this mischance, by inclosing it in an envelope with a card,) and proceeding to another street considerably farther up, they arrived at the dwelling of the Watkinson family, to the mistress of which the other Philadelphia letter was directed. It was one of a large block of houses all exactly alike, and all shut up from top to bottom, according to a custom more prevalent in New York than in any other city.

Here they were also unsuccessful; the servant who came to the door telling them that the ladies were particularly engaged and could see no company. So they left their second letter and card and drove off; continuing their ride till they reached the

Croton water works, which they quitted the carriage to see and admire. On returning to the hotel, with the intention after an hour or two of rest to go out again, and walk till near dinner-time, they found waiting them a note from Mrs. Watkinson, expressing her regret that she had not been able to see them when they called; and explaining that her family duties always obliged her to deny herself the pleasure of receiving morning visitors, and that her servants had general orders to that effect. But she requested their company for that evening, (naming nine o'clock as the hour,) and particularly desired an immediate answer.

"I suppose"—said Mrs. Morland—"she intends asking some of her friends to meet us, in case we accept the invitation; and therefore is naturally desirous of a reply as soon as possible. Of course we will not keep her in suspense. Mrs. Denham, who volunteered the letter, assured me that Mrs. Watkinson was one of the most estimable women in New York, and a pattern to the circle in which she moved. It seems that Mr. Denham and Mr. Watkinson are connected in business. Shall we go?"

The young people assented, saying they had no doubt of passing a pleasant evening.

The billet of acceptance having been written, it was sent off immediately, entrusted to one of the errand-goers belonging to the hotel, that it might be received in advance of the next hour for the dispatch-post—and Edward Morland desired the man to get into an omnibus with the note that no time might be lost in delivering it. "It is but right"—said he to his mother—"that we should give Mrs. Watkinson an ample opportunity of making her preparations, and sending round to invite her friends."

"How considerate you are, dear Edward"—said Caroline—"always so thoughtful of every one's convenience. What an excellent husband you will make. Your college friends must have idolized you."

"No"—said Edward—"they called me a prig." Just then a remarkably handsome carriage drove up to the private door of the hotel. From it alighted a very elegant woman, who in a few moments was ushered into the drawing-room by the head waiter, and on his designating Mrs. Morland's family, she advanced and gracefully announced herself as Mrs. St. Leonard. This was the lady at whose house they had left the first letter of introduction. She expressed her regret at not having been at home when they called; but said that on finding their letter, she had immediately come down to see them, and to engage them for the evening. "To night"—said Mrs. St. Leonard—"I expect as many friends as I can collect for a summer party. The occasion is the recent marriage of my niece, who with her husband has just returned from their bridal excursion, and they will be soon on their way to his residence in Baltimore. I think I can promise you an agreeable evening, as I expect some very delightful people, with whom I shall be most happy to make you acquainted."

Edward and Caroline exchanged glances, and could not refrain from looking wistfully at their mother, on whose countenance a shade of regret was very apparent. After a short pause she replied to Mrs. St. Leonard—"I am truly sorry to say, that we have just answered in the affirmative a previous invitation for this very evening."

"I am indeed disappointed"—said Mrs. St. Leonard, who had been looking approvingly at the prepossessing appearance of the two young people. "Is there no way in which you can revoke your compliance with this unfortunate first invitation—at least, I am sure, it is unfortunate for me. What a vexatious *contre-temps* that I should have chanced to be out when you called; thus missing the pleasure of seeing you at once, and securing that of your society for this evening? The truth is, I was disappointed in some of the preparations that had been sent home this morning, and I had to go myself and have the things rectified, and was detained away longer than I expected. May I ask to whom you are engaged this evening? Perhaps I know the lady—if so, I should be very much tempted to go and beg you from her."

"The lady is Mrs. John Watkinson"—replied Mrs. Morland—"Most probably she will invite some of her friends to meet us."

"That of course"—answered Mrs. St. Leonard—"I am really very sorry—and I regret to say that I do not know her at all."

"We shall have to abide by our first decision"—said Mrs. Morland—"By Mrs. Watkinson, mentioning in her note the hour of nine, it is to be presumed she intends asking some other company. I cannot possibly disappoint her. I can speak feelingly as to the annoyance (for I have known it by my own experience) when after inviting a number of my friends to meet some strangers, the strangers have sent an excuse almost at the eleventh hour. I think no inducements, however strong, could tempt me to do so myself."

"I confess that you are perfectly right"—said Mrs. St. Leonard—"I see you must go to Mrs. Watkinson. But can you not divide the evening, by passing a part of it with her and then finishing with me."

At this suggestion the eyes of the young people sparkled, for they had become delighted with Mrs. St. Leonard, and imagined that a party at her house must be every way charming. Also, parties were novelties to both of them.

"If possible we will do so"—answered Mrs. Morland—"and with what pleasure I need not assure you. We leave New York to-morrow, but we shall return this way in September, and will then be exceedingly happy to see more of Mrs. St. Leonard."

After a little more conversation Mrs. St. Leonard took her leave, repeating her hope of still seeing her new friends at her house that night; and enjoining them to let her know as soon as they returned to New York on their way home.

Edward Morland handed her to her carriage, and then joined his mother and sister in their commendations of Mrs. St. Leonard, with whose exceeding beauty were united a countenance beaming with intelligence, and a manner that put every one at their ease immediately.

"She is an evidence"—said Edward—"how superior our women of fashion are to those of Europe."

"Wait, my dear son"—said Mrs. Morland—"till you have been in Europe, and had an opportunity of forming an opinion on that point (as on many others) from actual observation. For my part, I believe that in all civilized countries the upper classes of people are very much alike, at least in their leading characteristics."

"Ah! here comes the man that was sent to Mrs. Watkinson"—said Caroline Morland. "I hope he could not find the house and has brought the note back with him. We shall then be able to go at first to Mrs. St. Leonard's, and pass the whole evening there."

The man reported that he *had* found the house, and had delivered the note into Mrs. Watkinson's own hands, as she chanced to be crossing the entry when the door was opened; and that she read it immediately, and said "Very well."

"Are you certain that you made no mistake in the house"—said Edward—"and that you really *did* give it to Mrs. Watkinson?"

"And it's quite sure I am, sir"—replied the man—"when I first came over from the ould country I lived with them awhile—and though when she saw me to-day, she did not let on that she remembered my doing that same, she could not help calling me Jeames. Yes, the rale words she said when I handed her the billy-dux was, 'very well, Jeames.'"

"Come—come"—said Edward, when they found themselves alone—"let us look on the bright side. If we do not find a large party at Mrs. Watkinson's, we may in all probability meet some very agreeable people there, and enjoy the feast of reason and the flow of soul. We may find the Watkinson house so pleasant as to leave it with regret even for Mrs. St. Leonard's."

"I do not believe Mrs. Watkinson is in fashionable society"—said Caroline—"or Mrs. St. Leonard would have known her. I heard some of the ladies here talking last evening of Mrs. St. Leonard, and I found from what they said that she is among the élite of the élite."

"Even if she is"—observed Mrs. Morland—"are polish of manners and cultivation of mind confined exclusively to persons of that class?"

"Certainly not"—said Edward—"the most talented and refined youth at our college, and he in whose society I found the greatest pleasure, was the son of a bricklayer."

In the ladies' drawing-room, after dinner, the Morlands heard a conversation between several of the female guests, who all seemed to know Mrs. St. Leonard very well by reputation, and they talked of her party that was to "come off" on this evening.

"I hear"—said one lady—"that Mrs. St. Leonard is to have an unusual number of lions."

She then proceeded to name a gallant general, with his elegant wife and accomplished daughter; a celebrated commander in the navy; two highly distinguished members of congress, and even an ex-president. Also several of the most eminent among the American literati, and two first-rate artists.

Edward Morland felt as if he could say—"Had I three ears I'd hear thee."

"Such a woman as Mrs. St. Leonard can always command the best lions that are to be found"—observed another lady.

"And then"—said a third—"I have been told, that she has such exquisite taste in lighting and embellishing her always elegant rooms. And her supper table, whether for summer or winter parties, is so beautifully arranged; all the viands are so delicious, and the attendance of the servants so perfect—and Mrs. St. Leonard does the honors with so much ease and tact."

"Some friends of mine that visit her"—said a fourth lady—"describe her parties as absolute perfection. She always manages to bring together those persons that are best fitted to enjoy each other's conversation. Still no one is overlooked or neglected. Then everything at her *re-unions* is so well proportioned—she has just enough of music, and just enough of whatever amusement may add to the pleasure of her guests;

and still there is no appearance of design or management on her part."

"And better than all"—said the lady who had spoken first—"Mrs. St. Leonard is one of the kindest, most generous, and most benevolent of women—she does good in every possible way."

"I can listen no longer"—said Caroline to Edward, rising to change her seat—"If I hear any more I shall absolutely hate the Watkinsons. How provoking that they should have sent us the first invitation. If we had only thought of waiting till we could hear from Mrs St. Leonard!"

"For shame, Caroline"—said her brother—"how can you talk so of persons you have never seen, and to whom you ought to feel grateful for the kindness of their invitation; even if it *has* interfered with another party, that I must confess seems to offer unusual attractions. Now I have a presentiment that we shall find the Watkinson part of the evening very enjoyable."

As soon as tea was over, Mrs. Morland and her daughter repaired to their toilettes. Fortunately, fashion as well as good taste, has decided that, at a summer-party, the costume of the ladies should never go beyond an elegant simplicity. Therefore our two ladies in preparing for their intended appearance at Mrs. St. Leonard's, were enabled to attire themselves in a manner that would not seem out of place in the smaller company they expected to meet at the Watkinsons. Over an under-dress of lawn, Caroline Morland put on a white organdy trimmed with lace, and decorated with bows of pink ribbon. At the back of her head was a wreath of fresh and beautiful pink flowers, tied with a similar ribbon. Mrs. Morland wore a black grenadine over a satin, and a lace cap trimmed with white.

It was but a quarter past nine o'clock when their carriage stopped at the Watkinson door. The front of the house looked very dark. Not a ray gleamed through the Venetian shutters, and the glimmer beyond the fan-light over the door was almost imperceptible. After the coachman had rung several times, an Irish girl opened the door, cautiously, (as Irish girls always do) and admitted them into the entry, where one light only was burning in a branch lamp. "Shall we go up stairs?"—said Mrs. Morland. "And what for would ye go up stairs?"—said the girl in a pert tone—" It's all dark there, and there's no preparations. Ye can lave your things here a hanging on the rack. Is it a party ye're expecting? Blessed are them what expects nothing."

The sanguine Edward Morland looked rather blank at this intelligence, and his sister whispered to him—"We'll get off to Mrs. St. Leonard's as soon as we possibly can. When did you tell the coachman to come for us?"

"At half past ten"—was the brother's reply.

"Oh! Edward, Edward!"—she exclaimed—"And I dare say he will not be punctual. He may keep us here till eleven."

"*Courage, mes enfants*"—said their mother—"*et parlez plus doucement.*"

The girl then ushered them into the back parlor, saying—"Here's the company."

The room was large and gloomy. A chequered mat covered the floor, and all the furniture was encased in striped calico covers, and the lamps, mirrors, &c., concealed under green gauze. The front parlor was entirely dark, and in the back apartment was no other light than a shaded lamp on a large centre-table, round which was assembled a circle of children of all sizes and ages. On a backless, cushionless sofa sat

Mrs. Watkinson, and a young lady, whom she introduced as her daughter Jane. And Mrs. Morland in return presented Edward and Caroline.

"Will you take the rocking-chair, ma'am?"—inquired Mrs. Watkinson.

Mrs. Morland declining the offer, the hostess took it herself, and see-sawed on it nearly the whole time. It was a very awkward, high-legged, crouch-backed rocking-chair, and shamefully unprovided with anything in the form of a footstool.

"My husband is away, at Boston, on business"—said Mrs. Watkinson. "I thought at first, ma'am, I should not be able to ask you here this evening, for it is not our way to have company in his absence; but my danghter Jane over-persuaded me to send for you."

"What a pity"—thought Caroline.

"You must take us as you find us, ma'am"—continued Mrs. Watkinson. "We use no ceremony with anybody; and our rule is never to put ourselves out of the way. We do not give parties (looking at the dresses of the ladies). Our first duty is to our children, and we cannot waste our substance on fashion and folly. They'll have cause to thank us for it when we die."

Something like a sob was heard from the centre table, at which the children were sitting, and a boy was seen to hold his handkerchief to his face.

"Joseph, my child"—said his mother—"do not cry. You have no idea, ma'am, what an extraordinary boy that is. You see how the bare mention of such a thing as our deaths has overcome him."

There was another sob behind the handkerchief, and the

Morlands thought it now sounded very much like a smothered laugh.

"As I was saying, ma'am"—continued Mrs. Watkinson—"we never give parties. We leave all sinful things to the vain and foolish. My daughter Jane has been telling me, that she heard this morning of a party that is going on to-night at the widow St. Leonard's. It is only fifteen years since her husband died. He was carried off with a three day's illness, but two months after they were married. I have had a domestic that lived with them at the time, so I know all about it. And there she is now, living in an elegant house, and riding in her carriage, and dressing and dashing, and giving parties, and enjoying life, as she calls it. Poor creature, how I pity her! Thank heaven, nobody that *I* know goes to her parties. If they did I would never wish to see them again in my house. It is an encouragement to folly and nonsense—and folly and nonsense are sinful. Do not you think so, ma'am?"

"If carried too far they may certainly become so"—replied Mrs. Morland.

"We have heard"—said Edward—"that Mrs. St. Leonard, though one of the ornaments of the gay world, has a kind heart, a beneficent spirit and a liberal hand."

"I know very little about her—"replied Mrs. Watkinson, drawing up her head—"and I have not the least desire to know any more. It is well she has no children; they'd be lost sheep if brought up in her fold. For my part, ma'am"—she continued—turning to Mrs. Morland—"I am quite satisfied with the quiet joys of a happy home. And no mother has the least business with any other pleasures. My innocent babes know nothing about plays, and balls, and parties; and they never shall. Do they look as if they had been accustomed to a life of pleasure?"

They certainly did not; for when the Morlands took a glance at them, they thought they had never seen youthful faces that were less gay, and indeed less prepossessing. There was not a good feature or a pleasant expression among them all. Edward Morland recollected his having often read, "that childhood is always lovely." But he saw that the juvenile Watkinsons were an exception to the rule.

"The first duty of a mother is to her children"—repeated Mrs. Watkinson. "Till nine o'clock, my daughter Jane and myself are occupied every evening in hearing the lessons that they have learnt for to-morrow's school. Before that hour we can receive no visitors, and we never have company to tea, as that would interfere too much with our duties. We had just finished hearing these lessons when you arrived. Afterwards the children are permitted to indulge themselves in rational play, for I permit no amusement that is not also instructive. My children are so well trained, that even when alone their sports are always serious."

Two of the boys glanced slyly at each other, with what Edward Morland comprehended as an expression of pitch-penny and marbles.

"They are now engaged at their game of astronomy"—continued Mrs. Watkinson. "They have also a set of geography cards, and a set of mathematical cards. It is a blessed discovery, the invention of these educational games; so that even the play-time of children can be turned to account. And you have no idea, ma'am, how they enjoy them."

Just then the boy Joseph rose from the table, and stalking up to Mrs. Watkinson, said to her—"Mamma, please to whip me."

At this unusual request the visitors looked much amazed, and Mrs. Watkinson replied to him—"Whip you my best Joseph—for what cause? I have not seen you do anything wrong this evening, and you know my anxiety induces me to watch my children all the time."

"You could not see me"—answered Joseph—"for I have not *done* anything very wrong. But I have had a bad thought, and you know Mr. Ironrule says that a fault imagined is just as wicked as a fault committed."

"You see ma'am, what a good memory he has"—said Mrs. Watkinson aside to Mrs. Morland. "But my best Joseph, you make your mother tremble. What fault have you imagined! What was your bad thought?"

"Ay"—said another boy—"What's your thought like?"

"My thought"—said Joseph—"was 'Confound all astronomy, and I could see the man hanged that made this game.'"

Oh! my child"—exclaimed the mother—stopping her ears—"I am indeed shocked. I am glad you repented so immediately."

"Yes"—returned Joseph—"but I am afraid my repentance won't last. If I am not whipped, I may have these bad thoughts whenever I play at astronomy, and worse still at the geography game. Whip me, ma', and punish me as I deserve. There's the rattan in the corner: I'll bring it you myself."

"Excellent boy!" said his mother—"You know I always pardon my children when they are so candid as to confess their faults."

"So you do"—said Joseph—"but a whipping will cure me better."

"I cannot resolve to punish so conscientious a child"—said Mrs. Watkinson.

"Shall I take the trouble off your hands!"—inquired Edward, losing all patience in his disgust at the sanctimonious hypocrisy of this young Blifil—"It is such a rarity for a boy to request a whipping, that so remarkable a desire ought by all means to be gratified."

Joseph turned round and made a face at him.

"Give me the rattan"—said Edward, half laughing, and offering to take it out of his hand. "I'll use it to your full satisfaction."

The boy thought it most prudent to stride off and return to the table, and ensconce himself among his brothers and sisters; some of whom were staring with stupid surprise, others were whispering and giggling in the hope of seeing Joseph get a real flogging.

Mrs. Watkinson having bestowed a bitter look on Edward, hastened to turn the attention of his mother to something else. "Mrs. Morland"—said she—"allow me to introduce you to my youngest hope." She pointed to a sleepy boy about five years old, who with head thrown back and mouth wide open, was slumbering in his chair.

Mrs. Watkinson's children were of that uncomfortable species who never go to bed; at least never without all manner of resistance. All her boasted authority was inadequate to compel them; they never would confess themselves sleepy; always wanted to "sit up," and there was a nightly scene of scolding, coaxing, threatening and manoeuvring to get them off.

"I declare"—said Mrs. Watkinson—"dear Benny is almost

asleep. Shake him up, Christopher. I want him to speak a speech. His schoolmistress takes great pains in teaching her little pupils to speak, and stands up herself and shows them how."

The child having been shaken up hard, (two or three others helping Christopher,) rubbed his eyes and began to whine. His mother went to him, took him on her lap, hushed him up, and began to coax him. This done, she stood him on his feet before Mrs. Morland, and desired him to speak a speech for the company. The child put his thumb into his mouth, and remained silent.

"Ma"—said Jane Watkinson—"you had better tell him what speech to speak."

"Speak Cato or Plato"—said his mother. "Which do you call it? Come now, Benny—how does it begin! 'You are quite right and reasonable, Plato.' That's it."

"Speak Lucius"—said his sister Jane. "Come now, Benny— say 'your thoughts are turned on peace.'"

The little boy looked very much as if they were *not*, and as if meditating an outbreak.

"No no—"—exclaimed Christopher—"let him say Hamlet. Come now, Benny—'To be or not be.'"

"It an't to be at all"—cried Benny—"and I won't speak the least bit of it for any of you. I hate that speech."

"Only see his obstinacy"—said the solemn Joseph. "And is he to be given up to?"

"Speak anything, Benny"—said Mrs. Watkinson—"anything so that it is only a speech."

All the Watkinson voices now began to clamor violently at the obstinate child—"Speak a speech! speak a speech!—speak a speech!" But they had no more effect than the reiterated exhortations with which nurses confuse the poor heads of babies, when they require them to "shake a day-day—shake a day-day!"

Mrs. Morland now interfered, and begged that the sleepy little boy might be excused; on which he screamed out that "he wasn't sleepy at all, and would not go to bed ever."

"I never knew any of my children behave so before"—said Mrs. Watkinson. "They are always models of obedience, ma'am. A look is sufficient for them. And I must say that they have in every way profited by the education we are giving them. It is not our way, ma'am, to waste our money in parties and fooleries, and fine furniture and fine clothes, and rich food, and all such abominations. Our first duty is to our children, and to make them learn everything that is taught in the schools. If they go wrong, it will not be for want of education. Hester, my dear, come and talk to Miss Morland in French."

Hester (unlike her little brother that would not speak a speech) stepped boldly forward, and addressed Caroline Morland with—"*Parlez-vous Français, mademoiselle? Comment vous pertez-vous? Comment se va madame votre mère? Aimez-vous la musique? Aimez-vous la danse? Bon jour—bon soir—bon repos. Comprenez-vous?*"

To this tirade, uttered with great volubility, Miss Morland made no other reply than—"*Oui—je comprends.*"

"Very well, Hester—very well, indeed"—said Mrs. Watkinson. "You see, ma'am"—turning to Mrs. Morland—"how very fluent she is in French; and she has only been learning eleven quarters."

After considerable whispering between Jane and her mother, the former withdrew, and sent in by the Irish girl a waiter with a basket of soda biscuit, a pitcher of water, and some glasses.

Mrs. Watkinson invited her guests to consider themselves at home and help themselves freely, saying—"We never let cakes, sweetmeats, confectionery, or any such things, enter the house, as they would be very unwholesome for the children, and it would be sinful to put temptation in their way. I am sure, ma'am, you will agree with me that the plainest food is the best for everybody. People that want nice things may go to parties for them; but they will never get any with me."

When the collation was over, and every child provided with a biscuit, Mrs. Watkinson said to Mrs. Morland—"Now, ma'am, you shall have some music from my daughter Jane, who is one of Mr. Bangwhanger's best scholars."

Jane Watkinson sat down to the piano, and commenced a powerful piece of six mortal pages, which she played out of time, and out of tune; but with tremendous force of hands; notwithstanding which, it had, however, the good effect of putting most of the children to sleep.

To the Morlands the evening had seemed already five hours long. Still it was only half-past ten, when Jane was in the midst of her piece. The guests had all tacitly determined that it would be best not to let Mrs. Watkinson know their intention to go directly from her house to Mrs. St. Leonard's party; and the arrival of their carriage would have been the signal of departure, even if Jane's piece had not reached its termination. They stole glances at the clock on the mantel. It wanted but a quarter of eleven, when Jane rose from the piano, and was congratulated by her mother on the excellence of her music. Still no carriage was heard to stop; no door-bell was heard to ring. Mrs. Morland expressed her fears that the coachman had forgotten to come for them.

"Has he been paid for bringing you here?"—asked Mrs. Watkinson.

"I paid him when we came to the door"—said Edward. "I thought perhaps he might want the money for some purpose, before he came for us."

"That was very kind in you, sir"—said Mrs. Watkinson—"but not very wise. There's no dependence on any coachman; and perhaps as he may be sure of business enough this rainy night, he may never come at all—being already paid for bringing you here."

Now, the truth was that the coachman *had* come at the appointed time, but the noise of Jane's piano had prevented his arrival being heard in the back parlor. The Irish girl had gone to the door when he rung the bell, and recognized in him what she called "an ould friend." Just then a lady and gentleman who had been caught in the rain came running along, and seeing a carriage drawing up at a door, the gentleman inquired of the driver if he could not take them to Rutgers Place. The driver replied that he had just come for two ladies and a gentleman whom he had brought from the Astor House.

"Indeed and Patrick"—said the girl who stood at the door—"if I was you I'd be after making another penny to-night. Miss Jane is pounding away at one of her long music pieces, and it won't be over before you have time to get to Rutgers and back again. And if you do make them wait awhile, where's the harm? They've a dry roof over their heads, and I warrant it's not the first waiting they've ever had in their lives; and it won't be the last neither."

"Exactly so"—said the gentleman; and regardless of the propriety of first sending to consult the persons who had engaged the carriage, he told his wife to step in, and following her instantly himself, they drove away to Rutgers Place.

Reader, if you were ever detained in a strange house by the non-arrival of your carriage, you will easily understand the excessive annoyance of finding that you are keeping a family out of their beds beyond their usual hour. And in this case, there was a double grievance; the guests being all impatience to get off to a better place. The children, all crying when wakened from their sleep, were finally taken to bed by two servant maids, and Jane Watkinson, who never came back again. None were left but Hester, the great French scholar, who, being one of those young imps that seem to have the faculty of living without sleep, sat bolt upright with her eyes wide open watching the uncomfortable visitors.

The Morlands felt as if they could bear it no longer, and Edward proposed sending for another carriage to the nearest livery stable.

"We don't keep a man now"—said Mrs. Watkinson, who sat nodding in the rocking-chair, attempting now and then a snatch of conversation, and saying "ma'am" still more frequently than usual. "Men servants are dreadful trials, ma'am, and we gave them up three years ago. And I don't know how Mary or Katy are to go out this stormy night in search of a livery stable."

"On no consideration could I allow the women to do so"—replied Edward. "If you will oblige me by the loan of an umbrella, I will go myself."

Accordingly he sat out on this business, but was unsuccessful at two livery stables, the carriages being all out. At last he found one, and was driven in it to Mr. Watkinson's house, where his mother and sister were awaiting him, all quite ready,

with their calashes and shawls on. They gladly took their leave;
Mrs. Watkinson rousing herself to hope they had spent a pleasant evening, and that they would come and pass another with
her, on their return to New York. In such cases how difficult it
is to reply even with what are called "words of course."

A kitchen lamp was brought to light them to the door; the
entry lamp having long since been extinguished. Fortunately
the rain had ceased; the stars began to re-appear; and the Morlands, when they found themselves in the carriage and on their
way to Mrs. St. Leonard's, felt as if they could breathe again.
As may be supposed, they freely discussed the annoyances of
the evening; but now those troubles were over, they felt rather
inclined to be merry about them.

"Dear mother"—said Edward—"how I pitied you for
having to endure Mrs. Watkinson's perpetual 'ma'aming' and
'ma'aming;' for I know you dislike the word."

"I wish"—said Caroline—"I was not so prone to be taken
with ridiculous recollections. But really to-night I could not get
that old foolish child's play out of my head—

'Here come three knights out of Spain
A courting of your daughter Jane.'"

"*I* shall certainly never be one of those Spanish knights"—
said Edward. "Her daughter Jane is in no danger of being ruled
by any 'flattering tongue' of mine. But what a shame for us to
be talking of them in this manner."

They drove to Mrs. St. Leonard's, hoping to be yet in time
to pass half an hour there; though it was now near twelve
o'clock, and summer parties never continue to a very late
hour. But as they came into the street in which she lived, they
were met by a number of coaches on their way home; and on

reaching the door of her brilliantly-lighted mansion, they saw the last of the guests driving off in the last of the carriages; and several musicians coming down the steps with their instruments in their hands.

"So there *has* been a dance, then"—sighed Caroline. "Oh! what we have missed. It is really too provoking."

"So it is"—said Edward—"but remember that to-morrow morning we set off for Niagara."

"I will leave a note for Mrs. St. Leonard"—said his mother—"explaining that we were detained at Mrs. Watkinson's by our coachman disappointing us. Let us console ourselves with the hope of seeing more of this lady on our return. And now, dear Caroline, you must draw a moral from the untoward events of to-day. When you are mistress of a house, and wish to show civility to strangers, let the invitation be always accompanied with a frank disclosure of what they are to expect. And if you cannot conveniently invite company to meet them, tell them at once that you will not insist on their keeping their engagement with *you*, if anything offers afterwards that they think they would prefer; provided only that they apprize you in time of the change in their plan."

"Oh, mamma"—replied Caroline—"you may be sure I shall always take care not to betray my visitors into an engagement which they may have cause to regret, particularly if they are strangers whose time is limited. I shall certainly, as you say, tell them not to consider themselves bound to me, if they afterwards receive an invitation which promises them more enjoyment. It will be a long while before I forget the Watkinson evening."

Wiser Than a God

KATE CHOPIN

> "To love and be wise is scarcely granted even to
> a god."
>
> – LATIN PROVERB

"You might at least show some distaste for the task, Paula," said Mrs. Von Stoltz, in her querulous invalid voice, to her daughter who stood before the glass bestowing a few final touches of embellishment upon an otherwise plain toilet.

"And to what purpose, Mutterchen? The task is not entirely to my liking, I'll admit; but there can be no question as to its results, which you even must concede are gratifying."

"Well, it's not the career your poor father had in view for you. How often he has told me when I complained that you were kept too closely at work, 'I want that Paula shall be at the head,'" with appealing look through the window and up into the gray, November sky into that far "somewhere," which might be the abode of her departed husband.

"It isn't a career at all, mamma; it's only a makeshift," answered the girl, noting the happy effect of an amber pin that she had thrust through the coils of her lustrous yellow hair. "The pot must be kept boiling at all hazards, pending the appearance of that hoped for career. And you forget that an occasion like this gives me the very opportunities I want."

"I can't see the advantages of bringing your talent down to such banale servitude. Who are those people, anyway?"

The mother's question ended in a cough which shook her into speechless exhaustion.

"Ah! I have let you sit too long by the window, mother," said Paula, hastening to wheel the invalid's chair nearer the grate fire that was throwing genial light and warmth into the room, turning its plainness to beauty as by a touch of enchantment. "By the way," she added, having arranged her mother as comfortably as might be, "I haven't yet qualified for that 'banale servitude,' as you call it." And approaching the piano which stood in a distant alcove of the room, she took up a roll of music that lay curled up on the instrument, straightened it out before her. Then, seeming to remember the question which her mother had asked, turned on the stool to answer it. "Don't you know? The Brainards, very swell people, and awfully rich. The daughter is that girl whom I once told you about, having gone to the Conservatory to cultivate her voice and old Engfelder told her in his brusque way to go back home, that his system was not equal to overcoming impossibilities."

"Oh, those people."

"Yes; this little party is given in honor of the son's return from Yale or Harvard, or some place or other." And turning to the piano she softly ran over the dances, whilst the mother gazed into the fire with unresigned sadness, which the bright music seemed to deepen.

"Well, there'll be no trouble about *that*," said Paula, with comfortable assurance, having ended the last waltz. "There's nothing here to tempt me into flights of originality; there'll be no difficulty in keeping to the hand-organ effect."

"Don't leave me with those dreadful impressions Paula; my poor nerves are on edge."

"You are too hard on the dances, mamma. There are certain strains here and there that I thought not bad."

"It's your youth that finds it so; I have outlived such illusions."

"What an inconsistent little mother it is!" the girl exclaimed, laughing. "You told me only yesterday it was my youth that was so impatient with the commonplace happenings of everyday life. That age, needing to seek its delights, finds them often in unsuspected places, wasn't that it?"

"Don't chatter, Paula; some music, some music!"

"What shall it be?" asked Paula, touching a succession of harmonious chords. "It must be short."

"The 'Berceuse,' then; Chopin's. But soft, soft and a little slowly as your dear father used to play it."

Mrs. Von Stoltz leaned her head back amongst the cushions, and with eyes closed, drank in the wonderful strains that came like an ethereal voice out of the past, lulling her spirit into the quiet of sweet memories.

When the last soft notes had melted into silence, Paula approached her mother and looking into the pale face saw that tears stood beneath the closed eyelids. "Ah! mamma, I have made you unhappy," she cried, in distress.

"No, my child; you have given me a joy that you don't dream of. I have no more pain. Your music has done for me what Faranelli's singing did for poor King Philip of Spain; it has cured me."

There was a glow of pleasure on the warm face and the eyes with almost the brightness of health. "Whilst I listened to you,

Paula, my soul went out from me and lived again through an evening long ago. We were in our pretty room at Leipsic. The soft air and the moonlight came through the open-curtained window, making a quivering fret-work along the gleaming waxed floor. You lay in my arms and I felt again the pressure of your warm, plump little body against me. Your father was at the piano playing the 'Berceuse,' and all at once you drew my head down and whispered, '*Ist es nicht wunderschön,* mama?' When it ended, you were sleeping and your father took you from my arms and laid you gently in bed."

Paula knelt beside her mother, holding the frail hands which she kissed tenderly.

"Now you must go, *liebchen*. Ring for Berta, she will do all that is needed. I feel very strong to-night. But do not come back too late."

"I shall be home as early as possible; likely in the last car, I couldn't stay longer or I should have to walk. You know the house in case there should be need to send for me?"

"Yes, yes; but there will be no need."

Paula kissed her mother lovingly and went out into the drear November night with the roll of dances under her arm.

II

The door of the stately mansion at which Paula rang was opened by a footman, who invited her to "kindly walk upstairs."

"Show the young lady into the music room, James," called from some upper region a voice, doubtless the same whose impossibilities had been so summarily dealt with by Herr Engfelder, and Paula was led through a suite of handsome apartments, the warmth and mellow light of which were very grateful, after the chill out-door air.

Once in the music room, she removed her wraps and seated herself comfortably to await developments. Before her stood the magnificent "Steinway," on which her eyes rested with greedy admiration, and her fingers twitched with a desire to awaken its inviting possibilities. The odor of flowers impregnated the air like a subtle intoxicant and over everything hung a quiet smile of expectancy, disturbed by an occasional feminine flutter above stairs, or muffled suggestions of distant household sounds.

Presently, a young man entered the drawing-room—no doubt, the college student, for he looked critically and with an air of proprietorship at the festive arrangements, venturing the bestowal of a few improving touches. Then, gazing with pardonable complacency at his own handsome, athletic figure in the mirror, he saw reflected Paula looking at him, with a demure smile lighting her blue eyes.

"By Jove!" was his startled exclamation. Then, approaching, "I beg pardon, Miss—Miss—"

"Von Stoltz."

"Miss Von Stoltz," drawing the right conclusion from her simple toilet and the roll of music. "I hadn't seen you when I came in. Have you been here long? and sitting all alone, too? That's certainly rough."

"Oh, I've been here but a few moments, and was very well entertained."

"I dare say," with a glance full of prognostic complimentary utterances, which a further acquaintance might develop.

As he was lighting the gas of a side bracket that she might

better see to read her music, Mrs. Brainard and her daughter came into the room, radiantly attired and both approached Paula with sweet and polite greeting.

"George, in mercy!" exclaimed his mother, "put out that gas, you are killing the effect of the candle light."

"But Miss Von Stoltz can't read her music without it, mother."

"I've no doubt Miss Von Stoltz knows her pieces by heart," Mrs. Brainard replied, seeking corroboration from Paula's glance.

"No, madam; I'm not accustomed to playing dance music, and this is quite new to me," the girl rejoined, touching the loose sheets that George had conveniently straightened out and placed on the rack.

"Oh, dear! 'not accustomed'?" said Miss Brainard. "And Mr. Sohmeir told us he knew you would give satisfaction."

Paula hastened to re-assure the thoroughly alarmed young lady on the point of her ability to give perfect satisfaction.

The door bell now began to ring incessantly. Up the stairs tripped fleeting opera-cloaked figures, followed by their black robed attendants. The rooms commenced to fill with the pretty hub-bub that a bevy of girls can make when inspired by a close masculine proximity; and Paula, not waiting to be asked, struck the opening bars of an inspiring waltz.

Some hours later, during a lull in the dancing, when the men were making vigorous applications of fans and handkerchiefs; and the girls beginning to throw themselves into attitudes of picturesque exhaustion—save for the always indefatigable few—a proposition was ventured, backed by clamorous entreaties, which induced George to bring forth his banjo. And an agreeable moment followed, in which that young man's skill met with a truly deserving applause. Never had his audience beheld such proficiency as he displayed in the handling of his instrument, which was now behind him, now over-head, and again swinging in mid-air like the pendulum of a clock and sending forth the sounds of stirring melody. Sounds so inspiring that a pretty little black-eyed fairy, an acknowledged votary of Terpsichore, and George's particular admiration, was moved to contribute a few passes of a Virginia break-down, as she had studied it from life on a Southern plantation. The act closed amid a spontaneous babel of hand clapping and admiring bravos.

It must be admitted that this little episode, however graceful, was hardly a fitting prelude to the magnificent "Jewel Song from 'Faust,'" with which Miss Brainard next consented to regale the company. That Miss Brainard possessed a voice, was a fact that had existed as matter of tradition in the family as far back almost as the days of that young lady's baby utterances, in which loving ears had already detected the promise which time had so recklessly fulfilled.

True genius is not to be held in abeyance, though a host of Engfelders would rise to quell it with their mundane protests!

Miss Brainard's rendition was a triumphant achievement of sound, and with the proud flush of success moving her to kind condescension, she asked Miss Von Stoltz to "please play something."

Paula amiably consented, choosing a selection from the Modern Classic. How little did her auditors appreciate in the performance the results of a life study, of a drilling that had made her amongst the knowing an acknowledged mistress of technique. But to her skill she added the touch and interpretation of the artist; and in hearing her, even Ignorance paid to her genius the tribute of a silent emotion.

When she arose there was a moment of quiet, which was broken by the black-eyed fairy, always ready to cast herself into a breach, observing, flippantly, "How pretty!" "Just lovely!" from another; and "What wouldn't I give to play like that." Each inane compliment falling like a dash of cold water on Paula's ardor.

She then became solicitous about the hour, with reference to her car, and George who stood near looked at his watch and informed her that the last car had gone by a full half hour before.

"But," he added, "if you are not expecting any one to call for you, I will gladly see you home."

"I expect no one, for the car that passes here would have set me down at my door," and in this avowal of difficulties, she tacitly accepted George's offer.

The situation was new. It gave her a feeling of elation to be walking through the quiet night with this handsome young fellow. He talked so freely and so pleasantly. She felt such a comfort in his strong protective nearness. In clinging to him against the buffets of the staggering wind she could feel the muscles of his arms, like steel.

He was so unlike any man of her acquaintance. Strictly unlike Poldorf, the pianist, the short rotundity of whose person could have been less objectionable, if she had not known its cause to lie in an inordinate consumption of beer. Old Engfelder, with his long hair, his spectacles and his loose, disjointed figure, was hors de combat in comparison. And of

Max Kuntzler, the talented composer, her teacher of harmony, she could at the moment think of no positive point of objection against him, save the vague, general, serious one of his unlikeness to George.

Her new-awakened admiration, though, was not deaf to a little inexplicable wish that he had not been so proficient with the banjo.

On they went chatting gaily, until turning the corner of the street in which she lived, Paula saw that before the door stood Dr. Sinn's buggy.

Brainard could feel the quiver of surprised distress that shook her frame, as she said, hurrying along, "Oh! mamma must be ill—worse; they have called the doctor."

Reaching the house, she threw open wide the door that was unlocked, and he stood hesitatingly back. The gas in the small hall burned at its full, and showed Berta at the top of the stairs, speechless, with terrified eyes, looking down at her. And coming to meet her was a neighbor, who strove with well-meaning solicitude to keep her back, to hold her yet a moment in ignorance of the cruel blow that fate had dealt her whilst she had in happy unconsciousness played her music for the dance.

III

Several months had passed since the dreadful night when death had deprived Paula for the second time of a loved parent.

After the first shock of grief was over, the girl had thrown all her energies into work, with the view of attaining that position in the musical world which her father and mother had dreamed might be hers.

She had remained in the small home occupying now but the half of it; and here she kept house with the faithful Berta's aid.

Friends were both kind and attentive to the stricken girl. But there had been two, whose constant devotion spoke of an interest deeper than mere friendly solicitude.

Max Kuntzler's love for Paula was something that had taken hold of his sober middle age with an enduring strength which was not to be lessened or shaken by her rejection of it. He had asked leave to remain her friend, and while holding the tender, watchful privileges which that comprehensive title may imply, had refrained from further thrusting a warmer feeling on her acceptance.

Paula one evening was seated in her small sitting-room, working over some musical transpositions, when a ring at the bell was followed by a footstep in the hall which made her hand and heart tremble.

George Brainard entered the room, and before she could rise to greet him, had seated himself in the vacant chair beside her.

"What an untiring worker you are," he said, glancing down at the scores before her. "I always feel that my presence interrupts you; and yet I don't know that a judicious interruption isn't the wholesomest thing for you sometimes."

"You forget," she said, smiling into his face, "that I was trained to it. I must keep myself fitted to my calling. Rest would mean deterioration."

"Would you not be willing to follow some other calling?" he asked, looking at her with unusual earnestness in his dark, handsome eyes.

"Oh, never!"

"Not if it were a calling that asked only for the labor of loving?"

She made no answer, but kept her eyes fixed on the idle traceries that she drew with her pencil on the sheets before her.

He arose and made a few impatient turns about the room, then coming again to her side, said abruptly:

"Paula, I love you. It isn't telling you something that you don't know, unless you have been without bodily perceptions. To-day there is something driving me to speak it out in words. Since I have known you," he continued, striving to look into her face that bent low over the work before her, "I have been mounting into higher and always higher circles of Paradise, under a blessed illusion that you—cared for me. But to-day, a feeling of dread has been forcing itself upon me—dread that with a word you might throw me back into a gulf that would now be one of everlasting misery. Say if you love me, Paula. I believe you do, and yet I wait with indefinable doubts for your answer."

He took her hand which she did not withdraw from his. "Why are you speechless? Why don't you say something to me!" he asked desperately.

"I am speechless with joy and misery," she answered. "To know that you love me, gives me happiness enough to brighten a lifetime. And I am miserable, feeling that you have spoken the signal that must part us."

"You love me, and speak of parting. Never! You will be my wife. From this moment we belong to each other. Oh, my Paula," he said, drawing her to his side, "my whole existence will be devoted to your happiness."

"I can't marry you," she said shortly, disengaging his hand from her waist.

"Why?" he asked abruptly. They stood looking into each other's eyes.

"Because it doesn't enter into the purpose of my life."

"I don't ask you to give up anything in your life. I only beg you to let me share it with you."

George had known Paula only as the daughter of the undemonstrative American woman. He had never before seen her with the father's emotional nature aroused in her. The color mounted into her cheeks, and her blue eyes were almost black with intensity of feeling.

"Hush," she said; "don't tempt me further." And she cast herself on her knees before the table near which they stood, gathering the music that lay upon it into an armful, and resting her hot cheek upon it.

"What do you know of my life," she exclaimed passionately. "What can you guess of it? Is music anything more to you than the pleasing distraction of an idle moment? Can't you feel that with me, it courses with the blood through my veins? That it's something dearer than life, than riches, even than love?" with a quiver of pain.

"Paula listen to me; don't speak like a mad woman."

She sprang up and held out an arm to ward away his nearer approach.

"Would you go into a convent, and ask to be your wife a nun who has vowed herself to the service of God?"

Paula seated herself on the sofa, all emotion seeming suddenly to have left her; and he came and sat beside her.

"Say only that you love me, Paula," he urged persistently.

"I love you," she answered low and with pale lips.

He took her in his arms, holding her in silent rapture against his heart and kissing the white lips back into red life.

"You will be my wife?"

"You must wait. Come back in a week and I will answer you." He was forced to be content with the delay.

The days of probation being over, George went for his answer, which was given him by the old lady who occupied the upper story.

"*Ach Gott! Fräulein Von Stoltz ist schon im Leipsic gegangen!*"—All that has not been many years ago. George Brainard is as handsome as ever, through growing a little stout in the quiet routine of domestic life. He has quite lost a pretty taste for music that formerly distinguished him as a skillful banjoist. This loss his little black-eyed wife deplores; though she has herself made concessions to the advancing years, and abandoned Virginia break-downs as incompatible with the serious offices of wifehood and matrimony.

You may have seen in the morning paper, that the renowned pianist, Fräulein Paula Von Stoltz, is resting in Leipsic, after an extended and remunerative concert tour.

Professor Max Kuntzler is also in Leipsic—with the ever persistent will—the dogged patience that so often wins in the end.

Lost on Dress Parade

O. HENRY

Mr. Towers Chandler was pressing his evening suit in his hall bedroom. One iron was heating on a small gas stove; the other was being pushed vigorously back and forth to make the desirable crease that would be seen later on extending in straight lines from Mr. Chandler's patent leather shoes to the edge of his low-cut vest. So much of the hero's toilet may be intrusted to our confidence. The remainder may be guessed by those whom genteel poverty has driven to ignoble expedient. Our next view of him shall be as he descends the steps of his lodging-house immaculately and correctly clothed; calm, assured, handsome—in appearance the typical New York young clubman setting out, slightly bored, to inaugurate the pleasures of the evening.

Chandler's honorarium was $18 per week. He was employed in the office of an architect. He was twenty-two years old; he considered architecture to be truly an art; and he honestly believed—though he would not have dared to admit it in New York—that the Flatiron Building was inferior in design to the great cathedral in Milan.

Out of each week's earnings Chandler set aside $1. At the end of each ten weeks with the extra capital thus accumulated, he purchased one gentleman's evening from the bargain counter of stingy old Father Time. He arrayed himself in the regalia of millionaires and presidents; he took himself to the quarter where life is brightest and showiest, and there dined with taste and luxury. With ten dollars a man may, for a few hours, play the wealthy idler to perfection. The sum is ample for a well-considered meal, a bottle bearing a respectable label, commensurate tips, a smoke, cab fare, and the ordinary etceteras.

This one delectable evening culled from each dull seventy was to Chandler a source of renascent bliss. To the society bud comes but one début; it stands alone sweet in her memory when her hair has whitened; but to Chandler each ten weeks brought a joy as keen, as thrilling, as new as the first had been. To sit among *bon vivants* under palms in the swirl of concealed music, to look upon the *habitués* of such a paradise and to be looked upon by them—what is a girl's first dance and short-sleeved tulle compared with this?

Up Broadway Chandler moved with the vespertine dress parade. For this evening he was an exhibit as well as a gazer. For the next sixty-nine evenings he would be dining in cheviot and worsted at dubious *table d'hôtes*, at whirlwind lunch counters, on sandwiches and beer in his hall bedroom. He was willing to do that, for he was a true son of the great city of razzle-dazzle, and to him one evening in the limelight made up for many dark ones.

Chandler protracted his walk until the Forties began to intersect the great and glittering primrose way, for the evening was yet young, and when one is of the *beau monde* only one day in seventy, one loves to protract the pleasure. Eyes bright, sinister, curious, admiring, provocative, alluring were bent upon him, for his garb and air proclaimed him a devotee to the hour of solace and pleasure.

At a certain corner he came to a standstill, proposing to himself the question of turning back toward the showy and fashionable restaurant in which he usually dined on the evenings of his especial luxury. Just then a girl scudded lightly around the corner, slipped on a patch of icy snow, and fell plump upon the sidewalk.

Chandler assisted her to her feet with instant and solicitous courtesy. The girl hobbled to the wall of the building, leaned against it, and thanked him demurely.

"I think my ankle is strained," she said. "It twisted when I fell."

"Does it pain you much?" inquired Chandler.

"Only when I rest my weight upon it. I think I will be able to walk in a minute or two."

"If I can be of any further service," suggested the young man, "I will call a cab, or——"

"Thank you," said the girl, softly but heartily. "I am sure you need not trouble yourself any further. It was so awkward of me. And my shoe heels are horridly common-sense; I can't blame them at all."

Chandler looked at the girl and found her swiftly drawing his interest. She was pretty in a refined way; and her eye was both merry and kind. She was inexpensively clothed in a plain black dress that suggested a sort of uniform such as shop girls wear. Her glossy dark-brown hair showed its coils beneath a cheap hat of black straw whose only ornament was a velvet ribbon and bow. She could have posed as a model for the self-respecting working girl of the best type.

A sudden idea came into the head of the young architect. He would ask this girl to dine with him. Here was the element that his splendid but solitary periodic feasts had lacked. His brief season of elegant luxury would be doubly enjoyable if he could add to it a lady's society. This girl was a lady, he was sure—her manner and speech settled that. And in spite of her extremely plain attire he felt that he would be pleased to sit at table with her.

These thoughts passed swiftly through his mind, and he decided to ask her. It was a breach of etiquette, of course, but oftentimes wage-earning girls waived formalities in matters of this kind. They were generally shrewd judges of men; and thought better of their own judgment than they did of useless conventions. His ten dollars, discreetly expended, would enable the two to dine very well indeed. The dinner would no doubt be a wonderful experience thrown into the dull routine of the girl's life; and her lively appreciation of it would add to his own triumph and pleasure.

"I think," he said to her, with frank gravity, "that your foot needs a longer rest than you suppose. Now, I am going to suggest a way in which you can give it that and at the same time do me a favour. I was on my way to dine all by my lonely self when you came tumbling around the corner. You come with me and we'll have a cozy dinner and a pleasant talk together, and by that time your game ankle will carry you home very nicely, I am sure."

The girl looked quickly up into Chandler's clear, pleasant countenance. Her eyes twinkled once very brightly, and then she smiled ingenuously.

"But we don't know each other—it wouldn't be right, would it?" she said, doubtfully.

"There is nothing wrong about it," said the young man,

candidly. "I'll introduce myself—permit me—Mr. Towers Chandler. After our dinner, which I will try to make as pleasant as possible, I will bid you good-evening, or attend you safely to your door, whichever you prefer."

"But, dear me!" said the girl, with a glance at Chandler's faultless attire. "In this old dress and hat!"

"Never mind that," said Chandler, cheerfully. "I'm sure you look more charming in them than any one we shall see in the most elaborate dinner toilette."

"My ankle does hurt yet," admitted the girl, attempting a limping step. "I think I will accept your invitation, Mr. Chandler. You may call me—Miss Marian."

"Come then, Miss Marian," said the young architect, gaily, but with perfect courtesy; "you will not have far to walk. There is a very respectable and good restaurant in the next block. You will have to lean on my arm—so—and walk slowly. It is lonely dining all by one's self. I'm just a little bit glad that you slipped on the ice."

When the two were established at a well-appointed table, with a promising waiter hovering in attendance, Chandler began to experience the real joy that his regular outing always brought to him.

The restaurant was not so showy or pretentious as the one farther down Broadway, which he always preferred, but it was nearly so. The tables were well filled with prosperous-looking diners, there was a good orchestra, playing softly enough to make conversation a possible pleasure, and the cuisine and service were beyond criticism. His companion, even in her cheap hat and dress, held herself with an air that added distinction to the natural beauty of her face and figure. And it is certain that she looked at Chandler, with his animated but self-possessed manner and his kindling and frank blue eyes, with something not far from admiration in her own charming face.

Then it was that the Madness of Manhattan, the Frenzy of Fuss and Feathers, the Bacillus of Brag, the Provincial Plague of Pose seized upon Towers Chandler. He was on Broadway, surrounded by pomp and style, and there were eyes to look at him. On the stage of that comedy he had assumed to play the one-night part of a butterfly of fashion and an idler of means and taste. He was dressed for the part, and all his good angels had not the power to prevent him from acting it.

So he began to prate to Miss Marian of clubs, of teas, of golf and riding and kennels and cotillions and tours abroad and threw out hints of a yacht lying at Larchmont. He could see that she was vastly impressed by this vague talk, so he endorsed his pose by random insinuations concerning great wealth, and mentioned familiarly a few names that are handled reverently by the proletariat. It was Chandler's short little day, and he was wringing from it the best that could be had, as he saw it. And yet once or twice he saw the pure gold of this girl shine through the mist that his egotism had raised between him and all objects.

"This way of living that you speak of," she said, "sounds so futile and purposeless. Haven't you any work to do in the world that might interest you more?"

"My dear Miss Marian," he exclaimed—"work! Think of dressing every day for dinner, of making half a dozen calls in an afternoon—with a policeman at every corner ready to jump into your auto and take you to the station, if you get up any greater speed than a donkey cart's gait. We do-nothings are the hardest workers in the land."

The dinner was concluded, the waiter generously feed, and the two walked out to the corner where they had met. Miss Marian walked very well now; her limp was scarcely noticeable.

"Thank you for a nice time," she said, frankly. "I must run home now. I liked the dinner very much, Mr. Chandler."

He shook hands with her, smiling cordially, and said something about a game of bridge at his club. He watched her for a moment, walking rather rapidly eastward, and then he found a cab to drive him slowly homeward.

In his chilly bedroom Chandler laid away his evening clothes for a sixty-nine days' rest. He went about it thoughtfully.

"That was a stunning girl," he said to himself. "She's all right, too, I'd be sworn, even if she does have to work. Perhaps if I'd told her the truth instead of all that razzle-dazzle we might—but, confound it! I had to play up to my clothes."

Thus spoke the brave who was born and reared in the wigwams of the tribe of the Manhattans.

The girl, after leaving her entertainer, sped swiftly crosstown until she arrived at a handsome and sedate mansion two squares to the east, facing on that avenue which is the highway of Mammon and the auxiliary gods. Here she entered hurriedly and ascended to a room where a handsome young lady in an elaborate house dress was looking anxiously out the window.

"Oh, you madcap!" exclaimed the elder girl, when the other entered. "When will you quit frightening us this way? It is two hours since you ran out in that rag of an old dress and Marie's hat. Mamma has been so alarmed. She sent Louis in the auto to try to find you. You are a bad, thoughtless Puss."

The elder girl touched a button, and a maid came in a moment.

"Marie, tell mamma that Miss Marian has returned."

"Don't scold, sister. I only ran down to Mme. Theo's to tell her to use mauve insertion instead of pink. My costume and Marie's hat were just what I needed. Every one thought I was a shopgirl, I am sure."

"Dinner is over, dear; you stayed so late."

"I know. I slipped on the sidewalk and turned my ankle. I could not walk, so I hobbled into a restaurant and sat there until I was better. That is why I was so long."

The two girls sat in the window seat, looking out at the lights and the stream of hurrying vehicles in the avenue. The younger one cuddled down with her head in her sister's lap.

"We will have to marry some day," she said dreamily—"both of us. We have so much money that we will not be allowed to disappoint the public. Do you want me to tell you the kind of a man I could love, Sis?"

"Go on, you scatterbrain," smiled the other.

"I could love a man with dark and kind blue eyes, who is gentle and respectful to poor girls, who is handsome and good and does not try to flirt. But I could love him only if he had an ambition, an object, some work to do in the world. I would not care how poor he was if I could help him build his way up. But, sister dear, the kind of man we always meet—the man who lives an idle life between society and his clubs—I could not love a man like that, even if his eyes were blue and he were ever so kind to poor girls whom he met in the street."

The Dead

JAMES JOYCE

Lily, the caretaker's daughter, was literally run off her feet. Hardly had she brought one gentleman into the little pantry behind the office on the ground floor and helped him off with his overcoat than the wheezy hall-door bell clanged again and she had to scamper along the bare hallway to let in another guest. It was well for her she had not to attend to the ladies also. But Miss Kate and Miss Julia had thought of that and had converted the bathroom upstairs into a ladies' dressing-room. Miss Kate and Miss Julia were there, gossiping and laughing and fussing, walking after each other to the head of the stairs, peering down over the banisters and calling down to Lily to ask her who had come.

It was always a great affair, the Misses Morkan's annual dance. Everybody who knew them came to it, members of the family, old friends of the family, the members of Julia's choir, any of Kate's pupils that were grown up enough, and even some of Mary Jane's pupils too. Never once had it fallen flat. For years and years it had gone off in splendid style, as long as anyone could remember; ever since Kate and Julia, after the death of their brother Pat, had left the house in Stoney Batter and taken Mary Jane, their only niece, to live with them in the dark, gaunt house on Usher's Island, the upper part of which they had rented from Mr Fulham, the corn-factor on the ground floor. That was a good thirty years ago if it was a day. Mary Jane, who was then a little girl in short clothes, was now the main prop of the household, for she had the organ in Haddington Road. She had been through the Academy and gave a pupils' concert every year in the upper room of the Antient Concert Rooms. Many of her pupils belonged to the better-class families on the Kingstown and Dalkey line. Old as they were, her aunts also did their share. Julia, though she was quite grey, was still the leading soprano in Adam and Eve's, and Kate, being too feeble to go about much, gave music lessons to beginners on the old square piano in the back room. Lily, the caretaker's daughter, did housemaid's work for them. Though their life was modest, they believed in eating well; the best of everything: diamond-bone sirloins, three-shilling tea and the best bottled stout. But Lily seldom made a mistake in the orders, so that she got on well with her three mistresses. They were fussy, that was all. But the only thing they would not stand was back answers.

Of course, they had good reason to be fussy on such a night. And then it was long after ten o'clock and yet there was no sign of Gabriel and his wife. Besides they were dreadfully afraid that Freddy Malins might turn up screwed. They would not wish for worlds that any of Mary Jane's pupils should see him under the influence; and when he was like that it was sometimes very hard to manage him. Freddy Malins always came late, but they wondered what could be keeping Gabriel: and that was what brought them every two minutes to the banisters to ask Lily had Gabriel or Freddy come.

'O, Mr Conroy,' said Lily to Gabriel when she opened the

door for him, 'Miss Kate and Miss Julia thought you were never coming. Good-night, Mrs Conroy.'

'I'll engage they did,' said Gabriel, 'but they forget that my wife here takes three mortal hours to dress herself.'

He stood on the mat, scraping the snow from his goloshes, while Lily led his wife to the foot of the stairs and called out: 'Miss Kate, here's Mrs Conroy.'

Kate and Julia came toddling down the dark stairs at once. Both of them kissed Gabriel's wife, said she must be perished alive, and asked was Gabriel with her.

'Here I am as right as the mail, Aunt Kate! Go on up. I'll follow,' called out Gabriel from the dark.

He continued scraping his feet vigorously while the three women went upstairs, laughing, to the ladies' dressing-room. A light fringe of snow lay like a cape on the shoulders of his overcoat and like toecaps on the toes of his goloshes; and, as the buttons of his overcoat slipped with a squeaking noise through the snow-stiffened frieze, a cold, fragrant air from out-of-doors escaped from crevices and folds.

'Is it snowing again, Mr Conroy?' asked Lily.

She had preceded him into the pantry to help him off with his overcoat. Gabriel smiled at the three syllables she had given his surname and glanced at her. She was a slim, growing girl, pale in complexion and with hay-coloured hair. The gas in the pantry made her look still paler. Gabriel had known her when she was a child and used to sit on the lowest step nursing a rag doll.

'Yes, Lily,' he answered, 'and I think we're in for a night of it.'

He looked up at the pantry ceiling, which was shaking with the stamping and shuffling of feet on the floor above, listened for a moment to the piano and then glanced at the girl, who was folding his overcoat carefully at the end of a shelf.

'Tell me, Lily,' he said in a friendly tone, 'do you still go to school?'

'O no, sir,' she answered. 'I'm done schooling this year and more.'

'O, then,' said Gabriel gaily, 'I suppose we'll be going to your wedding one of these fine days with your young man, eh?'

The girl glanced back at him over her shoulder and said with great bitterness: 'The men that is now is only all palaver and what they can get out of you.'

Gabriel coloured, as if he felt he had made a mistake and, without looking at her, kicked off his goloshes and flicked actively with his muffler at his patent-leather shoes.

He was a stout, tallish young man. The high colour of his cheeks pushed upwards even to his forehead, where it scattered itself in a few formless patches of pale red; and on his hairless face there scintillated restlessly the polished lenses and the bright gilt rims of the glasses which screened his delicate and restless eyes. His glossy black hair was parted in the middle and brushed in a long curve behind his ears where it curled slightly beneath the groove left by his hat.

When he had flicked lustre into his shoes he stood up and pulled his waistcoat down more tightly on his plump body. Then he took a coin rapidly from his pocket.

'O Lily,' he said, thrusting it into her hands, 'it's Christmas-time, isn't it? Just . . . here's a little . . .'

He walked rapidly towards the door.

'O no, sir!' cried the girl, following him. 'Really, sir, I wouldn't take it.'

'Christmas-time! Christmas-time!' said Gabriel, almost trotting to the stairs and waving his hand to her in deprecation.

The girl, seeing that he had gained the stairs, called out after him: 'Well, thank you, sir.'

He waited outside the drawing-room door until the waltz should finish, listening to the skirts that swept against it and to the shuffling of feet. He was still discomposed by the girl's bitter and sudden retort. It had cast a gloom over him which he tried to dispel by arranging his cuffs and the bows of his tie. He then took from his waistcoat pocket a little paper and glanced at the headings he had made for his speech. He was undecided about the lines from Robert Browning, for he feared they would be above the heads of his hearers. Some quotation that they would recognize from Shakespeare or from the Melodies would be better. The indelicate clacking of the men's heels and the shuffling of their soles reminded him that their grade of culture differed from his. He would only make himself ridiculous by quoting poetry to them which they could not understand. They would think that he was airing his superior education. He would fail with them just as he had failed with the girl in the pantry. He had taken up a wrong tone. His whole speech was a mistake from first to last, an utter failure.

Just then his aunts and his wife came out of the ladies' dressing-room. His aunts were two small, plainly dressed old women. Aunt Julia was an inch or so the taller. Her hair, drawn low over the tops of her ears, was grey; and grey also, with darker shadows, was her large flaccid face. Though she was stout in build and stood erect, her slow eyes and parted lips gave her the appearance of a woman who did not know where she was or where she was going. Aunt Kate was more vivacious.

Her face, healthier than her sister's, was all puckers and creases, like a shrivelled red apple, and her hair, braided in the same old-fashioned way, had not lost its ripe nut colour.

They both kissed Gabriel frankly. He was their favourite nephew, the son of their dead elder sister, Ellen, who had married T. J. Conroy of the Port and Docks.

'Gretta tells me you're not going to take a cab back to Monkstown tonight, Gabriel,' said Aunt Kate.

'No,' said Gabriel, turning to his wife, 'we had quite enough of that last year, hadn't we? Don't you remember, Aunt Kate, what a cold Gretta got out of it? Cab windows rattling all the way, and the east wind blowing in after we passed Merrion. Very jolly it was. Gretta caught a dreadful cold.'

Aunt Kate frowned severely and nodded her head at every word.

'Quite right, Gabriel, quite right,' she said. 'You can't be too careful.'

'But as for Gretta there,' said Gabriel, 'she'd walk home in the snow if she were let.'

Mrs Conroy laughed.

'Don't mind him, Aunt Kate,' she said. 'He's really an awful bother, what with green shades for Tom's eyes at night and making him do the dumb-bells, and forcing Eva to eat the stirabout. The poor child! And she simply hates the sight of it! . . . O, but you'll never guess what he makes me wear now!'

She broke out into a peal of laughter and glanced at her husband, whose admiring and happy eyes had been wandering from her dress to her face and hair. The two aunts laughed heartily, too, for Gabriel's solicitude was a standing joke with them.

'Goloshes!' said Mrs Conroy. 'That's the latest. Whenever it's wet underfoot I must put on my goloshes. Tonight even, he wanted me to put them on, but I wouldn't. The next thing he'll buy me will be a diving suit.'

Gabriel laughed nervously and patted his tie reassuringly, while Aunt Kate nearly doubled herself, so heartily did she enjoy the joke. The smile soon faded from Aunt Julia's face and her mirthless eyes were directed towards her nephew's face. After a pause she asked: 'And what are goloshes, Gabriel?'

'Goloshes, Julia!' exclaimed her sister. 'Goodness me, don't you know what goloshes are? You wear them over your . . . over your boots, Gretta, isn't it?'

'Yes,' said Mrs Conroy. 'Guttapercha things. We both have a pair now. Gabriel says everyone wears them on the continent.'

'O, on the continent,' murmured Aunt Julia, nodding her head slowly.

Gabriel knitted his brows and said, as if he were slightly angered: 'It's nothing very wonderful, but Gretta thinks it very funny because she says the word reminds her of Christy Minstrels.'

'But tell me, Gabriel,' said Aunt Kate, with brisk tact. 'Of course, you've seen about the room. Gretta was saying . . .'

'O, the room is all right,' replied Gabriel. 'I've taken one in the Gresham.'

'To be sure,' said Aunt Kate, 'by far the best thing to do. And the children, Gretta, you're not anxious about them?'

'O, for one night,' said Mrs Conroy. 'Besides, Bessie will look after them.'

'To be sure,' said Aunt Kate again. 'What a comfort it is to have a girl like that, one you can depend on! There's that Lily,

I'm sure I don't know what has come over her lately. She's not the girl she was at all.'

Gabriel was about to ask his aunt some questions on this point, but she broke off suddenly to gaze after her sister, who had wandered down the stairs and was craning her neck over the banisters.

'Now, I ask you,' she said almost testily, 'where is Julia going? Julia! Julia! Where are you going?'

Julia, who had gone half-way down one flight, came back and announced blandly: 'Here's Freddy.'

At the same moment a clapping of hands and a final flourish of the pianist told that the waltz had ended. The drawing-room door was opened from within and some couples came out. Aunt Kate drew Gabriel aside hurriedly and whispered into his ear: 'Slip down, Gabriel, like a good fellow and see if he's all right, and don't let him up if he's screwed. I'm sure he's screwed. I'm sure he is.'

Gabriel went to the stairs and listened over the banisters. He could hear two persons talking in the pantry. Then he recognised Freddy Malins' laugh. He went down the stairs noisily.

'It's such a relief,' said Aunt Kate to Mrs Conroy, 'that Gabriel is here. I always feel easier in my mind when he's here . . . Julia, there's Miss Daly and Miss Power will take some refreshment. Thanks for your beautiful waltz, Miss Daly. It made lovely time.'

A tall wizen-faced man, with a stiff grizzled moustache and swarthy skin, who was passing out with his partner, said: 'And may we have some refreshment, too, Miss Morkan?'

'Julia,' said Aunt Kate summarily, 'and here's Mr Browne

and Miss Furlong. Take them in, Julia, with Miss Daly and Miss Power.'

'I'm the man for the ladies,' said Mr Browne, pursing his lips until his moustache bristled and smiling in all his wrinkles. 'You know, Miss Morkan, the reason they are so fond of me is –'

He did not finish his sentence, but, seeing that Aunt Kate was out of earshot, at once led the three young ladies into the back room. The middle of the room was occupied by two square tables placed end to end, and on these Aunt Julia and the caretaker were straightening and smoothing a large cloth. On the sideboard were arrayed dishes and plates, and glasses and bundles of knives and forks and spoons. The top of the closed square piano served also as a sideboard for viands and sweets. At a smaller sideboard in one corner two young men were standing, drinking hopbitters.

Mr Browne led his charges thither and invited them all, in jest, to some ladies' punch, hot, strong and sweet. As they said they never took anything strong, he opened three bottles of lemonade for them. Then he asked one of the young men to move aside, and, taking hold of the decanter, filled out for himself a goodly measure of whiskey. The young men eyed him respectfully while he took a trial sip.

'God help me,' he said, smiling, 'it's the doctor's orders.'

His wizened face broke into a broader smile, and the three young ladies laughed in musical echo to his pleasantry, swaying their bodies to and fro, with nervous jerks of their shoulders. The boldest said: 'O, now, Mr Browne, I'm sure the doctor never ordered anything of the kind.'

Mr Browne took another sip of his whiskey and said, with sidling mimicry: 'Well, you see, I'm like the famous Mrs

Cassidy, who is reported to have said: "Now, Mary Grimes, if I don't take it, make me take it, for I feel I want it."'

His hot face had leaned forward a little too confidentially and he had assumed a very low Dublin accent so that the young ladies, with one instinct, received his speech in silence. Miss Furlong, who was one of Mary Jane's pupils, asked Miss Daly what was the name of the pretty waltz she had played; and Mr Browne, seeing that he was ignored, turned promptly to the two young men who were more appreciative.

A red-faced young woman, dressed in pansy, came into the room, excitedly clapping her hands and crying: 'Quadrilles! Quadrilles!'

Close on her heels came Aunt Kate, crying: 'Two gentlemen and three ladies, Mary Jane!'

'O, here's Mr Bergin and Mr Kerrigan,' said Mary Jane. 'Mr Kerrigan, will you take Miss Power? Miss Furlong, may I get you a partner, Mr Bergin. O, that'll just do now.'

'Three ladies, Mary Jane,' said Aunt Kate.

The two young gentlemen asked the ladies if they might have the pleasure, and Mary Jane turned to Miss Daly.

'O, Miss Daly, you're really awfully good, after playing for the last two dances, but really we're so short of ladies tonight.'

'I don't mind in the least, Miss Morkan.'

'But I've a nice partner for you, Mr Bartell D'Arcy, the tenor. I'll get him to sing later on. All Dublin is raving about him.'

'Lovely voice, lovely voice!' said Aunt Kate.

As the piano had twice begun the prelude to the first figure Mary Jane led her recruits quickly from the room. They had hardly gone when Aunt Julia wandered slowly into the room, looking behind her at something.

'What is the matter, Julia?' asked Aunt Kate anxiously. 'Who is it?'

Julia, who was carrying in a column of table-napkins, turned to her sister and said, simply, as if the question had surprised her: 'It's only Freddy, Kate, and Gabriel with him.'

In fact right behind her Gabriel could be seen piloting Freddy Malins across the landing. The latter, a young man of about forty, was of Gabriel's size and build, with very round shoulders. His face was fleshy and pallid, touched with colour only at the thick hanging lobes of his ears and at the wide wings of his nose. He had coarse features, a blunt nose, a convex and receding brow, tumid and protruded lips. His heavy-lidded eyes and the disorder of his scanty hair made him look sleepy. He was laughing heartily in a high key at a story which he had been telling Gabriel on the stairs and at the same time rubbing the knuckles of his left fist backwards and forwards into his left eye.

'Good-evening, Freddy,' said Aunt Julia.

Freddy Malins bade the Misses Morkan good-evening in what seemed an offhand fashion by reason of the habitual catch in his voice and then, seeing that Mr Browne was grinning at him from the sideboard, crossed the room on rather shaky legs and began to repeat in an undertone the story he had just told to Gabriel.

'He's not so bad, is he?' said Aunt Kate to Gabriel.

Gabriel's brows were dark but he raised them quickly and answered: 'O, no, hardly noticeable.'

'Now, isn't he a terrible fellow!' she said. 'And his poor

mother made him take the pledge on New Year's Eve. But come on, Gabriel, into the drawing-room.'

Before leaving the room with Gabriel she signalled to Mr Browne by frowning and shaking her forefinger in warning to and fro. Mr Browne nodded in answer and, when she had gone, said to Freddy Malins: 'Now, then, Teddy, I'm going to fill you out a good glass of lemonade just to buck you up.'

Freddy Malins, who was nearing the climax of his story, waved the offer aside impatiently but Mr Browne, having first called Freddy Malins' attention to a disarray in his dress, filled out and handed him a full glass of lemonade. Freddy Malins' left hand accepted the glass mechanically, his right hand being engaged in the mechanical readjustment of his dress. Mr Browne, whose face was once more wrinkling with mirth, poured out for himself a glass of whiskey while Freddy Malins exploded, before he had well reached the climax of his story, in a kink of high-pitched bronchitic laughter and, setting down his untasted and overflowing glass, began to rub the knuckles of his left fist backwards and forwards into his left eye, repeating words of his last phrase as well as his fit of laughter would allow him.

Gabriel could not listen while Mary Jane was playing her Academy piece, full of runs and difficult passages, to the hushed drawing-room. He liked music but the piece she was playing had no melody for him and he doubted whether it had any melody for the other listeners, though they had begged Mary Jane to play something. Four young men, who had come from the refreshment-room to stand in the doorway at the sound of the piano, had gone away quietly in couples after a few minutes.

The only persons who seemed to follow the music were Mary Jane herself, her hands racing along the keyboard or lifted from it at the pauses like those of a priestess in momentary imprecation, and Aunt Kate standing at her elbow to turn the page.

Gabriel's eyes, irritated by the floor, which glittered with beeswax under the heavy chandelier, wandered to the wall above the piano. A picture of the balcony scene in *Romeo and Juliet* hung there and beside it was a picture of the two murdered princes in the Tower which Aunt Julia had worked in red, blue and brown wools when she was a girl. Probably in the school they had gone to as girls that kind of work had been taught for one year. His mother had worked for him as a birthday present a waistcoat of purple tabinet, with little foxes' heads upon it, lined with brown satin and having round mulberry buttons. It was strange that his mother had had no musical talent though Aunt Kate used to call her the brains carrier of the Morkan family. Both she and Julia had always seemed a little proud of their serious and matronly sister. Her photograph stood before the pier-glass. She held an open book on her knees and was pointing out something in it to Constantine who, dressed in a man-o'-war suit, lay at her feet. It was she who had chosen the names of her sons for she was very sensible of the dignity of family life. Thanks to her, Constantine was now senior curate in Balbriggan and, thanks to her, Gabriel himself had taken his degree in the Royal University. A shadow passed over his face as he remembered her sullen opposition to his marriage. Some slighting phrases she had used still rankled in his memory; she had once spoken of Gretta as being country cute and that was not true of Gretta at all. It was Gretta who had nursed her during all her last long illness in their house at Monkstown.

He knew that Mary Jane must be near the end of her piece for she was playing again the opening melody with runs of scales after every bar and while he waited for the end the resentment died down in his heart. The piece ended with a trill of octaves in the treble and a final deep octave in the bass. Great applause greeted Mary Jane as, blushing and rolling up her music nervously, she escaped from the room. The most vigorous clapping came from the four young men in the doorway who had gone away to the refreshment-room at the beginning of the piece but had come back when the piano had stopped.

Lancers were arranged. Gabriel found himself partnered with Miss Ivors. She was a frank-mannered talkative young lady, with a freckled face and prominent brown eyes. She did not wear a low-cut bodice and the large brooch which was fixed in the front of her collar bore on it an Irish device and motto.

When they had taken their places she said abruptly: 'I have a crow to pluck with you.'

'With me?' said Gabriel.

She nodded her head gravely.

'What is it?' asked Gabriel, smiling at her solemn manner.

'Who is G.C.?' answered Miss Ivors, turning her eyes upon him.

Gabriel coloured and was about to knit his brows, as if he did not understand, when she said bluntly: 'O, innocent Amy! I have found out that you write for *The Daily Express*. Now, aren't you ashamed of yourself?'

'Why should I be ashamed of myself?' asked Gabriel, blinking his eyes and trying to smile.

'Well, I'm ashamed of you,' said Miss Ivors frankly. 'To

say you'd write for a paper like that. I didn't think you were a
West Briton.' A look of perplexity appeared on Gabriel's face.
It was true that he wrote a literary column every Wednesday
in *The Daily Express*, for which he was paid fifteen shillings.
But that did not make him a West Briton surely. The books he
received for review were almost more welcome than the paltry
cheque. He loved to feel the covers and turn over the pages of
newly printed books. Nearly every day when his teaching in the
college was ended he used to wander down the quays to the
second-hand booksellers, to Hickey's on Bachelor's Walk, to
Webb's or Massey's on Aston's Quay, or to O'Clohissey's in the
by-street. He did not know how to meet her charge. He wanted
to say that literature was above politics. But they were friends of
many years' standing and their careers had been parallel, first at
the University and then as teachers: he could not risk a grandi-
ose phrase with her. He continued blinking his eyes and trying
to smile and murmured lamely that he saw nothing political in
writing reviews of books.

When their turn to cross had come he was still perplexed
and inattentive. Miss Ivors promptly took his hand in a warm
grasp and said in a soft friendly tone: 'Of course, I was only
joking. Come, we cross now.'

When they were together again she spoke of the University
question and Gabriel felt more at ease. A friend of hers had
shown her his review of Browning's poems. That was how she
had found out the secret: but she liked the review immensely.
Then she said suddenly: 'O, Mr Conroy, will you come for an
excursion to the Aran Isles this summer? We're going to stay
there a whole month. It will be splendid out in the Atlantic.
You ought to come. Mr Clancy is coming, and Mr Kilkelly and

Kathleen Kearney. It would be splendid for Gretta too if she'd come. She's from Connacht, isn't she?'

'Her people are,' said Gabriel shortly.

'But you will come, won't you?' said Miss Ivors, laying her warm hand eagerly on his arm.

'The fact is,' said Gabriel, 'I have just arranged to go –'

'Go where?' asked Miss Ivors.

'Well, you know, every year I go for a cycling tour with some fellows and so –'

'But where?' asked Miss Ivors.

'Well, we usually go to France or Belgium or perhaps Germany,' said Gabriel awkwardly.

'And why do you go to France and Belgium,' said Miss Ivors, 'instead of visiting your own land?'

'Well,' said Gabriel, 'it's partly to keep in touch with the languages and partly for a change.'

'And haven't you your own language to keep in touch with – Irish?' asked Miss Ivors.

'Well,' said Gabriel, 'if it comes to that, you know, Irish is not my language.'

Their neighbours had turned to listen to the cross-examination. Gabriel glanced right and left nervously and tried to keep his good humour under the ordeal which was making a blush invade his forehead.

'And haven't you your own land to visit,' continued Miss Ivors, 'that you know nothing of, your own people, and your own country?'

'O, to tell you the truth,' retorted Gabriel suddenly, 'I'm sick of my own country, sick of it!'

'Why?' asked Miss Ivors.

Gabriel did not answer for his retort had heated him.

'Why?' repeated Miss Ivors.

They had to go visiting together and, as he had not answered her, Miss Ivors said warmly: 'Of course, you've no answer.'

Gabriel tried to cover his agitation by taking part in the dance with great energy. He avoided her eyes for he had seen a sour expression on her face. But when they met in the long chain he was surprised to feel his hand firmly pressed. She looked at him from under her brows for a moment quizzically until he smiled. Then, just as the chain was about to start again, she stood on tiptoe and whispered into his ear: 'West Briton!'

When the lancers were over Gabriel went away to a remote corner of the room where Freddy Malins' mother was sitting. She was a stout feeble old woman with white hair. Her voice had a catch in it like her son's and she stuttered slightly. She had been told that Freddy had come and that he was nearly all right. Gabriel asked her whether she had had a good crossing. She lived with her married daughter in Glasgow and came to Dublin on a visit once a year. She answered placidly that she had had a beautiful crossing and that the captain had been most attentive to her. She spoke also of the beautiful house her daughter kept in Glasgow, and of all the friends they had there. While her tongue rambled on Gabriel tried to banish from his mind all memory of the unpleasant incident with Miss Ivors. Of course the girl or woman, or whatever she was, was an enthusiast but there was a time for all things. Perhaps he ought not to have answered her like that. But she had no right to call him a West Briton before people, even in joke. She had tried to make him ridiculous before people, heckling him and staring at him with her rabbit's eyes.

He saw his wife making her way towards him through the waltzing couples. When she reached him she said into his ear: 'Gabriel, Aunt Kate wants to know won't you carve the goose as usual. Miss Daly will carve the ham and I'll do the pudding.'

'All right,' said Gabriel.

'She's sending in the younger ones first as soon as this waltz is over so that we'll have the table to ourselves.'

'Were you dancing?' asked Gabriel.

'Of course I was. Didn't you see me? What row had you with Molly Ivors?'

'No row. Why? Did she say so?'

'Something like that. I'm trying to get that Mr D'Arcy to sing. He's full of conceit, I think.'

'There was no row,' said Gabriel moodily, 'only she wanted me to go for a trip to the west of Ireland and I said I wouldn't.'

His wife clasped her hands excitedly and gave a little jump.

'O, do go, Gabriel,' she cried. 'I'd love to see Galway again.'

'You can go if you like,' said Gabriel coldly.

She looked at him for a moment, then turned to Mrs Malins and said: 'There's a nice husband for you, Mrs Malins.'

While she was threading her way back across the room Mrs Malins, without adverting to the interruption, went on to tell Gabriel what beautiful places there were in Scotland and beautiful scenery. Her son-in-law brought them every year to the lakes and they used to go fishing. Her son-in-law was a splendid fisher. One day he caught a beautiful big fish and the man in the hotel cooked it for their dinner.

Gabriel hardly heard what she said. Now that supper was coming near he began to think again about his speech and about the quotation. When he saw Freddy Malins coming across the room to visit his mother Gabriel left the chair free for him and retired into the embrasure of the window. The room had already cleared and from the back room came the clatter of plates and knives. Those who still remained in the drawing-room seemed tired of dancing and were conversing quietly in little groups. Gabriel's warm trembling fingers tapped the cold pane of the window. How cool it must be outside! How pleasant it would be to walk out alone, first along by the river and then through the park! The snow would be lying on the branches of the trees and forming a bright cap on the top of the Wellington Monument. How much more pleasant it would be there than at the supper-table!

He ran over the headings of his speech: Irish hospitality, sad memories, the Three Graces, Paris, the quotation from Browning. He repeated to himself a phrase he had written in his review: 'One feels that one is listening to a thought-tormented music.' Miss Ivors had praised the review. Was she sincere? Had she really any life of her own behind all her propagandism? There had never been any ill-feeling between them until that night. It unnerved him to think that she would be at the supper-table, looking up at him while he spoke with her critical quizzing eyes. Perhaps she would not be sorry to see him fail in his speech. An idea came into his mind and gave him courage. He would say, alluding to Aunt Kate and Aunt Julia: 'Ladies and Gentlemen, the generation which is now on the wane among us may have had its faults but for my part I think it had certain qualities of hospitality, of humour, of humanity, which the new and very serious and hyper-educated generation that is growing up around us seems to me to lack.' Very good:

that was one for Miss Ivors. What did he care that his aunts were only two ignorant old women?

A murmur in the room attracted his attention. Mr Browne was advancing from the door, gallantly escorting Aunt Julia, who leaned upon his arm, smiling and hanging her head. An irregular musketry of applause escorted her also as far as the piano and then, as Mary Jane seated herself on the stool, and Aunt Julia, no longer smiling, half turned so as to pitch her voice fairly into the room, gradually ceased. Gabriel recognised the prelude. It was that of an old song of Aunt Julia's – *Arrayed for the Bridal.* Her voice, strong and clear in tone, attacked with great spirit the runs which embellish the air and though she sang very rapidly she did not miss even the smallest of the grace notes. To follow the voice, without looking at the singer's face, was to feel and share the excitement of swift and secure flight. Gabriel applauded loudly with all the others at the close of the song and loud applause was borne in from the invisible supper-table. It sounded so genuine that a little colour struggled into Aunt Julia's face as she bent to replace in the music-stand the old leather-bound song-book that had her initials on the cover. Freddy Malins, who had listened with his head perched sideways to hear her better, was still applauding when everyone else had ceased and talking animatedly to his mother who nodded her head gravely and slowly in acquiescence. At last, when he could clap no more, he stood up suddenly and hurried across the room to Aunt Julia whose hand he seized and held in both his hands, shaking it when words failed him or the catch in his voice proved too much for him.

'I was just telling my mother,' he said, 'I never heard you sing so well, never. No, I never heard your voice so good as it is tonight. Now! Would you believe that now? That's the truth. Upon my word and honour that's the truth. I never heard your voice sound so fresh and so . . . so clear and fresh, never.'

Aunt Julia smiled broadly and murmured something about compliments as she released her hand from his grasp. Mr Browne extended his open hand towards her and said to those who were near him in the manner of a showman introducing a prodigy to an audience: 'Miss Julia Morkan, my latest discovery!'

He was laughing very heartily at this himself when Freddy Malins turned to him and said: 'Well, Browne, if you're serious you might make a worse discovery. All I can say is I never heard her sing half so well as long as I am coming here. And that's the honest truth.'

'Neither did I,' said Mr Browne. 'I think her voice has greatly improved.'

Aunt Julia shrugged her shoulders and said with meek pride: 'Thirty years ago I hadn't a bad voice as voices go.'

'I often told Julia,' said Aunt Kate emphatically, 'that she was simply thrown away in that choir. But she never would be said by me.'

She turned as if to appeal to the good sense of the others against a refractory child while Aunt Julia gazed in front of her, a vague smile of reminiscence playing on her face.

'No,' continued Aunt Kate, 'she wouldn't be said or led by anyone, slaving there in that choir night and day, night and day. Six o'clock on Christmas morning! And all for what?'

'Well, isn't it for the honour of God, Aunt Kate?' asked Mary Jane, twisting round on the piano-stool and smiling.

Aunt Kate turned fiercely on her niece and said: 'I know all about the honour of God, Mary Jane, but I think it's not at all honourable for the pope to turn out the women out of the choirs that have slaved there all their lives and put little whipper-snappers of boys over their heads. I suppose it is for the good of the Church if the pope does it. But it's not just, Mary Jane, and it's not right.'

She had worked herself into a passion and would have continued in defence of her sister for it was a sore subject with her but Mary Jane, seeing that all the dancers had come back, intervened pacifically: 'Now, Aunt Kate, you're giving scandal to Mr Browne who is of the other persuasion.' Aunt Kate turned to Mr Browne, who was grinning at this allusion to his religion, and said hastily: 'O, I don't question the pope's being right. I'm only a stupid old woman and I wouldn't presume to do such a thing. But there's such a thing as common everyday politeness and gratitude. And if I were in Julia's place I'd tell that Father Healey straight up to his face . . .'

'And besides, Aunt Kate,' said Mary Jane, 'we really are all hungry and when we are hungry we are all very quarrelsome.'

'And when we are thirsty we are also quarrelsome,' added Mr Browne.

'So that we had better go to supper,' said Mary Jane, 'and finish the discussion afterwards.'

On the landing outside the drawing-room Gabriel found his wife and Mary Jane trying to persuade Miss Ivors to stay for supper. But Miss Ivors, who had put on her hat and was buttoning her cloak, would not stay. She did not feel in the least hungry and she had already overstayed her time.

'But only for ten minutes, Molly,' said Mrs Conroy. 'That won't delay you.'

'To take a pick itself,' said Mary Jane, 'after all your dancing.'

'I really couldn't,' said Miss Ivors.

'I am afraid you didn't enjoy yourself at all,' said Mary Jane hopelessly.

'Ever so much, I assure you,' said Miss Ivors, 'but you really must let me run off now.'

'But how can you get home?' asked Mrs Conroy.

'O, it's only two steps up the quay.'

Gabriel hesitated a moment and said: 'If you will allow me, Miss Ivors, I'll see you home if you are really obliged to go.'

But Miss Ivors broke away from them.

'I won't hear of it,' she cried. 'For goodness' sake go in to your suppers and don't mind me. I'm quite well able to take care of myself.'

'Well, you're the comical girl, Molly,' said Mrs Conroy frankly.

'*Beannacht libh,*' cried Miss Ivors, with a laugh, as she ran down the staircase.

Mary Jane gazed after her, a moody puzzled expression on her face, while Mrs Conroy leaned over the banisters to listen for the hall-door. Gabriel asked himself was he the cause of her abrupt departure. But she did not seem to be in ill humour: she had gone away laughing. He stared blankly down the staircase.

At the moment Aunt Kate came toddling out of the supper-room, almost wringing her hands in despair.

'Where is Gabriel?' she cried. 'Where on earth is Gabriel? There's everyone waiting in there, stage to let, and nobody to carve the goose!'

'Here I am, Aunt Kate!' cried Gabriel, with sudden animation, 'ready to carve a flock of geese, if necessary.'

A fat brown goose lay at one end of the table and at the

other end, on a bed of creased paper strewn with sprigs of parsley, lay a great ham, stripped of its outer skin and peppered over with crust crumbs, a neat paper frill round its shin and beside this was a round of spiced beef. Between these rival ends ran parallel lines of side-dishes: two little minsters of jelly, red and yellow; a shallow dish full of blocks of blancmange and red jam, a large green leaf-shaped dish with a stalk-shaped handle, on which lay bunches of purple raisins and peeled almonds, a companion dish on which lay a solid rectangle of Smyrna figs, a dish of custard topped with grated nutmeg, a small bowl full of chocolates and sweets wrapped in gold and silver papers and a glass vase in which stood some tall celery stalks. In the centre of the table there stood, as sentries to a fruit-stand which upheld a pyramid of oranges and American apples, two squat old-fashioned decanters of cut glass, one containing port and the other dark sherry. On the closed square piano a pudding in a huge yellow dish lay in waiting and behind it were three squads of bottles of stout and ale and minerals, drawn up according to the colours of their uniforms, the first two black, with brown and red labels, the third and smallest squad white, with transverse green sashes.

Gabriel took his seat boldly at the head of the table and, having looked to the edge of the carver, plunged his fork firmly into the goose. He felt quite at ease now for he was an expert carver and liked nothing better than to find himself at the head of a well-laden table.

'Miss Furlong, what shall I send you?' he asked. 'A wing or a slice of the breast?'

'Just a small slice of the breast.'

'Miss Higgins, what for you?'

'O, anything at all, Mr Conroy.'

While Gabriel and Miss Daly exchanged plates of goose and plates of ham and spiced beef Lily went from guest to guest with a dish of hot floury potatoes wrapped in a white napkin. This was Mary Jane's idea and she had also suggested apple sauce for the goose but Aunt Kate had said that plain roast goose without any apple sauce had always been good enough for her and she hoped she might never eat worse. Mary Jane waited on her pupils and saw that they got the best slices and Aunt Kate and Aunt Julia opened and carried across from the piano bottles of stout and ale for the gentlemen and bottles of minerals for the ladies. There was a great deal of confusion and laughter and noise, the noise of orders and counter-orders, of knives and forks, of corks and glass-stoppers. Gabriel began to carve second helpings as soon as he had finished the first round without serving himself. Everyone protested loudly so that he compromised by taking a long draught of stout for he had found the carving hot work. Mary Jane settled down quietly to her supper but Aunt Kate and Aunt Julia were still toddling round the table, walking on each other's heels, getting in each other's way and giving each other unheeded orders. Mr Browne begged of them to sit down and eat their suppers and so did Gabriel but they said there was time enough, so that, at last, Freddy Malins stood up and, capturing Aunt Kate, plumped her down on her chair amid general laughter.

When everyone had been well served Gabriel said, smiling: 'Now, if anyone wants a little more of what vulgar people call stuffing let him or her speak.'

A chorus of voices invited him to begin his own supper and

Lily came forward with three potatoes which she had reserved for him.

'Very well,' said Gabriel amiably, as he took another preparatory draught, 'kindly forget my existence, ladies and gentlemen, for a few minutes.'

He set to his supper and took no part in the conversation with which the table covered Lily's removal of the plates. The subject of talk was the opera company which was then at the Theatre Royal. Mr Bartell D'Arcy, the tenor, a dark-complexioned young man with a smart moustache, praised very highly the leading contralto of the company but Miss Furlong thought she had a rather vulgar style of production. Freddy Malins said there was a negro chieftain singing in the second part of the Gaiety pantomime who had one of the finest tenor voices he had ever heard.

'Have you heard him?' he asked Mr Bartell D'Arcy across the table.

'No,' answered Mr Bartell D'Arcy carelessly.

'Because,' Freddy Malins explained, 'now I'd be curious to hear your opinion of him. I think he has a grand voice.'

'It takes Teddy to find out the really good things,' said Mr Browne familiarly to the table.

'And why couldn't he have a voice too?' asked Freddy Malins sharply. 'Is it because he's only a black?'

Nobody answered this question and Mary Jane led the table back to the legitimate opera. One of her pupils had given her a pass for *Mignon*. Of course it was very fine, she said, but it made her think of poor Georgina Burns. Mr Browne could go back farther still, to the old Italian companies that used to come to Dublin – Tietjens, Ilma de Murzka, Campanini, the great Trebelli, Giuglini, Ravelli, Aramburo. Those were the days, he said, when there was something like singing to be heard in Dublin. He told too of how the top gallery of the old Royal used to be packed night after night, of how one night an Italian tenor had sung five encores to *Let Me Like a Soldier Fall*, introducing a high C every time, and of how the gallery boys would sometimes in their enthusiasm unyoke the horses from the carriage of some great *prima donna* and pull her themselves through the streets to her hotel. Why did they never play the grand old operas now, he asked, *Dinorah, Lucrezia Borgia*? Because they could not get the voices to sing them: that was why.

'O, well,' said Mr Bartell D'Arcy, 'I presume there are as good singers today as there were then.'

'Where are they?' asked Mr Browne defiantly.

'In London, Paris, Milan,' said Mr Bartell D'Arcy warmly. 'I suppose Caruso, for example, is quite as good, if not better than any of the men you have mentioned.'

'Maybe so,' said Mr Browne. 'but I may tell you I doubt it strongly.'

'O, I'd give anything to hear Caruso sing,' said Mary Jane.

'For me,' said Aunt Kate, who had been picking a bone, 'there was only one tenor. To please me, I mean. But I suppose none of you ever heard of him.'

'Who was he, Miss Morkan?' asked Mr Bartell D'Arcy politely.

'His name,' said Aunt Kate, 'was Parkinson. I heard him when he was in his prime and I think he had then the purest tenor voice that was ever put into a man's throat.'

'Strange,' said Mr Bartell D'Arcy. 'I never even heard of him.'

'Yes, yes, Miss Morkan is right,' said Mr Browne. 'I remember hearing of old Parkinson but he's too far back for me.'

'A beautiful, pure, sweet, mellow English tenor,' said Aunt Kate with enthusiasm.

Gabriel having finished, the huge pudding was transferred to the table. The clatter of forks and spoons began again. Gabriel's wife served out spoonfuls of the pudding and passed the plates down the table. Midway down they were held up by Mary Jane, who replenished them with raspberry or orange jelly or with blancmange and jam. The pudding was of Aunt Julia's making and she received praises for it from all quarters. She herself said that it was not quite brown enough.

'Well, I hope, Miss Morkan,' said Mr Browne, 'that I'm brown enough for you because, you know, I'm all brown.'

All the gentlemen, except Gabriel, ate some of the pudding out of compliment to Aunt Julia. As Gabriel never ate sweets the celery had been left for him. Freddy Malins also took a stalk of celery and ate it with his pudding. He had been told that celery was a capital thing for the blood and he was just then under doctor's care. Mrs Malins, who had been silent all through the supper, said that her son was going down to Mount Melleray in a week or so. The table then spoke of Mount Melleray, how bracing the air was down there, how hospitable the monks were and how they never asked for a penny-piece from their guests.

'And do you mean to say,' asked Mr Browne incredulously, 'that a chap can go down there and put up there as if it were a hotel and live on the fat of the land and then come away without paying anything?'

'O, most people give some donation to the monastery when they leave,' said Mary Jane.

'I wish we had an institution like that in our church,' said Mr Browne candidly.

He was astonished to hear that the monks never spoke, got up at two in the morning and slept in their coffins. He asked what they did it for.

'That's the rule of the order,' said Aunt Kate firmly.

'Yes, but why?' asked Mr Browne.

Aunt Kate repeated that it was the rule, that was all. Mr Browne still seemed not to understand. Freddy Malins explained to him, as best he could, that the monks were trying to make up for the sins committed by all the sinners in the outside world. The explanation was not very clear for Mr Browne grinned and said: 'I like that idea very much but wouldn't a comfortable spring bed do them as well as a coffin?'

'The coffin,' said Mary Jane, 'is to remind them of their last end.'

As the subject had grown lugubrious it was buried in a silence of the table during which Mrs Malins could be heard saying to her neighbour in an indistinct undertone: 'They are very good men, the monks, very pious men.'

The raisins and almonds and figs and apples and oranges and chocolates and sweets were now passed about the table and Aunt Julia invited all the guests to have either port or sherry. At first Mr Bartell D'Arcy refused to take either but one of his neighbours nudged him and whispered something to him upon which he allowed his glass to be filled. Gradually as the last glasses were being filled the conversation ceased. A pause followed, broken only by the noise of the wine and by unsettlings of chairs. The Misses Morkan, all three, looked down at the tablecloth. Someone coughed once or twice and then a few gentlemen patted the table gently as a signal for silence. The silence came and Gabriel pushed back his chair and stood up.

The patting at once grew louder in encouragement and then ceased altogether. Gabriel leaned his ten trembling fingers on the tablecloth and smiled nervously at the company. Meeting a row of upturned faces he raised his eyes to the chandelier. The piano was playing a waltz tune and he could hear the skirts sweeping against the drawing-room door. People, perhaps, were standing in the snow on the quay outside, gazing up at the lighted windows and listening to the waltz music. The air was pure there. In the distance lay the park where the trees were weighted with snow. The Wellington Monument wore a gleaming cap of snow that flashed westward over the white field of Fifteen Acres.

He began: 'Ladies and Gentlemen, it has fallen to my lot this evening, as in years past, to perform a very pleasing task but a task for which I am afraid my poor powers as a speaker are all too inadequate.'

'No, no!' said Mr Browne.

'But, however that may be, I can only ask you tonight to take the will for the deed and to lend me your attention for a few moments while I endeavour to express to you in words what my feelings are on this occasion.

'Ladies and Gentlemen, it is not the first time that we have gathered together under this hospitable roof, around this hospitable board. It is not the first time that we have been the recipients – or perhaps, I had better say, the victims – of the hospitality of certain good ladies.'

He made a circle in the air with his arm and paused. Every-one laughed or smiled at Aunt Kate and Aunt Julia and Mary Jane who all turned crimson with pleasure. Gabriel went on more boldly: 'I feel more strongly with every recurring year that our country has no tradition which does it so much honour and which it should guard so jealously as that of its hospitality. It is a tradition that is unique as far as my experience goes (and I have visited not a few places abroad) among the modern nations. Some would say, perhaps, that with us it is rather a fail-ing than anything to be boasted of. But granted even that, it is, to my mind, a princely failing, and one that I trust will long be cultivated among us. Of one thing, at least, I am sure. As long as this one roof shelters the good ladies aforesaid – and I wish from my heart it may do so for many and many a long year to come – the tradition of genuine warm-hearted courteous Irish hospitality, which our forefathers have handed down to us and which we in turn must hand down to our descendants, is still alive among us.'

A hearty murmur of assent ran round the table. It shot through Gabriel's mind that Miss Ivors was not there and that she had gone away discourteously: and he said with confidence in himself: 'Ladies and Gentlemen, a new generation is growing up in our midst, a generation actuated by new ideas and new principles. It is serious and enthusiastic for these new ideas and its enthusiasm, even when it is misdirected, is, I believe, in the main sincere. But we are living in a sceptical and, if I may use the phrase, a thought-tormented age: and sometimes I fear that this new generation, educated or hyper-educated as it is, will lack those qualities of humanity, of hospitality, of kindly humour which belonged to an older day. Listening tonight to the names of all those great singers of the past it seemed to me, I must confess, that we were living in a less spacious age. Those days might, without exaggeration, be called spacious days: and if they are gone beyond recall let us hope, at least, that in gatherings such as this we shall still speak of them with pride and affection, still cherish in our hearts the memory of those dead and gone great ones whose fame the world will not willingly let die.'

'Hear, hear!' said Mr Browne loudly.

'But yet,' continued Gabriel, his voice falling into a softer inflection, 'there are always in gatherings such as this sadder thoughts that will recur to our minds: thoughts of the past, of youth, of changes, of absent faces that we miss here tonight. Our path through life is strewn with many such sad memories: and were we to brood upon them always we could not find the heart to go on bravely with our work among the living. We have all of us living duties and living affections which claim, and rightly claim, our strenuous endeavours.

'Therefore, I will not linger on the past. I will not let any gloomy moralising intrude upon us here tonight. Here we are gathered together for a brief moment from the bustle and rush of our everyday routine. We are met here as friends, in the spirit of good-fellowship, as colleagues, also to a certain extent, in the true spirit of *camaraderie*, and as the guests of – what shall I call them? – the Three Graces of the Dublin musical world.'

The table burst into applause and laughter at this allusion. Aunt Julia vainly asked each of her neighbours in turn to tell her what Gabriel had said.

'He says we are the Three Graces, Aunt Julia,' said Mary Jane.

Aunt Julia did not understand but she looked up, smiling, at Gabriel, who continued in the same vein: 'Ladies and Gentlemen, I will not attempt to play tonight the part that Paris played on another occasion. I will not attempt to choose between them. The task would be an invidious one and one beyond my poor powers. For when I view them in turn, whether it be our chief hostess herself, whose good heart, whose too good heart, has become a byword with all who know her, or her sister, who seems to be gifted with perennial youth and whose singing must have been a surprise and a revelation to us all tonight, or, last but not least, when I consider our youngest hostess, talented, cheerful, hard-working and the best of nieces, I confess, Ladies and Gentlemen, that I do not know to which of them I should award the prize.'

Gabriel glanced down at his aunts and, seeing the large smile on Aunt Julia's face and the tears which had risen to Aunt Kate's eyes, hastened to his close. He raised his glass of port gallantly, while every member of the company fingered a glass expectantly, and said loudly: 'Let us toast them all three together. Let us drink to their health, wealth, long life, happiness and prosperity and may they long continue to hold the proud and self-won position which they hold in their profession and the position of honour and affection which they hold in our hearts.'

All the guests stood up, glass in hand, and turning towards the three seated ladies, sang in unison, with Mr Browne as leader:

'For they are jolly gay fellows,
For they are jolly gay fellows,
For they are jolly gay fellows,
Which nobody can deny.'

Aunt Kate was making frank use of her handkerchief and even Aunt Julia seemed moved. Freddy Malins beat time with his pudding-fork and the singers turned towards one another, as if in melodious conference, while they sang with emphasis:

'Unless he tells a lie,
Unless he tells a lie.'

Then, turning once more towards their hostesses, they sang:

'For they are jolly gay fellows,
For they are jolly gay fellows,
For they are jolly gay fellows,
Which nobody can deny.'

The acclamation which followed was taken up beyond the door of the supper-room by many of the other guests and renewed time after time, Freddy Malins acting as officer with his fork on high.

The piercing morning air came into the hall where they were standing so that Aunt Kate said: 'Close the door, somebody. Mrs Malins will get her death of cold.'

'Browne is out there, Aunt Kate,' said Mary Jane.

'Browne is everywhere,' said Aunt Kate, lowering her voice.

Mary Jane laughed at her tone.

'Really,' she said archly, 'he is very attentive.'

'He has been laid on here like the gas,' said Aunt Kate in the same tone, 'all during the Christmas.'

She laughed herself this time good-humouredly and then added quickly: 'But tell him to come in, Mary Jane, and close the door. I hope to goodness he didn't hear me.'

At that moment the hall-door was opened and Mr Browne came in from the doorstep, laughing as if his heart would break. He was dressed in a long green overcoat with mock astrakhan cuffs and collar and wore on his head an oval fur cap. He pointed down the snow-covered quay from where the sound of shrill prolonged whistling was borne in.

'Teddy will have all the cabs in Dublin out,' he said.

Gabriel advanced from the little pantry behind the office, struggling into his overcoat and, looking round the hall, said: 'Gretta not down yet?'

'She's getting on her things, Gabriel,' said Aunt Kate.

'Who's playing up there?' asked Gabriel.

'Nobody. They're all gone.'

'O no, Aunt Kate,' said Mary Jane. 'Bartell D'Arcy and Miss O'Callaghan aren't gone yet.'

'Someone is fooling at the piano anyhow,' said Gabriel.

Mary Jane glanced at Gabriel and Mr Browne and said with a shiver: 'It makes me feel cold to look at you two gentlemen muffled up like that. I wouldn't like to face your journey home at this hour.'

'I'd like nothing better this minute,' said Mr Browne stoutly, 'than a rattling fine walk in the country or a fast drive with a good spanking goer between the shafts.'

'We used to have a very good horse and trap at home,' said Aunt Julia sadly.

'The never-to-be-forgotten Johnny,' said Mary Jane, laughing.

Aunt Kate and Gabriel laughed too.

'Why, what was wonderful about Johnny?' asked Mr Browne.

'The late lamented Patrick Morkan, our grandfather, that is,' explained Gabriel, 'commonly known in his later years as the old gentleman, was a glue-boiler.'

'O, now, Gabriel,' said Aunt Kate, laughing, 'he had a starch mill.'

'Well, glue or starch,' said Gabriel, 'the old gentleman had a horse by the name of Johnny. And Johnny used to work in the old gentleman's mill, walking round and round in order to drive the mill. That was all very well; but now comes the tragic part about Johnny. One fine day the old gentleman thought he'd like to drive out with the quality to a military review in the park.'

'The Lord have mercy on his soul,' said Aunt Kate compassionately.

'Amen,' said Gabriel. 'So the old gentleman, as I said, harnessed Johnny and put on his very best tall hat and his very best stock collar and drove out in grand style from his ancestral mansion somewhere near Back Lane, I think.'

Everyone laughed, even Mrs Malins, at Gabriel's manner and Aunt Kate said: 'O, now, Gabriel, he didn't live in Back Lane, really. Only the mill was there.'

'Out from the mansion of his forefathers,' continued Gabriel, 'he drove with Johnny. And everything went on beautifully until Johnny came in sight of King Billy's statue: and whether he fell in love with the horse King Billy sits on or whether he thought he was back again in the mill, anyhow he began to walk round the statue.'

Gabriel paced in a circle round the hall in his goloshes amid the laughter of the others.

'Round and round he went,' said Gabriel, 'and the old gentleman, who was a very pompous old gentleman, was highly indignant. "Go on, sir! What do you mean, sir? Johnny! Johnny! Most extraordinary conduct! Can't understand the horse!"'

The peals of laughter which followed Gabriel's imitation of the incident were interrupted by a resounding knock at the hall-door. Mary Jane ran to open it and let in Freddy Malins. Freddy Malins, with his hat well back on his head and his shoulders humped with cold, was puffing and steaming after his exertions.

'I could only get one cab,' he said.

'O, we'll find another along the quay,' said Gabriel.

'Yes,' said Aunt Kate. 'Better not keep Mrs Malins standing in the draught.'

Mrs Malins was helped down the front steps by her son and Mr Browne and, after many manoeuvres, hoisted into the cab. Freddy Malins clambered in after her and spent a long time settling her on the seat, Mr Browne helping him with advice. At last she was settled comfortably and Freddy Malins invited Mr Browne into the cab. There was a good deal of confused talk, and then Mr Browne got into the cab. The cabman settled his rug over his knees, and bent down for the address. The confusion grew greater and the cabman was directed differently by Freddy Malins and Mr Browne, each of whom had his head out through a window of the cab. The difficulty was to know where to drop Mr Browne along the route, and Aunt Kate, Aunt Julia and Mary Jane helped the discussion from the doorstep with cross-directions and contradictions and abundance of laughter. As for Freddy Malins he was speechless with laughter. He popped his head in and out of the window every moment to the great danger of his hat, and told his mother how the discussion was progressing, till at last Mr Browne shouted to the bewildered cabman above the din of everybody's laughter: 'Do you know Trinity College?'

'Yes, sir,' said the cabman.

'Well, drive bang up against Trinity College gates,' said Mr Browne, 'and then we'll tell you where to go. You understand now?'

'Yes, sir,' said the cabman.

'Make like a bird for Trinity College.'

'Right, sir,' said the cabman.

The horse was whipped up and the cab rattled off along the quay amid a chorus of laughter and adieus.

Gabriel had not gone to the door with the others. He was in a dark part of the hall gazing up the staircase. A woman was standing near the top of the first flight, in the shadow also. He could not see her face but he could see the terracotta and salmon-pink panels of her skirt which the shadow made appear black and white. It was his wife. She was leaning on the banisters, listening to something. Gabriel was surprised at her stillness and strained his ear to listen also. But he could hear little save the noise of laughter and dispute on the front steps, a few chords struck on the piano and a few notes of a man's voice singing.

He stood still in the gloom of the hall, trying to catch the air that the voice was singing and gazing up at his wife. There was grace and mystery in her attitude as if she were a symbol of something. He asked himself what is a woman standing on the stairs in the shadow, listening to distant music, a symbol of. If he were a painter he would paint her in that attitude. Her blue felt hat would show off the bronze of her hair against the darkness and the dark panels of her skirt would show off the light ones. *Distant Music* he would call the picture if he were a painter.

The hall-door was closed; and Aunt Kate, Aunt Julia and Mary Jane come down the hall, still laughing.

'Well, isn't Freddy terrible?' said Mary Jane. 'He's really terrible.'

Gabriel said nothing but pointed up the stairs towards where his wife was standing. Now that the hall-door was closed the voice and the piano could be heard more clearly. Gabriel held up his hand for them to be silent. The song seemed to be in the old Irish tonality and the singer seemed uncertain both of his words and of his voice. The voice, made plaintive by distance and by the singer's hoarseness, faintly illuminated the cadence of the air with words expressing grief:

'O, the rain falls on my heavy locks
And the dew wets my skin,
My babe lies cold . . .'

'O,' exclaimed Mary Jane. 'It's Bartell D'Arcy singing and he wouldn't sing all the night. O, I'll get him to sing a song before he goes.'

'O, do, Mary Jane,' said Aunt Kate.

Mary Jane brushed past the others and ran to the staircase, but before she reached it the singing stopped and the piano was closed abruptly.

'O, what a pity!' she cried. 'Is he coming down, Gretta?'

Gabriel heard his wife answer yes and saw her come down towards them. A few steps behind her were Mr Bartell D'Arcy and Miss O'Callaghan.

'O, Mr D'Arcy,' cried Mary Jane, 'it's downright mean of you to break off like that when we were all in raptures listening to you.'

'I have been at him all the evening,' said Miss O'Callaghan, 'and Mrs Conroy, too, and he told us he had a dreadful cold and couldn't sing.'

'O, Mr D'Arcy,' said Aunt Kate, 'now that was a great fib to tell.'

'Can't you see that I'm as hoarse as a crow?' said Mr D'Arcy roughly.

He went into the pantry hastily and put on his overcoat. The others, taken aback by his rude speech, could find nothing to say. Aunt Kate wrinkled her brows and made signs to the others to drop the subject. Mr D'Arcy stood swathing his neck carefully and frowning.

'It's the weather,' said Aunt Julia, after a pause.

'Yes, everybody has colds,' said Aunt Kate readily, 'everybody.'

'They say,' said Mary Jane, 'we haven't had snow like it for thirty years; and I read this morning in the newspapers that the snow is general all over Ireland.'

'I love the look of snow,' said Aunt Julia sadly.

'So do I,' said Miss O'Callaghan. 'I think Christmas is never really Christmas unless we have the snow on the ground.'

'But poor Mr D'Arcy doesn't like the snow,' said Aunt Kate, smiling.

Mr D'Arcy came from the pantry, fully swathed and buttoned, and in a repentant tone told them the history of his cold. Everyone gave him advice and said it was a great pity and urged him to be very careful of his throat in the night air. Gabriel watched his wife, who did not join in the conversation. She was standing right under the dusty fanlight and the flame of the gas lit up the rich bronze of her hair, which he had seen her drying at the fire a few days before. She was in the same attitude and seemed unaware of the talk about her. At last she turned towards them and Gabriel saw that there was colour on her cheeks and that her eyes were shining. A sudden tide of joy went leaping out of his heart.

'Mr D'Arcy,' she said, 'what is the name of that song you were singing?'

'It's called *The Lass of Aughrim*,' said Mr D'Arcy, 'but I couldn't remember it properly. Why? Do you know it?'

'*The Lass of Aughrim*,' she repeated. 'I couldn't think of the name.'

'It's a very nice air,' said Mary Jane. 'I'm sorry you were not in voice tonight.'

'Now, Mary Jane,' said Aunt Kate, 'don't annoy Mr D'Arcy. I won't have him annoyed.'

Seeing that all were ready to start she shepherded them to the door, where good-night was said: 'Well, good-night, Aunt Kate, and thanks for the pleasant evening.'

'Good-night, Gabriel. Good-night, Gretta!'

'Good-night, Aunt Kate, and thanks ever so much. Good-night, Aunt Julia.'

'O, good-night, Gretta, I didn't see you.'

'Good-night, Mr D'Arcy. Good-night, Miss O'Callaghan.'

'Good-night, Miss Morkan.'

'Good-night, again.'

'Good-night, all. Safe home.'

'Good-night. Good-night.'

The morning was still dark. A dull, yellow light brooded over the houses and the river; and the sky seemed to be descending. It was slushy underfoot; and only streaks and patches of snow lay on the roofs, on the parapets of the quay and on the area railings. The lamps were still burning redly in the murky air and, across the river, the palace of the Four Courts stood out menacingly against the heavy sky.

She was walking on before him with Mr Bartell D'Arcy, her shoes in a brown parcel tucked under one arm and her hands holding her skirt up from the slush. She had no longer any grace of attitude, but Gabriel's eyes were still bright with happiness. The blood went bounding along his veins; and the thoughts went rioting through his brain, proud, joyful, tender, valorous.

She was walking on before him so lightly and so erect that he longed to run after her noiselessly, catch her by the shoulders and say something foolish and affectionate into her ear. She seemed to him so frail that he longed to defend her against something and then to be alone with her. Moments of their secret life together burst like stars upon his memory. A heliotrope envelope was lying beside his breakfast-cup and he was caressing it with his hand. Birds were twittering in the ivy and the sunny web of the curtain was shimmering along the floor: he could not eat for happiness. They were standing on the crowded platform and he was placing a ticket inside the warm palm of her glove. He was standing with her in the cold, looking in through a grated window at a man making bottles in a roaring furnace. It was very cold. Her face, fragrant in the cold air, was quite close to his; and suddenly he called out to the man at the furnace: 'Is the fire hot, sir?'

But the man could not hear with the noise of the furnace. It was just as well. He might have answered rudely.

A wave of yet more tender joy escaped from his heart and went coursing in warm blood along his arteries. Like the tender fire of stars moments of their life together, that no one knew of or would ever know of, broke upon and illumined his memory. He longed to recall to her those moments, to make her forget the years of their dull existence together and remember only their moments of ecstasy. For the years, he felt, had not quenched his soul or hers. Their children, his writing, her household cares had not quenched all their souls' tender fire. In one letter that he had written to her then he had said: 'Why is it that words like these seem to me so dull and cold? Is it because there is no word tender enough to be your name?'

Like distant music these words that he had written years before were borne towards him from the past. He longed to be alone with her. When the others had gone away, when he and she were in the room in the hotel, then they would be alone together. He would call her softly: 'Gretta!'

Perhaps she would not hear at once: she would be undressing. Then something in his voice would strike her. She would turn and look at him . . .

At the corner of Winetavern Street they met a cab. He was glad of its rattling noise as it saved him from conversation. She was looking out of the window and seemed tired. The others spoke only a few words, pointing out some building or street.

The horse galloped along wearily under the murky morning sky, dragging his old rattling box after his heels, and Gabriel was again in a cab with her, galloping to catch the boat, galloping to their honeymoon.

As the cab drove across O'Connell Bridge Miss O'Callaghan said: 'They say you never cross O'Connell Bridge without seeing a white horse.'

'I see a white man this time,' said Gabriel.

'Where?' asked Mr Bartell D'Arcy.

Gabriel pointed to the statue, on which lay patches of snow. Then he nodded familiarly to it and waved his hand.

'Good-night, Dan,' he said gaily.

When the cab drew up before the hotel, Gabriel jumped out and, in spite of Mr Bartell D'Arcy's protest, paid the driver. He gave the man a shilling over his fare. The man saluted and said: 'A prosperous New Year to you, sir.'

'The same to you,' said Gabriel cordially.

She leaned for a moment on his arm in getting out of the cab and while standing at the kerbstone, bidding the others good-night. She leaned lightly on his arm, as lightly as when she had danced with him a few hours before. He had felt proud and happy then, happy that she was his, proud of her grace and wifely carriage. But now, after the kindling again of so many memories, the first touch of her body, musical and strange and perfumed, sent through him a keen pang of lust. Under cover of her silence he pressed her arm closely to his side; and, as they stood at the hotel door, he felt that they had escaped from their lives and duties, escaped from home and friends and run away together with wild and radiant hearts to a new adventure.

An old man was dozing in a great hooded chair in the hall.

He lit a candle in the office and went before them to the stairs. They followed him in silence, their feet falling in soft thuds on the thickly carpeted stairs. She mounted the stairs behind the porter, her head bowed in the ascent, her frail shoulders curved as with a burden, her skirt girt tightly about her. He could have flung his arms about her hips and held her still, for his arms were trembling with desire to seize her and only the stress of his nails against the palms of his hands held the wild impulse of his body in check. The porter halted on the stairs to settle his guttering candle. They halted, too, on the steps below him. In the silence Gabriel could hear the falling of the molten wax into the tray and the thumping of his own heart against his ribs.

The porter led them along a corridor and opened a door. Then he set his unstable candle down on a toilet-table and asked at what hour they were to be called in the morning.

'Eight,' said Gabriel.

The porter pointed to the tap of the electric-light and began a muttered apology, but Gabriel cut him short.

'We don't want any light. We have light enough from the street. And I say,' he added, pointing to the candle, 'you might remove that handsome article, like a good man.'

The porter took up his candle again, but slowly, for he was surprised by such a novel idea. Then he mumbled good-night and went out. Gabriel shot the lock to.

A ghastly light from the street lamp lay in a long shaft from one window to the door. Gabriel threw his overcoat and hat on a couch and crossed the room towards the window. He looked down into the street in order that his emotion might calm a little. Then he turned and leaned against a chest of drawers with his back to the light. She had taken off her hat and cloak and was standing before a large swinging mirror, unhooking her waist. Gabriel paused for a few moments, watching her, and then said: 'Gretta!'

She turned away from the mirror slowly and walked along the shaft of light towards him. Her face looked so serious and weary that the words would not pass Gabriel's lips. No, it was not the moment yet.

'You looked tired,' he said.

'I am a little,' she answered.

'You don't feel ill or weak?'

'No, tired: that's all.'

She went on to the window and stood there, looking out. Gabriel waited again and then, fearing that diffidence was about to conquer him, he said abruptly: 'By the way, Gretta!'

'What is it?'

'You know that poor fellow Malins?' he said quickly.

'Yes. What about him?'

'Well, poor fellow, he's a decent sort of chap, after all,' continued Gabriel in a false voice. 'He gave me back that sovereign I lent him, and I didn't expect it, really. It's a pity he wouldn't keep away from that Browne, because he's not a bad fellow, really.'

He was trembling now with annoyance. Why did she seem so abstracted? He did not know how he could begin. Was she annoyed, too, about something? If she would only turn to him or come to him of her own accord! To take her as she was would be brutal. No, he must see some ardour in her eyes first. He longed to be master of her strange mood.

'When did you lend him the pound?' she asked, after a pause.

Gabriel strove to restrain himself from breaking out into brutal language about the sottish Malins and his pound. He longed to cry to her from his soul, to crush her body against his, to overmaster her. But he said: 'O, at Christmas, when he opened that little Christmas-card shop in Henry Street.'

He was in such a fever of rage and desire that he did not hear her come from the window. She stood before him for an instant, looking at him strangely. Then, suddenly raising herself on tiptoe and resting her hands lightly on his shoulders, she kissed him.

'You are a very generous person, Gabriel,' she said.

Gabriel, trembling with delight at her sudden kiss and at the quaintness of her phrase, put his hands on her hair and began smoothing it back, scarcely touching it with his fingers. The washing had made it fine and brilliant. His heart was brimming over with happiness. Just when he was wishing for it she had come to him of her own accord. Perhaps her thoughts had been running with his. Perhaps she had felt the impetuous desire that was in him, and then the yielding mood had come upon her. Now that she had fallen to him so easily, he wondered why he had been so diffident.

He stood, holding her head between his hands. Then, slipping one arm swiftly about her body and drawing her towards him, he said softly: 'Gretta, dear, what are you thinking about?'

She did not answer nor yield wholly to his arm. He said again, softly: 'Tell me what it is, Gretta. I think I know what is the matter. Do I know?'

She did not answer at once. Then she said in an outburst of tears: 'O, I am thinking about that song, *The Lass of Aughrim*.'

She broke loose from him and ran to the bed and, throwing

her arms across the bed-rail, hid her face. Gabriel stood stock-still for a moment in astonishment and then followed her. As he passed in the way of the cheval-glass he caught sight of himself in full length, his broad, well-filled shirt-front, the face whose expression always puzzled him when he saw it in a mirror, and his glimmering gilt-rimmed eyeglasses. He halted a few paces from her and said: 'What about the song? Why does that make you cry?'

She raised her head from her arms and dried her eyes with the back of her hand like a child. A kinder note than he had intended went into his voice.

'Why, Gretta?' he asked.

'I am thinking about a person long ago who used to sing that song.'

'And who was the person long ago?' asked Gabriel, smiling.

'It was a person I used to know in Galway when I was living with my grandmother,' she said.

The smile passed away from Gabriel's face. A dull anger began to gather again at the back of his mind and the dull fires of his lust began to glow angrily in his veins.

'Someone you were in love with?' he asked ironically.

'It was a young boy I used to know,' she answered, 'named Michael Furey. He used to sing that song, *The Lass of Aughrim*. He was very delicate.'

Gabriel was silent. He did not wish her to think that he was interested in this delicate boy.

'I can see him so plainly,' she said, after a moment. 'Such eyes as he had: big, dark eyes! And such an expression in them – an expression!'

'O, then, you are in love with him?' said Gabriel.

'I used to go out walking with him,' she said, 'when I was in Galway.'

A thought flew across Gabriel's mind.

'Perhaps that was why you wanted to go to Galway with that Ivors girl?' he said coldly.

She looked at him and asked in surprise: 'What for?'

Her eyes made Gabriel feel awkward. He shrugged his shoulders and said: 'How do I know? To see him, perhaps.'

She looked away from him along the shaft of light towards the window in silence.

'He is dead,' she said at length. 'He died when he was only seventeen. Isn't it a terrible thing to die so young as that?'

'What was he?' asked Gabriel, still ironically.

'He was in the gasworks,' she said.

Gabriel felt humiliated by the failure of his irony and by the evocation of this figure from the dead, a boy in the gasworks. While he had been full of memories of their secret life together, full of tenderness and joy and desire, she had been comparing him in her mind with another. A shameful consciousness of his own person assailed him. He saw himself as a ludicrous figure, acting as a pennyboy for his aunts, a nervous, well-meaning sentimentalist, orating to vulgarians and idealising his own clownish lusts, the pitiable fatuous fellow he had caught a glimpse of in the mirror. Instinctively he turned his back more to the light lest she might see the shame that burned upon his forehead.

He tried to keep up his tone of cold interrogation, but his voice when he spoke was humble and indifferent.

'I suppose you were in love with this Michael Furey, Gretta,' he said.

'I was great with him at that time,' she said.

Her voice was veiled and sad. Gabriel, feeling now how vain it would be to try to lead her whither he had purposed, caressed one of her hands and said, also sadly: 'And what did he die of so young, Gretta? Consumption, was it?'

'I think he died for me,' she answered.

A vague terror seized Gabriel at this answer, as if, at that hour when he had hoped to triumph, some impalpable and vindictive being was coming against him, gathering forces against him in its vague world. But he shook himself free of it with an effort of reason and continued to caress her hand. He did not question her again, for he felt that she would tell him of herself. Her hand was warm and moist: it did not respond to his touch, but he continued to caress it just as he had caressed her first letter to him that spring morning.

'It was in the winter,' she said, 'about the beginning of the winter when I was going to leave my grandmother's and come up here to the convent. And he was ill at the time in his lodgings in Galway and wouldn't be let out, and his people in Oughterard were written to. He was in decline, they said, or something like that. I never knew rightly.'

She paused for a moment and sighed.

'Poor fellow,' she said. 'He was very fond of me and he was such a gentle boy. We used to go out together, walking, you know, Gabriel, like the way they do in the country. He was going to study singing only for his health. He had a very good voice, poor Michael Furey.'

'Well; and then?' asked Gabriel.

'And then when it came to the time for me to leave Galway and come up to the convent he was much worse and I wouldn't be let see him so I wrote him a letter saying I was going up to Dublin and would be back in the summer, and hoping he would be better then.'

She paused for a moment to get her voice under control, and then went on: 'Then the night before I left, I was in my grandmother's house in Nuns' Island, packing up, and I heard gravel thrown up against the window. The window was so wet I couldn't see, so I ran downstairs as I was and slipped out the back into the garden and there was the poor fellow at the end of the garden, shivering.'

'And did you not tell him to go back?' asked Gabriel.

'I implored of him to go home at once and told him he would get his death in the rain. But he said he did not want to live. I can see his eyes as well as well! He was standing at the end of the wall where there was a tree.'

'And did he go home?' asked Gabriel.

'Yes, he went home. And when I was only a week in the convent he died and he was buried in Oughterard, where his people came from. O, the day I heard that, that he was dead!'

She stopped, choking with sobs, and, overcome by emotion, flung herself face downward on the bed, sobbing in the quilt. Gabriel held her hand for a moment longer, irresolutely, and then, shy of intruding on her grief, let it fall gently and walked quietly to the window.

She was fast asleep.

Gabriel, leaning on his elbow, looked for a few moments unresentfully on her tangled hair and half-open mouth, listening to her deep-drawn breath. So she had that romance in her life: a man had died for her sake. It hardly pained him now to think how poor a part he, her husband, had played in her life.

He watched her while she slept, as though he and she had never lived together as man and wife. His curious eyes rested long upon her face and on her hair: and, as he thought of what she must have been then, in that time of her first girlish beauty, a strange, friendly pity for her entered his soul. He did not like to say even to himself that her face was no longer beautiful, but he knew that it was no longer the face for which Michael Furey had braved death.

Perhaps she had not told him all the story. His eyes moved to the chair over which she had thrown some of her clothes. A petticoat string dangled to the floor. One boot stood upright, its limp upper fallen down: the fellow of it lay upon its side. He wondered at his riot of emotions of an hour before. From what had it proceeded? From his aunt's supper, from his own foolish speech, from the wine and dancing, the merrymaking when saying good-night in the hall, the pleasure of the walk along the river in the snow. Poor Aunt Julia! She, too, would soon be a shade with the shade of Patrick Morkan and his horse. He had caught that haggard look upon her face for a moment when she was singing *Arrayed for the Bridal*. Soon, perhaps, he would be sitting in that same drawing-room, dressed in black, his silk hat on his knees. The blinds would be drawn down and Aunt Kate would be sitting beside him, crying and blowing her nose and telling him how Julia had died. He would cast about in his mind for some words that might console her, and would find only lame and useless ones. Yes, yes: that would happen very soon.

The air of the room chilled his shoulders. He stretched himself cautiously along under the sheets and lay down beside his wife. One by one, they were all becoming shades. Better pass boldly into that other world, in the full glory of some passion, than fade and wither dismally with age. He thought of how she who lay beside him had locked in her heart for so many years that image of her lover's eyes when he had told her that he did not wish to live.

Generous tears filled Gabriel's eyes. He had never felt like that himself towards any woman, but he knew that such a feeling must be love. The tears gathered more thickly in his eyes and in the partial darkness he imagined he saw the form of a young man standing under a dripping tree. Other forms were near. His soul had approached that region where dwell the vast hosts of the dead. He was conscious of, but could not apprehend, their wayward and flickering existence. His own identity was fading out into a grey impalpable world: the solid world itself which these dead had one time reared and lived in, was dissolving and dwindling.

A few light taps upon the pane made him turn to the window. It had begun to snow again. He watched sleepily the flakes, silver and dark, falling obliquely against the lamplight. The time had come for him to set out on his journey westward. Yes, the newspapers were right: snow was general all over Ireland. It was falling on every part of the dark central plain, on the treeless hills, falling softly upon the Bog of Allen and, farther westward, softly falling into the dark mutinous Shannon waves. It was falling, too, upon every part of the lonely churchyard on the hill where Michael Furey lay buried. It lay thickly drifted on the crooked crosses and headstones, on the spears of the little gate, on the barren thorns. His soul swooned slowly as he heard the snow falling faintly through the universe and faintly falling, like the descent of their last end, upon all the living and the dead.

The Spectre Bridegroom

A Traveller's Tale

WASHINGTON IRVING

"He that supper for is dight,
He lyes full cold, I trow, this night!
Yestreen to chamber I him led,
This night Gray-Steel has made his bed."

SIR EGER, SIR GRAHAME, AND SIR GRAY-STEEL

On the summit of one of the heights of the Odenwald, a wild and romantic tract of Upper Germany, that lies not far from the confluence of the Main and the Rhine, there stood, many, many years since, the Castle of the Baron Von Landshort. It is now quite fallen to decay, and almost buried among beech-trees and dark firs; above which, however, its old watch-tower may still be seen, struggling, like the former possessor I have mentioned, to carry a high head, and look down upon the neighboring country.

The baron was a dry branch of the great family of Katzenellenbogen, and inherited the relics of the property, and all the pride of his ancestors. Though the warlike disposition of his predecessors had much impaired the family possessions, yet the baron still endeavored to keep up some show of former state. The times were peaceable, and the German nobles, in general, had abandoned their inconvenient old castles, perched like

eagles' nests among the mountains, and had built more conveni-
ent residences in the valleys: still the baron remained proudly
drawn up in his little fortress, cherishing, with hereditary invet-
eracy, all the old family feuds; so that he was on ill terms with
some of his nearest neighbors, on account of disputes that had
happened between their great-great-grandfathers.

The baron had but one child, a daughter; but Nature, when
she grants but one child, always compensates by making it a
prodigy; and so it was with the daughter of the baron. All the
nurses, gossips, and country cousins, assured her father that she
had not her equal for beauty in all Germany; and who should
know better than they? She had, moreover, been brought up
with great care under the superintendence of two maiden
aunts, who had spent some years of their early life at one of
the little German courts, and were skilled in all the branches
of knowledge necessary to the education of a fine lady. Under
their instructions she became a miracle of accomplishments.
By the time she was eighteen, she could embroider to admiration, and had worked whole histories of the saints in tapestry,
with such strength of expression in their countenances, that
they looked like so many souls in purgatory. She could read
without great difficulty, and had spelled her way through several church legends, and almost all the chivalric wonders of
the Heldenbuch. She had even made considerable proficiency
in writing; could sign her own name without missing a letter,
and so legibly, that her aunts could read it without spectacles.
She excelled in making little elegant good-for-nothing lady-like
nicknacks of all kinds; was versed in the most abstruse dancing
of the day; played a number of airs on the harp and guitar; and
knew all the tender ballads of the Minnelieders by heart.

Her aunts, too, having been great flirts and coquettes in their younger days, were admirably calculated to be vigilant guardians and strict censors of the conduct of their niece; for there is no duenna so rigidly prudent, and inexorably decorous, as a superannuated coquette. She was rarely suffered out of their sight; never went beyond the domains of the castle, unless well attended, or rather well watched; had continual lectures read to her about strict decorum and implicit obedience; and, as to the men—pah!—she was taught to hold them at such a distance, and in such absolute distrust, that, unless properly authorized, she would not have cast a glance upon the handsomest cavalier in the world—no, not if he were even dying at her feet.

The good effects of this system were wonderfully apparent. The young lady was a pattern of docility and correctness. While others were wasting their sweetness in the glare of the world, and liable to be plucked and thrown aside by every hand, she was coyly blooming into fresh and lovely womanhood under the protection of those immaculate spinsters, like a rosebud blushing forth among guardian thorns. Her aunts looked upon her with pride and exultation, and vaunted that though all the other young ladies in the world might go astray, yet, thank Heaven, nothing of the kind could happen to the heiress of Katzenellenbogen.

But, however scantily the Baron Von Landshort might be provided with children, his household was by no means a small one; for Providence had enriched him with abundance of poor relations. They, one and all, possessed the affectionate disposition common to humble relatives; were wonderfully attached to the baron, and took every possible occasion to come in swarms and enliven the castle. All family festivals were commemorated by these good people at the baron's expense; and when they were filled with good cheer, they would declare that there was nothing on earth so delightful as these family meetings, these jubilees of the heart.

The baron, though a small man, had a large soul, and it swelled with satisfaction at the consciousness of being the greatest man in the little world about him. He loved to tell long stories about the dark old warriors whose portraits looked grimly down from the walls around, and he found no listeners equal to those who fed at his expense. He was much given to the marvellous, and a firm believer in all those supernatural tales with which every mountain and valley in Germany abounds. The faith of his guests exceeded even his own: they listened to every tale of wonder with open eyes and mouth, and never failed to be astonished, even though repeated for the hundredth time. Thus lived the Baron Von Landshort, the oracle of his table, the absolute monarch of his little territory, and happy, above all things, in the persuasion that he was the wisest man of the age.

At the time of which my story treats, there was a great family gathering at the castle, on an affair of the utmost importance: it was to receive the destined bridegroom of the baron's daughter. A negotiation had been carried on between the father and an old nobleman of Bavaria, to unite the dignity of their houses by the marriage of their children. The preliminaries had been conducted with proper punctilio. The young people were betrothed without seeing each other; and the time was appointed for the marriage ceremony. The young Count Von Altenburg had been recalled from the army for the purpose, and was actually on his way to the baron's to receive his bride. Missives had even been received from him, from Wurtzburg, where he was accidentally detained, mentioning the day and hour when he might be expected to arrive.

The castle was in a tumult of preparation to give him a suitable welcome. The fair bride had been decked out with uncommon care. The two aunts had superintended her toilet, and quarrelled the whole morning about every article of her dress. The young lady had taken advantage of their contest to follow the bent of her own taste; and fortunately it was a good one. She looked as lovely as youthful bridegroom could desire; and the flutter of expectation heightened the lustre of her charms.

The suffusions that mantled her face and neck, the gentle heaving of the bosom, the eye now and then lost in reverie, all betrayed the soft tumult that was going on in her little heart. The aunts were continually hovering around her; for maiden aunts are apt to take great interest in affairs of this nature. They were giving her a world of staid counsel how to deport herself, what to say, and in what manner to receive the expected lover.

The baron was no less busied in preparations. He had, in truth, nothing exactly to do: but he was naturally a fuming, bustling little man, and could not remain passive when all the world was in a hurry. He worried from top to bottom of the castle with an air of infinite anxiety; he continually called the servants from their work, to exhort them to be diligent; and buzzed about every hall and chamber, as idly restless and importunate as a blue-bottle fly on a warm summer's day.

In the mean time, the fatted calf had been killed; the forests had rung with the clamor of the huntsmen; the kitchen was crowded with good cheer; the cellars had yielded up whole oceans of *Rhein-wein* and *Ferne-wein;* and even the great Hei-delburg tun had been laid under contribution. Every thing was ready to receive the distinguished guest with *Saus und Braus* in the true spirit of German hospitality—but the guest delayed to make his appearance. Hour rolled after hour. The sun, that had poured his downward rays upon the rich forest of the Odenwald, now just gleamed along the summits of the mountains. The baron mounted the highest tower, and strained his eyes in hope of catching a distant sight of the count and his attendants. Once he thought he beheld them: the sound of horns came floating from the valley, prolonged by the moun-tain echoes. A number of horsemen were seen far below, slowly advancing along the road; but when they had nearly reached the foot of the mountain, they suddenly struck off in a different direction. The last ray of sunshine departed—the bats began to flit by in the twilight—the road grew dimmer and dimmer to the view; and nothing appeared stirring in it but now and then a peasant lagging homeward from his labor.

While the old castle of Landshort was in this state of per-plexity, a very interesting scene was transacting in a different part of the Odenwald.

The young Count Von Altenburg was tranquilly pursuing his route in that sober, jog-trot way, in which a man travels toward matrimony when his friends have taken all the trouble and uncertainty of courtship off his hands, and a bride is waiting for him, as certainly as a dinner at the end of his journey. He had encountered, at Wurtzburg, a youthful companion in arms, with whom he had seen some service on the frontiers—Herman Von Starkenfaust, one of the stoutest hands and worthiest hearts of German chivalry, who was now returning from the

army. His father's castle was not far distant from the old fortress of Landshort, although an hereditary feud rendered the
families hostile, and strangers to each other.

In the warm-hearted moment of recognition, the young
friends related all their past adventures and fortunes; and the
count gave the whole history of his intended nuptials with a
young lady whom he had never seen, but of whose charms he
had received the most enrapturing descriptions.

As the route of the friends lay in the same direction, they
agreed to perform the rest of their journey together; and, that
they might do it the more leisurely, set off from Wurtzburg at
an early hour, the count having given directions for his retinue
to follow and overtake him.

They beguiled their wayfaring with recollections of their
military scenes and adventures; but the count was apt to be a
little tedious, now and then, about the reputed charms of his
bride, and the felicity that awaited him.

In this way they had entered among the mountains of the
Odenwald, and were traversing one of its most lonely and
thickly-wooded passes. It is well known that the forests of
Germany have always been as much infested by robbers as
its castles by spectres; and, at this time, the former were particularly numerous, from the hordes of disbanded soldiers
wandering about the country. It will not appear extraordinary,
therefore, that the cavaliers were attacked by a gang of these
stragglers, in the midst of the forest. They defended themselves with bravery, but were nearly overpowered, when the
count's retinue arrived to their assistance. At sight of them the
robbers fled, but not until the count had received a mortal
wound. He was slowly and carefully conveyed back to the city

of Wurtzburg, and a friar summoned from a neighboring convent, who was famous for his skill in administering to both soul and body; but half of his skill was superfluous: the moments of the unfortunate count were numbered.

With his dying breath he entreated his friend to repair instantly to the castle of Landshort, and explain the fatal cause of his not keeping his appointment with his bride. Though not the most ardent of lovers, he was one of the most punctilious of men, and appeared earnestly solicitous that his mission should be speedily and courteously executed. "Unless this is done," said he, "I shall not sleep quietly in my grave!" He repeated these last words with peculiar solemnity. A request, at a moment so impressive, admitted no hesitation. Starkenfaust endeavored to soothe him to calmness; promised faithfully to execute his wish, and gave him his hand in solemn pledge. The dying man pressed it in acknowledgment, but soon lapsed into delirium—raved about his bride—his engagements—his plighted word; ordered his horse, that he might ride to the castle of Landshort; and expired in the fancied act of vaulting into the saddle.

Starkenfaust bestowed a sigh and a soldier's tear on the untimely fate of his comrade; and then pondered on the awkward mission he had undertaken. His heart was heavy, and his head perplexed; for he was to present himself an unbidden guest among hostile people, and to damp their festivity with tidings fatal to their hopes. Still there were certain whisperings of curiosity in his bosom to see this far-famed beauty of Katzenellenbogen, so cautiously shut up from the world; for he was a passionate admirer of the sex, and there was a dash of eccentricity and enterprise in his character that made him fond of all singular adventure.

Previous to his departure he made all due arrangements with the holy fraternity of the convent for the funeral solemnities of his friend, who was to be buried in the cathedral of Wurtzburg, near some of his illustrious relatives; and the mourning retinue of the count took charge of his remains.

It is now high time that we should return to the ancient family of Katzenellenbogen, who were impatient for their guest, and still more for their dinner; and to the worthy little baron, whom we left airing himself on the watch-tower.

Night closed in, but still no guest arrived. The baron descended from the tower in despair. The banquet, which had been delayed from hour to hour, could no longer be postponed. The meats were already overdone; the cook in an agony; and the whole household had the look of a garrison that had been reduced by famine. The baron was obliged reluctantly to give orders for the feast without the presence of the guest. All were seated at table, and just on the point of commencing, when the sound of a horn from without the gate gave notice of the approach of a stranger. Another long blast filled the old courts of the castle with its echoes, and was answered by the warder from the walls. The baron hastened to receive his future son-in-law.

The drawbridge had been let down, and the stranger was before the gate. He was a tall, gallant cavalier, mounted on a black steed. His countenance was pale, but he had a beaming, romantic eye, and an air of stately melancholy. The baron was a little mortified that he should have come in this simple, solitary style. His dignity for a moment was ruffled, and he felt

disposed to consider it a want of proper respect for the important occasion, and the important family with which he was to be
connected. He pacified himself, however, with the conclusion,
that it must have been youthful impatience which had induced
him thus to spur on sooner than his attendants.

"I am sorry," said the stranger, "to break in upon you thus
unseasonably—"

Here the baron interrupted him with a world of compliments and greetings; for, to tell the truth, he prided himself
upon his courtesy and eloquence. The stranger attempted, once
or twice, to stem the torrent of words, but in vain; so he bowed
his head, and suffered it to flow on. By the time the baron
had come to a pause, they had reached the inner court of the
castle; and the stranger was again about to speak, when he was
once more interrupted by the appearance of the female part of
the family, leading forth the shrinking and blushing bride. He
gazed on her for a moment as one entranced; it seemed as if
his whole soul beamed forth in the gaze, and rested upon that
lovely form. One of the maiden aunts whispered something in
her ear: she made an effort to speak; her moist blue eye was
timidly raised; gave a shy glance of inquiry on the stranger; and
was cast again to the ground. The words died away; but there
was a sweet smile playing about her lips, and a soft dimpling of
the cheek that showed her glance had not been unsatisfactory.
It was impossible for a girl of the fond age of eighteen, highly
predisposed for love and matrimony, not to be pleased with so
gallant a cavalier.

The late hour at which the guest had arrived left no time for
parley. The baron was peremptory, and deferred all particular

conversation until the morning, and led the way to the untasted banquet.

It was served up in the great hall of the castle. Around the walls hung the hard-favored portraits of the heroes of the house of Katzenellenbogen, and the trophies which they had gained in the field and in the chase. Hacked corslets, splintered jousting-spears, and tattered banners, were mingled with the spoils of sylvan warfare; the jaws of the wolf and the tusks of the boar grinned horribly among cross-bows and battle-axes, and a huge pair of antlers branched immediately over the head of the youthful bridegroom.

The cavalier took but little notice of the company or the entertainment. He scarcely tasted the banquet, but seemed absorbed in admiration of his bride. He conversed in a low tone, that could not be overheard—for the language of love is never loud; but where is the female ear so dull that it cannot catch the softest whisper of the lover? There was a mingled tenderness and gravity in his manner, that appeared to have a powerful effect upon the young lady. Her color came and went as she listened with deep attention. Now and then she made some blushing reply, and when his eye was turned away, she would steal a sidelong glance at his romantic countenance, and heave a gentle sigh of tender happiness. It was evident that the young couple were completely enamored. The aunts, who were deeply versed in the mysteries of the heart, declared that they had fallen in love with each other at first sight.

The feast went on merrily, or at least noisily, for the guests were all blessed with those keen appetites that attend upon light purses and mountain air. The baron told his best and longest stories, and never had he told them so well, or with such great effect. If there was any thing marvelous, his auditors were lost in astonishment; and if any thing facetious, they were sure to laugh exactly in the right place. The baron, it is true, like most great men, was too dignified to utter any joke but a dull one; it was always enforced, however, by a bumper of excellent Hockheimer; and even a dull joke, at one's own table, served up with jolly old wine, is irresistible. Many good things were said by poorer and keener wits that would not bear repeating, except on similar occasions; many sly speeches whispered in ladies' ears, that almost convulsed them with suppressed laughter; and a song or two roared out by a poor but merry and broad-faced cousin of the baron, that absolutely made the maiden aunts hold up their fans.

Amidst all this revelry, the stranger-guest maintained a most singular and unseasonable gravity. His countenance assumed a deeper cast of dejection as the evening advanced; and, strange as it may appear, even the baron's jokes seemed only to render him the more melancholy. At times he was lost in thought, and at times there was a perturbed and restless wandering of the eye that bespoke a mind but ill at ease. His conversations with the bride became more and more earnest and mysterious. Lowering clouds began to steal over the fair serenity of her brow, and tremors to run through her tender frame.

All this could not escape the notice of the company. Their gayety was chilled by the unaccountable gloom of the bridegroom; their spirits were infected; whispers and glances were interchanged, accompanied by shrugs and dubious shakes of the head. The song and the laugh grew less and less frequent; there were dreary pauses in the conversation, which were at length succeeded by wild tales and supernatural legends. One dismal story produced another still more dismal, and the baron nearly frightened some of the ladies into hysterics with the history of the goblin horseman that carried away the fair Leonora; a dreadful story, which has since been put into excellent verse, and is read and believed by all the world.

The bridegroom listened to this tale with profound attention. He kept his eyes steadily fixed on the baron, and, as the story drew to a close, began gradually to rise from his seat, growing taller and taller, until, in the baron's entranced eye, he seemed almost to tower into a giant. The moment the tale was finished, he heaved a deep sigh, and took a solemn farewell of the company. They were all amazement. The baron was perfectly thunder-struck.

"What! going to leave the castle at midnight? Why, every thing was prepared for his reception; a chamber was ready for him if he wished to retire."

The stranger shook his head mournfully and mysteriously. "I must lay my head in a different chamber to-night!"

There was something in this reply, and the tone in which it was uttered, that made the baron's heart misgive him; but he rallied his forces, and repeated his hospitable entreaties.

The stranger shook his head silently, but positively, at every offer; and, waving his farewell to the company, stalked slowly out of the hall. The maiden aunts were absolutely petrified— the bride hung her head, and a tear stole to her eye.

The baron followed the stranger to the great court of the castle, where the black charger stood pawing the earth, and snorting with impatience. When they had reached the portal, whose deep archway was dimly lighted by a cresset, the stranger paused, and addressed the baron in a hollow tone of voice, which the vaulted roof rendered still more sepulchral.

"Now that we are alone," said he, "I will impart to you the reason of my going. I have a solemn, an indispensable engagement—"

"Why," said the baron, "cannot you send some one in your place?"

"It admits of no substitute—I must attend it in person—I must away to Wurtzburg cathedral—"

"Ay," said the baron, plucking up spirit, "but not until tomorrow—to-morrow you shall take your bride there."

"No! no!" replied the stranger, with tenfold solemnity, "my engagement is with no bride—the worms! The worms expect me! I am a dead man—I have been slain by robbers—my body lies at Wurtzburg—at midnight I am to be buried—the grave is waiting for me—I must keep my appointment!"

He sprang on his black charger, dashed over the drawbridge, and the clattering of his horse's hoofs was lost in the whistling of the night blast.

The baron returned to the hall in the utmost consternation, and related what had passed. Two ladies fainted outright, others sickened at the idea of having banqueted with a spectre. It was the opinion of some, that this might be the wild huntsman, famous in German legend. Some talked of mountain-sprites, of wood-demons, and of other supernatural beings, with which the good people of Germany have been so grievously harassed since time immemorial. One of the poor relations ventured to suggest that it might be some sportive evasion of the young cavalier, and that the very gloominess of the caprice seemed to accord with so melancholy a personage. This, however drew on him the indignation of the whole company, and especially of the baron, who looked upon him as little better than an infidel; so that he was fain to abjure his heresy as speedily as possible, and come into the faith of the true believers.

But whatever may have been the doubts entertained, they were completely put to an end by the arrival, next day, of regular missives, confirming the intelligence of the young count's murder, and his interment in Wurtzburg cathedral.

The dismay at the castle may well be imagined. The baron shut himself up in his chamber. The guests, who had come to rejoice with him, could not think of abandoning him in his distress. They wandered about the courts, or collected in groups in the hall, shaking their heads and shrugging their shoulders, at the troubles of so good a man; and sat longer than ever at table, and ate and drank more stoutly than ever, by way of keeping up their spirits. But the situation of the widowed bride was the most pitiable. To have lost a husband before she had even embraced him—and such a husband! if the very spectre could be so gracious and noble, what must have been the living man? She filled the house with lamentations.

On the night of the second day of her widowhood, she had retired to her chamber, accompanied by one of her aunts, who insisted on sleeping with her. The aunt, who was one of the best tellers of ghost-stories in all Germany, had just been recounting one of her longest, and had fallen asleep in the very midst of it. The chamber was remote, and overlooked a small garden. The niece lay pensively gazing at the beams of the rising moon, as they trembled on the leaves of an aspen-tree before the lattice. The castle clock had just tolled midnight, when a soft strain of music stole up from the garden. She rose hastily from her bed, and stepped lightly to the window. A tall figure stood among the shadows of the trees. As it raised its head, a beam of moonlight fell upon the countenance. Heaven and earth! She beheld the Spectre Bridegroom! A loud shriek at that moment burst upon her ear, and her aunt, who had been awakened by the music, and had followed her silently to the window, fell into her arms. When she looked again, the spectre had disappeared.

Of the two females, the aunt now required the most soothing, for she was perfectly beside herself with terror. As to the young lady, there was something, even in the spectre of her lover, that seemed endearing. There was still the semblance of manly beauty; and though the shadow of a man is but little calculated to satisfy the affections of a love-sick girl, yet, where the substance is not to be had, even that is consoling. The aunt declared she would never sleep in that chamber again; the niece, for once, was refractory, and declared as strongly that she would sleep in no other in the castle: the consequence was, that she had to sleep in it alone: but she drew a promise from her aunt not to relate the story of the spectre, lest she should be denied the only melancholy pleasure left her on earth—that of inhabiting the chamber over which the guardian shade of her lover kept its nightly vigils.

How long the good old lady would have observed this promise is uncertain, for she dearly loved to talk of the marvellous, and there is a triumph in being the first to tell a frightful story; it is, however, still quoted in the neighborhood, as a memorable instance of female secrecy, that she kept it to herself for a whole week; when she was suddenly absolved from all further restraint by intelligence brought to the breakfast-table one morning that the young lady was not to be found. Her room was empty—the bed had not been slept in—the window was open, and the bird had flown.

The astonishment and concern with which the intelligence was received, can only be imagined by those who have witnessed the agitation which the mishaps of a great man cause among his friends. Even the poor relations paused for a moment from the indefatigable labors of the trencher; when the aunt, who had at first been struck speechless, wrung her hands, and shrieked out, "The goblin! the goblin! she's carried away by the goblin!"

In a few words she related the fearful scene of the garden, and concluded that the spectre must have carried off his bride. Two of the domestics corroborated the opinion, for they had heard the clattering of a horse's hoofs down the mountain about midnight, and had no doubt that it was the spectre on his black charger, bearing her away to the tomb. All present were struck with the direful probability; for events of the kind are extremely common in Germany, as many well-authenticated histories bear witness.

What a lamentable situation was that of the poor baron! What a heart-rending dilemma for a fond father, and a member of the great family of Katzenellenbogen! His only daughter had either been rapt away to the grave, or he was to have some wood-demon for a son-in-law, and perchance a troop of goblin grandchildren. As usual, he was completely bewildered, and all the castle in an uproar. The men were ordered to take horse, and scour every road and path and glen of the Odenwald. The baron himself had just drawn on his jack-boots, girded on his sword, and was about to mount his steed to sally forth on the doubtful quest, when he was brought to a pause by a new apparition. A lady was seen approaching the castle, mounted on a palfrey, attended by a cavalier on horseback. She galloped up to the gate, sprang from her horse, and, falling at the baron's feet, embraced his knees. It was his lost daughter, and her companion—the Spectre Bridegroom! The baron was astounded. He looked at his daughter, then at the spectre, and almost doubted the evidence of his senses. The latter, too, was wonderfully improved in his appearance since his visit to the world of spirits. His dress was splendid, and set off a noble figure of manly symmetry. He was no longer pale and melancholy. His fine countenance was flushed with the glow of youth, and joy rioted in his large dark eye.

The mystery was soon cleared up. The cavalier (for, in truth, as you must have known all the while, he was no goblin) announced himself as Sir Herman Von Starkenfaust. He related his adventure with the young count. He told how he had hastened to the castle to deliver the unwelcome tidings, but that the eloquence of the baron had interrupted him in every attempt to tell his tale. How the sight of the bride had completely captivated him, and that, to pass a few hours near her, he had tacitly suffered the mistake to continue. How he had been sorely perplexed in what way to make a decent retreat, until the baron's goblin-stories had suggested his eccentric exit. How, fearing the feudal hostility of the family, he had repeated his visits by stealth—had haunted the garden beneath the young lady's window—had wooed—had won—had borne away in triumph—and, in a word, had wedded the fair.

Under any other circumstances the baron would have been inflexible, for he was tenacious of paternal authority, and devoutly obstinate in all family feuds: but he loved his daughter; he had lamented her as lost; he rejoiced to find her still alive; and, though her husband was of a hostile house, yet, thank Heaven, he was not a goblin! There was something, it must be acknowledged, that did not exactly accord with his notions of strict veracity, in the joke the knight had passed upon him of his being a dead man; but several old friends present, who had served in the wars, assured him that every stratagem was excusable in love, and that the cavalier was entitled to especial privilege, having lately served as a trooper.

Matters, therefore, were happily arranged. The baron pardoned the young couple on the spot. The revels at the castle were resumed. The poor relations overwhelmed this new member of the family with loving-kindness; he was so gallant, so generous—and so rich. The aunts, it is true, were somewhat scandalized that their system of strict seclusion and passive obedience should be so badly exemplified, but attributed it all to their negligence in not having the windows grated. One of them was particularly mortified at having her marvelous story marred, and that the only spectre she had ever seen should turn out a counterfeit; but the niece seemed perfectly happy at having found him substantial flesh and blood—and so the story ends.

After the Ball

LEO TOLSTOY

"So you contend a man cannot judge independently of what is good and what is bad, that it is all a matter of environment—that man is a creature of environment. But I contend it is all a matter of chance. And here is what I can say about myself. . . ."

This is what our respected friend Ivan Vasilyevich said at the conclusion of a discussion we had been having about the necessity of changing the environment, the conditions in which men live, before there could be any talk about the improvement of the individual. As a matter of fact, no one had said it was impossible to judge independently of the good and the bad, but Ivan Vasilyevich had a habit of answering thoughts of his own stimulated by a discussion, and recounting experiences from his own life suggested by these thoughts. Often he become so absorbed in the story that he forgot his reason for telling it, especially since he always spoke with great fervor and sincerity. That is precisely what happened in the present case.

"At least I can make this claim with regard to myself. My own life has been molded in that way and no other—not by environment, but by something quite different."

"By what?" we asked.

"That is a long story. If you are to understand, I must tell it all to you."

"Then do."

Ivan Vasilyevich considered a moment and shook his head.

"Yes," he said, "my whole life was changed by a single night, or rather, a morning."

"Why? What happened?"

"It happened that I was deeply in love. I had often been in love before, but never so deeply. It took place a long time ago—her daughters are married women by this time. Her name was B., Varenka B. She was still strikingly beautiful at fifty, but in her youth, when she was eighteen, she was a dream: tall, slender, graceful, and majestic—yes, majestic. She always held herself as erect as if she were unable to bend, with her head tipped slightly backward; this, combined with her beauty and height, even though she was so thin as to be almost bony, gave her a queenly air that would have been intimidating if it had not been for her gay, winning smile, her mouth, her glorious shining eyes, and her whole captivating, youthful being."

"Ivan Vasilyevich certainly does lay it on thick!"

"However thick I were to lay it on, I could not make you understand what she was really like. But that is beside the point. The events I shall recount took place in the forties.

"I was then a student at a provincial university. I don't know whether it was a good or a bad thing, but in those days there were none of your study circles, none of your theorizing, at our university; we were just young and lived in the way of young folk—studying and having a good time. I was a very gay and energetic youth, and rich in the bargain. I owned a spirited carriage horse and used to take the girls out for drives (skating had not yet become the fad); I went on drinking parties with my fellow students (in those days we drank nothing but champagne; if we were out of money, we drank nothing, for we never drank vodka as they do now); but most of all I enjoyed parties and balls. I was a good dancer and not exactly ugly."

"Come, don't be modest," put in one of the listeners. "We've all seen your daguerreotype. You were a very handsome youth."

"Perhaps I was, but that isn't what I wanted to tell you. When my love was at its height I attended a ball given on the last day of Shrovetide by the Marshal of Nobility, a good-natured old man, wealthy, and fond of entertaining. His wife, as amiable as he was, stood beside him to receive us. She was wearing a velvet gown and a diamond tiara in her hair, and her aging neck and shoulders, plump and white, were exposed, as in the portraits of Empress Yelizaveta Petrovna. The ball was magnificent. The ballroom was charming, there were famous serf singers and musicians belonging to a certain landowner who was a lover of music, the food was abundant, the champagne flowed in rivers. Much as I loved champagne, I did not drink—I was drunk with love. But I danced till I dropped. I danced quadrilles, and waltzes, and polonaises, and it goes without saying that I danced as many of them as I could with Varenka. She was wearing a white dress with a pink sash, white kid gloves that did not quite reach her thin, pointed elbows, and white satin slippers. A wretched engineer named Anisimov cheated me out of a mazurka with her. I have never forgiven him for that. He invited her the moment she entered the ballroom, while I had been delayed by calling at the hairdresser's for my gloves. And so instead of dancing the mazurka with her, I danced it with a German girl I had once had a crush on. But I am afraid I was very neglectful of her that evening; I did not talk to her or look at her, for I had eyes for no one but a tall, slender girl in a white dress with a pink sash, with radiant, flushed, dimpled cheeks and soft, gentle eyes. I was not the only one; everyone looked at her and admired her, even the women, though she outshone them all. It was impossible not to admire her.

"Formally I was not her partner for the mazurka, but as a matter of fact I did dance it with her—at least most of it. Without the least embarrassment she danced straight to me down the length of the whole room, and when I leapt up to meet her without waiting for the invitation, she smiled to thank me for guessing what she wanted. When we had been led up to her and she had not guessed my nature, she had given a little shrug of her thin shoulders as she held out her hand to another, turning upon me a little smile of regret and consolation.

"When the figures of the mazurka changed into a waltz, I waltzed with her for a long time, and she smiled breathlessly and murmured '*encore*.' And I waltzed on and on with her, quite unaware of my own body, as if it were made of air."

"Unaware of it? I'm sure you must have been very much aware of it as you put your arm about her waist—aware of not only *your* body, but of hers as well," said one of the guests.

Ivan Vasilyevich suddenly turned crimson and almost shouted:

"That may apply to you, modern youth—all you think of is the body. In our day things were different. The more deeply I loved a girl, the more incorporeal she seemed to me. Today you are aware of legs, ankles, and other things; you disrobe the ladies with whom you are in love, but for me, as Alphonse Karr has said—and a very good writer he was—the object of my love was always clad in bronze raiment. Far from exposing, we tried to hide nakedness, as did the good son of Noah. But you cannot understand this."

"Pay no attention to him. Go on with your story," said another of the listeners.

"Well, I danced mostly with her and did not notice the passage of time. The musicians were so exhausted—you know how it always is at the end of a ball—that they kept playing the mazurka; mamas and papas were rising from the card tables in the drawing room in anticipation of supper; footmen were rushing about. It was going on for three o'clock. We had to take advantage of the few minutes left us. I invited her once more, and for the hundredth time we passed down the length of the room.

"'Will I be your partner for the quadrille after supper?' I asked her as I took her back to her place.

"'Oh, yes, if they do not take me home,' she said with a smile.

"'I won't let them,' I said.

"'Give me my fan,' she said.

"'I am sorry to give it back to you,' I said as I handed her her little white fan.

"'Here, then, to keep you from being sorry,' she said, plucking a feather out of the fan and giving it to me.

"I took the feather, unable to express my rapture and gratitude except with a glance. I was not only gay and content—I was happy, I was blissful, I was benevolent, I was no longer myself, but some creature not of this earth, who knew no evil and could do nothing but good.

"I tucked the feather in my glove and stood riveted to the spot, unable to move away from her.

"'Look, they are asking Papa to dance,' she said, indicating a tall, stately man who was her father, a colonel, in silver epaulettes, standing in the doorway with the hostess and some other women.

"'Varenka, come here,' called the hostess in the diamond tiara.

"Varenka made for the door and I followed her.

"'Do talk your father into dancing with you, *ma chère*. Please do, Pyotr Vladislavich,' said the hostess to the colonel.

"Varenka's father was a tall, handsome, stately, and well-preserved old man. He had a ruddy face with a white mustache curled *à la* Nicholas I, white side whiskers that met his mustache, hair combed forward over his temples, and the same smile as his daughter's lighting up his eyes and lips. He was very well built, with a broad chest swelling out in military style and with a modest display of decorations on it, with strong shoulders and long, fine legs. He was an officer of the old type with a military bearing of the Nicholas school.

"As we came up to the door the colonel was protesting that he had forgotten how to dance, but nevertheless he smiled, reached for his sword, drew it out of its scabbard, handed it to a young man eager to offer his services, and, drawing a suede glove on to his right hand ('Everything according to rule,' he said with a smile), he took his daughter's hand and struck a pose in a quarter turn, waiting for the proper measure to begin.

"As soon as the mazurka phrase was introduced he stamped one foot energetically and swung out with the other, and then his tall heavy figure sailed round the ball-room. He kept striking one foot against the other, now slowly and gracefully, now quickly and energetically. The willowy form of Varenka floated beside him. Imperceptibly and always just in time, she kept lengthening or shortening the step of the little white satin feet to fit his.

"All the guests stood watching the couple's every movement. The feeling I experienced was less admiration than a sort of deep ecstasy. I was especially touched by the sight of the colonel's boots. They were good calfskin boots, but they were heelless and had blunt toes instead of fashionable pointed ones. Obviously they had been made by the battalion cobbler. 'He wears ordinary boots instead of fashionable ones so that he can dress his beloved daughter and take her into society,' I thought to myself, and that is why I was particularly touched by his blunt-toed boots. Anyone could see he had once danced beautifully, but now he was heavy and his legs were not flexible enough to make all the quick and pretty turns he attempted. But he went twice round the room very well, and everybody applauded when he quickly spread out his feet, then snapped them together again and fell, albeit rather heavily, on one knee. And she smiled as she freed her caught skirt and floated gracefully round him. When he had struggled back to his feet, he touchingly put his hands over his daughter's ears and kissed her on the forehead, then led her over to me, who he thought had been her dancing partner. I told him I was not.

"'It doesn't matter; you dance with her,' he said, smiling warmly as he slipped his sword back into the scabbard.

"Just as the first drop poured out of a bottle brings a whole stream in its wake, so my love for Varenka released all the love in my soul. I embraced the whole world with love. I loved the hostess with her diamond tiara, and her husband, and her guests, and her footmen, and even the wretched Anisimov, who was clearly angry with me. As for her father with his blunt-toed boots and a smile so much like hers—I felt a rapturous affection for him.

"The mazurka came to an end and our hosts invited us to the supper table. But Colonel B. declined, saying that he must be up early in the morning. I was afraid he would take Varenka with him, but she remained behind with her mother.

"After supper I danced the promised quadrille with her. And while it had seemed that my happiness could not be greater, it went on growing and growing. We said nothing of love; I did not ask her, nor even myself, whether she loved me. It was sufficient that I loved her. The only thing I feared was that something might spoil my happiness.

"When I got home, undressed myself and thought of going to bed, I realized that sleep was out of the question. I held in my hand the feather from her fan and one of her gloves, which she had given to me when I put her and her mother into their carriage. As I gazed at these keepsakes I saw her again at the moment when, choosing one of two partners, she had guessed my nature and said in a sweet voice, 'Too proud? Is that it?' then joyfully held out her hand to me; or when, sipping champagne at the supper table, she had gazed at me over her glass with loving eyes. But I saw her best as she danced with her father, floating gracefully beside him, looking at all the admiring spectators with joy and pride for his sake as well as her own. And involuntarily the two of them became merged in my mind and enveloped in one deep and tender feeling.

"At that time my late brother and I lived alone. My brother had no use for society and never went to balls. He was getting ready to take his examinations for a master's degree and was leading the most exemplary of lives. He was asleep. I felt sorry for him as I looked at his head buried in the pillow, half covered by the blanket—sorry because he did not know and did not share the happiness which was mine. Petrusha, our serf valet, met me with a candle and would have helped me undress, but I dismissed him. I was touched by the sight of the man's sleepy face and disheveled hair. Trying to make no noise, I tiptoed to my own room and sat down on the bed. I was too happy, I could not sleep. I found it hot in the room, and so without taking off my uniform I went quietly out into the hall, put on my greatcoat, opened the entrance door, and went out.

"It had been almost five o'clock when I left the ball; about two hours had passed since, so that it was already light when I went out. It was typical Shrovetide weather—misty, with wet snow melting on the roads and water dripping from all the roofs. At that time the B.'s lived on the outskirts of town, at the edge of an open field with a girls' school at one end and a space used for promenading at the other. I went down our quiet little bystreet and came out upon the main street, where I met passersby and carters with timber loaded on sledges whose runners cut through the snow to the very pavement. And everything—the horses bobbing their heads rhythmically under their lacquered yokes, and the carters with bast matting on their shoulders plodding in their enormous boots through the slush beside their sledges, and the houses on either side of the street standing tall in the mist—everything seemed particularly dear and significant.

"When I reached the field where their house stood I saw something big and black at the promenade end of it, and I heard the sounds of a fife and drum. My heart had been singing all this time, and occasionally the strains of the mazurka

337

had come to my mind. But this was different music, harsh and sinister.

"'What could it be?' I wondered, and made my way in the direction of the sounds, down the slippery wagon road that cut across the field. When I had gone about a hundred paces I began to distinguish in the mist a crowd of people. They were evidently soldiers. 'Drilling,' I thought, and continued on my way in the company of a blacksmith in an oil-stained apron and jacket who was carrying a large bundle. A double row of soldiers in black coats were standing facing each other motionless, their guns at their sides. Behind them stood a fifer and a drummerboy who kept playing that shrill tune over and over.

"'What are they doing?' I asked the blacksmith who was standing next to me.

"'Driving a Tatar down the line for having tried to run away,' replied the blacksmith brusquely, glaring at the far end of the double row.

"I looked in the same direction and saw something horrible coming toward me between the rows. It was a man bare to the waist and tied to a horizontal gun held at either end by a soldier. Beside him walked a tall officer in a greatcoat and forage cap whose figure seemed familiar to me. The prisoner, his whole body twitching, his feet squashing through the melting snow, advanced through the blows raining down on him from either side, now cringing back, at which the soldiers holding the gun would pull him forward, now lunging forward, at which the soldiers would jerk him back to keep him from falling. And next to him, walking firmly, never lagging behind, came the tall officer. It was her father, with his ruddy face and white mustache and side whiskers.

"At every blow the prisoner turned his pain-distorted face to the side from which the blow had come, as if in surprise, and kept repeating something over and over through bared white teeth. I could not make out the words until he came closer to me. He was sobbing rather than speaking them. 'Have mercy, brothers; have mercy, brothers.' But the brothers had no mercy, and when the procession was directly opposite me I saw one of the soldiers step resolutely forward and bring his lash down so hard on the Tatar's back that it whistled through the air. The Tatar fell forward, but the soldiers jerked him up, and then another blow fell from the opposite side, and again from this, and again from that. . . . The colonel marched beside him, now glancing down at his feet, now up at the prisoner, drawing in deep breaths of air, blowing out his cheeks, slowly letting the air out between pursed lips. When the procession passed the spot where I was standing I got a glimpse of the prisoner's back through the row of soldiers. It was something indescribable: striped, wet, crimson, outlandish. I could not believe it was part of a human body.

"'God in heaven!' murmured the blacksmith standing next to me.

"The procession moved on. The blows kept falling from both sides on the cringing, floundering creature, the drum kept beating, the fife shrilling, and the tall, stately colonel walking firmly beside the prisoner. Suddenly the colonel stopped and went quickly over to one of the soldiers.

"'Missed? I'll show you!' I heard him say in a wrathful voice. 'Here, take this! And this!' And I saw his strong hand in its suede glove strike the small weak soldier in the face because the man's lash had not come down hard enough on the crimson back of the Tatar.

"'Bring fresh whips!' shouted the colonel. As he spoke he turned round and caught sight of me. Pretending not to recognize me, he gave a vicious, threatening scowl and turned quickly away. I felt so ashamed that I did not know where to turn my eyes, as if I had been caught doing something disgraceful. With hanging head I hurried home. All the way I kept hearing the rolling of the drum, the shrilling of the fife, the words, 'Have mercy, brothers,' and the wrathful, self-confident voice of the colonel shouting, 'Here, take this! And this!' And the aching of my heart was so intense as to be almost physical, making me feel nauseated, so that I had to stop several times. I felt I must throw up all the horror that this sight had filled me with. I do not remember how I reached home and got into bed, but the moment I began to doze off I saw and heard everything all over again. I jumped up.

"'There must be something he knows that I do not know,' I said to myself, thinking of the colonel. 'If I knew what he knows, I would understand, and what I saw would not cause me such anguish.' But rack my brains as I might, I could not understand what it was the colonel knew, and I could not fall asleep until evening, and then only after having gone to see a friend and drinking myself into forgetfulness.

"Do you suppose I concluded that what I had seen was bad? Nothing of the sort. 'If what I saw was done with such assurance and was accepted by everyone as being necessary, it means they know something I do not know,' was the conclusion I came to, and I tried to find out what it was. But I never did. And not having found out, I could not enter military service, as it had been my intention to do, and not only military service, but any service at all, and so I turned out to be the good-for-nothing that you see."

"We know very well what a 'good-for-nothing' you turned out to be," said one of the guests. "It would be more to the point to say how many people would have turned out to be good-for-nothing had it not been for you."

"Now that's a foolish thing to say," said Ivan Vasilyevich with real vexation.

"Well, and what about your love?" we asked.

"My love? From that day on my love languished. Whenever we went out walking and she smiled that pensive smile of hers, I could not help recalling the colonel out in the field, and this made me feel uncomfortable and unhappy, and I gradually stopped going to see her. My love petered out.

"So that is what sometimes happens, and it is incidents like this that change and give direction to a man's whole life. And you talk about environment," he said.

The Twelve Dancing Princesses

BROTHERS GRIMM

There was a king who had twelve beautiful daughters. They slept in twelve beds all in one room; and when they went to bed, the doors were shut and locked up; but every morning their shoes were found to be quite worn through as if they had been danced in all night; and yet nobody could find out how it happened, or where they had been.

Then the king made it known to all the land that if any man could discover the secret, and find out where it was that the princesses danced in the night, he should have the one he liked best for his wife, and should be king after his death; but whoever tried and did not succeed, after three days and nights should be put to death.

A king's son soon came. He was well entertained, and in the evening was taken to the chamber next to the one where the princesses lay in their twelve beds. There he was to sit and watch where they went to dance; and, in order that nothing might pass without his hearing it, the door of his chamber was left open. But the king's son soon fell asleep; and when he awoke in the morning he found that the princesess had all been dancing, for the soles of their shoes were full of holes. The same thing happened the second and third night, so the king ordered his head to be cut off. After him came several others;

but they had all the same luck, and all lost their lives in the same manner.

Now it chanced that an old soldier, who had been wounded in battle and could fight no longer, passed through the country where this king reigned, and as he was travelling through a wood, he met an old woman, who asked him where he was going. 'I hardly know where I am going, or what I had better do,' said the soldier; 'but I think I should like very well to find out where it is that the princesses dance, and then in time I might be a king.'

'Well,' said the old dame, 'that is no very hard task, only take care not to drink any of the wine which one of the princesses will bring to you in the evening; and as soon as she leaves you pretend to be fast asleep.' Then she gave him a cloak, and said, 'As soon as you put that on you will become invisible, and you will then be able to follow the princesses wherever they go.'

When the soldier heard all this good counsel, he determined to try his luck: so he went to the king, and said he was willing to undertake the task. He was as well received as the others had been, and the king ordered fine royal robes to be given him; and when the evening came he was led to the outer chamber. Just as he was going to lie down, the eldest of the princesses brought him a cup of wine; but the soldier threw it all away secretly, taking care not to drink a drop. Then he laid himself down on his bed, and in a little while began to snore very loud as if he was fast asleep.

When the twelve princesses heard this they laughed heartily; and the eldest said, 'This fellow too might have done a wiser thing than lose his life in this way!'

Then they rose up and opened their drawers and boxes, and took out all their fine clothes, and dressed themselves at the glass, and skipped about as if they were eager to begin dancing. But the youngest said, 'I don't know why it is, but while you are all so happy I feel very uneasy; I am sure some mischance will befall us.'

'You simpleton,' said the eldest, 'you are always afraid; have you forgotten how many kings' sons have already watched in vain? And as for this soldier, even if I had not given him his sleeping draught, he would have slept soundly enough.'

When they were all ready, they went and looked at the soldier; but he snored on, and did not stir hand or foot, so they thought they were quite safe; and the eldest went up to her own bed and clapped her hands, and the bed sank into the floor and a trap-door flew open. The soldier saw them going down through the trap-door one after another, the eldest leading the way; and thinking he had no time to lose, he jumped up, put on the cloak which the old woman had given him, and followed them; but in the middle of the stairs he trod on the gown of the youngest princess, and she cried out to her sisters, 'All is not right; someone took hold of my gown.'

'You silly creature!' said the eldest, 'it is nothing but a nail in the wall.'

Then down they all went, and at the bottom they found themselves in a most delightful grove of trees; and the leaves were all of silver, and glittered and sparkled beautifully. The soldier wished to take away some token of the place; so he broke off a little branch, and there came a loud noise from the tree. Then the youngest daughter said again, 'I am sure all is not right – did not you hear that noise? That never happened before.'

But the eldest said, 'It is only our princes, who are shouting for joy at our approach.'

Then they came to another grove of trees, where all the leaves were of gold; and afterwards to a third, where the leaves were all glittering diamonds. And the soldier broke a branch from each; and every time there was a loud noise, which made the youngest sister tremble with fear; but the eldest still said, it was only the princes, who were crying for joy. So they went on till they came to a great lake; and at the side of the lake there lay twelve little boats with twelve handsome princes in them, who seemed to be waiting there for the princesses.

One of the princesses went into each boat, and the soldier stepped into the same boat as the youngest. As they were rowing over the lake, the prince who was in the boat with the youngest princess and the soldier said, 'I do not know why it is, but though I am rowing with all my might we do not get on so fast as usual, and I am quite tired: the boat seems very heavy today.'

'It is only the heat of the weather,' said the princess. 'I feel very warm too.'

On the other side of the lake stood a fine illuminated castle, from which came the merry music of horns and trumpets. There they all landed, and went into the castle, and each prince danced with his princess; and the soldier, who was all the time invisible, danced with them too; and when any of the princesses had a cup of wine set by her, he drank it all up, so that when she put the cup to her mouth it was empty. At this, too, the youngest sister was terribly frightened, but the eldest always silenced her. They danced on till three o'clock in the morning, and then all their shoes were worn out, so that they were obliged to leave off. The princes rowed them back again over the lake (but this time the soldier placed himself in the boat with the eldest princess); and on the opposite shore they took leave of each other, the princesses promising to come again the next night.

When they came to the stairs, the soldier ran on before the princesses, and laid himself down; and as the twelve sisters slowly came up, very much tired, they heard him snoring in his bed; so they said, 'Now all is quite safe;' then they undressed themselves, put away their fine clothes, pulled off their shoes, and went to bed. In the morning the soldier said nothing about what had happened, but determined to see more of this strange adventure, and went again the second and third night; and everything happened just as before; the princesses danced each time till their shoes were worn to pieces, and then returned home. However, on the third night the soldier carried away one of the golden cups as a token of where he had been.

As soon as the time came when he was to declare the secret, he was taken before the king with the three branches and the golden cup; and the twelve princesses stood listening behind the door to hear what he would say. And when the king asked him, 'Where do my twelve daughters dance at night?' he answered, 'With twelve princes in a castle under ground.' And then he told the king all that had happened, and showed him the three branches and the golden cup which he had brought with him. Then the king called for the princesses, and asked them whether what the soldier said was true; and when they saw that they were discovered, and that it was of no use to deny what had happened, they confessed it all. And the king asked the soldier which of them he would choose for his wife; and he answered, 'I am not very young, so I will have the eldest.' And they were married that very day, and the soldier was chosen to be the king's heir.

Permissions Acknowledgements